HAUME

HATI-HEU

ANA-HO

HA'A-TUATUA

UMMIT

VALLEY
of TEARS

TAI-PI-VAI
Tai-pi tribes

HAKA-PA'A
Hapa'a tribes

HO'O-UMI

TAI-O-HAE
Tei'i tribes

NUKU HIVA
THE MARQUESAS

THUNDER FROM THE SEA

*'Thunder in the mountains
is good, but thunder from the sea
is different'*—Priest Kohu

THUNDER FROM THE SEA

WILLOWDEAN
CHATTERSON HANDY

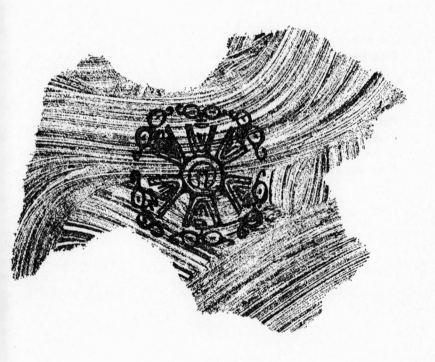

THE UNIVERSITY PRESS OF HAWAII HONOLULU 1973

Upsala College
Library
East Orange, N. J. 07019

The University Press of Hawaii
Copyright © 1973 by E. S. C. Handy
Library of Congress Catalog Card
Number 73 80210
ISBN 0-8248-0284-5
Printed in Australia
First published in Australia 1973
by the Australian National
University Press

Foreword

How often has one wished for a really convincing interpretation of the traumatic changes in island life and thought brought about by the advent of the European on the Pacific scene?

Such an interpretation, if it is to be meaningful to more than a few specialists must, I believe, be written as a novel (or at least in partly fictional, partly biographical form) and by one who through temperament and training is able to get beneath the surface of island life and visualise the attitudes, motivations, and values of the islanders through their own eyes.

Within a decade or two we shall have some notable indigenous novelists, but for the present the writer must be someone who has lived with understanding among the people of Oceania and has the imagination and involvement to capture the drama and pathos of the cultural revolution taking place around them.

Many have essayed such a task; and among them will be found most of the great masters of South Sea literature who have touched the islands with genius. But not one of them was able to depict characters who thought and behaved like islanders rather than Europeans, for to do so requires a degree of participation in another society which few have attempted and fewer still achieved. Of the handful who did, all had, I thought, been either mute or at the best descriptive narrators. We see the finest examples of such observers' accounts in the 'beachcomber books', and especially those by Mariner, Edward Robarts and Vason; yet while they give us invaluable insights into functioning island societies at the dawn of European contact we are left wondering how individuals felt and thought and acted within the ambit of these communities, where social and environmental conditioning produced men and women so fascinatingly different from ourselves.

Some time ago I found that there was indeed such an unpublished manuscript in existence; that it had been written by Willowdean Chatterson Handy, a versatile and sympathetic American anthropologist who had lived for twelve years among the Polynesians, notably in the Marquesas (on which she had already published seven books, monographs and articles), and had been five more writing her quasi-historical account of all that our coming must have meant to their world.

I suppose that the writing provided the catharsis which the author was in need of after her long and intimate association with one of the most attractive, most misunderstood and mistreated of all the Polynesian peoples, for she had done little to secure its publication.

However, she let me borrow her copy; and I shall never forget the feeling of mounting excitement with which I first read it. The mental images of Nukuhiva itself and the procession of dramatic events centred there round the culture hero Pakoko ('Ironwood') were intensely vivid and, unlike those in most novels, they were lasting. For weeks afterwards my mind kept returning to some event in Pakoko's life and, in particular, to the final scene—the last, hopeless battle in the swirling mountain mists between the remnant of his followers and the French invaders, which is portrayed with such skill that one is left with a feeling of justification, almost of triumph, rather than of tragedy and helplessness.

Steeped in the literature of Oceania since a child, I felt convinced that Willowdean Handy had produced one of those rare works which would be treasured from the start by the cognoscenti of island belles-lettres and will eventually come to be acknowledged as one of the classics of Polynesia. Confirmation came from the writers, poets and literary critics who read the manuscript, and, in the words of the Australian novelist Kylie Tennant, felt that it was 'a tremendous book, and one about which I am most enthusiastic'.

Willowdean Handy has clearly offended the accepted commercial canons of South Sea fiction, in which the image of Polynesia is essentially feminine: 'a neater, sweeter maiden, in a cleaner, greener land', as Fairchild expresses it. From the time of the discoverers, Tahiti, and by extension Polynesia, had become the home of the mythical Noble Savage, created by the Rousseauesque philosophical speculators of the eighteenth century, and thus of the exemplars of what is known in the jargon of literary criticism as 'soft primitivism'; and as a result South Sea novels came to be written to a formula as unlike reality as the average western or science fiction paperback.

Anything less conformable to the stereotype of escapist Paradise literature than *Thunder from the Sea* would be hard to imagine. Lacking even the apparently essential 'white man, brown woman' motif, it has the authenticity of a modern field study, with its characters and main events drawn from historical sources; and yet once launched into the narrative the reader is carried through without a break to its dramatic culmination by the sheer vitality of the plot and the sensitivity of its denouement.

Willowdean Chatterson Handy is no longer with us, but her *Thunder from the Sea* has found the perceptive publisher its author wished for, and I predict will become an imperishable memorial to the gifted woman who has written the only South Sea novel which successfully transcends cultural boundaries. It is fitting that a work in itself so distinctive should have the additional distinction of being the first novel to be published by the Australian National University Press.

H. E. Maude, Canberra, 1972

vii

Preface

I had a sorcerer's fancy to bring the dead to life, not to prove that they were better or worse than the living, but just to see what they were like.

My friend Hapu wept because a gendarme called him a savage. He cried out 'Je ne suis pas sauvage! Je suis homme!' I agreed with him in a way. He was certainly not a savage; but as a man he was as frustrated as a human being can be and continue to live. (He has died since, in his early thirties, and I am surprised that he endured so long.)

What I wanted to know was this: when Hapu's ancestors were living their own lives in the latter part of the eighteenth century and the early years of the nineteenth, what were they—savages or men or both? I had read contemporary accounts of their sex orgies at harvest times, of their physical cruelties during war and religious rites and their mental cruelties in the practice of witchcraft; but, as a resident of the white man's world of the twentieth century, I was not impressed by these traits as being exclusively Marquesan. Furthermore, I knew that there was a margin for error in these accounts, since all of them were written by white men from an outsider's point of view, and all of them were written after a new and terrifying culture, whose outstanding features were guns, spirituous liquors, consuming diseases and incomprehensible taboos, had disturbed the indigenous culture traits of these Polynesians of the South

Seas. What had Hapu's ancestors been like from their own point of view when their lives were under their own control? With what qualities did they meet exploiters and reformers during the years of cultural upheaval?

I had no conjuror's skill to materialize the Marquesans who lived on the island of Nuku Hiva a hundred and fifty years ago. I was not even psychic enough to hear the drums of the ancients beating up-valley on full moon nights, which some whites claim to have heard. But I felt that I held enough of the pieces of the picture-puzzle in my hands to try to suggest at least the ancient Marquesan scene in novel form. I knew the rules of the game as the old-time people played it, as well as they can be known today, both from the confidences of their living descendants and from a study of ethnological details incorporated in early records. I knew their verbal concepts as recorded when their language was spoken correctly, as well as a good many of their psychological reactions which were reported by contemporaries. I did not have to manufacture characters nor the main events of their lives. Discoverers, explorers, captains of whaling ships, agents for the sandal-wood trade, deserters from all manner of ships, Naval officers, missionaries, colonial officials, settlers, all remarked the outstanding native individuals of their era and left their notations of appearance, character and behaviour for me to mull over until imagination reconstructed men from the skeletons delineated.

Naturally, imagination had to breathe the breath of life into those dead nostrils, but an imagination closely circumscribed and supervised by fact. I have not attempted to comment on the lives those ancients lived. Who am I to praise or condemn? I am not a Marquesan. I have merely looked and listened, tasted and felt, as the emotions I myself am familiar with were applied to situations undreamed of in my own life. To my own satisfaction, however, the question has been answered: were they savages or men or both?

For others, who watch the lives of these people of another race and another epoch unfold, will any conviction of kinship eventuate? I do not know. Perhaps those who think more of the mould of culture than of the human being who is moulded by it had better keep away from this book. Perhaps they would be repelled by it. But there are some who will comprehend the human stuff that was thrown into the crucible of cataclysmic change when white men were expanding their horizons more than a century ago. For them I have written what may have been the life of Pakoko, whom we know to have been the chief warrior, or 'Ironwood', of Nuku Hiva.

Willowdean Chatterson Handy

Contents

xiii

Author's Note

THERE is nothing arbitrary or personal in the choice of style and vocabulary used in this novel. I have tried to suggest the Marquesan mode of verbal expression, in so far as I could without awkwardness or obscurity. I have followed the native custom of using frequent exclamations and questions, for it seems to me reflective of their emotional intensity and fluidity. I have held myself as rigidly as possible to the use of their limited number of nouns and verbs, since this, perhaps, exhibits the level of their intellectual development, when taken in connection with their inventiveness in supplementing them with similes and metaphors drawn from nature and work. I have brought out their use of onomatopoetic expressions as ejaculations in describing events, and have translated literally their attempts to name mental states in terms of physical equivalents (as, confused—'hung up', 'swinging') or of bodily symptoms (embarrassed—'in a voice without an echo').

For the sake of clarity for English readers I have had to make compromises in literalness of vocabulary and in grammatical order, but I believe that this approximation of the Marquesan verbal expression helps me to convey the native as he actually was.

I hope the reader will feel that in a literary way this novel is worthy of the material embodied in it. For twenty years I have been trying to let the Marquesan people speak for themselves through me, by recording their arts and crafts, and by lecturing on their culture traits. For five years I have worked on this summation of what I know of them as human beings. They and their culture had too many fine aspects to be thrown away wantonly and without discrimination. It seemed to me worth while to salvage what was good, if only in the form of a literary memorial; and if I have succeeded in establishing, thus, what was eradicated so thoughtlessly and selfishly by great nations concerned only with their own temporary interests—and even whims—I shall feel that the arduous labor has been well spent.

If the Marquesan case versus expanding white nations can make the people of this day think about the disastrous consequences to human beings which sudden and drastic changes in culture entail, then I shall be satisfied. However, neither I nor my Marquesan friends would want anything to appear on their behalf that was not well done. I hope you will consider that it is.

Willowdean Chatterson Handy

Glossary

ena	a plant *(Curcuma domestica)* from whose roots yellow and saffron dyes were made
Ferane	French people
ihi	a nut-bearing tree *(Inocarpus edulis)*
kaoha	greeting, farewell, thanks, love
Katorika	Catholic missionaries
kava	a drink made from the root of the *Piper methysticum*
Komana	Commander
manowa	man-of-war, warship
mei	the breadfruit tree *(Artocarpus incisus)* whose large starch-filled fruit were the staff of life
Menike	American people
noni	a shrub-like tree *(Morinda citrifolia)* with edible fruits also used medicinally
Peketane	British people
peto	'pet'—a foreigner's dog
Protetane	Protestant missionary
puhi	onomatapoetic word from the sound of a gun-blast; hence a gun
Setani	Satan
tapa	material beaten from the bark of various trees

temanu	a tall straight tree *(Calophyllum inofillum)* from which large war canoes were made
ti	a shrub *(Cordyline terminalis)* whose long stout leaves had many domestic uses
tiki	ancestral image carved of wood or stone
toa	the ironwood tree *(Casuarina equisetifolia);* from its exceptionally hard wood war clubs were made—warriors were called by its name, Toa or Ironwood
Wee Wees	French people, from oui, oui

Personal and Clan Names

Veo	Pakoko's true father, Chief of Meau
Ehua	his true mother; daughter of the exiled Chief of Haavao
Fatu	his foster father; his mother's brother
Kohu	his foster brother, Fatu's son; later priest of Haavao
Hina	his father's brother's daughter; hence his 'sister'
Mauhau	his cousin; his father's sister's son
Oehitu	his cousin; his father's sister's son
Kiato-nui	his father's adopted son; hence Pakoko's 'brother'
Kena	his adopted brother Kiato-nui's true mother
Hono	his grandfather's sister's son; a Chief of Tahu Ata
Tea-roru	his father-in-law; Chief of the Hapaas of Hakapaa
Metani	his formally mated wife; daughter of Tea-roru
Tohi-kai	his friend with whom he exchanged names; Chief of Taipivai

Hiatai	his first-born son by Chiefess Metani; called Paia-roru in his mother's valley
Pae-tini	his daughter by Metani; adopted by Kiato-nui
Taa	his nephew; son of his sister Tita and Kohu; later Priest of the Teiis
Tini	his father-in-law's brother's son, hence his wife Metani's 'brother'
Haape	his son Hiatai's Hapaa cousin, appointed Regent of Meau
Veketu	his grandson; son of his foster daughter Mata-heva and Taa
Moana	his brother Kiato-nui's great-grandson
Vae-kehu	his granddaughter; daughter of Pae-tini
Moana-tini	his granddaughter Vai-kehu's adopted son; Tohi-kai's grandson
Kepua	his younger son by Metani; foster son of Tohi-kai of Taipivai; Priest of the Taipis
Teii	clan name of the people of Taiohae valley
Hapaa	clan name of the people of Hakapaa valley
Taipi	clan name of the people of Taipivai valley
Taioa	clan name of the people of Hakaui valley

1 THE LONG RED GIRDLE

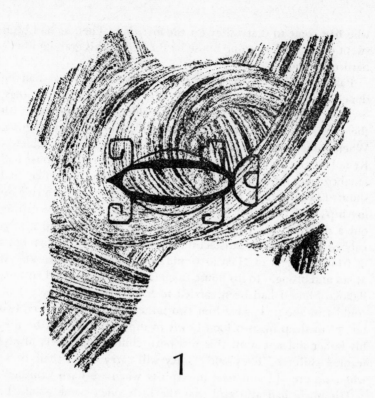

1

As if he were walking in sleep, Pakoko wandered across the cold black stones of his father's high terrace, felt his way down the notched log to the beach below, and plodded through yesterday's tossed up sands. Skimming lightly along this morning's clean flat shore, he followed a way he had taken many times because he liked to be the first to leave traces of his feet on land still wet from the night sea's licking, but today he did not look back to see his toes and heels running after him.

The little boy was agitated without knowing why. He had wept because he had seen eye water running over his father's cheeks. When he had tried to comfort him, he had been frightened by Chief Veo's turning his face to the mat, digging his finger nails into the leaves. He had found himself alone in sudden deep silence, for all the relatives had stopped their laughing to look sideways at the father and the son, as if they were strangers

3

who had come to that valley for the first time. Then he had been swept outside the sleeping house by the back of his grandmother's hard old hand.

Pakoko looked at the sand through his tears. What had he done? He could not ask his uncle, who always explained things, because he had gone to summon the elders for a meeting with the chief. Alone and uneasy, he considered this cloudy thing. When a messenger had come in the night to say that Chiefess Kena had given birth to a son, all the dwellers in Veo's house had laughed and flung themselves about in joy, until Pakoko had shouted to his father, 'Now I shall have a little brother to ride on my hip', and the Chief had looked at him as if he were calling out a death. Uncle Fatu, with whom the boy lived, had always rubbed his chin with satisfaction when telling how the first-born of Chiefess Kena of Haavao would be adopted by Chief Veo of Meau and brought to his house to be fed. This was a good custom. Pakoko himself had been carried to his uncle's house before he could run about. It gave him two fathers and two mothers, two houses to sleep in, two food bowls to dip into. Could it be that his father did not want this new-born child? No, fathers always wanted children. They said, 'They will carry us on their backs when we are old and feed our spirits when we have vanished'.

His uncle had also said that the little one's name would be Kiato-nui and that he would be chief over all the branches of Taiohae. This was good, because Uncle Fatu's father had been driven away from the sub-valley, Haavao, by Chiefess Kena's father and this land had been ruled ever since separately from the other water courses of the big valley.

Indeed, Uncle Fatu had ridden Pakoko on his hip all the way up Haavao's path to the backbone of the land, in order to show him why Haavao was so important. Standing with their backs to Red Stone Mountain, they two had looked down on the heads of innumerable trees and on the white feet of the sea coming and going far below. Sweeping his arms all around him, as if to embrace the towering mountains and their ridges sloping down to the ocean, the uncle had said, 'This is the land of Nuku Hiva, which the god Tikki fished up from the sea.' When they had looked back again at the bowl of the valley of Taiohae, it was small because Nuku Hiva was so big. There were many families living on the island, just as little fish live on a big shark, nibbling at his skin for their food. There were Hapaas and, beyond them, Taipis on the east, nestling in the hollows of the big fish's wrinkles, and Taioas on the west. But in Taiohae valley there were the Teiis, the best people of all. This was the first time that Pakoko had heard that he was a Teii. He had been given many names by his relatives, but he had never been called a Teii. 'Teii! Teii! I am a Teii!' he had cried, jumping first on one foot and then on the other.

Then Uncle Fatu had made his nephew look at the Teii's land of Taiohae. 'See, it is like a big hand with five fingers,' he had said. They had been able to see the fingers clearly because the sun was making shining streaks of their streams which wiggled between the rocky ridges that separated them. Hoata, the thumb; Meau, the pointing finger; Haavao, the middle finger; Pakiu, the erect finger; and the twin valleys of Hikoei and Haka-pehi, the little finger: these were the branches of Taiohae.

Pakoko had liked Haavao best even before his uncle had told him why. Haavao was the only branch with a path from the sea up to the high level of Nuku Hiva. Haavao, open at both ends, held the great path to war, to conquest and, alas, to defeat. But most important, Haavao was Uncle Fatu's dear land. 'My dear land of Haavao,' he still called this powerful valley, although he had been just a little fellow when his father, the true chief, was forced to seek lands in distant seas. Looking down on its controlling place in the palm of Taiohae, he had cried out in pain, 'Alas, this finger of Haavao was broken from the hand when Chiefess Kena's father seized the land and ever since the hand has been without strength.'

The little boy had felt the fire in his uncle's eyes burn his own cheeks. 'I know!' he had agreed. 'Kena's father crawled from a lost and broken canoe onto the sands of Haavao. He was nothing but a food-beggar when the true chief made him his Fire Keeper.' Pakoko had narrowed his eyes and hardened his tongue. 'Your father was a foolish chief,' he had declared.

'Hush!' Fatu had commanded, looking from side to side as if that spirit might be listening. 'Hear this!' he had continued, for he was always careful to explain to his nephew the ancient customs of his people, 'My father exchanged names with the poor fellow who was washed up on his shore.'

'I would not give my name to a nobody,' the boy had protested, lifting his chin.

'Perhaps you are right,' the uncle had agreed. 'Only a grasping beggar would take advantage of a name to claim its rights. No matter. A name given is a knot tied. And remember this: your names are proof of your privileges and your property. Never forget this: to give your name to another is to give him everything you have — if he is rat enough to ask for it.'

The boy had opened his eyes wide. 'Did he ask your father for his land of Haavao?'

'He asked for one step up at a time,' Uncle Fatu had answered with a bitter tongue, 'first for his sheath of fire embers, then for his woman, then for the things a chief carries, his staff, his fan, his conch shell sounder. Finally . . . '

Pakoko had been swelling up, red and tight, with anger. 'He was a lizard and your father was a fly. He was eating him, bit by bit.'

'Something like that.' The uncle's eyes misted and his lips trembled. 'Finally, my father had to flee for his life, leaving your mother and me with Chief Veo's father.'

'Was the Chief of Haavao my mother's father, too?' The little fellow had not thought of that. 'Then Haavao is my dear land, too!' he had declared.

Hand in hand, those two had stood, gazing with affection on their land with its plantations of breadfruit, banana and coconut trees and its patches of taro and sweet potatoes. A land of abundance! They had murmured a greeting together, 'Kaoha to our dear land of Haavao.'

Then the man had told the boy the thing that had made a sea of joy flood over him. 'Soon, Haavao will be restored to Taiohae. Your grandfather on your father's side saw to that. He was not soft wood, that father of Chief Veo. He also exchanged names with the usurper of Haavao but he was the namesake who asked first for what he wanted.'

'Oh!' Pakoko had cried. 'He asked for the land back again!'

6

'In a way, yes. He asked for the fellow's first grandchild to be given to his son, Chief Veo, and he promised to make him chief of all lands in Taiohae.'

Oh, what a clever grandfather! The boy remembered that old man who had fallen into his bathing pool and drowned because he was too weak to pull himself out. He had always thought he was a foolish old thing, but it seemed he was a man of light.

How joyfully Pakoko and his uncle had waited for the coming of Chiefess Kena's first-born! 'It is good,' the boy said stubbornly on this strange day of the child's birth. Why then were the relatives sitting in his father's sleeping house with swollen eyelids and heavy hands? He was tired of questioning. The sun had stuck his legs over the mountains and was walking with him along the beach, warming the sands, making the waters sparkle. Birds were singing. When the little fellow felt running water slapping his ankles, he saw that he was crossing the stream that flowed down from Haavao's uplands. He patted the water with his palms and scooped up handsful of pebbles. 'Kaoha to my dear land of Haavao!' he murmured in greeting. He decided to throw a pinch of his morning breadfruit over his shoulder for his clever grandfather who had tied Haavao again to the other branches of Taiohae. He ran back to his father's cook house, suddenly very hungry.

Outside the open-fronted warrior's hall, the boy waited. There were many men inside, looking black in the shade of the thatch and sitting as still as the images which held up the roof. The white beards were the brothers of his clever grandfather, the elders who stood firm behind the young chiefs of the finger valleys of Taiohae. Behind these folk of the high level sat the masters, all of them Pakoko's friends. The Master Stone Cutter often carried him on his hip when he went about encouraging his workers. The Master Drum Maker always let him hold the plaited fibres and the bone rings when he pulled the shark's skin tight over the hollow log. The Master Image Striker's work was taboo, but he sometimes threw broken combs out of the tattooing house for his small friend. Pakoko's eyes shone when he made out Chief Veo on his high seat at the end of the house, for his father looked like a single perfect ornament among all those landsmen. His skin glistened, his hair was carefully coiled like sea shells on either side of his head, the very long knotted tail of his white loin cloth was folded neatly over his knee. But as the son peered at the handsome chief, he knew that his father was troubled, for his eyes were sunken in their bowls and his fingers were picking at the mat.

Pakoko's own anxiety returned. He wanted to press against his father's breast for comfort, but he could not enter that house of wise men until Uncle Fatu, who directed Chief Veo's craftsmen, had named the ornaments to be carried to Chiefess Kena and pointed out their makers. The boy always kept his distance and never interrupted when his uncle put on the coconut leaf cap and cape of the Master Manager. It made him feel strange to see Fatu wear anything but a coarse mat over his back, tied under his chin. He never wore ornaments or fine *tapa*. He often said, 'I have been reduced to nothing and nothing I have,' but he was not a mean fellow when he put on his high cap and thick cape of leaves. It seemed as if he had stepped up to a level that was out of reach.

When the count of ornaments was complete, Pakoko ran across the mats and crawled within the folded legs of Chief Veo. He had sought safety in this nest, but he was almost frightened by a fierce clasping of legs and arms about him and by his inability to turn and see Uncle Fatu who was speaking so sharply to his father.

'Harden your feet when your path is stony,' the uncle commanded.

'It is not my path!' The cry leapt from Veo's throbbing throat.

'Your father's spirit will hear you!' his brother-in-law warned.

'He hears,' Veo agreed bitterly. 'He is still the chief. Before he died, he never let go his hold on the steering paddle of the canoe of our land. Now his breath body still guides our going. It was his desire that Chiefess Kena's first-born should succeed me, not mine. Who am I to choose a path? I am nothing but driftwood pushed about by running water.'

Everyone in that house was astonished at this outburst. Was this the chief who cared only for dressing himself handsomely, who let others do his work without shadowing them, who nodded and smiled and consented gently to any request? Pakoko scarcely knew his own father. His breathing quickened and he rooted deeper into that heaving breast. He felt himself lifted and rushed through the heavy silent air of the house and out into gentle fragrant breezes. He did not know along what paths the stamping feet of Chief Veo were carrying the two of them, but he was not afraid. He was quivering with joy.

The singing of wind through ironwood trees made Pakoko raise his face. Here was a place he did not know.

'There is your grandfather,' panted Veo.

On a high stone terrace in a clearing, an image sat in a canoe. He was bending low over his paddle, pushing it through the swift current of wind. His red *tapa* robes were billowing, the black feathers of his headband were swimming behind him. The boy was almost without breath for a whisper. 'Where is he going?'

'To the skies,' Veo answered. 'Yet he lingers.' Oh but his tongue was rancid! 'He is still the chief here. He is the one who is choosing Kiato-nui to sit in the highest seat of Taiohae.' He held his son at arm's length and hooked eyes with him. 'You know that is not my work?'

Pakoko nodded, but he was lost in fog again. 'Don't you want Haavao to be joined to the other branches?' he asked.

'Naturally, that is good,' the Chief said impatiently. 'But who is this Kiato-nui that he should be given our great names? You were born with a right to our names and Haavao's as well. You are my High Chief of Taiohae!' Words and sobs tumbled out together in a troubled stream.

Pakoko drew his black brows down level. 'I do not want to be a chief,' he protested. 'I want to be . . . '

The father fondled his foolish child, who scarcely knew enough to come when called. 'Yes, I know, you said you wanted to be a Master Fisherman.'

'That was when I was a little fellow.' The boy hung his head. 'I shall be a Master Chanter. I shall know all names and all words with power. I shall tell chiefs and masters what to do.'

Chief Veo put the boy down on his own feet and stared at him. Here was a thought to be chewed on, certainly. He himself had never had satisfaction in carrying a chief's staff. Why, the boy had a stomach full of light! The father began to feel soft and smooth, as if he were a piece of limp seaweed floating on still water. 'Well,' he asked finally, putting a tender finger under the boy's firm chin and tilting his small face upwards, 'What do you want to do now?'

'I want to catch shrimps!' Pakoko cried, and dragged his father away to the stream.

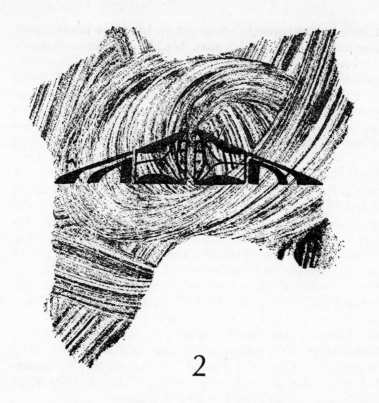

2

IN the dark of his sleeping house, Uncle Fatu knew that his woman had rolled her mat, tucked it behind the head rest of the bed space, and crawled across the front stones. He sat up, blinking at the bright patch of day which dazzled him when she removed the cover from the low entrance. He could see her dark against the soft radiance outside, with face uplifted as if she were straining to see things far away. That was exactly what she was doing, he knew. Presently she would come to warn him of something about to happen. She ought to be a priestess, but she was too lazy for such strict work. All she wanted to do was to sit dreaming with the whites of her eyes showing. Fatu sighed. Their son Kohu was the same. There he lay now in the far corner of the fern-padded matting, his eyes fixed on air, his lips incessantly whispering to his foster brother, Pakoko. They encouraged each other to waste time, those two boys. All the while the man was shaking his head over the idleness of his family, his careful hands were rolling and folding his mats. He had learned not to disregard his woman's visions, but he was scarcely ready for the word she brought to him now when she turned away from the doorway.

'This is the day when Chiefess Kena will bring her child to Brother Veo's house,' she told him. Fatu sat back on his heels and let his hands fall on his thighs. This was not an easy word to swallow. He must peck at it awhile. Could this be the day? There was the custom of exchanging gifts. Those from Veo's family had gone to Kena's family only yesterday. She had not had time to collect the return gifts. But Kena was not one to take a long time doing a few things. Perhaps . . . But there was the invitation. Chief Veo had asked that the child be brought for the feast of Big Breadfruit. Six moons must rise and sleep before that harvest could be picked. Besides, the making of the new chief's sacred possessions could not be hurried. True. But would Chiefess Kena wait nine twenties of nights to see her son wrapped in the long red girdle of a High Chief? Never! At least, not idly sitting on her mats in Haavao. She was a woman who could not let a man finish his work without grabbing his tool to show him how. Undoubtedly, she would come to Meau to shadow the workers preparing for Kiato-nui's feast of consecration. Yes, his woman had once again foretold a true thing. Today, Chiefess Kena would bring her child to Brother Veo's house.

At once Fatu was in such a hurry that he wanted to blow his family and their belongings out of his house with one puff. Where else but in this house could Chiefess Kena and her son be entertained while they waited for the building of the new house planned for the new chief? The place must be cleared and cleaned, the bundles untied from its rafters, fresh ferns and new mats brought for its sleeping space, its stones brushed and polished. A hole must be opened in the thatch, through which the child could be lowered, for the taboo infant could not be carried under the framework of his doorway. There were so many things to pick up that Fatu did not know which to handle first.

He was about to shout at his woman who sat dreaming and his nephew and son who were strangely silent, when a whistling, coming from the roof, startled him. Was a god about to speak to him? Shrill words trilled through the house. 'I see Chiefess

Kena coming down from the uplands, carrying a new child in her arms.' Before the man could gather his wits, another tongue began to sound the familiar words of the earth-growing chant, 'Joined long ago the big roots, ah, the big roots of the land.' At this moment, the sun burst through the rim of the valley and stuck a leg through the open doorway, so that Uncle Fatu could see his son Kohu lying along a rafter, making strange noises through a twisted mouth, and his nephew Pakoko intoning the chant through cupped hands. 'You two drag sacred things in the mud!' he cried.

Pakoko looked at him with round, innocent eyes. 'But I am a Master Chanter and Kohu is a Diviner.'

'You have not been taught the true sounding of the ancient words,' the uncle replied sharply. 'As for you, Kohu, I have told you many times that a man cannot decide when a god will enter him to use his tongue. He must wait to be chosen and you haven't been . . . ' he paused, uneasily, then added, 'Have you?'

'I do not know,' Kohu answered, looking through his father with pale, unseeing eyes.

To cover his shivering, Fatu jerked his nephew to his feet. 'Go to your father's house, Pakoko,' he commanded, 'and shake his dwellers awake.'

Pakoko was bursting with his news when he slid aside the cover of Chief Veo's house and crawled inside. The risen sun entered with him, touching the white *tapa* rolls in which his relatives were wrapped and lying side by side all along the bed space. His father and his mother, his father's mother and brothers and sisters, their mates and their children all lay quietly, unaware of the great day which had come. Seeing the chief's conch hanging on his treasure pole, glistening in the bright light, the boy thought that only the sounder could announce his wonderful news. He stretched to reach it and, puffing out his cheeks, blew such noise through the house that everyone was lifted on end. *Tapas* and mats flew about like birds driven in a thunder storm. Open-mouthed, wide-eyed faces appeared in the gloom as if lit by a white flash of lightning. Pakoko made his own tongue as loud as he could. 'Chiefess Kena is on the path with her taboo child!' The boy was riding high on the glorious tempest he had raised, but he was a kite soon jerked to earth.

'Lies!' The old people handled his word roughly. When he boasted that Kohu had seen them coming, the fathers mocked him. 'Kohu is an insect who thinks he is a bird,' they jeered. Even Chief Veo laughed at him. 'You boys deceive yourselves with your tricks,' he said.

But Pakoko stood firm. 'My aunt saw them, too.'

Ah! Here was a different matter. The Chief's older sister often saw things before they happened. Veo sat up with a jerk, wincing as if a spear had touched tender flesh. Of course! Chiefess Kena would not sit on her heels while he performed the works that would raise her son to the high seat of government. She would come with her staff to drive him faster than his feet and hands could move. He wiped the sweat from his forehead and turned his eyes towards his woman, begging her to contradict him, but he could not coax her eyes from her tightly clasped hands. As he sat, helplessly wondering what to do, his mother's voice, raised in sudden alarm that her children and grandchildren would not be presentable when the Haavao family arrived, gave him a push. 'Go to the bathing pool!' she was commanding old and young alike. Veo fumbled about for his shell of sweet oil and a new loin cloth, but these were instantly taken from him by his brother who was his Fire Keeper and guardian of all his taboo possessions. There was nothing for him to do but creep outside with the children and follow the path to the stream.

Pakoko was running back and forth as if he were responsible for the procession of children who lingered on the path, breaking spiders' webs stretched from leaf to leaf, spying out bright colored land shells, climbing flower trees for tightly rolled blossoms. He made the big girl Hina go first, although he knew she wanted to stay behind to watch him. He was a big boy and needed no shadowing. Let her carry his fat little sister. That was her work now.

Hina had had the care of some little one in the Chief's household ever since she was big enough to carry a child on her hip. She had no brothers and sisters of her own, for her mother was dead and her father slept in the men's house with the warriors he led. The cousins whom she had helped take their first steps had been heavy or fretful or dirty, all save Pakoko. He was different. She had not needed the grandmother's word that the children of brothers were as close as brothers and sisters themselves. She knew that Pakoko was especially hers. He was still her own, even though he would no longer let her hover over him. Now, while she thudded along the path to the running water, changing Pakoko's little sister from one aching arm to the other, she kept turning around to smile at her boy. Her eyes caressed his slender, active limbs, while she thought, 'Perhaps when we have bathed, Pakoko will let me rub him with sweet oil.'

In the sleeping house, Chiefess Ehua sat apart from the aimless scurrying of her women relatives who ran about like ants, lowering their bundles from the rafters, picking up rolls of *tapa* and flinging them down, tying on ornaments and untying them. She sat staring at her own finery, at a porpoise tooth headband which lay on top. This fine work from the island of Ua Pou was the only family treasure left her. She had never been able to wear it, for thinking that it had encircled her mother's proud head at that last feast when she was Chiefess of the Haavao branch of Taiohae. But now the daughter of the exiled woman touched the wreath as if it were an old friend she was recalling to her side. Now she could hold up her head under those pricking points, for was she not to be the mother of the Chief of Haavao? A smile, pale and flitting as sun on a day of showers, ran lightly across her lips.

When the tempest of preparation had whirled out of the house, a gentle voice from the far end of the room made Ehua lift her eyes. 'It will be a sweet thing to have that little outsider in this house,' Chief Veo's younger sister was saying, as she pressed her own newly born son against her breasts.

After the young woman had melted into the sunshine beyond the door, Ehua turned her words over and over. True, the new child Kiato-nui would be a stranger in this valley. A child alone. The Chiefess trembled, remembering how unfamiliar faces had pressed upon her long ago when her father gave her to a foster father and sailed away in search of new lands. An outsider Ehua had always been in Meau, a child alone. True, her brother Fatu was nearby, but he had never cared for anything but the lost land of Haavao. There was also her son Pakoko, but he had been taken from her as soon as he was weaned and given to his uncle. Her little daughter clung now only to the big girl who hovered over her. Even her mate Veo had wandered away from her as soon as his son was big enough to play with him. Yes, Chiefess Ehua was alone and Kiato-nui would be alone. But they would be mother and son!

Ehua stood up, like a reed after the wind has passed. She must make herself clean and sweet, so that the child would love her. She followed the others to the bathing place.

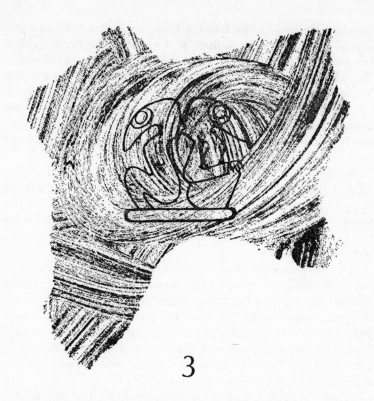

3

WHERE was Chief Veo when an old woman from Haavao
announced the arrival of Chiefess Kena, calling out the
names of her grandfathers-far-below? Where was that
householder with his welcoming shout, 'Come here! Come here!'
Only the deep silence of the valley answered the cascade of Kena's
names. The folk on Chief Veo's terrace were in a panic, hurrying
here, hurrying there, searching for their chief. The Keeper of the
Fire, carrying Veo's staff and fan, had thought his brother was
following him from the bathing pool. Hearing that the procession
from Haavao was actually on the path, he had pulled his chief
from his red stone basin, where he was floating and dozing, and
made him ready to welcome them. He had rubbed him with oil
till his tattooed designs popped out like black leaves against a
white night. He had watched him twist his hair in a new way on
top of his head and part his beard into two bunches tied under

his chin. He had run back to the house to fetch a red loin cloth instead of an every-day white. He had looked at his chief and cried out in admiration, 'You are like a comet in the sky of stars!' But when he had turned to speak to him on the way back to the house, he had found him gone. Where was Chief Veo? His stone seat was empty, his speaking stone stood up bare. When the old woman from Haavao intoned the name of Kiato-nui, the chief was not there to bid his visitors enter the opening in the wall and cross his feast place to his terrace.

Suddenly, the old woman who had chanted and the man who carried the child were pushed aside and Chiefess Kena herself darted upon the paving. As swiftly as a booby dives for fish, the woman flew across the open space, her hard black eyes fixed on the empty stone, her sharp beak pointing, her spreading *tapas* winging behind her.

The anxious women on the terrace were not too confused to see that Chiefess Kena wore her finery as if she were expecting a feast. 'She has tied her cape on one shoulder as if she were an unopened bud,' whispered one. She had frizzled her hair and pulled it through a band of sheer white *tapa* into a fluff on top. Chiefess Ehua tossed her own shoulder-length locks which were proper for a mated woman but she wished that she had had the time to bleach her skin so fair and white.

When the visiting Chiefess stood below Veo's high terrace, her nostrils were wide open, her breathing too rapid for a word of greeting to her son's new family. Indeed, she looked at them without *kaoha*. It was only the promise of her dead father which brought her here to throw away her first-born on a mat-sitting chief who had no desires. She knew well enough that if any work were done to raise Kiato-nui to power, she herself would have to do it.

'Have you brought the Chief of Haavao?' a small voice asked.

Kena's head turned quickly on her bird-like neck and her eyes pecked at the little boy who squatted on the stones above.

Before she could answer Pakoko, Chief Veo's drawl called her attention. 'I am waiting to receive him,' he said with a loud tongue. As he came from the shadow of his taboo food house, he was encouraged by the support of his relatives who lifted their heads in relief and edged closer to him, but, exposed to the visitor's piercing eyes, his feet began to drag and his tongue to limp. 'B-b-bring him here,' he stammered.

Chiefess Kena herself gave the call that brought her men and women-at-the-side running. Behind them came her mate carrying the child as if he were a whale's tooth ornament displayed on his breast. Delicately as a dancer, the heavy man climbed the notched log to the terrace and stood at ease beside Kena, holding his son high for all to see his beauty.

There was a polite clicking of tongues, but only Pakoko spoke. He pulled at his uncle's girdle. 'May I ride him on my hip?' he asked.

'Not yet,' whispered Fatu. 'The little Chief is still covered with clouds of taboo.'

Pakoko nodded. Perhaps there had never been such a sacred chief. The boy could scarcely keep his feet still in his great desire to serve this god.

But there were other wonderful things to draw Pakoko's gaze. When he saw the gifts which Kena's Fire Keeper was flinging at Chief Veo's feet, he ran round and round them, naming the masters who had made them as the Chiefess named them and counting off their cost after her. Piles of fine mats, rolls of white breadfruit bark *tapa,* rolls of red banyan bark *tapa,* whale's tooth earrings, carved bone earrings, tortoise-shell headbands, cocks' feather headbands, white beard plumes, wristlets and anklets of curled black hair: great riches were given by Chiefess Kena to Chief Veo.

Veo's dwellers protested that they could not accept such precious things, but when Kena said, '*Kaoha* to you all,' they pounced upon them, laughing and screaming, pushing and shoving, grabbing their desires. With satisfaction Kena watched Chief Veo who stood with covered eyes and hanging hands. 'He is ashamed,' she thought. 'He sees that I have given him twice or three times what he gave me.' But when the Chiefess saw Pakoko thrust a short picking pole under the contending relatives and draw out a prize, a small but perfect whale's tooth, she muttered, 'That boy is a pig of a different breed.'

When Chiefess Kena saw that her serving women were carrying her bundles to Fatu's house, she shook her head. 'We will wait for the building of a new house,' she said.

Chief Veo choked. The woman had come before she was invited. There had not been time to build the child a new house. Was he so sacred that he could not breathe common air, this grandson of an eater of lizards? The Chief opened his mouth to say this bold word, but Kena was waiting for no orders from him and her question swept past him.

'Where is the Master House Builder?' she asked.

'I will find him,' Pakoko offered, leaping up.

Chiefess Kena's quick reply checked his spring as if it had been a noose flung about his neck. 'No!' she commanded. 'Let another go. Your work is here. You are the big boy who will shadow the High Chief. Go to his father and learn.'

Oh but there was a high sea of joy lifting Pakoko off his feet and rushing him across the terrace to see his baby!

Uncle Fatu could not resist a barbed word. 'Pakoko will never betray his chief,' he said, and met the answering spear from her eyes without flinching.

Chief Veo was like a fish struggling to loosen a hook that dug deeper and deeper into his flesh. Why couldn't he speak to claim other work for Pakoko? Why must he stand biting his nails when the Master House Builder looked to him for 'Yes' or 'No' to Kena's demand for the finishing of a new house before the fall of this sun? Why couldn't he give his Fire Keeper a sign of denial when he was asked to prepare a house-entering feast? Nobody consulted Chief Veo. He was tossed aside as if he were the worn out skin of an eel. Why stand here torturing himself? He stumbled towards his taboo house and made the ladder swing as he climbed to its quiet perch. 'Bring me a bowl of *kava*,' he called to his Fire Keeper. At least he would be allowed to drink himself to sleep.

When the terrace of Pakoko's dead grandfather had been cleared of charred house posts, rotten mats and the hidden litters of pigs, and the relatives had brought their shares of posts, rafters and lashings for the new house, Pakoko followed Chiefess Kena as she looked over their offerings to make sure that all were of the best quality. The little boy had never seen a woman who knew the way of taboo work and his admiration for her grew as he saw her going about among the workers, telling them how to make things firm and strong. He watched her pushing the thatch-makers to make their fingers go faster, rapping their knuckles with a stick when they made mistakes. When she was challenged by the irritated old woman who set the pace for the coconut leaf mat-makers, he clapped his hands because she sat down with them to plait a mat. He sucked in his breath over her great skill and screamed with laughter over her clever imitations of masters and chiefs, which made her opponents laugh and make mistakes. When she outstripped all others in this work, he cried out, 'Chief Veo will give you a fat pig for this fine mat!' But her mocking glance at him threw him into confusion. Indeed, he stepped back as if he had come too close to a fire. He began to look at this strange chiefess from a distance. Perhaps the folk of Meau were right when they whispered that Chiefess Kena changed into a wild woman at night, with eyes that popped out and a long mouldy tongue that licked the ground!

In his taboo house, Chief Veo groped for his drinking shell. It was empty. The big bowl was empty, too. Where was his Fire Keeper? What was that noise that made his ears ache? When he remembered that the wood strikers were building a new house on his father's terrace, he sat up trembling, not from too much *kava* drinking, not from anger, but from fear. He had forgotten the song for the new house! He crawled to the edge of his platform, slid down the post, and stumbled across the paving. He tried to steady his shaking knees as he walked the path to the house of the Master Chanter. When he neared a shed of freshly cut coconut leaves and heard the clapping of hands and sounding of tongues, he sat down in relief. The good old master knew his work. He should have a handsome present for this. The Chief began to sing softly with the young people, as they repeated the words again and again.

> Around Red Stone Mountain is a band of mist,
> Girdle of the land, that sacred cloud,
> Head wreath of Kiato-nui, that fiery breath,
> Hair coil of Ehua, mother of the Chief.
> This is their song.

When he was sleepy, he tiptoed away to his bathing pool and slid into the quiet waters.

Chiefess Kena also heard the clapping and chanting and

directed Pakoko to lead her to the taboo house of instruction.
The boy went ahead, but he kept looking back over his shoulder
to see if she had changed into a wild woman, and when he had
brought her within hearing of the words, he was afraid she had.
He did not run away when she began to rush about, trampling
ferns and breaking bushes outside the circle of taboo sticks that
protected the singers, but he waited out of reach on the path.

When the Master Chanter came with his young people from
the house that was set apart, Chiefess Kena demanded, 'Whose
song do you sing?' But she gave him no chance to answer. 'Am I
not the mother of the High Chief of Taiohae?' she asked.

The old man stood firm. 'Of the Chief of Haavao only, as yet.'

'Isn't Red Stone Mountain the head of Haavao?' she snapped.
Seeing his unwilling nod, she continued, 'Your words are wrong.
The hair coil is mine, not Ehua's.'

The aged Master knew when it was waste time to fight a storm.
He led his youngsters back into the house to make the song over.

At the time of fires, the new house stood up, taboo, untouchable, until the Master Chanter gave it a name and linked it with
that first house of the gods, built for the woman of Atea. When it
was freed for use, Chief Veo and Chiefess Ehua entered with their
new child and his uncles and aunts and sat around torches stuck
between the stones. While the smoky flames ate the greasy nuts,
one by one, from tip to butt of the midrib that strung them
together, knots were tied in the loin cloth of the house, which
hung down over the sleeping space, and the young people outside
on the terrace began to sing of this sacred girdle.

> Around Red Stone Mountain is a band of mist,
> Girdle of the land, that sacred cloud,
> Head wreath of Kiato-nui, that fiery breath,
> Hair coil of Kena, mother of the Chief.
> This is their song.

Chief Veo's breathing stopped. Were his ears lying? No. The
words came again, swirling through the house, mingling with the
smoke and flame, 'Hair coil of Kena, mother of the Chief.' Had
he and Ehua adopted this child or had they not? He was stifling
in the clouds of fragrance of flowers, sweet oil and fire. He swam
through the heated air into the night's cold breath outside. There

was Kena's mocking face, fitfully lighted by torches. He shouted at her, 'Very well. Since you are the mother, you will take your child back to your house.'

The aged Master Chanter blotted out the greedy eyes of the chiefess, as he came close to whisper fiercely. 'Will you bring your father's spirit down upon us in anger?'

Fatu's hot breath fanned Veo's neck behind. 'You must not throw away the land of Haavao!'

The Chief was encircled by hard eyes. There was no way out for him. When his Fire Keeper slipped his ceremonial staff under his arm, he leaned on it like a broken old man. He did not call back his insult to Kena. Let these wise men mend matters. All he wanted was to creep away and drown himself in a sea of sleep. 'Bring *kava*,' he muttered thickly as he climbed into his taboo house.

In the men's house, words were flung about like stones without aim. The brother of Chief Veo, who was his Ironwood, leader of his brave-faced warriors, said that the chief's insult had given Chiefess Kena cause for war. The Master Chanter said that the Meau names given to the child could not be withdrawn and that Kena would use them to rule all Taiohae from Haavao. Fatu, sitting outside the circle of wise men, as was his custom, was disgusted with their windy talk. Kena making war, Kena ruling from Haavao, these were not the things to consider. How could the insult be wiped out and forgotten, that was the question. Fatu never grew red and swollen with anger, but his skin tightened over his bones, his eyes narrowed to slits and his mouth drew into a knot. If the elders in that house had looked at him, sitting humbly behind them, they might have trembled. Fatu was thinking savagely that the time for which he had waited all his life had come, the time for the return of Haavao to the control of a Chief of Taiohae, but that just as the great day was marching towards him, Chief Veo had stuck out his foot and tripped it up. Impatiently, he left the men who argued back and forth and went out into the night. He was Chief Veo's Master Manager. It was his duty to arrange this affair without loss to the childish chief he served. He must think of a way.

In front of his own house sat Chiefess Kena, eating by the light of a torch held by her Fire Keeper. He had brought packages of food wrapped for the guests to take home from the house-entering feast and her mate was kneeling beside her opening the leaves and spreading out the good things. How she enjoyed her food. The faster she ate, the better she liked it. Sucking pastes and crunching bones, she ate like a Brave Face preparing to go to war. Was she getting ready for a fight? She was talking constantly with a full mouth, but Fatu could make nothing of her mumbling save that it sprang from contentment rather than anger. If food could make her forget . . . Yes, that was it. Give her a feast quickly. Why wait for Big Breadfruit picking for Kiato-nui's feast of consecration as chief? The storage holes were full of paste, not too sour. The pens were crowded with fattening pigs, not too thin. There would be a memorial feast for Chief Veo's dead father and on the third day, Kena's son would be girdled with the long red loin cloth of sovereignty. Fatu would not wait till morning to propose this thing to Chiefess Kena, lest she nourish her displeasure during the night until it was too strong to strangle. His muscles twitched with eagerness, but he would not proceed without the proper forms. He ran to the men's house for his cap and cape of office.

When Chiefess Kena's stomach was tight and heavy, she thought of her soft mats which she had ordered spread in Fatu's house. That old place would do well enough for her. She cared nothing for herself. As soon as she had seen her son suitably housed, she had ceased to think of a place to sleep. She had gladly laid the burden of her hungry, helpless child in Chiefess Ehua's arms. She had more important work than chewing shrimps and breadfruit for the infant. Her work was to make him the most important chief on Nuku Hiva.

At his doorway, Fatu was waiting for Chiefess Kena. In his tall cap and cape of spraying leaflets, he looked as impressive as a chief's staff. 'Chief Veo is sick,' he began.

'Nonsense,' she snapped. 'He is soaked in *kava*.'

Fatu would not let his eyes waver. 'His desire is to make your son High Chief of Taiohae at once, on the third day of a gift-offering festival for his father's spirit.'

'Nothing of the kind,' the woman crossed him. 'His desire is for me and my son to go back to Haavao.' Fatu couldn't have opened his tight mouth if Kena had let him. 'I know what is in your intestines, also, Fatu.' She smiled at him and for the first time he could not keep his fear from shaking his hand as he held on to his thin beard. 'Why are you trembling?' she asked. 'You and I are of one thought in this matter. We both want Kiato-nui to rule over all of Taiohae. Yes?' She grinned and gouged him suddenly with a sharp finger. 'Oh, it is not to please you that I will work for this. It was my father's desire. He worked for me. I work for him. But I won't insult my son by offering him a feast of peelings and scrapings from an old harvest. We will wait for Big Breadfuit. That will give Chief Veo time to build Kiato-nui's new feast place.'

Fatu's surprise betrayed his caution. 'This feast place is still good!' he protested. 'It was built by Chief Veo's own father when Veo himself was made chief.'

'I know,' the woman answered, pointing her eyes so that they touched the quick and made him flinch. 'That old line of chiefs is ended now.' When she saw that this hook had caught in his intestines, she continued, 'There is no Master Stone Builder in Taiohae who can set up stones big enough for Kiato-nui, the Great. If it is your habit to tell Chief Veo what you have com-manded in his name'—she grinned and stuck her thumb again into his stomach—'just say that you have asked me to bring my mother's Taipi brother here to build pavings and walls and terraces fit for the god, Kiato-nui.' Chiefess Kena yawned, and drew the screen across the door opening, leaving Chief Veo's Master Manager in the dark.

Fatu passed a slow hand across his bewildered eyes. Kena had asked the one thing Chief Veo would never grant. Did she know that, this clever woman who could not be deceived? These stones were his foundation. His father had set them up for him. On them he had been lifted up and shown to his people. He had been old enough to hear the praises of the Teiis for their little new chief, because his consecration had been put off until his father had recovered from an accident which made one side of his body useless. On the great day of his feast, Veo had felt himself altogether a chief of power and he still clung for support to the memory of it.

As Fatu turned to the men's house to get what rest he could, he saw Pakoko creeping towards his father's taboo house. Ah!

The boy would climb up and Chief Veo would not send him away. Chief Veo's ears were never full of wax when Pakoko spoke to him. Chief Veo's desire was always Pakoko's desire. Yes, that was true. The uncle felt his force returning. 'Pakoko, come here,' he called. When he had pulled the little fellow to one side, away from ears behind the thatch, he stooped down and talked to him quietly. 'What great thing would you like to give our new Chief of Haavao and Taiohae?' he asked.

'A conch shell with a tassel,' Pakoko answered promptly.

'That is a little thing. Can't you think of a big thing? You know it is the custom to build a big feast place for superior chiefs.'

His uncle thought of such wonderful things. The boy's eyes sparkled. 'Big enough for all the people of Haavao to sit on with all the people of the other branches of Taiohae!' he cried.

'Exactly,' Uncle Fatu agreed. 'If you ask your father, perhaps he will buid one for your little brother.'

'I will ask him now!' The boy started for the taboo house. Fatu followed him and lifted him up to the hole in the floor. 'Tell him that there is a master in the valley of the Taipis who can move stones big enough for a god's feast place.'

'I will!' the boy whispered as he drew his feet up into the dark house.

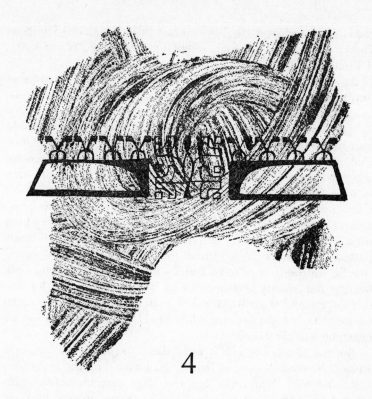

4

NEVER in his life had Pakoko been so happy. It was his work, this building of Kiato-nui's enormous establishment of house platforms, and temple terraces with a walled-in paving between them. Hadn't he asked Chief Veo to build it? His father took him to watch the procession of relatives coming from every watercourse to lay smooth boulders at the feet of the great Master Stone Builder who had come from Taipivai. The Chief let him plant the taboo sticks around the special house for the master and his skilled stone dressers and stalwart rock movers. The father and the son sat outside, watching them enter this place set apart for their consecration after they had cleansed themselves in the salty sea. Together they listened to the Master Chanter's song of the building of the first great terrace of the gods, until Pakoko himself could repeat the names of the mothers who gave birth to rocks and red tufa and beach boulders for this work. Over and over the boy intoned those wonderful names of Father Clear Space's women, 'Smoking Headland', 'Blood Rain', 'Glistening Feather'.

As soon as the Master began to lay down the 'rat's path' that outlined the great structures, Uncle Fatu went along with Pakoko to explain every work, so that the expert would not be bothered by questions. But when the heavy work of carrying big rocks on crossed shoulder poles and splitting facing blocks from Red Stone Mountain began, the Master forbade all chiefs and chiefesses and masters from following him about. He said it tangled his lines to have Chief Veo begging him to leave old stones where they were, and Chiefess Kena commanding him to change his plan, and Master Manager Fatu hurrying him to finish everything before Big Breadfruit harvest. He was free to follow the old-time pattern only when Veo retired to drink more *kava* than he should, and Kena went to pick and scratch at the aunts who were beating out twenty arm lengths of banyan bark *tapa* for the child's ceremonial girdle, and Fatu ran from house to house to see that the dwellers gave their best food to their pigs for a speedy fattening for the feast.

But the Master did not forbid Pakoko to run on his footsteps. Indeed, he used the boy as bait to draw after him the child who had come with him from Taipivai. Not that he wanted him around, this son of a Taipi chief, but he wanted to keep him out of mischief. Against his desire, he had brought Tohi-kai with him. Forbidden by his father to acompany the Master, the boy had hidden himself under a pile of bailers in the shell of the canoe until the end of the sea path to Taiohae was in sight. Then the little fellow had jumped up and given orders as loud a tongue as any chief. What could a mere Master do but hear them?

For Pakoko this Taipi boy was not an unwelcome guest. Indeed, he was the very flower on the wave of his sea of happiness. The little Teii had never had a friend from the outside before. No one had ever given him a gift of friendship. When Tohi-kai had seen that Kiato-nui was a little one unable to walk, he had seized the handsome stilts sent by his father to the new chief and given them to Pakoko. The little Taipi had closed his ears to Chiefess Kena's sharp outcry and to the Master Stone Builder's gruff protest. He had turned his back on them and pressed his gift upon Pakoko. '*Kaoha* to my friend', he had said. Chief Veo had been so pleased that he had taken a roll of *tapa* out of his ear hole and tied it around the visitor's wrist to make him taboo and free from harm in Taiohae. Pakoko, without words to answer, because of his swollen breath, had run for his anklets of curled hair as a return gift. '*Kaoha* to my friend', he had panted.

After that, from the time the sun splintered the crest of the mountain until he fell into the sea, those two little fellows were chirping together like birdlets, as they followed the Master from work to work. Often Tohi-kai wearied of such entertainment and commanded his new friend to turn aside with him to steal a bunch of bananas which had caught his skipping eyes in a nearby cook house, or to raid an oven whose pungent smoke announced its opening. Pakoko laughed with his relatives over the little Taipi's cleverness as a thief, but he kept running back to be sure that work on Kiato-nui's great feast place was going forward properly.

When the stonework was finished, Pakoko saw a tree of flames begin to sprout and branch on the highest terrace of the new sacred place and he knew that this was the sign that the Diviner and the Master Chanter were about to blow away the clouds of taboo from the stones. This was the time when all folk must hide during the seven days of the gods' feasting. The boy knew the saying, 'No fire, no work, no running about', but he did not follow his relatives as they ran to their houses to cover themselves. He followed Tohi-kai, who had peeped before at sacred things and had not died. He laughed as they crawled through the underbrush. Uncle Fatu would think they were in Father Veo's house and Veo would think they were in the shed Fatu had built for his family.

The boys climbed a hillside beyond the terraces and hid themselves in a cave behind a cascade of *ieie* vines. When they had made a hole in this screen, they looked below. The old men were leaning against their stone slabs, swinging their fans and sounding words of power. The Clubs who served the Priest were stripping leaves from a long bundle. Pakoko's breathing stopped when he saw that inside lay a man, stiff and still, a victim caught for the gods, but Tohi-kai said this was no longer a man but a fish for the gods to eat. Tohi-kai had seen all this before. He began breaking ferns to make a soft seat. But Pakoko's eyes clung like vines to the sacred work below. He watched the Clubs smear that pale face with red and close the ears with hibiscus blooms and the mouth with bad-smelling *noni* fruits. He trembled and fell flat when all the old men bent over as if a strong wind had blown them down. Was it a big bird that was floating past them? 'That is the Diviner,' said Tohi-kai. Pakoko did not know the god who lived far up valley in a sky-piercing house, but he had heard of his great power. It was said that he could fly through the air on his ironwood stick and that he could hear the talk of birds. Pakoko crawled outside the cave to see this wonder, but he was just a natural man, with a shaven head bound with a wreath, with a white beard that was tangled in a neckband of boars' teeth. But no! He was different. His mouth was pulled to one side and when he chanted it did not move. His voice came from the sky, like an echo!

'Here is your food, Oh Grandfathers-far-below! Come, eat! When you are full, send food to men! Cover this feast place with good food!' The voice fluttered in the tree tops, and the Priest followed it up, up, flying from terrace to terrace, up to the top where the fire quivered and swayed. His long white *tapa* and his short red *tapa* stretched out on the wind behind him. Up above, coming and going in the fire's breath, in and out among the pale banyan roots that dripped like rain from the clouds hanging among the leaves, he led his white-robed Clubs. Now they were piling the fruits of the land and the sea before the bent legs of the *tikis*. Big, heavy, black, those images, with shut eyes and folded arms. No man knew their thoughts. Only the Priest knew. Only he saw the dead chiefs and priests of the Teiis entering them. Only he asked them for plenty and was heard. '*Ou, ou, ou!*' he sang in a voice high and thin as a spirit's. Then, heavy as a stone, his voice fell on those below, 'Come, be brave!'

Pakoko jumped up to answer but Tohi-kai caught his ankle and pulled him down beside him. 'That is not an invitation for you,' he said. 'I could go if I wanted,' he boasted. 'I am taboo in this valley but you're just a piece of lichen clinging to the chief.'

The Teii child recoiled. Lichen! He was nobody's hanger-on. Was the Taipi laughing at him or trying to make him laugh? He could not dig into his eyes, that gleamed behind enlaced lashes. He shivered a little and turned for comfort to the scene below.

The Brave Faces in full battle dress were following the red-robed Master Chanter now, as he pointed his three bound sticks towards the sky as a sign to the temple assistants to carry the victim up to the topmost terrace. When the old man turned to receive the god's fish, Pakoko saw that he held the great tortoise-shell fish hook on which the gods pulled their food to the sky. Many stories the boy had heard of this great hook as he sat clapping and singing old words with his relatives. Now he was seeing with naked eyes how the Master fastened the point in the dead man's mouth, how that lifeless form was raised slowly towards the clouded leaves. The boy felt the power of the old man's chant, pulling, pulling him, as he intoned the familiar story of the Priest's helpers who hid behind rocks watching for those that wandered alone on the sands. Terror shook him as he heard of the baskets of delicious food held out as bait for catching the relatives of the victim, for there were the baskets of young coconuts, sure enough, tied to the arms of the dead. He covered his eyes but he could not shut out the lament of those who had been caught for the gods.

> Grasping-fingered sea! Oh Ki-i-ia!
> Long-armed sea! Oh Ki-i-ia!
> Why were we on the sand? Oh Ki-i-ia!
> Digging crawfish! Oh Ki-i-ia!
> Grasping-fingered sea! Oh Ki-i-ia!

When Pakoko looked again, the body had been lowered to the paving and the red-robed celebrant was kneeling beside it. He seemed to be talking to the gods themselves. The little fellow had told his father that he wanted to be a Master Chanter. Now he was sure of it. But when he saw the old man gouge out the eyes of the victim and eat them, he felt dizzy and wanted to vomit.

Tohi-kai laughed at him. 'I shan't be sick when I eat the eyes. It is a good thing you are not a chief. You would faint.'

'I won't when I am a Master Chanter.' Pakoko encouraged himself, louder than he had meant, and the old man raised his burning eyes. Was he looking straight into the cave? The boy turned to ashes and crumpled down onto the ground. 'Do not eat me!' he begged 'I shall never break another taboo!' He pressed his face against the red soil. He had seen too many bright things of the sky. Like a shrimp's old shell, he lay still and empty.

Even Tohi-kai crawled far back into the cave and went to sleep.

Because the assistants of the Teii Priest had caught the fish for their gods on the sands of the valley of Hakapaa, the Hapaa Chief, Tea-roru, struck back swiftly to avenge this seizure of his relative. He sent men before the light was bright to cut girdles in the skin of breadfruit trees in upper Meau valley. When Chief Veo was told, he ground his teeth. 'Tea-roru is a rotten rat!' he cried.

Chiefess Kena rushed to the women's cook house to find the coconut sheath of embers. She herself would fan it into flame, running to all the branches of Taiohae to rouse the people to dig ovens for many Hapaas. 'A man for every tree killed!' she screamed.

But Master Manager Fatu blocked her path. 'One work at a time,' he warned. 'What do you want—war with the Hapaas or a feast of consecration for your son? Choose!'

'Both!' she demanded with a lift of her heavy chin. 'Kiato-nui is a new post with strength to hold up one roof over this entire island.' She would not give in to this son of a driven chief.

Fatu stared at the foolish woman. Not even in ancient times had a chief conquered all tribes. 'First, let Kiato-nui put one roof over all the branches of Taiohae,' he answered with scorn.

She knew he was right, but she could not admit it. 'I was thinking of Veo's rights,' she said, 'but since he does not care . . .' She stamped out the flame in the sheath. 'As for me, I prefer to tie the Hapaas to Kiato-nui by adopting a child of their chiefly level. It will last longer than conquest.'

Naturally, the Master Manager did not intend that Chief Veo should let this cause for war go unprotested, but even a greedy woman must wait for revenge until after Big Breadfruit had been eaten at a feast for her son. The Council of Masters was of one mind with him and Chief Veo nodded and smiled when they decided to send a messenger to the Hapaa chief to arrange for a talk about putting a cover on this flame of war that had been lighted.

When the meeting between the two chiefs had been agreed upon, Chief Veo was not in the procession as it climbed to the backbone of the land. There were Veo's two brothers, the one-eyed Ironwood and the watchful Fire Keeper. There was the Master Chanter carrying a big coconut leaf and after him the Master Fisherman with four men bearing a heavy turtle on their crossed shoulder poles. Master Manager Fatu went along to see that Chief Veo kept his appointment. If Chief Veo had not insisted that Pakoko should accompany him, he might have been leading this important group of Teiis, but he had many things to show his son and could not be bothered with a path. The Fire Keeper, who carried his brother's staff and fan and feather headdress, kept turning his ears to hear the voices of those two shouting, now from a breadfruit grove, now from a mulberry plantation, now from a thicket of sugar cane. Fatu threw little pebbles in the direction of their laughter, wherever it mingled with the calls of birds or the fury of waterfalls. Both men were afraid that Veo's play with Pakoko would make him forget where he was going. But the battle-scarred Ironwood, going on this peace mission with dragging feet, hoped it would. A fire smothered might never be rekindled.

Chief Veo kept backing off from the path that led to the Valley of Tears where he must shout at the Hapaas with a loud tongue and demand what he wanted. What did he want? Chiefess Kena wanted war, Fatu wanted peace. But nobody had asked the Chief's desires, not even the Master Fisherman who had chosen for the ceremony a little turtle which the Hapaas would laugh at.

It was no wonder that the Fire Keeper wiped the sweat from his forehead and sat down to rest when he had finally tied the red and yellow feathers on Chief Veo's head and put his staff and fan into his hands, for there, above the sea of rippling, waist-high grass in the Valley of Tears, the feathers of the Hapaa party stood up shining in the sun.

Uncle Fatu caught his nephew by the arm and pointed to a bald red rock standing in the clear. 'That is the end of Teii land. On the other side, the Hapaas will catch you and feed you to their gods,' he told Pakoko.

The boy's eyes widened, remembering a thing he had seen. He crept in the shadow of his elders until he heard the greetings shouted between the enemy chiefs. Then he stood up to see. Looking at the tall, well-built chief of the Hapaas, he called up to his father in amazement, 'You said he was a rotten rat!'

All the grand old words of the Teiis and the Hapaas fell on the ground like stones. Veo's breathing stopped. Fatu's went out in a roar. 'Come here!'

The Hapaa Chief was a wind striking swiftly, lifting the boy high into the air. 'What do you say I am?' he questioned the small face across from his own that was frightful with bands of tattooing.

Pakoko felt the strength ooze out of his toes. For a space he could not move his tongue, then he would not, because he knew that Chief Tea-roru was holding him on the Hapaa side of the red rock. 'Put me down on my own land,' he said between closed teeth.

When the man had complied, stooping to the child's level, holding his eyes firmly, the boy repeated stubbornly, 'You are a rotten rat.'

No one moved or breathed until Tea-roru said, 'You will be an Ironwood.'

'No,' the little fellow crossed him, 'I will be a Master Chanter.'

'An old man's work,' the Hapaa said in disgust. He stood up with a rush. 'Give him my fan,' he called to his Fire Keeper. 'You want to smother war until Big Breadfruit is picked and eaten?' he asked Chief Veo. The Teii being without breath to answer, he demanded, 'Yes or no?'

'Yes!' shouted Fatu before it was too late.

'There is my turtle.' Chief Tea-roru made a sign to his Master Fisherman. 'He is larger than yours. Are you satisfied?'

'Yes,' the Master Chanter answered for Chief Veo, and when the turtles had been exchanged he stepped forward to dig a hole for the big coconut leaf he had brought to plant as a sign of peace.

'Wait!' the Hapaa commanded. 'There is one condition. I want that boy for a son-in-law. Yes or no?'

Do men say yes or no to the sea when it storms in precipices? The Teiis looked at Pakoko with round eyes and the boy looked

34

only at his beautiful white fan with the carved bone handle. He waved it gently, this side, that side, as he began to sound old words.

> Joined long ago the big roots,
> Ah, the big roots of the land.

'Good. Our roots will be joined,' said Tea-roru. 'Now you may plant the coconut leaf.' He hurried away to his own valley without looking back.

Chief Veo carried his son on his hip all the way down to his house. 'Don't leave me! Don't go!' he begged.

'No,' Pakoko promised. 'I don't want to be eaten by the Hapaas.'

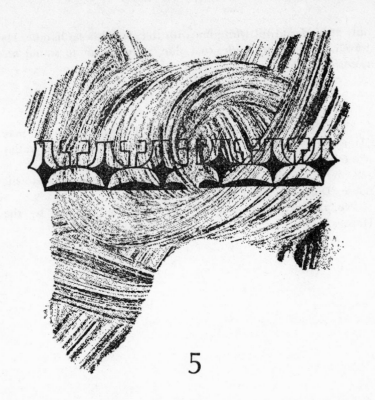

5

Now that the Hapaas had consented to peace during the rainy moons of ripening breadfruit and fattening pigs, the chiefs of the Teiis declared a taboo on all fruits of the land and sea. Little Breadfruit harvest was not eaten but stored in deep hillside holes. Nobody grumbled about using sour breadfruit paste from old storage holes and such women's food as limpets scraped from rocks by the sea. Stomachs felt heavy just with the thought of the great feast to come and saliva dripped when the masters repeated Chief Veo's count of the knots of breadfruit, bundles of fish and litters of fat pigs that would be collected.

As soon as oven holes were covered and oven stones put away in baskets, Chiefess Kena took her relatives back to her own house in Haavao. The folk of Meau whispered that she had no intention of closing her own cook house and that her Fire Keeper would look the other way when she went about picking breadfruit from her own trees. Let her go! Now work and laughter could run along together in Chief Veo's valley. Now he could come down from his taboo house and make anything or nothing last as long as he pleased. Now Chiefess Ehua could enfold the sacred child in her arms as petals curl about a bud, without being told to feed him.

There were so many taboo works going on that Pakoko wore his legs out running from houses to streams and from mountains to sands. When rain kept the workers under thatch, he watched the careful fingers of the makers of Kiato-nui's hair ornaments. When rain grew afraid of the light and workers came out under dirty skies, he lay on wet leaves beside the muddy stream where his grandmother and aunts were beating the soaking pulp of banyan bark into Kiato-nui's long, long girdle. While the Master Fisherman was overhauling his canoes, he stayed day and night in the expert's house. He could not touch the taboo cord as the women rolled it nor the nets as the men mended torn eyes, but he encouraged the workers with handclapping. In the obscurity of rain clouds and taboo clouds, the little boy kept close to the Master Planter when he splashed through the mud in breadfruit groves to tie to the tree trunks big coconut leaves as a sign that the growing fruits were untouchable.

Pakoko thought that he had made his own breadfruit tree doubly safe by naming it 'The Head of Pakoko,' but, alas, one day he found his foster brother, Kohu, in its branches. 'Come down from my tree! You are standing on my head!' yelled the outraged owner.

Terrified at the fury of his brother and the bellowing of his father who came running like the wind, little Kohu lost his hold when Pakoko shook the tree and fell onto the ground, mashing the breadfruit clasped in his arms. Hearing Fatu's agonized cry, 'My son has defiled Pakoko's head!' all the relatives burst out of the houses onto the terraces chattering like birds after fish. Chief Veo shook Pakoko in a frenzy of fear for his son. Fatu slapped his Kohu as he wept for his safety. The big girl, Hina, twisted her hands together, longing to comfort her boy, Pakoko. The Fire Keeper ran for the Master who could untie this bad thing.

Pakoko broke away from his father's hand and said in a hollow voice, 'Now I must kill Kohu and eat his eyes.' This made everybody stare at the boy. Where had he picked that up? It made Uncle Fatu pull him aside and talk to him quietly until the Master came to remove the insult to the boy's head. Then Pakoko said to the Master, 'Kohu is just a child. He did not know he was a taboo breaker.' The man was busy, giving orders for coconut fibres, hibiscus blooms, coconut water, many things. Pakoko pulled at his leaf cape. 'I will not kill him if you make my head well again.' Receiving no answer, he kept feeling his head uneasily until he forgot everything but the Master's work of mixing a strange drink to undo the harm.

No one gave ear to Kohu's moans until his father saw that his right foot was turning backward. 'His leg is broken!' he cried.

Again there was a commotion, with everyone running here and there—for the Master Bone Mender, for ironwood sticks, for new *tapa*. Now it was Pakoko's turn to weep, for he had shaken his foster brother out of the tree onto sharp stones below. While the Master slit the leg and fitted a smooth stick inside and wrapped it tight, the boy squatted close to the sufferer and whispered encouragement. His tears splashed on Kohu's closed eyes. 'I made you fall,' he lamented.

When the pain had eased, Kohu opened his eyes to Pakoko. 'While I was in the air,' he whispered, 'I was like the Priest, flying on his ironwood stick.'

'The light is nearly bright!' The Fire Keeper shook Chief Veo awake. 'Stand up!'

Veo pretended to be snoring. He knew very well that this was the day to seek pigs for his father's spirit. He knew that he must take little Kiato-nui with him, but he would put off that work as long as he could. During the moons when Chiefess Ehua had fed the child the soft pulp of very ripe breadfruit from her own mouth, Veo had refused to see or touch the little one. He was forced to give him the high seat of Taiohae but not the seat on his hip. That belonged to Pakoko. The Chief was about to roll farther over on the taboo mats, when, in the fluttering light of a single torch, he saw his son's shadow stretching to the rafters. 'What are you doing?' he asked sharply, sitting up to see.

'Here is your sweet oil,' the boy answered, handing him his shell.

What was there to bellow about? The child had not stepped on his father's mat, nor touched his loin cloth that was propped out of harm's way on a stick inside the taboo space. Yet Veo bellowed at him. 'The sun is not yet standing up. Go back to your uncle's house where you belong.' Now, why had he said that? Why had he driven the boy outside? Had he offended him? The Chief threw off his *tapas* as if they were smothering him. He dashed the oil over his body and left it sticky and uneven. He screwed his hair about on either side without taking any care. He grabbed a torn *tapa* and pulled it between his legs and tied it without tail behind or flap in front. He rushed out of his sleeping house.

There were the sons and the grandsons of the dead chief waiting. Pakoko, riding on the Fire Keeper's shoulders, was shouting to the other children, 'I will bring back two pigs for every one of yours.' He did not look at his father at all.

The Chief was angry because Pakoko was thinking of something different. He was angry because his son had to ride on the shoulders of a man who was not a chief. He looked about for Kiato-nui and he was pricked again to see that his woman carried the little fellow as if he were a precious coconut. Chiefess Ehua also was as inconstant as a breeze. He snatched the child from her, flung him over his shoulder and held him there with hard fingers. 'Go along,' he commanded his brothers. 'Go where you please. I shall take Haavao and Meau.' He jumped from the terrace and started across the paving.

'Not so fast!' The quick, sharp voice of his brother-in-law was in his ear. What had come over Fatu? He was Master Manager of work. Did he think he must also direct the chief? 'For a space I will climb with you,' he was saying.

Veo rubbed his teeth together and hastened his legs, but the pat, pat, of Fatu's feet echoed his own. He jumped over the high roots of black leaved *ihi* trees, but Fatu jumped too. He tore his skin on thorny vines, but Fatu followed through the brambles.

Where the path branched, Fatu shouted, 'This way!' and pointed towards the ironwood grove circling the taboo terrace of the dead chief. 'Your father wants to see you and his grandson begging pigs for his spirit,' he said.

Driven by the tongue behind him, Chief Veo dragged his toes

through the fallen hair of the trees. Yes, his father was watching him, too, always directing him. Standing at the edge of the clearing, he would not uncover his eyes to see the sky-going canoe and the paddler inside it, but he could not close his ears to the whispering of his brother-in-law beside him.

'Your father is very, very weary of this long going,' Fatu was telling him. 'Only twice have you fed him and he is without strength to climb to the skies. He is without gifts to ask for entrance there.'

Veo raised his head like a startled bird. Was he himself keeping his father from seeking that beautiful land? Had he been stingy? Deeply moved, he called out, 'I will go quickly, my father. I will bring you innumerable pigs.'

The child on Veo's shoulder made a noise. He was laughing. He was stretching out his arms towards the image with its fluttering capes and streaming feathers.

Chief Veo lifted Kiato-nui down and stared at him. He knew his grandfather. He wanted him. 'He is yours!' the father cried. He turned shining eyes on his companion. 'Did you see that?' He laughed. 'He is a birdlet just out of his shell, and yet he knows the work of a chief. He is offering his grandfather all his pigs.'

'The god will send breadfruit and children in return,' the Master Manager said, wiping his eyes. Then he struck Veo's behind with his bundle of sticks. 'Go,' he commanded.

Holding Kiato-nui on his head, the Chief visited the houses of his relatives, shouting at each, 'Pigs for the grandfather! Pigs for the grandfather!'

'Sound the names of your grandfathers for the pigs!' was the answer from each terrace.

'O Ani is the father; Nohoana, his woman.' Beginning thus with Sky and Uniting, Veo kept naming the faces of the gods and men all the way up from the beginning to Kiato-nui himself. The child began to beat on his head for the father, for the woman, for the father, for the woman. Veo laughed and the child laughed.

'Here is a child who makes a song before he talks. Here is a new shoot who knows his roots. A sacred child of power comes asking pigs for his grandfather's spirit. Give! Give! Give so that Kiato-nui may push him into the sky, so that we may have a new god to send us abundance!'

Those two went from house to house, laughing and calling sacred names and looking back to count the fat pigs swinging on poles as more and more carriers followed them. What open hands the valley folk turned towards them! What loud *kaohas* they shouted to the grandfather, the father and the son! How they praised Chief Veo for tying the branch of Haavao with the other branches of Taiohae in one unbreakable bundle! How they admired the beautiful child! Indeed, Veo himself began to see the little fellow's straight back and round limbs and big, black eyes and head sloping to a peak.

Those eyes rested on Veo's face until he felt their soft touch and gave the child his own eyes in return. Then Kiato-nui smiled with wide open mouth.

'He knows me!' Veo exclaimed. He tossed the little one up and caught him with soft hands.

When Chief Veo returned to his own terrace at the fall of the sun, he was carrying the child in his arms, pressed against his breast. Pakoko was waiting for him, the tale of the pigs he had brought back spilling out of his mouth in a loud stream.

'Hush! He is asleep,' Veo whispered, never taking his eyes from the small round face wedged in his folded arm. He went on soft feet past his own sleeping house, past the taboo house and into the new house built for Kiato-nui.

Pakoko bit his lip to keep it from trembling and squatted near the bamboo pickets that screened the little Chief's house. He waited until the evening fires fell into ashes, then crept forlornly through the dark to his mat in Uncle Fatu's house.

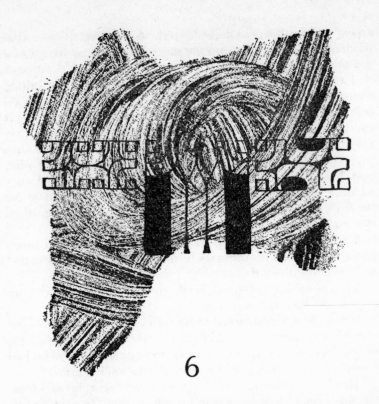

6

WHEN the stars, Sparkling and Pig, were a moon old and Big Litter swung again across the sky, Chief Veo's shell blew away the clouds of taboo and the folk of Taiohae gave their hands and backs to gathering the great abundance set aside for the old and the new chiefs. Innumerable new breadfruit were bending the trees, three two-hundreds of pigs were groaning under fat in their pens. The names of the little fish in the sea had been changed to those of big ones. Chief Veo's messenger ran through every branch of Taiohae and through the valleys of the Taipis, Haapas and Taioas, calling out to the relatives, 'Here is your invitation! Here is your invitation!' How handsome he was, wrapped in folds and folds of white *tapa!* His gay scarf fluttering behind him set the young men to shaking their hips and the young women to oiling their skins.

Before dawn on the first day of the festival, the Fire Keeper summoned helpers to fill the ovens. 'Stand up! Stand up!' His call echoed through the great silence of the valley. Shivering in the cold shades, men and boys raked away the embers of the firewood that had burned through the night, flung green sticks and leaf mats on the glowing red stones inside the deep holes, and lowered forties and forties of pigs and innumerable baskets of bananas, yams and taro down upon them. Shutting all the sweet smells inside with a covering of bark and soil, they warmed themselves by dancing round and round the holes.

'*Owhe-te-pepe, owhe-te-pepe, owhe-te-pepe!*' The voice of the big drum was calling at the new feast place, its beats slow and level as an old man's tongue. Chief Veo was stepping to its pulse across the new stones, holding the baby Kiato-nui on his hip. 'Look at your smooth paving, little Coconut,' he begged. He guided the child's hand over the faces carved on the walls. '*Tikis.* Say, *Tikis*,' he urged. He climbed onto a terrace ringing round a big *temanu* tree and set the boy against a stone back rest. 'Now sing like an old man!' he commanded. Kiato-nui's answer was always a wide-open smile or a gurgle in his throat which made Veo laugh out loud. The Chief could not stop showing all these grand things to his son. He ran to the clean earth in the centre of the paving, where it was beaten hard for the feet of dancers. 'Here, little Chief, show yourself!' He made the little feet go pat, pat on the land. Then he lay on his back and looked up at the terraces at the far end of the paving, up to the sacred place where the images of the grandfathers-far-below pierced the sky. Holding the child above him, he cried to them, 'Look down! Look down! See your new shoot!'

'See me!' called the little boy for any ear to hear.

Yes, all the folk of Nuku Hiva were coming to see this little new Chief. They would fill the new bamboo sheds on the enclosing terraces. They would see the child being carried about the feast place on the heads of his uncles and aunts. 'Here is where the Chiefs will sit. Here is where the high-born women will sit.' Veo pointed out the sweet smelling bowers and made Kiato-nui laugh at the red and yellow *ti* leaves swinging from their roofs. He held him up to pat the stiff and shining coconut leaves plaited around their posts. Ah. The sea was rising high in Chief

Veo. 'Oh! Oh! Oh! Oh!' Joy rushed out of his mouth. 'Long is this feast place, wide is this feast place, high is this feast place of Kiato-nui!'

Now the sun was standing up and six long drums, two arms high, were calling with quick, quick tongues, *'Owhe-te-pepe, owhe-te-pepe, owhe-te-pepe!'* Veo could hear canoes scraping on the sand and feet pounding the paths. Hurrying to Kiato-nui's terrace, he looked suddenly into Pakoko's red eyes staring at him from a high stone. 'Come!' he called gaily. 'Let us say *kaoha* to our food friends!'

The boy did not move. His eyes were hard. The father stepped back, as if struck by a stone from a sling. In his breast a current twisted through the high sea of his joy, black and agitated. Pakoko's eyes that had always pulled him close were pushing him away! What had happened to the son while the father was busy making ready this great feast? 'He has been turning aside from me!' the Chief remembered. Why were they two no longer going together? 'Come with me,' he pleaded. When Pakoko neither moved nor blinked, Veo grew angry. The boy was full of black bile. He was making his ears wood. He was crossing his own father. 'What bad thing have you done?' he shouted. 'Have you stolen food from the trees?' He looked hastily at the packages tied to branches stuck in between the stones. Was anything missing?

High and shrill sounded a woman's chant. 'Oh we are the family of Hopu! Oh Hopu! Ho-o-o-oi! Oh Nati is the woman! Ho-o-o-oi!' The folk of Hoata were crying their arrival. They were waiting at the opening in the massive walls of the feast place. Chief Veo could not be bothered with that stubborn boy, Pakoko. He climbed Kiato-nui's terrace to call his welcome and walk back and forth on the stones, holding up the sacred child for all to see. He knew that they were pleased with their new chief. They could scarcely tear their eyes away to see the seats set apart for them on the new paving. Turning their backs on the Fire Keeper, who was trying to point them out with his staff with flying ribbons, they lingered near the baby. What strong *kaoha* flowed from their bright eyes and smiling lips! Chief Veo swung his hips to the beat of the drums. He began to feel like a yellow-stained youngster. He thought of bawdy old jokes and

called them out, making the women laugh to cover their embarrassment, making the men slap their thighs.

Yes, the Chief of Meau was a father-man, standing up whole.
He had a first-born sent by the gods. The long waiting was over.
He could just sit quietly now, watching Kiato-nui stand up on
the prow of the canoe of this land. He would be a good father.
He would hold the steering paddle, just to let the little one feel
confident, but he would let his son go where he pleased.

The white day blazed. The tall drums rocked faster and faster
as the names of all relatives from other valleys were called out for
seats on the new paving of Chief Kiato-nui. The women of the
high level folk were crowding their terrace, standing up and
moving about to show themselves to one another and to the
common water on the stones below. They were like wind-tossed
flowers, their bobbing heads banded with red and yellow feathers
or carved tortoise-shell plaques and crested with sprays of white
hair. They were wrapped round and round and round with crisp
white *tapa* that made them light as balls of sea foam. Chiefess
Kena was rustling about from group to group, clapping her
hands sharply for her women-at-the-side to bring mats or eye-
shades or drinking coconuts, as if she were the hostess. Chiefess
Ehua was nowhere to be seen, for she had gone to the little
Chief's cook house to prepare food for him. The Chiefess from
Hakaui was not there, because she was in the birth house waiting
for the little one who would be the mate of Kiato-nui. The little
Hapaa girl, who would one day be joined to Pakoko, was sitting
with very straight back on the edge of the terrace, turning her
serious eyes from face to face of those below, as if she wanted to
remember her new relatives. Ah, there was one who would never
have to give orders with a loud tongue to show she was a chiefess.
The watchers on the paving beckoned to Pakoko to come see that
little Metani but they could not make him see them.

Pakoko had witnessed other harvest festivals without knowing
their excitements, because he had been such a little fellow, and
today, though he was a big boy able to laugh and shout and feast
with his elders, he could not join their play. He was like a bare
rock lying at midday on the edge of a sea that dashed against his
feet but left him hot and dry and still. He could not dip into the
flood of joy around him, he could not run away nor even turn

his head and close his eyes, for he had to face unflinching the cruel sun that burned him. With hard dry eyes fixed on Chief Veo and his new son, he missed no gesture of tenderness, no cry of pride of the new father. Ever since the day of pig begging he had felt the uneasiness of one who is alone while others are together, but today he had soaked in so much pain that he felt numb.

As he lay forsaken, thrown away, he felt the thudding of the feet of the visiting Chiefs as they passed him on their way to the men's house where the Fire Keeper had spread their leaves for food. Pakoko knew that quick light feet were pausing beside him and he heard a robust voice calling down to him, 'Well, little son-in-law, why aren't you looking at the beautiful gifts of betrothal I have brought your family?' The boy could not turn over to thank the Hapaa Chief, for he had to see where Chief Veo was carrying Kiato-nui. Only when he saw him enter the little Chief's sleeping house could he look up, but then Chief Tea-roru had gone on, grumbling about stubborn children with wax in their ears, leaving Pakoko more desolate than before. Still, his following eyes began to see the procession of high level men and he felt the same awe that was making the watchers on the paving below fall on their hands and knees and hide their faces against the stones. The chiefs' tall staffs with top knots of curled black hair stood up high above them, a forest of taboo sticks beside which they marched unafraid. Pakoko drew a deep breath, as if their serene dignity had cooled the fever of his distress.

Just then a tickling on the soles of his feet made him jerk around, but he halted his ready kick, for there was his friend, Tohi-kai, who had come with his father to Kiato-nui's feast. Pakoko got up slowly and stood looking at the little Taipi as if to discover some flaw in him. When a slow grin finally lighted his bleak face, Tohi-kai said, 'Come, play.' But another said, 'Not now. Come, eat.' That was his friend's father, a short man, but impressive because of his weight and blackness. Looking up at him, Pakoko thought he might fall over on him and crush him. His eyes went to the man's girdle to see if there was food tied there, for the Teiis often said that the Taipi chief hid food in his clothes for fear he might have to give some away. But no, only the mouth of the stingy man was drawn into a knot. Perhaps after all his intestines were not hard, for Tohi-kai paid no attention to his father but did as he pleased. 'Come,' he commanded Pakoko and pulled him after him.

It seemed as if Pakoko had forgotten all about his own father's *kaoha* for another. With his friend by his side, he raced over terraces and walls and pavings as if he had never seen them before. Now it was he who pulled Tohi-kai about, making him stand still or run. In front of a big *temanu* tree, which was circled by old men leaning against their stone back rests, he made him halt to listen to their chanting. The whitened fans of the masters swinging from side to side, their leaf-fringed caps and capes rising and falling had set the folk on the paving to swaying. Their red voices, following the swelling tones of the drums, had quickened the boys' breathing. For a space the two boys were no longer Pakoko and Tohi-kai, but just two ripples hurrying along in flowing water. When the warriors, those invincible Brave Faces with hair ornaments on their legs, came rushing across the stones and leaping upon their terrace, the children yelled and jumped with those around them. Teiis, Taipis, Hapaas, Taioas, fighters from all tribes, mingled. They were all big hearts, high jumpers, fast runners, silent snarers. Following their Ironwoods, with skulls of vanquished foes dangling from their girdles, they made their own sun and wind with their flashing pearl shells, glistening cocks' plumes, quivering bird tails, swirling black hair skirts and billowing *tapas*. They were a storm howling across the feast place, blowing all watchers about like frenzied leaves.

The appearance of the Diviner and the Master Chanter on the sacred terraces smothered the tumultuous joy with a hush of fear and respect. High and low alike waited with lowered eyes while the first shares of food were offered to the gods, while the Master Chanter blessed those who had brought pigs and the Diviner murmured *kaohas* to the grandfathers-far-below and begged them for another abundance like this one. But when the conch blew, declaring that food was free for all, the hurricane was loosed again.

Men pushed and shoved, clamoring for their shares. There were mountains of breadfruit ready to roast on little fires that were beginning to crackle all over the feast place. Packages of sweets were tied to branches as thick as leaves. Canoes full of breadfruit paste were being carried from the cook houses. Fishermen came with dripping leaf-wrapped bundles tied to their shoulder poles. "Five twenties of fish for the family of Honeno!' shrieked one, clawing at the wet leaves. 'Ours is the first share!' protested another. 'Make a path! Make a path!' commanded the Fire Keeper, waving his staff and leading the fishermen to the leaves spread for their catch, holding back the crowd while they emptied their shining flood of black, white, yellow and red. When he had counted out the shares, he tossed them to the families to whom they belonged. There were fish for all, again and again. There were hundreds and hundreds of pigs carried on rafts from every oven in Taiohae. When the bearers brought the smoking hot flesh to the Fire Keeper, he could scarcely swing his arm because of the press about him, as he cut off the heads of the pigs for the priests and the customary choice bits for the chiefs, masters and fighters. When he was throwing the others their just shares, there was such sucking of juice and cracking of bones that men could not hear their names called and grabbed the shares of their neighbors, so that the Fire Keeper had to strike apart those who quarreled and fought, although there was plenty for all and baskets full left over to be carried home. Even the women, who were served different food from their own ovens and who ate as daintily as little fish, said that their stomachs were too heavy to carry and that they must lie down before eating more. As for Pakoko and Tohi-kai, they ate everything offered them by friendly folk until the Teii's eyes began to turn in circles and he ran off alone into the bush, and the Taipi pushed aside a half-eaten package of sweetened taro and crawled into the shade to sleep.

'*Tuti-tuti-tuti!*' sang the little drums, shaking the drowsy feasters awake to see the tiny dancers being carried by the Priest's helpers to the centre of the feast place. They stood shyly while the grandmothers, just touching them with the tips of their fingers, unwound the lengths of *tapa* wrapped about their delicate bodies. They looked like little clouds unfurling. When they danced, their feet were raindrops on the land, their hands leaves trembling in a shower. These little ones and their dances were for the dead grandfather who was now a god. They came and went so swiftly that the spirit who watched seemed to have drawn them up into clear space.

The free youngsters took their place, half-grown boys and girls with yellow-stained skins and *tapas* gleaming in the sunlight. The crowds pressed close to see the young women kneading the land with their supple toes, agitating the air with their fluttering fingers, stirring up the intestines of every man there. Pakoko came running to follow, like the tail of a kite, the youths who circled around the young women. Flesh crawling, water dripping, the watchers began to beat with hollow palms on arm-pits, in time with the song of the old men under the *temanu* trees.

> Grandfather, join our play!
> Here is your song of greeting,
> Like a flute, like a shell for sweetness.
> Here is your yellow neck wreath,
> Fragrance filling your nostrils.
> Here are the seven plays of love,
> Bodies burning and melting.
> Grandfather, join our play!

The little boy imitated the entranced movements of the young men as they approached their mates from above, below, behind, kneeling, sitting, standing and lizard-like.

'*Owhe-te-pepe, owhe-te-pepe, owhe-te-pepe!*' urged the big drums, gathering the god Atea and all his children on the feast place into one beat. Shaking were the drums, shaking were the fathers and mothers, shaking was the land with the desire of the god. Shaking were the voices of the old men as they intoned the stages in the growth of the land.

> Joined long ago the big roots,
>   Ah, the big roots of the land.
> Joined long ago the big roots,
>   Ah, the rootlets of the land.
> Joined long ago the big roots,
>   Ah, the fastenings of the land.
> Joined long ago the big roots,
>   Ah, the girdle of the land.
> Joined long ago the big roots,
>   Ah, the knot of the land.

Beside this solemn chant, all other songs were moon babblings for Pakoko. Whenever he heard it, the little boy had to throw himself down on the land and gaze up at the sky, as if he were pressed between Level Below and Level Above, awaiting birth. He left the dancers now and dropped down close to the old men's terrace. Rocked gently by the sea of tone, which reached for him and receded, touched him and withdrew, he fell asleep.

All the children of Clear Space, filled with the god's seeds, slept. Free youngsters, laced together, limp, content as little pigs full of breast water, slept in nests under vines on the sands or in fern-lined hollows under upland bush. Mothers and fathers slept where they had fallen on the stones of the feast place. Grandmothers, rolled in *tapa* with armsful of babies, slept with one hand tending sputtering lighted nuts. Grandfathers, blowing noisily through their noses, belching and passing wind, slept between their comings and goings into the bush. All folk slept, until the red of the next sun and the tired voice of the big drum called the women to lament the dead chief in dance and song.

On the second day of the great memorial festival, Master Manager Fatu left the women to their grief-wailing and nude dancing to see that all was in order for the stilt races and the girdling ceremony of the following day. Hearing wild laughter and loud talk coming from the taboo terrace where the champions were housed, he went to see why those set apart for tomorrow's great trial of skill were not gathering strength in silence. The picked stilt runners of the four great valleys of Nuku Hiva were entertaining themselves by teaching the way of the stilt game. The two boys, Pakoko and his friend, Tohi-kai, were running back and forth in front of the men, learning to kick and jump on their sky-legs. Uncle Fatu made a sour mouth. That little Taipi chief was pushing Pakoko beyond his harvests. Only a father-man should wear the kind of stilts the child had given Pakoko, sacred ironwood sky-legs with carved footrests bound to the shafts with red and black cords. Not even champions had better to run on.

Fatu's nephew spied him and came stumbling and swaying towards him. 'Tohi-kai and I will be the first to run for the two sides of the island!' he cried.

'Down with the Teiis of the west!' yelled Tohi-kai, running after him.

'Down with the Taipis of the east!' shouted Pakoko, turning to kick him off his wooden legs.

The men on the terrace howled with laughter, but Uncle Fatu went away grumbling. Tomorrow's contest was not a child's game. It was a sacred work to make sure that the sun would walk over Taiohae on his long sky-legs. *Tuh! Tuh!* Men no longer took the god's ways seriously.

But next day, when Uncle Fatu sat on a wall to see the little Teii and Taipi run the course to decide which team should be given the inside track, he had to keep lowering his chin, lest he look too proud. He liked the way his nephew walked on his long legs, keeping them steady and looking to neither side, even while Tohi-kai laughed and capered, fell off his stilts and mounted with a shake of his behind.

When the starter's hand went up, the two boys were lifted up and pushed along by the roars of the watchers. Pakoko's mouth was shut tight, his eyes fastened on the stones ahead. He knew that his friend was kicking out to make men laugh, but he would not look. When Tohi-kai felt his breathing and his legs began to ache, he wondered why he should break his bones with such hard going. If his sticks caught in a crack between stones, he would surely fall. That was just what happened. 'My stilts slipped on the greasy stones,' he said piteously to the Master Stone Builder who picked him up. But Pakoko stumbled on, weary and panting, over the stones, over the stones, until he saw the opening in the walls and slid through it. He was still clinging to his sky-legs when Uncle Fatu lifted him up and carried him above the sea of noise swirling round him. 'Pakoko has won the inside course for the Teiis!' All men were praising him.

Sitting beside Uncle Fatu, Pakoko watched the great contest of Nuku Hiva teams. While the Teiis and Taioas contended, then the Taipis and Hapaas, the watchers on the walls sat kicking their heels against the stones, calling encouragement or taunts to the runners, but when the winners, Teiis and Taipis, ran against each other, everyone stood up to yell in deadly earnest. Here were not two currents racing smoothly around the course, but an agitated sea of waves dashing to and fro all over the paving.

Men were leaping in front of their enemies, striking them down with their wooden legs. Men were swaying, pounded and pressed, but still planting themselves in the path of their adversaries. Sometimes the overthrown rolled under the rushing sticks and lay still, trodden and bleeding. The on-coming, stumbling over the fallen, piled up, wood and bones together. 'Teii! Teii!' Yells fought with yells. 'Taipi! Taipi!'

Into the third corner of the feast place plunged those still in the race, four Teiis and four Taipis. They lined up, a row of savage kickers jabbing and punching at those pressed against the walls. Suddenly a stilt flew through the air. 'One Taipi down!' screamed those close to the corner. The Teii, who had thrown him, leapt over him, broke free from the walls and ran with long smooth steps. Teiis and Taipis were sucked after him in a turbulent stream. The end ran to meet them. Four Teiis, but only three Taipis, crowded through the opening in the walls and threw themselves down, panting and groaning, under the coconut trees.

Fatu lifted his foster son up again and ran with the crowds to touch the victors. 'It was Pakoko who brought good to the Teiis!' he shouted. Those running alongside shouted with him, 'It was Pakoko who won the inside course!' The boy stood up on his uncle's shoulders and called to everyone, 'I made the Taipis fall!'

'You will be my Ironwood, Pakoko,' Tohi-kai called up to him, but he wasn't allowed to run along with his wonderful friend, for 'Old Stingy', his father, caught his arm and pulled him back from giving too much.

The Taipi Chief was ashamed of his son. 'You ran without caring,' he complained.

Tohi-kai made his eyes big and round. 'I should not overthrow my friend, should I?'

The quick-handed Hapaa Chief, Tea-roru, reached up to pull Pakoko off Fatu's back. 'Come with me, little Ironwood,' he said, 'It is time to eat.'

Uncle Fatu, hearing the Taipi and the Hapaa contending for an Ironwood, turned away with the boy, muttering loud enough for all to hear, 'Your Chief, Kiato-nui, has work for you, my nephew.'

But it was Chief Veo who was waiting for Pakoko. He held

out his arms for him, gave him a seat on his hip, and walked back and forth showing him proudly. Both of them forgot that they had been following different paths.

When Kiato-nui was carried onto the feast place to be made Chief of all Teiis, his brother, Pakoko, was not seen nor heard nor named. Worn out by his great work, the boy had fallen asleep, but he was awakened by the calling of the Chief's shell. He could hear men singing below, towards the sea.

> Here am I, Tanaoa,
> Master of the sea.
> My robe is the wind,
> The northeast wind is my robe.

He turned his ears towards the mountains as voices floated down in answer.

> Here am I, Tiki,
> Who cried, 'Let Nuku Hiva be land!'
> Hina-with-the-face-of-sand is my woman,
> Banyan and Ute are my planting.

Pakoko went outside onto the terrace to see what great work was being performed.

There was the child, Kiato-nui, white as a new moon, riding upon Uncle Fatu's head. The aunts following were carrying the long red loin cloth they had beaten and the wristlets and anklets of their curled hair. Now they were all bending their heads to hold a big gourd on top, while the Master Chanter filled it with water from the sea and water from the uplands and washed the little one in it. When the Master had wrapped him in his new girdle, he gave him again to Fatu, who lifted him high for all to see and carried him slowly around the paving, the aunts walking before and behind with the ends of his loin cloth on their heads. 'Kiato-nui! Kiato-nui!' All the people on the terraces, all those on the paving below were shouting. '*Kaoha* to our High Chief! *Kaoha* to our High Chief!

Pakoko was a leaf blown about in a sudden storm. Where were his stilts? He was the one who had won the inside course for the Teiis! He jumped from the high stones onto his sky-legs and went clattering across the paving. Where was he going? To ride

53

on the head of Uncle Fatu? He was the foster son of that uncle, he was the first-born! Why were the crowds laughing? He could make them laugh, as Tohi-kai had made them laugh. Better than that! He would show them how he could dance on his sky-legs. He made the sticks walk stiff and straight as the older aunts were walking. Then he tripped over the stones with his younger aunt's light step. When he joined the procession, switching his behind, mimicking Uncle Fatu, the laughter died.

'*Fi! Fi! Fi!*' Were the Teiis blowing shame upon him? The boy's breathing stopped and his cold hands dropped the stilts. He began to run on his own feet. Where? Where? He could not see his way through his tears. High walls were on this side of him, on that. He ran back and forth, beating them with his sore hands until he found the opening. Outside, he ran without direction, over rocks, under bushes, through streams, until the land itself rose up against him. 'You shall not stop me!' he screamed, flinging himself against the cliffs. Exhausted, he felt his way numbly, on and on. '*Fi! Fi! Fi!*' When the wind began to echo the mocking cries of his kinsmen, he ceased tearing himself to pieces. He knew where he was now, for this was the whispering of wind in ironwood trees. He was near that sacred grove where his grandfather was paddling towards the sky. The odour of roasted pig awakened his curiosity. This flesh had been sent from the feast to the dead chief. Was the spirit satisfied? Had he really climbed to the skies? Pakoko crept quietly towards the clearing in the grove. He must see for himself.

Te! Someone was moving about. Ah, it was Uncle Fatu. Pakoko watched him untie a knot in his girdle, take out a handsome whale's tooth, the only ornament left him by his defeated father, and fling it into the canoe of the dead chief. The boy heard him call out in a burst of joyful gratitude, '*Kaoha* to the chief who has brought Haavao back from the Teiis!'

Pakoko had forgotten all about the return of Haavao to Taiohae. While he had been mocking his uncles and his aunts, they had been performing this wonderful work. He was ashamed. He could not look up when his uncle saw him and came towards him. But when he felt Fatu's strong hands lifting him, when he looked down into his uncle's face that was bright as the sun, he knew he had been pulled out of an angry sea in which he had nearly drowned. His voice was hoarse from screaming but his whisper was full of joy. 'Our dear land of Haavao has come back!'

Walking down to Chief Veo's terraces, Uncle Fatu answered his nephew's questions. 'Certainly, the dead grandfather's spirit has gone to the skies,' he said. 'He has been fed and he has been given the most precious things to offer for his entrance into the highest place.' The man's hand touched his girdle where his whale's tooth had been hidden. 'Now he is a god,' he added. 'He will make a just return for these things and for everything we give in future.'

'But we cannot give him anything more if he has gone away,' Pakoko protested.

'Why not? He will have a stone image, a resting place on the sacred terrace. He has a priest to tell us his desires and talk back and forth between us. He has a grandson whom he has chosen to take his seat as father of all Teiis. He has us to work for him and for his heir.'

The boy stood still to consider this. 'Does he want me to work for him?' he asked.

'You, above all others,' Uncle Fatu assured him proudly.

On Kiato-nui's terrace, Sister Hina was running back and forth, calling Pakoko's name. 'Have you forgotten your work?' she asked, pulling him up onto the high stones. 'Here is your child.' She thrust the little chief into the boy's arms and ran away to find his little sister.

Pakoko's eyes held a question as he looked at his uncle. He had not yet been allowed to touch the little fellow.

Uncle Fatu nodded. 'Didn't you see the Master Chanter wash away his taboo? But be careful of his sacred head.'

Pakoko clasped his hands tightly to keep the heavy child from falling. His legs trembled a little as he pressed his heels hard against the stones and carried Kiato-nui into his sleeping house. But he felt very strong. He was a big boy now, with work to do for the god.

II YELLOW ROBES

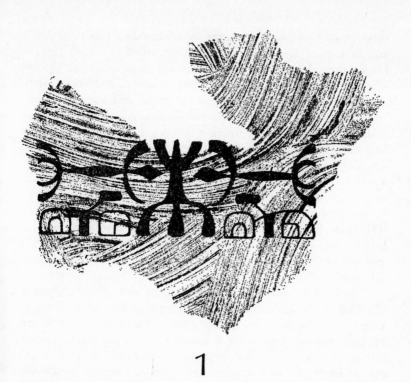

1

PAKOKO was feeling his breathing on this white night of the pregnant moon. Behind him, white waves mounted white sands. Before him, like a waterfall, the long branches of a *pikake* bush poured over a stone wall. Laughing low, he plunged into it, tearing off streamers of white stars, twisting them with trembling fingers into a headband. He was drunk with his own fragrance, for he had rubbed his skin with yellow oil and dipped his girdle in the scented stain.

'Where are you going? Where are you going?' The little ones following him made a song of their question. Why did they never go anywhere themselves? Pakoko was disgusted with them.

There was his foster brother, Kohu, who was afraid to sleep outside his father's house. He was as fast a growing sprout as Pakoko himself, but he was still as shy as a crab that scurries for a hole in the sand at the sound of a footfall. When the adventurous youth told of the strange things he had seen in this house and that, poor Kohu had nothing to boast of but the visions of his white-eyed dreaming as he lay in the dark corner of his own sleeping space. What the retiring boy whispered to Pakoko's little sister as they nestled together in the night and wandered hand and hand in the day, no one knew. She was a fat child who cried easily and moved slowly, but she was not a bother to Kohu who kept her by his side continually. If that little girl wanted a drinking coconut, the thin lad with the crooked leg could climb a tree easily, but if Pakoko made him climb a low stone wall, he always fell and hurt himself. Indeed, Kohu was no good at all to his daring foster brother. Worse, he was a thorn constantly scratching Pakoko's skin, making him uncomfortable, making him remember how he had shaken the little fellow out of a tree and broken his leg. Alas, perhaps that was why Kohu was different!

There were Pakoko's cousins, Mauhau and Oehitu, children of Chief Veo's beautiful younger sister and visitors from other valleys. Handsome as his mother and strong as his Taipi father, Mauhau should have been a companion for his active cousin, but he had attached himself to Chief Kiato-nui as a shell fish fastens itself to a rock and no prying could loosen him. Pakoko was disgusted with the youth who preferred to run errands for a child rather than run about for his own pleasure. Mauhau's younger brother, Oehitu, was different. Pakoko often felt the little fellow's big eyes upon him during his most secret errands, but he could never persuade him to join his play.

Kiato-nui himself seemed to pull and push Pakoko all at the same time, so that the older brother felt himself torn in two pieces, one for and one against the loving, demanding child. When the little Chief beamed his *kaoha* all over his round face, Pakoko always gave him his desires, but he always felt tricked, because Kiato-nui's desires were always for things that his brother did not want to give. When he was a baby, the big boy had tried to hover over him because he had been given this work by the god. Then, it had made him angry when Chief Veo insisted on carrying the little one on his hip or keeping him beside him on his mat. But when Kiato-nui was big enough to run about on his own legs, yet still clung to his older brother, Pakoko was glad when he saw Chief Veo beckoning his cherished son. He was even glad when he heard the father say to his woman, 'Pakoko keeps me stirred up but Kiato-nui smooths me.' That made him feel free to follow his secret paths and to sleep in strange houses where the folk cried, '*Kaoha,* friend, what we have is yours.'

As usual, on this bright moon night, brothers and cousins were swarming round Pakoko, hampering his flight, gumming his wings.

'Where am I going?' the lad called back. 'I am going to fly with Handsome Wreath on his palm leaf!'

'I am going with you,' a slow, soft voice drawled.

Pakoko looked in quick anger at the fat little boy squatting on his terrace, stretching out his arms to be lifted. He tried to strike down Kiato-nui's eyes but they nested confidingly in his. What could he do but carry this soft little beggar on his back? As the child's arms slid around him, the older boy shivered. He would not look at that upturned face, radiant with *kaoha.*

The other boys watched, swinging between following or staying with the little girls who appeared and disappeared in the shadows. Pakoko's sister was carrying Chiefess Ehua's new child and the big girl, Hina, had her arms about the two of them. When the white light splashed on his sister's pointed breasts and the tiny hand playing with them, Pakoko was bathed in a hot sea. He shouted hoarsely, 'You are always spying.'

'Are you going to play with the night moths?' Hina asked, her eyes roving over the youth's yellow soaked garments.

Why did Pakoko mock this older sister who had fed him from her own mouth when he was a birdlet? It was not his desire, yet he scoffed at her now. 'What do you know of the free young people with hot desires? They do not call your name on their flutes.'

It was a true word. No lovers called Hina to wear the yellow and play till cock's crow. Weary after work from red day to fires, Hina always slept the night away alone on her mat. Many were the good words of the mothers and aunts. 'Hina is strong, she digs taro easily. Hina is tall, she can cut the bananas. Hina's hands are quick, she catches baskets full of fish from pools in the rocks. Hina's eyes are sharp, she finds the best pandanus leaves for mats and baskets.'

Pakoko clenched his hands at her silence. Why didn't she carry her mat to an easier house? Watching her long, slender fingers twisting together, his stomach was suddenly sick. How those nails could scratch a fellow's cheeks!

'Carry the child to the house,' his sister said, laying him in Hina's arms. 'We go to watch something.' She caught Kohu's hand and pulled him along with her.

The others stood wavering until Kiato-nui said quietly, 'Go back to the sleeping house.' They turned their moon-white faces towards the little Chief but threw no word at him as they climbed the stones and vanished.

Pakoko stuck his lips out when he saw how easily they heard. As he ran along the wall of the feast place, he decided he would shake this solid Chief into little pieces, but suddenly he heard a flute calling and he forgot Kiato-nui altogether.

> Here is your song of greeting,
> Like a flute, like a shell for sweetness.

The song was coming from the terrace of the Master Bird Catcher.

'We will sing with them.' Kiato-nui's warm breath enwreathed Pakoko's neck.

Coming upon the 'night moths' glistening in the pale moon shine, the young women seated in a long row, the men kneeling before them, the two brothers clasped one another close. Pakoko rocked back and forth with the girls, slowly as a heart beats. Kiato-nui's breathing flowed with his as they grunted with the men, 'Ah-eh! Ah-eh! Ah-eh-heh!' They two were carried back and forth on that pulsing male tide, agitated by the high bird-like cries that dove through it now and then. The women sang solemnly:

> Ardently desiring am I!
> My love is a fragrant wreath,
> My love is a fragrant wreath.

> Ardently desiring the sprout,
> The flower of the swelling bulb!
> My love is a fragrant wreath.

A madness is in me
To reach innumerable coconut blooms!
My love is a fragrant wreath.

You are swollen with the sprout.
My love is a fragrant wreath,
My love is a fragrant wreath.

When the men thrust their strong right arms up into the quivering air and struck the hollows of their right elbows with their left palms, Pakoko burst with the swelling inside him. 'Who-ah-hee-who!' he cried wildly and fled along the down-going path.

'Where are you going?' Kiato-nui asked, when he was set down upon his own terrace.

Pakoko grinned at him. 'Where you can't follow,' he boasted. 'You are sacred. You would spoil your head. I am free!' He capered away into the black shade.

When he reached the moon-splashed beach, he found boys and girls scooping a hole in the warm sands. He pushed inside it, twisting and turning until he was comfortable. He lay on his back, staring at the luminous sky. Whispering, giggling, pale hands straying through black hair, fingers pinching soft flesh, he played with his friends, floating all night on the warm, sweet waves of a fragrant sea.

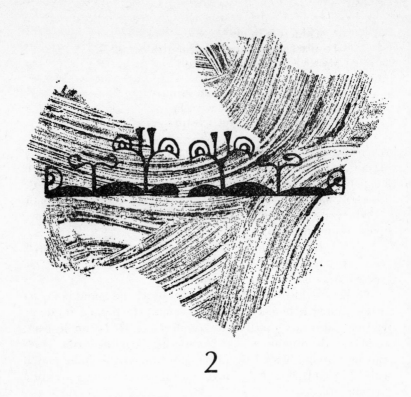

2

'GIVE me the mark of a young man,' Pakoko begged the
Master of Circumcision.

'That is a taboo work in a special house,' the Master
answered. 'I must have many pigs. There must be many young
people to fetch and carry. The word must come from Chief
Kiato-nui.'

Couldn't a fruit ripen until Kiato-nui was ready with his
picking pole and net? Pakoko ground his teeth, but he made his
lips smile and his tongue gentle when he put the thought into
his Chief's stomach. He knew that sweet words would make the
boy soft as ripe breadfruit.

True enough. A taboo house was built and Kiato-nui invited
his brothers and cousins inside. Pakoko was content when he sat
down close to the Master to watch his work, shut away from
common folk, within the circle of taboo sticks, inside walls that

smelled of upland forests, under gay streamers of red and white *tapa* that swam and dived on the gentle winds. When the Master unrolled his tools and spread them out, all the lad's force went into his eyes. Here was cutting finer than image carving, so swift and true that he had time for breathing only two or three times before Kiato-nui was carried away from the ancestral stone and he himself was beckoned to come.

Holding his precious things with care, the ironwood stick on which his skin had been slit by the Master's sharp-edged stone and a sun-warmed black rock for healing, Pakoko was whisked back to his own mat, scarcely knowing anything had happened to him. To make certain, he kept looking at his leaf-wrapped wound and feeling for the rolls of *tapa* stuck through the holes pierced in his ears also. Now he was a fruit-picking pole himself! Now he would play in earnest!

The work being finished, the five boys were waiting for healing inside the taboo house. Kiato-nui, who always heard the first time, lay without moving, holding a warm stone to his wound. Kohu, propped on one elbow, tapped the beat of a work song on the mat with his thin fingers. Mauhau went about showing his cut, boasting that he would be the first to heal. Oehitu sat with his eye to a hole in the plaitwork of the walls. 'The others are walking back and forth,' he complained. 'They are not shut up inside a house.'

'We are taboo,' Pakoko announced. 'We are different.'

Kohu sat up. 'Yes, we are different. We could have a secret tongue.' When he began to make upside down words, the others gathered around him, leaning close to hear.

When the healing was finished and the boys were walking to the sea to wash away their sacredness, they threw strange words at one another. 'They were taught to us by birds,' Kohu said to those who ran alongside, listening. Pakoko nodded. He made the procession of circumcised walk close together, as if they were hiding something very, very sacred. They were set apart. They were different from everybody else.

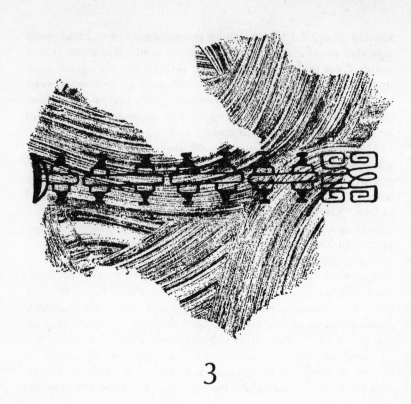

3

URING the moon called 'Thunder and Lightning', when rainy skies lay on the backbone of the land, and thunder shouted to the rocks, and cloud legs walked down the valleys, the Teiis sat inside their houses making return gifts for the family of Kiato-nui's betrothed mate in Haka-ui. In Chief Veo's sleeping house, his women folk were leaning on their hard elbows plaiting fine checkerwork mats. Unhurried they worked, soothed by the gentle hum of indoor living, as the rain tapped the thatch, fingernails snapped in laying down the strips of pandanus, children murmured and young women sang of love as they waited for the night. Now and then they broke the smooth flow of working together with sharp stabs of criticism aimed at the big girl, Hina, who gave too much help to the children she shadowed, too little to her elders. Instead of working out the stiffness of dried leaves and slitting them with a thorn into uniform widths for the workers, she was continually giving crying children their desires. Nobody meant to be unjust, but with everybody giving orders, Hina was often caught between crossing requests. Finally, when Chiefess Ehua begged her to stop the noise of the children who were agitating the unborn child inside her, and the grandmother complained that she could not make mats with a helper who was always carrying children to the cook house for food, Hina sat without working for a space, then got up quietly and began to lower her bundle from the rafters.

Even the children stopped crying and there was no sound but the sliding of rope over wood. The mat makers could not make their fingers go on. They could only stare while the young woman rolled her mat, tied it and slid herself towards the entrance of the house. Then the skies fell, for they knew the thought of their fine worker. She was going to an easier house! She would become lichen clinging to another chief! The grandmother shrieked, the aunts begged, Chiefess Ehua wept, but Hina slid the mats from the opening with a firm hand.

But Hina did not go out just yet, for her way was blocked by Kiato-nui, who stood just outside and called down to her, 'Tell my mother I have come.'

The pregnant woman heard and held out her hands. 'It is Kiato-nui with my shell fish!' she rejoiced. 'Hurry! The child inside me is begging for shell fish.'

The women sat back on their heels with sighs of relief. The little Chief would not let Hina go, that was certain. They waited while Kiato-nui chewed a mouthful of *noni* leaves before entering. Pakoko had said to him, 'If you forget the taboo about entering the house of a pregnant woman, I will kill you.' He had not forgotten. He spat the pulp carefully where any wandering breath body or evil spirit would smell it and turn away, before he put one foot over the red stone door slab and stooped to enter. 'I scraped the shell fish from the rocks myself,' he called to his mother, pushing before him a wet basket smelling of the sea. He stood up inside, moved heavily on soft quiet feet towards her corner, and set the basket down beside her. He knew that it was forbidden to eat inside a sleeping house, but his mother had asked for these dainties and he could not refuse her. He would see that she dropped nothing on the floor. Hovering over her, he watched her eat, shaking with laughter because she forgot to nibble as a woman should but chewed and sucked with noisy pleasure. When she had finished, he commanded her to sleep.

Then Kiato-nui turned to the others. 'Why are you looking at Hina with red eyes?' he asked.

He could make nothing of the storm of angry cries that blew from every side, until Hina herself lifted her strong chin and said, 'I am going to serve in the house of Chiefess Kena.'

At mention of his true mother, Kiato-nui became slower and heavier than he was by nature. He was like a man who picks his way carefully from rock to rock along the shore when the tide is high. 'Has Chiefess Kena asked you to come?' he inquired, after a long silence.

'Many times,' the young woman answered. She knew well enough that he would not prevent her leaving his household if he thought that Chiefess Kena desired her.

'Go, then,' said the young chief with a sigh.

Hina crawled outside quickly, clasping her bundle to her breast, smiling faintly. But when she stood in the rain, looking at the men's house where Pakoko was sitting with his elders learning to make ornaments, her face was not wet with water from the sky but from her own eyes. '*Kaoha*, little Coconut,' she cried harshly. After this anguished farewell, she made herself run to Haavao's path.

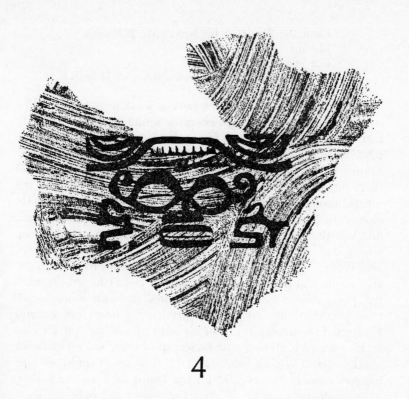

4

LISTENING to the Master Chanter's old tale, Pakoko had not
heard Hina's cry at breaking apart.

> Whence comes fire?
> From the head of Mahuike.
> Taboo that fire
> From the head of Mahuike.

To the beat of the words, the youth ran his fingers over the
outside of his bowl of red *temanu* wood. Truly, it was smooth as
a bird's breast. As if he were breaking open Mahuike's head to
get the sacred fire, he struck his gouge into the wood to hollow
the inside.

Beside him Kohu leaned against a post, idly running his thin
fingers along the sharp edge of a shell scraper, moving his lips
with those of the Master.

Then the fire from his head gave Mahuike.
The fire flew inside trees,
The fire flew inside rocks.
Scattered over the land was the fire of Mahuike.

Pakoko raised his head and took a good long breath. How sweet the smell of men! How good the sounds of work! The rub, rub, rubbing of Chief Veo's fine rat's tooth on tortoise-shell, the pricking of the Ironwood's keen point on bone, the squeak of the Master House Builder's colored cords as he twisted and pulled them into lashings binding a house post. 'I go faster than all the others,' thought Pakoko, quickening the *ta, ta, ta* of his gouge. He looked down at the little Chief, Kiato-nui, who had come inside and was drawing on a stone with a piece of charcoal, drawing, wiping away, drawing again. Always the same image—*tiki, tiki, tiki*. What a slow learner! Pakoko gave no trouble to his teachers. Indeed, he had no need of being taught. Didn't he see the *tiki's* face every day on house posts, coconut shell bowls, stone breadfruit pounders, ironwood clubs, drum cord rings, everywhere? He turned the smooth breast of his bowl up and cut quickly into it. He covered it all over with images until there was no space for another mark. What a beautiful bowl! The youth could not tear his eyes from it. It was good for the family of Kiato-nui's mate. This would be a *kaoha* for poor Kohu who had only one good leg. Pakoko held up his work proudly. 'Finished!' he exclaimed.

The Master looked closely at the images, shook his head and began to draw on his stone. 'This is the way of the *tiki* face,' he said. 'You have left out the lines joining the eyes and the ears.'

Pakoko drew down his brows and stared at his bowl. 'Next time, then,' he muttered. He snatched up his work and pushed it towards Kohu. '*Kaoha!*' he said with a loud tongue.

'Shame!' cried Chief Veo. 'Will you give your brother an untrue thing?' His word made Kohu withdraw his outstretched hand.

Through a sudden mist of tears, Pakoko again reached for his bowl. He threw it with all his force outside the house. He followed it and beat it to pieces with an axe. He did not return to the men's house, but chose three fine taro roots and two coconuts from the cook house and fled to the house of friends.

From the family of the Master Fisherman he was sure of warm *kaoha*. These friends were not criticizing him all the time, making him a nobody. They listened to his stories of the chiefly level, smoothing him with their soft eyes and gentle laughter. Indeed, when he came this day splashing through the mud, the Master beckoned him into his taboo house to watch the carving of a slender canoe paddle, a gift for the new stone god just completed by the fisherman's son.

Pakoko lay on his back, feasting his eyes on the images black as night on flashing white where the smoked wood was being cut away. 'Fish teeth, fish bones, bonito tails,' he named them.

'Yes,' agreed the Master. He pointed to the next row. 'Here are a man and a woman, coupled to bring new fish.'

'They say I do not know the images!' The youth's tongue was rancid as old breadfruit paste.

'Eyes are quick, hands are slow,' the Master said. 'Children can name the images, but only Masters can cut them.' He sat without moving, regarding his work for a long time. 'See this paddle,' he said finally. 'If the images are not true, how can the gods know our desires?'

Pakoko sat up suddenly. 'Do the gods know the true images?'

'No other,' answered the fisherman.

Pakoko moved to the open-front of the house and looked hard at the flowering sea. 'I see something,' he said at last and went outside.

The Master Fisherman laughed softly and said to his son, 'When I was a lad who had eaten only fifteen harvests, I was just as green a coconut.'

The fathers in the men's house did not look up from their carving when Pakoko brought a block of green wood and began to shape it. While that moon was going into the black, they did not count the days of sun when the youth continued working inside the house while they themselves stretched their legs on the steaming land. But his father, Chief Veo, began to complain to Uncle Fatu. 'The boy is not a master. He should not be tracing images on the logs of the sleeping space and saying their names in the darkness. He should be running wild with free youngsters, naming the images on a woman's skin.'

But Uncle Fatu would not draw the boy aside. From behind

he watched the work of Pakoko. It was unfolding as surely as a many petalled flower. One day he was too swollen for silence. He let his praise burst out. 'Here is the work of a Master!'

No one crossed this saying. Indeed, all the men sucked in their saliva as if they were eating good breadfruit. When Kiato-nui could not find a single slip of the rat's tooth, he said, 'These are images with power. When I marry they will bring my woman many children.'

'*Kaoha*, brother,' Pakoko said quietly, pushing the finished bowl towards him. He got up, stretched himself and went out into the rain. The cold drops from the leaf ends on the roof pounded him until he was wide awake. What sweet smelling smoke! Were his friends raiding an oven somewhere? He was hungry. He felt as if he had been chewing sand. He saw a yellow *tapa* running past. '*Who-ah-hee-who*!' He cried joyfully and raced after him.

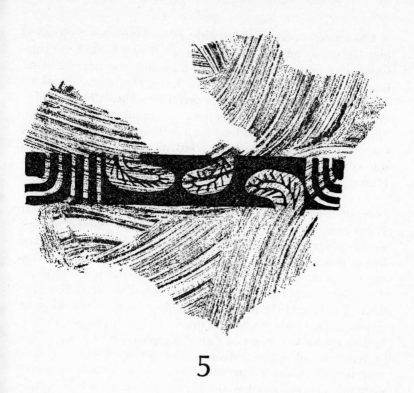

5

DIPPING his paddle deep into the strong sea, Chief Veo sang the ocean god's song:

> The wetting of the big roots of the land,
> Of the little roots of the land,
> Of the land of Nuku Hiva!
> The going of the canoe of the land
> Upon the waters of Tahaoa!
> Uia!

The fishing canoe slid swiftly down the slope of a valley of water, labored up the mountain beyond, shivered at the sea's slap in the face, and mounted the flowering crest. Again! Again! 'Ho, ho, ho, ho,' the paddles sang. Today Chief Kiato-nui had freed the giant ray fish from taboo. Today was set apart for the play of the high level folk.

Chief Veo's liver was quiet without *kava* now. No one pushed him for yes or no. He had only to stand firm behind the little Chief and watch for his desires. Kiato-nui was never a wind blowing hard in one direction, but just a gentle breeze making everybody feel good. He soothed even his mother, Chiefess Kena, giving her presents before she sent a coconut sheath for them, filling her oven with rich food even in times of scarcity. Indeed, some folk whispered that he was fattening her and her adopted son so that they would be too heavy to be carried down from Haavao to Meau to visit him.

Veo watched the youths of his household as they stood on the prow of the canoe, one by one, at the bidding of the Master Fisherman. How easily Kiato-nui listened! He planted his feet exactly where the man pointed and stood up like a mast unshaken by the pounding waves. Pakoko, slipping and sliding, was swinging his spear before he could stand firm on the jumping prow. That thin, long-legged youth had the intestines of a child. His desire was to peel the moon with his finger nail, to run when he should walk, to jump when he should feel with his toes, to fling himself on his face when he should sit quietly breathing.

Watching his nephew, Mauhau, ride the slippery prow as if he were its beak, Chief Veo rested on his paddle. Already the fisherman was showing this boy the expert movements of the fishing spear. The Chiefess Kena had pointed to Mauhau when he was still a little fellow. 'There is your head warrior, your Ironwood,' she had told Kiato-nui. What a great effort the youth was making to know war! Even the one-eyed Ironwood of the Teiis said his work was good when he jumped from rock to rock in a waterfall or climbed man-eating cliffs or lay still as a dead man when hiding. Chief Veo was sure he would spear the ray at his first dive.

His younger brother, Oehitu, sat watching the others. His uncle regarded him curiously when he called out directions to Mauhau. The lad knew the way of it but he would not try to spear the fish himself.

There was 'Crippled Heron' taking his place, reaching timidly for the fisherman's hand. As Kohu felt the dancing prow fall beneath him into a deep valley, his feet went up, his head went down, *pati*, against the sharp chin of the canoe's face. The youth lay with arms and legs jerking, with head turning from side to side. When the fisherman picked him up, he slipped through his arms and lay still on the flooring, limp as seaweed.

The Master turned to Chief Veo and asked with a trembling tongue, 'Was there a god inside him?' Veo looked at Kiato-nui, waiting for his word.

'Turn the canoe about,' the little Chief commanded. 'The gods have sent me a priest.'

Indeed it was so. Sitting in his sky-piercing house, gazing into his bowl of *kava,* the Diviner had seen the fall of the god into Kohu. The youth's mother had always known that her son could see breath bodies wandering in the valley. Now she went about saying over and over again, 'As soon as Kohu has tired of his yellow robes, he will stop playing and go to live on the sacred place.' Whenever the relatives came to look at him, Kohu covered his eyes and his crooked leg began to twitch. 'The god is hovering near,' the mother whispered.

What did he see? What did he hear? Pakoko lay beside him, hoping to know.

Finally, Kohu whispered, 'The god is like a bird. When he comes, he scratches my leg with his claws and I feel his wings in my hair.' On the day when Kiato-nui called his brothers and cousins to go again for the ray, Kohu beckoned to Pakoko. 'I can see the big fish in distant seas,' he told his brother.

Pakoko giggled. 'So can I,' he whispered and began to chant old words:

> Is the big ray dead?
> Torokia-e!
> Yes, the spear is in his wing,
> Torokia-e!

Kohu was angry. 'When the ray comes and you are standing on the prow pointing your spear, this is what my song will be:

> Whose are you, spear?
> Torokia-e!
> You are Pakoko's spear.
> Torokia-e!
> Is the big ray dead?
> Torokia-e!
> No, the spear is in the sea.
> Torokia-e!

Now it was Pakoko's turn to tremble with anger. Was Kohu trying to throw a god's power against him?

When the Master Fisherman had taught those youths to stand firm in any sea and dive at any point with spears held straight and true, he nodded to Kiato-nui and the little Chief gave the command to paddle the canoe into the path of the rays.

At the sight of a big black fish spreading his wings ahead of them, Pakoko leapt up, whirled his spear and yelled, 'Who-ah-hee-who!'

Chief Veo clapped his hand over that loud mouth. 'This is the way of it,' he said. The father was going to fling the first spear! He pointed his weapon carefully and tightened his muscles for a spring. There he went, his legs and arms in one line with the shaft. *Ta!* The spear struck. It was standing up quivering in the socket of one wing of the ray and Chief Veo was climbing back into the canoe before the fish could move.

Pakoko was suffocated. His father was magnificent! His work was wonderful! The boy jumped to his feet, eager to work with him.

'Sit down!' bellowed the fisherman. No need to call. Pakoko sat down hard as the rope tying the spear to the canoe jerked and the ray dashed for the open sea, dragging his captors behind. 'Paddle!' commanded the Master, and they all stirred up the water, digging deep, pushing hard, keeping the beak of the canoe in the wake of the fish's tail. When the monster dived suddenly beneath them, the fisherman was ready with his long tailed paddle to push them clear of that slippery back rising under them. They were off, but the fish was a solid wave towering beside them. Now he was falling! *Va! Vakakina!* Smash! The canoe's up-turned tail was crushed by the fish's powerful wing. *Koro-koro-koro!* The sea gushed into the shell. 'Use the bailer!' the fisherman shouted to Mauhau. Running, spinning, diving, jumping, that big fish fought in dying circles. Finally, the Master called to Kiato-nui, 'Spear him, little Chief.'

The boy stood up, waited for the man's 'Go!' and fell overboard like a stone tied to a fishing line. Chief Veo scooped his son from the sea. How easy! There was the spear standing up in the wing, trembling.

Pakoko's breathing was tearing his breast. Sweat and tears

were pouring into his open mouth. When the fisherman nodded to him to fling the next spear, he left his seat like a stone from a sling. He caught the point of his spear in the sideboards, jerked it free, and dived without alighting on any perch. Where was the fish? Pakoko's spear had pierced only whirling waters. Shaking the long hair out of his eyes, he looked up and saw a black cloud over him. It was falling! He could not move. He was like a man who had walked into a cloud of taboo. He waited for death. But someone caught his feet and pulled him from under the solid sky. A swimmer was dragging him from the sucking pool. It was his father who was lifting him over the sideboards of the canoe and climbing in after him.

Lying on the prow, Pakoko sought Veo's eyes as if he were a very young child, but the Chief had covered his face with his hands. The youth saw miserably that they were all disappointed. Kiato-nui's mouth was a dot in his fat face, Mauhau's eyes were red, the fisherman's hands hung down. Into the dismal silence, Pakoko dropped a bright word. 'I will strike again.'

Kiato-nui's level voice flowed over him. 'Turn the canoe landward,' he said.

No! Pakoko got up and looked wildly for his spear. But where was the fish? Two upright spears were riding out to sea! 'He has gotten away!' he cried. Then he saw that the ropes had been cut to save him. He hung his head and wept. But he could not think long of his shame, for another thought was twisting and turning inside him. What had Kohu said? 'The spear is in the sea!' Then it was true that Kohu could see afar with the whites of his eyes!

Pakoko did not follow his relatives from the beach, but remained with the Master Fisherman. Indeed, he did not again set foot on Kiato-nui's terraces until he helped his friends carry a load of fish to the little Chief's feast place where he was pounding his first breadfruit paste. Skin streaked with brine, long hair unbound for work, Pakoko swung his hips with the leaf-wrapped bundles that swayed on his shoulder pole. He had helped spread the big net in the deep sea and these fish were his share of the first net full. He laid them side by side in front of his brother.

Kiato-nui looked up with that radiant smile that always made Pakoko quiver, but he was not allowed to speak even a *kaoha*.

Chief Veo was teaching him a new thing, guiding his hand with the stone pestle, and he would not let the ceremony be broken. The father's hard eyes drove the youth away. Pakoko turned his back as if he wore a hard shell there that could not be pierced. A moment before he had been a bird flying to his nest to bring food to the little ones. He had wanted to tell how he had made a friend of Master Ocean, how he had worked with the fishing folk, harpooning a ray, noosing a shark while swimming underneath, tearing an octopus from his hole, how he had learned the words to chant to the god, Tanaoa. Now he was empty of all desire and he wandered about dragging his feet.

He went to stand beside Kohu who was perched on a wall with his crooked leg folded under him. He stood watching him. That brother's eye lids were twitching, the whites were turned towards the uncles and aunts who lay underneath the heavy wooden trough in which Kiato-nui was mixing the breadfruit paste. His lips were moving with the words of the Master Chanter.

Ta! Ta! Ta! Ta!
The pounding of the harvest
With the male stone.

Pakoko nudged him. 'What do you see?' he demanded.

Kohu turned his soft brown eyes down. 'I see Kiato-nui's sacredness running through his hands into the uncles and aunts.'

'Is his power great, yours little?' Pakoko asked, mocking, but serious also.

'A chief has power, yes,' Kohu whispered. 'But a diviner has power, power, power. Without a priest, a chief cannot be properly born, he cannot be nourished, he cannot build a good house nor a conquering canoe, he cannot have children nor breadfruit nor fish, he cannot make war nor peace, he cannot be healed of sickness nor enter the skies when he is dead.'

Pakoko trembled at the piercing force of these proud words. But this was just his brother, Kohu, 'Crippled Heron'. He said to him in their secret upside down talk, 'You are not a priest yet,' and he pulled his lower eyelid down to show the white in his derision. He was wasting time with this loud mouth, but he had scarcely turned away from him when unearthly cries and a commotion among the people behind him made him run back.

78

Kohu was rushing about on the bottom terrace of the sacred place itself, his eyes white, his crooked leg dragging sideways. Certainly there was a god inside him, flinging him about like a leaf in a strong wind! See! The god had thrown him across a fallen coconut trunk. He was making him vomit, emptying him of common food. Perhaps the god would make him call for a fish. The watchers shrank back, trying to hide, lest they be seized. When the Priest appeared on the top terrace and pointed with his ironwood stick, they fell flat and covered their faces.

Pakoko watched the Clubs pick up Kohu as if he were a precious treasure and carry him up above to the god's house. He heard Kiato-nui say to his Fire Keeper, 'This breadfruit I have beaten is for Priest Kohu.' Priest Kohu, with power, power, power! Pakoko sat down hard, without force even to stand up.

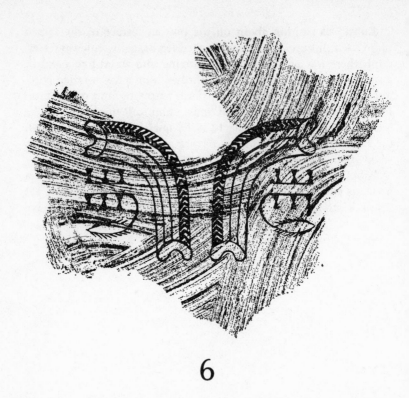

6

U NCLE Fatu was hanging a piece of *tapa* across his house to set apart a space for Kohu whenever he wanted to return from the sacred place to sleep with Chief Veo's daughter. Those cousins had always been like the lashes of a single eye, sleeping enlaced together whenever the boy had a trembling fit or the girl a crying spell. Apart, they were tossed about. Together, they were quiet. Now that Kohu was dwelling in the old Priest's house while he received instruction, she was a pigeon weeping the nights away. 'I will make a perch for them,' Fatu thought. Perhaps, now that blood had come to the girl, she would bear a child to fill her empty arms.

While he was tying the *tapa* to the rafters with Pakoko's help, he was thinking also that the time had come to complete the joining rites of his foster son with the daughter of the Hapaa Chief. Fatu was worn out with Pakoko's play. Every bowl in the place was filled with his flowers soaking in yellow oil, every mat was stained with the drippings from his dyed *tapas*, every sun was noisy with his learning to call names on his nose flute, every moon stormy with his goings and comings with the night moths. Long ago, the food gifts of betrothal had been exchanged between the Teii and Hapaa families, but now the knot of peace was wearing thin. With Pakoko actually made the half of Metani, the youth might be stopped from running wild in the mountains and the lashing binding the two valleys might be strengthened at the same time.

As if he were about to trap an octopus, Uncle Fatu let a glittering pearl shell down before Pakoko's eyes. 'They say that your woman, Metani, has no equal for beauty in all this island.'

The youth lifted startled eyes. When the uncle threw a stone without aim, it was time to dodge. 'I do not know,' he muttered, covering his eyes.

'You have seen her.'

'I have not heard her,' he complained. He remembered how still she had been, sitting between her parents at the time of the gift-giving. While her relatives were tearing to pieces the very walls and roof of Fatu's food-storage house in their scramble to carry off all his possessions, she had not joined in the screaming and laughing but had sat like an image. 'She never plays,' he added.

'Perhaps she is shy,' the man suggested.

'She is puffed up,' the nephew contended. 'Why not? She can throw away breadfruit without caring.'

'She is a High Chiefess,' agreed Fatu.

'And I am an insignificant fisherman,' Pakoko answered.

'No!' Fatu was shocked. 'Her father hangs you high on his treasure pole.'

'Yes, Chief Tea-roru would like me for a man-at-the-side.' Pakoko was working himself into a sweat. 'But I will not be lichen clinging to anyone.'

The Uncle felt the rope slipping out of his hands. He must noose this wild young thing. 'He has chosen you before all others for his son-in-law. He wants to see you sleeping beside his daughter.'

'I want to build my own sleeping house for my woman!'

Pakoko could not stop the strong sea that flooded him.

Fatu crossed him. 'She is a Chiefess. She will build the house.'

'Then I will make myself a chief!' What was he saying? Pakoko had vomited something that he did not know was in his stomach. He had said the Chief Veo, 'I do not want to be a chief. I want to be a Master Chanter.' What did he really want?

'There is one Chief, Kiato-nui,' Fatu said firmly. 'It is your work to keep him on the high seat, so that Haavao may be safe from Hapaa invaders. Chiefess Kena is not an easy mother and her adopted son wants to go back to his Hapaa family. She stuffs him full of food to keep him contented, but one of these nights he might run away. With you in the house of the Chiefess of the Hapaas, it will not matter.'

Now here was a net with not a single eye through which Pakoko could escape. He was caught. But he went on flopping about, just the same. 'I am just a child. I have just begun to play,' he whimpered.

Uncle Fatu breathed easily again. 'Of course you shall have your play. When you and Metani are tied together as two halves, you can break apart for play any time.'

Before Pakoko knew what was happening to him, he was wakened at dawn by drumming and chanting in the men's house and told to make himself ready for the joining rites. Alas, he was without interest as he coiled his two long locks in shells, one on either side, just as Father Veo had worn his long ago. Alas, he had lost his father. Perhaps he was trying to get rid of him now. He looked at himself in a bowl of water for a long time but he was not cheered at the sight of his feather headband. He tied his whale's tooth about his neck with a jerk. This was one of Chiefess Kena's gifts when she brought Kiato-nui to Meau. That woman was to blame for all his troubles. She needn't think that this poor little whale's tooth would pay for them.

The long walk up the Path of War, across the Valley of Tears and down into Hakapaa valley seemed without end. Pakoko had to drag his feet as the stiff old legs of the Name Singer set the pace of the marchers. Not even her loud tongue trilling the great names of his ancestors, nor the ripple of drums and blasts of shells that greeted him along the way put breath into his empty skin. He summoned courage to pull his eye lid down when a

friend called out to ask him where he had thrown his yellow
tapas. He was not an old man ended. He would be back to run
with the free youngsters after one night in the house of his
father-in-law.

When his ears picked up distant chanting, Pakoko began to
measure the path to the terrace where Metani must be sitting
like an image between her father and her mother. Step by step
he drew nearer, name by name her genealogy became clearer,
until her grandfathers and his were mingling. At last he was
pushing his heavy legs across the stone paving of Chief Tea-roru's
feast place in answer to his quick, bright call, 'Come here!' And
Chief Tea-roru was running to meet them, rubbing noses with
everyone, sweeping them all onto his terrace with the force of
a wind from the sea. Pakoko was the center of a whirlpool that
turned round him without touching him. He was alone, unnoticed. Perhaps he could escape! His legs were trembling but he
could make them run behind the houses, off the terrace, into a
plantation of sugar cane. No one stopped him. No one threw a
noose. Was he free?

He saw Metani before she saw him, but he could not back
away before she turned from the stalk of sugar cane she was
breaking. Then he could not move because of the radiant *kaoha*
flooding her eyes. It was the same look of greeting which Kiato-
nui always gave him and it sucked the foundation from under
him as if he stood on sand licked by the sea.

'You said you liked sugar cane,' she said, handing him the
stalk.

He could not untie his tongue. He liked sugar cane. When had
he told her?

'When you came with the food gifts,' she answered as if he
had asked.

He stripped off the hard skin with his teeth and chewed the
juicy pulp. 'Good.' His headband kept slipping over his eye and
he took it off.

'Hang it on the cane,' she said as he was about to throw it on
the ground. When he had fastened it up high, he sat down to
feast. She kept handing him new pieces. 'Do you like taro?' she
asked.

'Not much,' he answered through the juice.

'Oh,' she said in disappointment. 'The leaves of my upland taro are turning yellow. I thought perhaps you would know where to put the irrigation ditch.'

'I am not a planter,' he said with a rough tongue. Was she showing off?

'But your hands look like hot hands that make things grow.'

'Do they?' He spread them out and looked at them. 'Where is your taro?' he asked.

She led him to the running water. As she drew her filmy *tapas* between her legs and tied them up, she warned him, 'Take off your anklets. The water is wet.' They both laughed and laughed as he unbound them.

'This thing keeps swinging,' he complained, removing his whale's tooth.

'Is that the one you fished from the pile of Chiefess Kena's gifts?' she asked. When he stared at her, she laughed. 'Kena told it over and over. "Pakoko is a pig that roots for treasure." ' She mimicked the rancid-mouthed Chiefess. Pakoko could not follow her swift changes. He had thought she was laughing but now she was stamping her foot. 'Who is Kena to call you a pig?' she demanded. 'Haavao is your land, not hers.'

He was ready to say, 'Kiato-nui is Chief of Haavao, not I,' but he bit back the words. That would make her remember that he sat on no high seat. He began to splash upstream.

'If you were on your stilts, you would not spatter me,' she cried.

He turned and looked at her with shining eyes. 'Did you see me win that day?' he asked, but he could not wait for an answer. He felt her eyes clinging to his face like vines and he had to tear them loose. 'We will go see those taro terraces,' he said.

'Oh you won't care for them,' she said, as she followed him from stone to stone. 'You will not like planting. You will be an Ironwood. My father says so.'

He stopped still. 'You tell your father . . .'

'That you will be a Master Chanter. I know.' She was making fun of him. 'But my father always seizes what he wants.'

He knew it! There was a noose waiting for him on Chief Tea-roru's terraces! He looked about for a path, but turned to her to see why her voice was suddenly different. Her eyes were almost like Kohu's, for they were looking through him at something far off. She had power, yes! She was a great Chiefess. Pakoko felt like a little boy.

'You must lead our warriors against the Taipis and put a stop to their cruelties,' she said solemnly. 'My people are afraid to sleep because of their night raids. The old Chief of Taipivai wants fish, fish, fish to offer his god for the strengthening of the young Chief, Tohi-kai.'

'Tohi-kai is my friend,' he boasted.

'Yes.' She knew that too. 'But he is not worthy. He is soft wood.'

Pakoko remembered how Tohi-kai had caught his stilt in the paving and thrown himself down when he saw that the race would be difficult. He knew that the Taipi was soft wood but he was angry that this girl should look down upon his friend. 'If Tohi-kai is soft wood,' he said, 'his father is hard wood and he keeps rubbing him to start a fire.'

Metani turned her eyes to his. 'You are clever and you are constant,' she said. 'You will find a way to make Tohi-kai our friend.'

Again she had overturned his canoe. He did not know whether he was floating or drowning.

The breaking of branches and the crying of a conch shell silenced them. She was a little girl again with wide frightened eyes. 'Don't let them make you—before all those people,' she begged miserably.

She had been running away too! She didn't want him to touch her! Didn't she like him? Looking into her soft eyes, he could scarcely keep himself from being sucked into her. He pulled back, shivering. Why should he be stung by her withdrawal? It was his desire also to be free. 'When they spread the *tapa* over us,' he promised, 'I will pretend.'

'Until we have our own house,' she whispered.

He felt better. That was what he wanted also.

Their fathers were on the bank calling them, Fatu with a hard tongue, Tea-roru through gusts of laughter. The Hapaa Chief pointed at Pakoko. 'Look at that fellow!' he cried. 'He has already examined his woman. Is she a ripe breadfruit, tasting sweet?'

'Yes,' aswered the youth, faintly, lowering his eyes. He was astonished to see that Metani was clinging to him. He pushed her away and swung his hips as he splashed through the water to the bank.

'Good,' Tea-roru commended him. 'We will shorten the ceremony and get on to the food bowls.'

Those two young people were carried through the rites as if they were birds with outstretched wings borne on the wind. Underneath the *tapa* which the relatives spread over them, they lay limp but shaken with silent laughter until those seated around them began to throw rude jokes at them. Then they made themselves stiff and still and Pakoko stuffed his fist into his mouth to hold back the word he wanted to fling back at them. When the food bowls were set out for the men on the one side and the women on the other, the eyes of the two young people kept talking across the space between as if they had a secret language. When they were sitting in the family circle about the torch lights, clapping and singing old tales, they vied with one another to make their tongues loud and trilling.

Stretched out at last on their share of the family sleeping space, they turned their backs to one another, but each could feel the warmth of the other. Pakoko was thinking about this strange girl who was like a friend. He rolled over and touched her face to show his *kaoha,* but he drew back his hand quickly. It was wet! She needn't weep. He had told her he would wait. He crawled outside the house into the cold night and sat there until the murmuring of another sun brought him companionship.

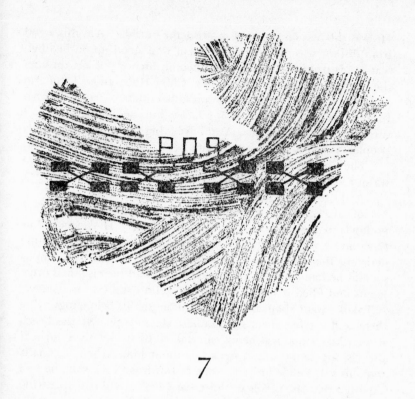

7

PAKOKO stood on the head of a coconut tree and shouted *kaoha* to the sun. This was his canoe, a leaf canoe floating on the southeast wind, rising and falling on its supports, lashing the current flowing past with rattling streamers. This was his land-seeking canoe!

When he had returned to Taiohae from the joining ceremony, he had told Chief Tea-roru that he must perform many important works. Now he kept picking up things and throwing them down. He joined this and that group of free young people and wandered with them, but they were the same boys and girls he had known. They were going to the same nests in the bush, to the same cook houses for stolen food. He wanted to see a new thing, a new land. He kept looking for a visiting canoe.

At last he saw a mat sail stained red in the morning light with paddles that scattered bright bubbles along the sea's shining path.

He was the first on the sand to greet the outsider. Was this a god from distant seas, this handsome man who stood up on his high seat as his paddlers carried the canoe on their shoulders through the unfurling sea? He said he was Chief Hono from Tahu Ata and that he was the son of Grandfather Mauia's sister. Pakoko rubbed noses with him as a relative but he thought he had surely come from the skies. 'You have a big canoe, seats for many people!' were his words of greeting.

The Chief laughed, but not to mock him. 'You would like to warm a seat with your bottom?' he asked.

'I want to seek new lands,' Pakoko said.

'So!' answered Chief Hono, looking sideways at him. 'I have no lands to give, but my island is good for play. Have you yellow *tapas* and a shell of sweet oil, my fine fellow?' Seeing the burning desire in the youth's eyes, he promised to take him with him as soon as he had emptied his canoe of shell and tortoise shell ornaments and filled it with roots for the yellow stain, in exchange.

Pakoko went about in a dream, gathering his belongings, tying them and retying them in bundles. He scarcely left the beach while Chief Hono was being entertained by his relatives, for fear the visiting canoe would depart without him. When he finally took his seat beside his handsome cousin from Tahu Ata, he half expected that the power of this great Chief would stir up a wind that would blow them to his island in a single night.

For many moons, the relatives of Tahu Ata held nothing back from Pakoko. On Nuku Hiva, he had been but a hand or a foot or a back for Chief Kiato-nui. Here he was a singer and a dancer who could make the flesh even of old women crawl. Naturally, he resisted when Kiato-nui sent Mauhau with a canoe full of gifts for Chief Hono and a command to Pakoko to return for instruction in chanting. This was a work the youth had longed for, but not just now. He wound his arms around his cousin and begged him to join the good play of Tahu Ata.

Mauhau shook his head. 'Kiato-nui wants to build the taboo house now.'

'I cannot leave now,' Pakoko protested. 'On the fifteenth night of the moon, I must sing and dance at the praise-song festival for Chief Hono's new woman.'

'Yes or no?' Mauhau planted his feet.

'No.' Pakoko shut his mouth tight.

When the canoe from Taiohae had vanished in the salt spray, Pakoko felt a spear thrust troubling him, but he laughed the prick away. The Master Chanter knew his burning desire for the words of power. He would wait for him.

Ah, what a beautiful festival! Night was just fleeing when Pakoko came down from the uplands with free young people, carrying bundles of bamboo and hibiscus sticks and armsful of coconut leaves, sweet ferns and vines for their taboo house, which they were going to build on Chief Hono's terrace. They were singing:

> Climbing for perfumes for the Chiefess,
> Questioned the handsome youth in the flower tree,
> 'Why are you here, Swallow and Tropic Bird?'
> 'Seeking sweet songs for our Chiefess.'

When they were inside their leafy bower, fashioning songs for the Chief's new woman, these gay youngsters praised Pakoko. 'He has never been taught, but he makes songs as easily as birds,' they said. They thought he was wonderful, these new friends. He was wonderful! What a beautiful red voice he had! He was like a fisherman with many fish on many lines. He pulled them here, he pushed them there. He made them laugh, he made them tremble. Ah. When he had been taught the old words of the gods, then indeed he would make men come or go! He felt that prick of fear again but flicked it away.

For eight nights the young people made songs and dances and dipped their *tapas* in yellow and made their skins white as coconut meat. The hair plucker came with his sharp shells and cut and shaved as they desired. Pakoko coiled his hair in a single ball on top in Chief Hono's way, but, alas, when he looked at himself in a bowl of water, he saw that it was not like Hono's after all. 'What is the matter with my head?' he asked the Chief's son who was his friend.

The young man answered carefully, as if wrapping bits of food in leaves and hiding them. 'Nothing, you are handsome.'

'But not a dancer,' Pakoko moaned, 'not without feathers. How can I trace a circle on the stones when I dip my head?'

Certainly it was the desire of the Chief's son to open his hands to his gay visitor, but he remembered his father's saying, 'To give twice without receiving once is throwing good breadfruit to a pig.' Pakoko had nothing to give. The young man covered his eyes and spoke with a thick tongue, 'Your hair will trace the circle.'

'Even a white hair plume would be something,' the Teii suggested, turning his soft, begging eyes upon his friend. When Hono's careful son laughed and tossed him his own bunch of white beards, Pakoko whispered a little praise song to him and made him wiggle with pleasure.

As the free youngsters scampered through the white night to the Chief's terrace to sing and dance, Pakoko slipped into the dark house of Hono's woman-before. 'It is I, Pakoko, your son's friend,' he said in reply to the blind woman's query.

Pakoko admired this old woman because she had made no trouble when Chief Hono had asked her consent to bring a new woman into his house. She had been mated to the chief's older brother, who had gone on a long voyage for red feathers and had never returned. There was a song which said that she was blind because she had worn her eyes out looking for his return, but everyone knew that it was because she had eaten pig which was forbidden to her. The youth was prepared to ask her for what he desired, openly, as was his right as a visiting relative, but when he saw the dark house and felt her fingers runnning over his face to be sure of his identity, he could not resist the play of stealing what he wanted. He laid his friend's plume of white hair in her hand. 'The dance for the new chiefess is about to begin,' he said, his breath running fast. 'Your son will not wear this beard. Give me his headband of cocks' feathers.'

'He wants the cocks' feathers?' she asked sharply.

Pakoko gave a sidewise answer. 'Where is his bundle?' He stumbled through the unlighted house, feeling along the back thatch for a hanging rope. 'Is it the last bundle at the end?' he asked.

'Yes, the last,' she agreed. The old mother's hands were smoothing the hair of the white beard. 'Yes,' she admitted, with a deep breath of relief, 'this is his plume. Here is the knot in the mending of the band.'

When Pakoko felt the long smooth feathers he sought, he laid them aside, refolded the package, pulled it to the rafters and fastened the cord. 'I have it, old one,' he whispered. As he passed her, he stooped and rubbed her cold, wrinkled nose with his own spread nostrils.

'You will take it to him?' she inquired anxiously.

'He is waiting for me at Chief Hono's feast place,' he answered evasively and ran away quickly lest she hear him laughing.

On the Chief's terrace, his beautiful young woman was sitting on a pile of soft mats while Hono called out the names of his kinsmen who were bringing flowers from every valley of Tahu Ata. She was leaning against a fan of blossoms spread out behind her, as if she were drowning in their fragrance. Now and then she plunged her arms into the sea of wreaths that climbed higher and higher around her. Smiling radiantly, she was listening to her praises sung by Hono's son.

> Oh new moon, flashing white,
> We turn our eyes to you,
> Above, in the sky,
> Brighter than the stars.

Pakoko shivered, looking at her white and flashing skin. Dizzy and moon-sick, he heard his own song offering gushing through his open throat as if it were wind in flower trees.

> Overturned are our coconut shells of sweet oil,
> Fallen to earth are our faded flowers.
> Only you are a pleasure to our nostrils,
> Only you dazzle our eyes.

How red, how agitating his voice! How long and slender his legs! Pakoko looked down upon them as he danced. Delicately, yet unrelentingly his feet were treading the land as if they were kneading the flesh of that beautiful fruit plucked by Chief Hono. He made his black feathers beckon to her. He knew that the whirling fringes of his hair cape and skirt were whipping her till she tingled. He could feel that he was pulling her, winding her into the circle as he turned. Yes, she was sliding down from the high stone terrace onto the paving, dancing with him as he sucked her into the whirlpool. She threw back her head and caught him with her luminous eyes. Neither one could break away. In an ecstasy they turned together, faster and faster, closer and closer.

Suddenly, Pakoko felt that they were whirling in cold blackness. Voices of men, flutes and drums had died. He could see Chief Hono standing, tall as a god, on his terrace. His eyes were red in their black stripes of tattooing. His upraised arm held his ceremonial club as if he were about to throw it. Wind rushed into the young man's ears, but he did not falter nor fall. He finished his turning, lowered his outstretched leg slowly, alighted as gently as a butterfly. For the first time, he touched his companion, turning her swiftly towards the Chief. 'The woman of Clear Space waits for her mate!' his quick tongue cried.

'Let the god seize his woman!' Every tongue there took up the cry.

Chief Hono lowered his club and leaned upon its carved head. He smiled at his fearless young kinsman with a twisted mouth and let his eyes cover him bit by bit. When they came to the feather headband, the twin of his own, he began to shake with laughter. 'You magnificent thief!' he shouted, making the crowds roar and slap their thighs.

But deep silence fell as Chief Hono climbed onto his speaking stone to answer Pakoko's challenge. His people lifted their eyes to him and watched him treading majestically on one foot, while he flung the other straight and far. With arms like wings, and a crested head, he stooped and rose in thrilling circles. The images on his rippling skin opened, closed, opened, closed, until flesh called to flesh. 'Oh Chief! O hot sun!' all his people called to him.

Wet-eyed, unnoticed, the young woman went back to her flower-covered mats and hid herself under their sweetness, waiting in her nest. When Chief Hono came, she lay soft and unresisting while he beat her and promised her death another time. She was content.

In the morning, Hono sent Pakoko back to his own island in a canoe loaded with gifts, the stolen headband of feathers laid carefully on top. 'You need no instruction in words of power, my cousin,' he told him, 'but go!'

8

WHEN the third sun reddened the mat of Hono's voyaging canoe and Pakoko saw Nuku Hiva standing up out of the sea, he threw off the mats that had sheltered him from the burning days, scraped away the bleaching paste, oiled his fair skin and put on all his new finery to show himself to the relatives of Taiohae. Many were on the sands, shading their eyes with their hands, as the canoe ran onto the land. He knew they were saying, 'Who is this fine fellow?' He ran from house to house, rubbing noses with high and low. 'Can this be Fatu's boy, Pakoko?' they were asking one another. He threw himself into his uncle's arms, his aunt's, his mother's, and pranced before their wet eyes.

But Chief Veo held him off. 'Tie your finery to a rafter,' he said, 'and help me find a *pao'o* fish.'

A *pao'o* fish! Why did he want that thing which was not good eating? Pakoko didn't like to ask. Perhaps he should know. Besides, he was dripping with *kaoha* for his father. He wanted to help him. But while he paused to dip his fingers into the bowl of sweet breadfruit paste which Uncle Fatu brought him, he said off-hand, 'That *pao'o* fish, it is called "Life-giving." What is it good for?'

The uncle answered, not meeting his eyes, 'If it is laid on the mouth and the hand of those who have been taught old words, it helps them to remember their learning.'

Those who have been taught! Pakoko overturned his food bowl as he stood up. Where was Kiato-nui? Where was Mauhau? Where were all the young people? For the first time he heard the humming that rippled the silence of the valley. Chanting! They were all being taught! They had not waited for him!

Hot and cold, quivering and jerking, Pakoko broke through bushes until he found the taboo house where his brothers and sisters and cousins were filling their stomachs with the ancient wisdom. He reached for the taboo sticks to pull them up but dared not touch them. He stood looking with haggard, burned-out eyes at the sacred house and at the perch in front, bound with red and white, where the spirits of the dead would alight when the fathers and mothers called their names and the sons and daughters sang to them. He was not one of them. He never had been one of them. He must go somewhere, do something. He could not stand there like an empty old skin.

Passing the sacred terraces, he saw the Priest inspecting a Taipi man who had been seized as an offering to please the gods at the chanting festival. Fortunate youth! He at least would be raised to the skies. Pakoko would just as soon be caught as a fish. Why not?

He turned into Haavao's Path of War, just wandering. When little stones came rolling down upon him, he would have hidden among the bamboos, but the down-comer called to him, '*Kaoha*, Little Coconut.'

He saw his sister, Hina, coming towards him. She carried her mat and bundle. 'Where are you going?' he asked listlessly.

'Who knows?' she asked lightly. 'Away from the house of Chiefess Kena. Her floors are hard. Her foster son is greedy, greedy. She herself is sacred, sacred, sacred! I am going to

Kiato-nui's chanting festival to look about for another householder. If I like my mother's sister of Haka-ui, I shall go to her place.'

Pakoko spoke in a tiny voice. 'I have no place to go.'

Hina smiled. 'Aren't you ready yet to go to the house of your joined woman? Metani is waiting for you and the Hapaas think you do not like her.'

Metani! He had forgotten her. But he would not go empty-handed, without learning in his stomach even! 'I will not be lichen clinging to her!' he cried.

'Is it power you want?' Hina asked with such *kaoha* that it started a rain of tears. She let him cry, pressed against her breast. 'Power may be seized in many ways,' she said gently. 'A young man may exchange names with a chief.'

'And become his man-at-the-side or his betrayer,' he answered with a bitter tongue.

'Is there no woman for whom you care?' she asked.

'Only you,' he sobbed. Then he lifted his face, his eyes wide and startled. 'That is a true word! Hina, I will build a house for you!'

Had she been struck by a flung stone? 'Our fathers are brothers!' she gasped, recoiling. 'Our joining is forbidden!'

'Old lies!' he replied. He bound her arms to her sides as he encircled her. 'If the fathers refuse, we will join ourselves.'

'No!' she begged, struggling to free herself.

'Yes, yes!' He was laughing as he slid to his knees and pressed his mouth into her thigh. 'You are my woman!'

'I am your sister!' she panted. 'Don't touch me!'

He heard her great fear and sat back on his heels to see her.

'It is play you want, not power,' she said, ashamed and angry. 'Any house will give you that. Stop at the first one.' She snatched her mat and bundle and fled, sobbing.

Was it play he wanted? No, he was sick to death of women! He sat for a long time looking down on the valley where he was nothing but a moon sick fool. Finally, when the sun had fallen off the sky's foundation and the sea was blowing his cold breath up the valley, he turned from that beloved land. 'Yes, power may be seized,' he whispered.

On quick, hard feet he climbed to the crest and hurried along the high level, slapping his arms to warm them and shouting to scare away any wild women who might be lurking to trap him. He waded through the tall grass of the Valley of Tears, but he did not turn down into the valley of Metani, Chiefess of the Hapaas. On, on he walked, to the man-eating precipice, the back wall of the valley of the Taipis. He stood on the edge, looking down into the black. There were many fires below. Were those cruel enemies roasting and eating his relatives? Certainly they would seek one to balance the young man seized for Kiato-nui's chanting festival. Pakoko's hair stood up, but he slid his foot over the edge of the rocks until his toes found a hole, and groped until his hand found a swinging vine. Then down, down he lowered himself. He was going to exchange names with Chief Tohi-kai.

III WHALES' TEETH

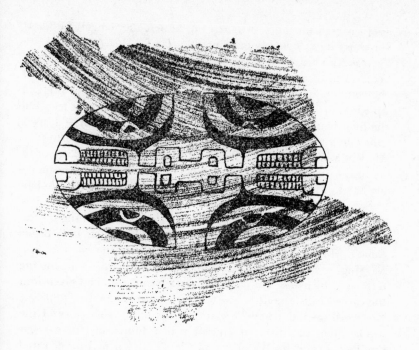

1

BREATHING violently, Pakoko flattened himself against the
slippery rocks at the foot of the cliffs of Taipivai. Cold
fingers still clutched his bowels. Horrible, that painful
descent in the blackness! He was afraid to look back at the deep
crack down which the waterfall, Two Eels, roared and foamed.
Sliding, falling, clutching at tiny rat's tooth moss and brittle
stems of ferns, he had crept down alongside it. He had heard the
panting of wild women, felt their cold breath blowing past, seen
their fiery eyes winking from black caves. His skin was raw
from the licking of their rough tongues, his limbs aching from
their violent embraces. Behind him stood up the man-eating
precipice, the back wall protecting the Taipis from all enemies
coming by land. Before him opened out the vast night-filled
valley of the man-eaters. 'Forward, courage!' It was as if he heard
again the Priest summoning the Brave Faces. Groping with his

toes through the cold, swift stream, he left the dangers he knew for those he could only imagine.

Was his own breathing pounding in his ears? No, he heard the beat of drums. Were they calling for revenge for the death of the young man seized for Kiato-nui's chanting festival? His tipped up ear caught the sound of faint laughter and capering feet. On the high bank above the stream, the trailing fire-breath of a sugar cane torch suddenly lit a band of young people scampering by. Ah, not war, but a feast. Pakoko followed in the shadows until he heard that these were nose-rubbers from Hiva Oa, a meandering band of singers who had come to praise young Chief Tohi-kai.

Shivering, but laughing too, Pakoko joined them as they entered the circle of yellow torches and red fires burning on the walls of the feast place. There was the old Chief, old 'Bitter Kava', white-haired and tight-mouthed, scowling at the hip-wagging youngsters. Several young men were with him on the terrace. Which was Tohi-kai, Pakoko's friend who had given him the carved stilts, the little boy who had worn his anklets long ago? Not until an indolent fellow turned his back as if weary of the whole affair and diverted himself with a bunch of bananas was the Teii sure of his Taipi friend. Yes, Tohi-kai had never cared for anything very long.

The sea rose high in Pakoko when he saw Tohi-kai toss his empty banana skins to his Fire Keeper, slide lazily off the stones of the terrace and stroll across the paving to the kneeling men and women. Now he could make himself known to his friend. But Tohi-kai held out his hands for a girdle and cape of yellow *ti* leaves and knelt with the singers. Not until the young Chief tired of this, did Pakoko offer his own song in a clear, high voice that might have been a bird's song for his beloved.

> Oh Tohi-kai is my friend!
> Broken our sky-legs,
> Worn out our anklets,
> Only our *kaoha* remains.
> This is my song for Tohi-kai,
> For Tohi-kai, my friend.

As the singer approached, the young Chief leaned forward examining his long, thin face with high cheek bones and thrust out chin, his sparkling eyes and laughing mouth. 'Is it Pakoko?' he whispered. Seeing the level black brows lift in relief, he laughed and cried out, 'Now there will be such play as men sing of from sea to sea!'

The Teii and the Taipi twined their arms about one another and whispered together. The nose-rubbers, treading a circle around them, began to sing of friends.

The playing ended, the ovens emptied, gifts pressed upon the visitiors, the fires were allowed to fall into ashes and the Hiva Oans straggled off to sleep before going on to another valley. Seeing that one fellow remained with Tohi-kai, the old Chief fastened his eyes upon him. Had his moon-struck son invited one of these yellow-smeared do-nothings to stay with him? He was worn out with Tohi-kai's playmates who slept all day and played all night and ate the shares of the Brave Faces whenever the ovens were opened. He spread his bent legs, clasped his bony hands behind his back, and waited while the young Chief and Pakoko crossed the paving, hand in hand.

The Teii was shaken by his own breath, but he made his feet go without jerking and kept his tongue busy with light words. He would not tremble before that shark waiting for him. He would wait at ease for the question that must come.

'Who is this?' the old Chief demanded.

It was Tohi-kai who began to tremble. Pakoko stood up whole and spoke boldly. 'I am Pakoko, son of Chief Veo of Taiohae, foster son of Fatu.' During the sudden cold silence, he saw the Taipi's hard eyes turn to fire, knew that his fingers were jerking as if itching for a sling. When his name went humming among the listeners, he waited with hands intertwined till his knuckles turned white. He heard the hum become a roar. 'Here is a Teii to balance our dead! Here is a fish for our gods!' He was deafened by the thunder of the Brave Faces who were walling him in. 'Death to the Teii! Death to the Teii!' Now he must speak! He must ask Tohi-kai to give him his name! What were the words for such a request? He did not know. Where was his gift? He had none. At last he trembled and turned to his friend with begging eyes.

The sun must have stuck out a ray on that dark night, for Pakoko's face was alight as Tohi-kai put his palms on his friend's breast and said, 'This is Tohi-kai, I am Pakoko.' He ripped the band from the white plume on his head, wrapped it around the Teii's wrist and tied it. 'Hear, all of you! To this one I have given my name and a sign that he is taboo in this valley.'

Pakoko's eyes fell upon that band. He had his name-friend, but he had bound himself to an enemy chief! Was this the path to power?

When Pakoko called out his name, 'Tohi-kai', every house was open to him and all things were his. He knew that the Taipis hid their eyes from him and turned aside when he approached. He knew that the Brave Faces fingered their slings whenever he entered the men's house and that the Priest's Clubs were listening for a command to noose him for their god. But he sat upon no thorns. He was taboo. He could not be touched.

His *kaoha* for Tohi-kai was a fever that burned him. He was continually feeling the young Chief's fingers lightly touching his breast as he silenced the angry bellowing of the man-eaters by giving him his own name. Pakoko could never make a just return for this, but he put all his effort into seeking Tohi-kai's desires. Before the sun was standing up, he was making a tour of the valley, spying out houses where workers were digging roots for yellow stain or grating coconuts for oil or filling ovens with special feast-time foods or beating *tapas* or carving ornaments. When the work was finished, he was always on hand with Tohi-kai's coconut sheath to collect the young Chief's share. Any house that refused was sure to be raided by the free young people or robbed by laughing thieves who stuck hooks through the thatch and pulled out what they wanted.

Tohi-kai himself lay longer and longer on his mats. All day he was rubbed by pretty young girls whom his name-friend summoned. Only after fires he got up, wrapped himself in yellow-drenched garments and strings of potent flowers, and went into the night to dance and sing and play. Oh what strong *kaoha* this Taipi Chief returned to his name-friend who filled his house with delights and made him the most talked of chief on Nuku Hiva! He held back none of his riches from him. It was his boast that Tohi-kai who was Pakoko and Pakoko who was Tohi-kai shared all things exactly alike. Looking at their finery, no one could point out the chief, no one the wandering Teii. Those two together were called 'Tohi-ka-kai', because Tohi-kai was doubled.

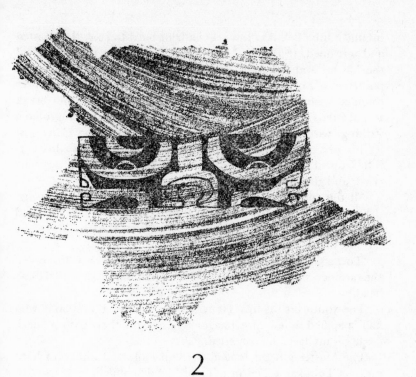

2

T OHI-KAI'S father was in a ferment of anger. Without Pakoko, his son had had hard ears, but with him he was a wild moon-child running away when called. The old Chief began to hear the murmuring of his people. They said that the taboos were being used to plunder the valley and that their children were being led to run wild in the mountains like pigs. 'I'll shut them all up in a taboo house and turn their laughing into crying!' the old Chief declared. He commanded his Image-Striking Master to prepare a place for tattooing his first-born. 'Tell all the young people that, whenever Tohi-kai is resting, they may have your work free for themselves,' he commanded the Master.

The old man was right. When the excitement of building the taboo houses and raiding the Chief's premises for food had given way to waiting for a turn to be tattooed during Tohi-kai's resting times, the boys and girls were as easy to handle as breast water infants. Only Tohi-kai was a breadfruit hard to cook. He twisted and screamed, trying to shake off the four learners who helped the Master and to escape the hands that were driving the bone points into his foot. He howled to drown the words of power sounded with the striking of the mallet, but he could not break the Master's steady rhythm, striking, wiping the spurting blood, striking, wiping, striking, wiping. Finally, the young Chief just let his breath run out and he lay limp and still with his eyes rolled up. That brought him rest. 'He has fainted!' the learners cried, and the Master let them carry him to his mat.

All the young men in Tohi-kai's house jumped up, shouting, 'I am first!' But Pakoko pushed ahead. 'I am Tohi-kai,' he said firmly and stretched himself in front of the Master. 'Make the face on my heel laugh,' he commanded gaily.

'To begin with the feet is for the first-born of a Chief only,' the tattooer reproved him and slid himself along towards Pakoko's head.

The youth bit his lips. He was to be marked as a nobody who had snatched a few face images free! 'Begin then with a black circle on my face,' he conceded.

The Master put his tools down and looked at him with hard eyes. 'Is Tohi-kai a Teii or a Taipi?' he demanded.

Pakoko's tongue was almost too dry to make the sound, 'Taipi,' as he turned up his face to be punctured with the three stripes of his people's enemy tribe. But when the teeth of the comb began to bite into his forehead, he laughed. He had laid out his path. He would ask for no days of rest until his skin was covered with images from head to foot. Then who would know the beginning, head or foot? 'You are slow, old man!' he challenged the Master, and laughed and laughed as the tiny rootlets of pain grew and spread over his head.

The Master's mallet answered the loud words of this Teii boaster, 'Ta! Ta! Ta! Ta!' Pricking with a fine, pointed bird bone, and digging with two big teeth cut in an enemy's bone he pushed his work vigorously. The learners could hold this proud fool down until the heavy black stripes and the fine 'men' and 'teeth' and 'fish tails' between them were finished. That would make the fellow scream for rest.

The roots of pain sprouted vines that twined about Pakoko's

head in a tight lashing, making the flesh swell between. The Master's song came to him like an Ironwood's mocking yell as he called his enemy an insect, an abscessed head, a filthy mat. But Pakoko would not cry for rest. 'You are weary,' his thick lips mumbled. 'Ask for breadfruit paste to make you strong.' And when the Master's answer was to dig the many toothed comb deep into the top of his shaved head, his bones shuddered and his teeth knocked together, but he would not ask for rest. His voice was dying, but he spoke, 'Make—the Brave Face—up there —pull down the lid of his eye.'

'Yes,' the Master answered gently. His voice was different now. His song was a strong arm lifting this brave youth above the sea of blood, carrying him through the splintering bone. Faces were watching, faces twisted with horror. Tohi-kai's voice was crying, 'Stop!' Even the Master was asking, 'Is it enough?'

'Go on!' wailed the stubborn fellow.

'Friend, shall I start the "Swallow" on your shoulder?' When the question ran slowly into Pakoko's enormous ears, he nodded and chanted crazily:

> Swallow up above,
> Where will you perch up above?
> I will perch on the rain shield,
> On the rain shield of Handsome Wreath.

He howled the words until the Swallow's claws tore out his lungs and his wings fanned away his breath. *Hahu!* He did not know that the learners were carrying him to the sleeping space for rest.

Pakoko was awakened in black night by a scratching at the back roof and a piercing whisper calling Tohi-kai. 'My son,' breathed the old Chief, 'it is said that the fellow from Taiohae is taking your place.'

'Why not?' Tohi-kai answered. 'I am resting. My foot is a rotten sore.'

'Only your foot!' grieved the father. 'I must give the Master twenties and twenties of pigs, arms and arms of *tapa,* many moons of work from all of my relatives, and for what? For images tapped into the skin of a nose-rubber from Taiohae!'

'You have taught me not to empty an oven at one sitting,' the son taunted him. 'If I were covered in one taboo house, I would have no new images to show at other tattooing festivals.'

The old man's voice quivered as if he were wailing for the dead. 'Endure a little,' he begged. 'Do not let the people say, "He cried too much to have his images struck," or perhaps, "He does not deserve a new name for his tattooing." '

Here was a new thought that tickled Tohi-kai. It would make this old 'Thunder and Lightning' grumble and flash. 'That is just,' he said. 'I will give the tattooing name to Pakoko.'

The skies fell! The old Chief could scarcely make sense for sputtering. 'Pakoko! You give him your skin! What you don't give, he takes! Who carried off the best things when the young people tore up my storage houses? Who got the carved house posts, the fine mats with hair fringes, the fattest pigs and ripest breadfruit? Pakoko! Hush! You said he stole to build this house for you, to feed you. Are you stupid? It was for himself, alone!'

'But it is the custom to give all to one's namesake,' said Tohi-kai.

The father opened his mouth to roar, but nothing would come out. He stumbled away, beating his hands together in anguish.

When the deep silence of the valley had swallowed even the traces of his feet and hands, Pakoko tried to make words with his scab-stiffened lips. He wanted to say, 'My *kaoha* is not a lie,' but only breath bubbled through his putrid mouth. Gulping in the night's cold breath, he lived; drowning in the sea of throbbing pain, he died. Reviving, fainting, reviving, fainting, he was like a breath body that appears and disappears.

When the fever left him, he woke to sweet air and the songs of birds. The hideous dreams were gone with the dark. He looked at Tohi-kai's swollen foot and laughed. 'Porpoise tail,' he called him.

Tohi-kai's eyes narrowed. Was Pakoko mocking him, ridiculing his undecorated body? 'You are stealing the Master's time from me,' he whined. 'You are stripping me of my skin.'

Pakoko laughed. He thought that Tohi-kai was imitating his father. He reached stiffly for a shell of banana juice and patted the liquid gently on his friend's bad foot.

Tohi-kai was smoothed all over. 'Your face is nasty,' he jeered. He fed Pakoko soft breadfruit paste through the bleeding crack that had been his mouth. The two friends leaned together, back to back, giggling and weeping.

As the moon of the Pig went into blackness and the moon of Abundance began to swell, Tohi-kai endured the Master's mallet now and then, but more often he was stretched out on his mats, leaning on one elbow, smiling, listening, watching. What piercing screams! What frightful wounds! Perhaps there had never been so many brave young men in any valley before. Certainly there was not another chief with a man-at-the-side whose skin had been completely covered in one taboo house. He looked proudly at Pakoko's mutilated body lying like a bloated fish rotting on the sand. Then he stuck out his own foot and admired the delicate blue tracery of 'turtles' and 'bonito tails.' It was the only tattooed foot in that house, save Pakoko's, and his friend's lacked the distinguishing marks of a chief. Tohi-kai laughed and his teeth showed very sharp and very white.

On full moon day of that harvest, when all the young men in the taboo house had heard the old Chief's conch shell releasing them for the work of decorating its posts and rafters with upland vines and colored leaves, when they had obeyed the Master's signal to wash the dried blood and scaly skin from their healed bodies in the stinging sea water, Pakoko sat with the others, rubbing his patterned skin with oil. He could not tear his eyes from the brilliant bands of images that covered him, three on his face, seven on his body, seven on his arms, seven on his legs and feet. He drew his *tapa* tight between his legs, so as not to cover a single design. He turned to Tohi-kai with *kaoha* streaming from his eyes, only to meet an empty regard.

'And what new thing will you show me at my next tattooing feast, my fine fellow?' When the young Chief's tongue licked this question as if it were a sweet morsel, it freed everyone in that house for mocking laughter.

Pakoko shrank as if he were a wet mat drying quickly in the hot sun. Still, he pressed out a laugh and a word. 'I shall think of something,' he boasted. He swung his hips as he obeyed the Master's invitation to be seated before the leaves spread for the feast and made a space for himself with pointed elbows.

When the Master had dipped a shell of *kava* for each young man and was lifting the cover from a large bird-bodied bowl, all eyes and tongues forgot their hardness and bitterness. Here was a taboo thing that stopped even Tohi-kai's taunts, for not one here had ever eaten the flesh of a man before. 'Here is the frightfulness of a Brave Face and the grace of a dancer,' the Master intoned as he passed a morsel to each. 'Be powerful on the battle field and on the feast place.'

Pakoko's hand was heavy with the power he was about to imbibe as he lifted the hot, juicy bit towards his mouth, but he saw that the eyes of the others were sliding sideways towards him and that they were nudging one another. Instantly, he knew their thought. He was being offered the flesh of a kinsman! He could not move his hand that was half-way to his mouth. Where was he? By what path had he come? Where was he going? Ah. He was about to seize power. Power must be his! Slowly he put the morsel into his mouth and swallowed it. Then he turned his eyes upon this one, that one, the next, forcing each to lower his eyes, until he regarded Tohi-kai, who looked back unflinching. Were those fixed eyes hard or soft? The Teii could not tell.

Tohi-kai said in a voice level as the sea on a windless day, 'It is the custom to give a new name to the first-born when he is tattooed. The first-born is Tohi-kai and there is Tohi-kai.' He pointed at Pakoko. 'The name is Kea, "Hard Shell."'

The Master dropped a word into the silent pool. 'The young man has paid for it.'

'Not yet,' the young Chief answered, 'but he will.'

Everybody laughed, Pakoko also, but he was wondering uneasily what the old Chief would do.

Since he was the one with the new name, Pakoko Kea led the procession of young people who showed their patterns on the feast place to all the Taipis bidden to come. Why wasn't the sea rising high in him as he pranced in front? True, there were no cries of admiration as he passed, no shaking of hips as he made his images open and close by flicking his skin. But before, he had cared nothing for the bad eyes and sour mouths of these hostile Taipis and now he was drowning in a bitter sea. Was it because Tohi-kai's eyes had hardened and his tongue put on a barb? Surely his friend could not believe the old Chief's lies. He had taken for himself only what Tohi-kai had pushed away. In front of the old Chief's terrace, Pakoko had to turn slowly to show him his beautiful skin. It was like turning round and round on a spit in licking flames.

The old man could not keep back his bile. He poured filthy words over the outsider who had taken his son's place of honor. 'You diseased brain! You dirty mat!' he shouted. 'Get out of my sight! You have made my son a louse in your stinking hair! Carry him, then, on your fouled head. I am ended here. I know nothing of the way of insects.'

Pakoko caught this wave full in the face. It left him gasping but it did not knock him down. 'I have given Tohi-kai my name and all my effort,' he said with dignity.

'Your effort for what?' the father bellowed. 'To drag down what I have tried to raise to power! All you care for is play!'

The sting of old words poisoned and numbed Pakoko. His sister, Hina, had said scornfully, 'It is play you want, not power.' He had come here to seize power. Had he missed his path? He drooped and hung his head.

But Tohi-kai was standing up whole now. 'You say you are ended here,' he addressed his father. 'Is it your desire to seek a new land?' He waited for his answer, swinging the long tail of his loin cloth gently from side to side.

It was the old man's turn to quiver. He answered in short gasps. 'Perhaps—I must. I will not look—at a moon prattler—carrying the chief's staff—in this great valley.'

'Good,' said Tohi-kai as if he tossed his father a package of breadfruit paste, 'I will build a double voyaging canoe for you and give you seven forties of paddlers. The Priest will watch for the stars that will guide you.' In the wink of an eye, that easy running tongue had turned everything upside down.

The old Chief was like a mighty tree struck by lightning. His cry tore through him as if it split him from leaf to root. 'In distant seas, I will hide my shame!' He fled inside his house.

During the moons of work for the great voyage of the old Chief, Pakoko hid himself in Tohi-kai's taboo house. Had the black bands crossing his face changed him completely? Tohi-kai examined him from the corners of his eyes. Pakoko looked like an Ironwood about to swing a man-eating club. Why? The young Taipi had freed his friend from all danger. Once the old shark was in the deep sea, the little fish could play as they pleased.

Yet Pakoko turned his back and muttered, 'I have no stomach for play,' when his friend begged him to come to a new nest where an opening bud was waiting for them in the soft moonshine.

But on the day of the sea-going, Pakoko could not miss seeing that enormous double canoe go land-seeking. He walked boldly along the path from Tohi-kai's upland terraces to his father's place far below. There folk had come from every part of the big valley to watch the filling of baskets and tying of bundles for the departure. One old woman after another raised her voice in tremulos of weeping. 'Oh Chief, you are going away! Far! Long! How many moons? Alas, the Chief leaves his house. He throws away his land. He breaks the flow of love to and fro. The Chief will never come back! Weep!' When the old man came onto his terrace, the heads of the families crawled to him and laid their parting gifts at his feet. He stood up among them, seeing them reflected in his tears. Angrily, Pakoko wiped his hand across his eyes. Was land-seeking a thing to weep about? He turned away from those foolish mourners and ran ahead to the beach. Picking his way over the tangled hibiscus roots in the wet place where the sea slept on the land, he crossed the open grasslands above the sands and sat down to watch.

The Fire Keeper, standing on the platform between the two long canoes, was shouting at his men-at-the-side to spread ferns underneath for sleeping places for the women and children and to lay the Chief's mats on the level above. The Master Fisherman was leaning on his steering paddle, nodding as he heard the names of the stars which the Priest had caught in his *kava* bowl. The Name Singer, an old woman bent under her load of oven stones, climbed over the sideboards, sat down in her place, and began to chant the names of the grandfathers. Her high tremulo pulsed above all other sounds, above the whispering of the sea and the whistling of the wind through bunches of hair strung along the sideboards, above the grunts and groans of workers, the shrill questions of women and the clapping of young people.

Those who were going with the old Chief followed the Name Singer. Eyes wide open and staring into the air, they walked, as if they saw already the distant land where they would unroll their mats, hang their bundles, heat their oven stones and plant their breadfruit roots and *tapa* shoots. When the women had climbed inside the canoes and fitted themselves into the shells, the paddlers took their seats and the bailers made themselves comfortable with their water-lickers in their hands.

At last the old Chief came down onto the grassy slope and stood still for a moment, a mountain looking seaward. Every one there, Pakoko included, bowed down and laid his face against the land. Tohi-kai suddenly cried out with a child's trembling tongue, 'Father!' Was he about to call him back? The mountain did not turn but signalled to his men to lift him and carry him to his seat on the platform. He sat with his back to the land, staring at the sky's foundation.

The paddlers stirred up the shallow waters, digging deeper and deeper. The Master Chanter's song floated back on the breeze. 'My canoe, my canoe is putting to sea.'

'You will find a land of abundance!' sang the Priest from the shore.

3

SHIVERING in the sea's thickening breath, Pakoko and Tohi-kai sat close together long after the vanishing of that big canoe. They were like little fellows who did not know what thing to pick up next.

The Master Stone Builder sat down beside them. 'My work is yours, nephew,' he said. 'Shall we build a new feast place?'

'What's the matter with the old one?' Tohi-kai answered, impudent as a pig. Then he threw a knowing look to Pakoko, 'We two have different play.'

'Different work!' The Teii crossed both uncle and nephew. 'We will build a sea wall!' When the others looked at him as if he had gone crazy, he pulled them to their feet and made them look back at the great valley of Taipivai and its man-eating precipice beyond. 'There is the land wall that shuts out enemies from that side, but here the valley is wide open.' He turned them seaward. 'This is bad, this sleeping water hidden under tangled vines and trees. Enemies from the sea cannot be seen when they come creeping to the houses of fishermen to seize men for their gods.'

Tohi-kai brushed him aside. 'This valley is invincible.'

The Master's eys were playful as little fish jumping in a sunny pool. 'Shall we noose the sun while we finish this great work?' he asked, but seeing Pakoko's face darken, he added, 'The grandfathers built no sea walls. I have no pattern.'

'I will show you the way of it,' Pakoko boasted. 'See, it will stand where the good land begins, taller than the tallest man.' He dragged the two Taipis to the eastern ridge and to the western ridge and pointed out where the arms of the wall would clasp the valley's arms.

Tohi-kai watched his friend from the corners of his eyes. Was the fellow slyly covering his thought from the uncle's view? With the Master occupied down by the sea, there would be no old man to speak against the play of young people up above. Tohi-kai began to smile upon this clever work.

The Master looked down from the ridge upon the marshlands and the rising land above. 'I could stand the stones up in a curve, very thick at the bottom, strong. Well, why not?' he asked at last. 'But I must have food for many workers for many moons.'

Oh this was a splendid thought! 'For many, many, many moons!' Tohi-kai promised. Behind his uncle's back, he rolled up his eyes, but Pakoko gave no answering sign of mocking.

Indeed, the Teii began to count with the Master the number of knots of breadfruit, the number of nets of fish required each day for the workers. The two walked up valley together ahead of their Chief, not even looking to see if he followed, Tohi-kai switched from side to side, breaking branches and kicking little stones. What was Pakoko's play? Was he pretending work or not?

As the stone building went forward, Pakoko tried to pull Tohi-kai along with him as a fisherman draws a fish on a line. Sometimes the Chief came along with a rush, but often he broke the line and ran away to play with other friends. When Pakoko shadowed the Master in the day and slept in the taboo house in the night, Tohi-kai taunted him. 'You say this work is for me, to put a stop to enemy raids, but there is an easier way to make friends of the Hapaas. Your woman is their Chiefess. I will build a house for her and you will bring her here.'

Pakoko's mouth tightened. He was still an insignificant man-at-the-side to a moon-struck youth. When he had made Tohi-kai a chief without an equal on Nuku Hiva, he might build that house, not now. He made his eyes very soft and said, 'When I have balanced your *kaoha* for me, I will think of her.'

'Then I will build a house for my own woman,' the Chief said. He swung the ends of his loin cloth as he watched his friend.

But Pakoko reached eagerly for this new bait for his fishing line. He summoned the Master House Builder and began to drag Tohi-kai here and there to encourage the wood strikers and carvers and mat makers.

Tohi-kai's woman had scarcely unrolled her mat in his new house before the Chief began to throw away food in many little feasts—when his head was shaved, when he went on a visit, when he received a new ornament. Pakoko thought of a new work. He brought the Master Stone Builder to the Chief's taboo house and over a bowl of *kava* he proposed to build the largest breadfruit storage hole on Nuku Hiva. He held up his hand when Tohi-kai opened his mouth to protest. 'Isn't it a good thing to put famine far away from this valley?'

Tohi-kai stuck out his lips. 'Our skies are always open, our land is never dry,' he declared.

'But your father and his people had to go land-seeking.' Pakoko waited for his friend to swallow this hook.

Sure enough, Tohi-kai understood. He had seen the bad eyes of the Taipis sliding sidewise to watch him and his friend ever since the old Chief's departure. He knew that some whispered that the Teii had driven the old man away, but some said that his son had shamed him. Now here was a clever way to make a bad thing good. He echoed Pakoko's suggestion. 'Yes, my father went land-seeking because there was not enough food for all in this valley. Undoubtedly we must make an end of famine, so that no one else must go.'

The Master Stone Builder could direct two works. Certainly he could. He was feeling like a young man these days, with such great work going on. 'I will make a storage hole six arms deep and four across and my children and my children's children will fill it with harvests.' Before Chief Tohi-kai could snatch back his consent, he went to find workers, and Pakoko carried the word to the planters that breadfruit was taboo until the new hole had been filled.

When the enormous hole was finished and the breadfruit paste inside it had risen almost to its stone lips, Pakoko ran round and round it, laughing. Ten men were inside it, standing up the last row of *ti* leaves to protect the last layer of paste. Twenties and twenties of women were wearing down the mountains of breadfruit piled beside them as they took them one by one and curled off their peels with sharp shells. Twenties and twenties were plaiting coconut leaf mats to add to the draining baskets that dotted the cleared hillside. All the little girls and boys of the valley were carrying the peeled ripe breadfruit to innumerable men who squeezed the soft flesh from the cores into the baskets. A long line of men in pairs bore canoe-loads of dry paste on their shoulders and emptied them into the hole. Pakoko jumped inside with those who were tramping down the harvest. He joined their singing:

> I-i-i-i! Lift the new paste,
> Throw it down, pile it up!
> Fill the big hole of Tohi-kai.

Chief Tohi-kai came to see his hole before it was covered over with leaves and bark and earth. Pakoko greeted him with a song:

> The stomach of the land is full.
> Here is the food bowl of the Taipis,
> Of old men and infants who suck,
> Of Brave Faces who swallow heaviness before war,
> Of the Chief who throws nothing away,
> Who drives the mother of famine from his valley.

The Taipis were enjoying this abundance, just looking at it. They were proud of their Chief who looked ahead. If the sky turned to wood and the land to sand, there would still be good food for Tohi-kai's people. They called out their praise to him. And Tohi-kai answered in song, making his voice gush out in tremulo.

Thinking of my father, I weep!
I weep for an old man who fled from scarcity.
Seeing this enormous bowl of food, I weep!
I weep for a hungry father looking in vain for food.
Here is food for you, my father!
We will make a feast for you.

'No feasting from this hole,' Pakoko begged. 'Cover this hole with your taboo.'

'Do you begrudge my father his share?' the Chief asked.

What answer could Pakoko make to that? He could only turn away to hide his anger and grief. Watching, the Taipis began to whisper that there was a quarrel betwen the two friends who were like the lashes of an eye. Some said that the Teii had refused food to the old Chief and that Tohi-kai would take back the name he had given him.

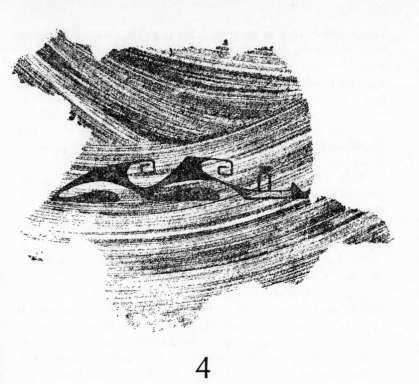

4

NDEED there was a breaking apart. Pakoko did not return to
Tohi-kai's terraces at the time of fires. He built himself a hasty
shelter in the uplands where he could be alone. He was worn
out trying to make his friend a chief of substance. He was
ashamed that he had given his name to a man who could plant
no new breadfruit and store no old. And he himself was still an
empty-handed food beggar. Slowly, his *kaoha* for Tohi-kai was
dying.

He began to think of his joined woman, Metani. Hina had
told him that the Hapaas thought he did not like their Chiefess.
What did the woman herself think? Remembering how he had
touched her cheeks and found them wet, he stood up suddenly.
Perhaps she had wanted him to seize her! He remembered her
delicate hands breaking sugar cane for him and her straight legs
wading ahead of him in the stream. Were they covered with fine

images now? She had never seen his tattooing. Would she know him? He found himself walking along a path. Where was he going? Perhaps Metani should be taught to play. A silent, inner laughter made him quiver. He would say nothing of building a house for her. How could he? He stopped suddenly. Perhaps she would not know him! The night was black. He would not tell her his name! It seemed as if there were eyes in his hands and feet which could see the footholds and vines climbing the precipice at the back of Taipivai. Before he knew it he was running across the high level and turning down into the path to Hakapaa. He felt as if he were going to his mark as a spear goes, quivering and singing, but flung by some hand not his own. Here was the feast place, here were the terraces of the high born, here was the house of the Chiefess Metani.

Pakoko put his mouth to the back roof and breathed her name, 'Metani!'

A quick, startled voice questioned, 'What name are you calling?' When he repeated it, a whisper stirred the leaves against his face. 'Where are your hands?' He thrust them through the matting and felt her fingers flutter over them. Then a dove's low laughing was in his ears. 'Come to the opening,' she murmured.

He watched the wood slide quietly back. A star's pale light showed her dark eyes and her open mouth. She was a bud, waiting for the sun. Did he touch her? Did she touch him? They were two flowers on a single stalk, tossed violently in a hot wind.

So sweet was this stolen play that, when night fled, Pakoko found himself walking through the red mists on the mountains, repeating his promise, 'Tonight again.' Or was it hers?

Smiling too sweetly, Tohi-kai beckoned to Pakoko. 'Come with me to my bathing pool, Kea.'

Ah! The tattooing name! Calling him that, the Chief would complain of Pakoko's hard shell and try to break it. The Teii followed the Taipi as if he were walking on slippery mud.

'Friend Kea,' Tohi-kai murmured above the song of the torrent that leapt into the stone-lined pool, 'I do not like your running away to another valley, even for a night.'

'*Afuru, afuru, afuru,*' roared the torrent in Pakoko's ears. He thought he would drown in these shallow waters. Anger gave him strength to sit up. 'You were spying!' He spat it out.

Floating limp as seaweed, Tohi-kai looked up at him through slits. 'I must give my Ironwood work.'

'This is the end!' Pakoko stood up.

'Do you want to take my band off your wrist?'

Without thinking, Pakoko covered the band with his other hand. This was his very life in Taipivai. He knew he was a fish on a hook. He must not tear himself to pieces. He made himself soft and stroked the band with gentle fingers. 'Not your binding of *kaoha*,' he whispered. By the time he had dropped to his knees his eyes were drowned in tears. 'You have your woman, I want mine,' he begged.

Tohi-kai threw his arms about his friend. 'I have told you to bring her here.'

'But,' said Pakoko piteously, 'I have no land, no terraces, no house, no plantations, no ornaments. I have nothing to offer a Chiefess.'

The hook held! Tohi-kai could afford to play his fish a little. He jumped up and pulled Pakoko after him in a swift ascent of the stream and one of its branches. Climbing a hill that over-looked a small upland valley, he swept his arm from ridge to ridge. 'Friend, this is your land!' he cried.

Pakoko was stirred by winds coming from two sides. Here was a chief's open hand, here were riches and power, perhaps. For them, he gave *kaoha*, yes, *kaoha nui*, much love. But here also was a tightening of the woven band about his wrist. Here also was a noose for Metani, a Hapaa hostage in a Taipi valley. Well, he must look in one direction at a time. Now he could see only this good land, this high valley wet with the sky's breath, very, very good for growing roots for yellow stain. How many pigs had his cousin, Chief Hono of Tahu Ata, given for a canoe full of this precious root that grew only on Nuku Hiva? Twenty pigs, yes! Pakoko saw himself sending innumerable canoes full of *ena* roots to Tahu Ata. He saw them returning filled with treasure. He would break his rafters with the bundles of ornaments tied to them. He was dizzy in this sweet, upland air.

'When will you bring our woman, Tohi-kai?' the Chief asked slyly, calling him by his own name.

Yes, that would be it—our woman. Pakoko answered smoothly, 'As soon as I have made this valley worthy of her. As soon as I have covered it with plantations and built a feast place and terraces and houses. Chiefess Metani is not a wild pig to root about in the mountains,' he reminded his friend.

With that Tohi-kai had to be content. At least he had given Pakoko many, many moons of work far from his own big valley. At least he would be free for a time of the rub-rubbing of that hard wood against his own soft desires. Now let this Teii show what he could do in bringing riches to the chief who had befriended him.

5

WHEN Pakoko's first canoe came back from Tahu Ata filled with exchanges for his *ena* roots—sucking pigs, fine *tapas*, forehead shells with pierced tortoise-shell patterns overlaid, incised tortoise-shell headbands, he sat on his terrace, spreading them out, counting them. These were his own things! He ran his hands over the pigs to see that they were without blemish. He built a stone wall about them and exchanged yellow stain roots for ripe breadfruit for them to eat. At the great fall of the sun, he wrapped the ornaments from Tahu Ata in *tapa* and tied them carefully out of reach. During the black night, he lay on his sleeping space looking up at the dim shapes of his things. In the morning's gentle shining, he saw that his bundles were still tied to his rafters.

However, his rafters were many, his bundles few. He fed twenty men while they uprooted a grove of light nut trees and pierced the land for more *ena* roots. His canoe went out and came in, out and in. His rafters began to bend.

One day Tohi-kai sent a messenger with a coconut sheath to Pakoko's house. 'Gifts for the first-born of Chief Tohi-kai!' he was calling.

Pakoko's hands trembled as he lowered his bundles and laid aside the fine things asked for. But when the messenger, clicking his tongue, exclaimed, 'You are like a chief with many treasures!' he swelled up. He would give like a chief. He walked ahead of his precious things and when he came to Tohi-kai's terrace, he named his gifts with a loud tongue and threw them down as if they amounted to nothing.

'You are just,' said the Taipi Chief. 'Truly the land belongs to the grandfathers and the fruits of it are the grandson's.'

Were Pakoko's bundles only bubbles that vanished at a touch? Certainly, they were disappearing with every feast. Tohi-kai wanted pigs and a roll of wrinkled white *tapa* for his dead aunt. Tohi-kai wanted arms and arms of red banyan *tapa* for his first-born. Tohi-kai wanted stone paste pounders and fine mats for the house for his child. Alas, Pakoko's rafters were not bending now.

There was a man from Taiohae who was joined to a Taipi woman in Pakoko's upland valley, and the Teii had called his tribesman as a paddler for his canoe. To him he whispered, 'Speak in secret to my cousin, Chief Hono. Say to him, "Hold back ten pigs from every canoe full. When there are one hundred coming to Pakoko, send him instead a whale's tooth breast ornament." ' Pointing to the man's loin cloth, Pakoko added, 'You will hide it there and bring it to me in deep black of night.'

After that, Pakoko was always laughing. He laughed when he encouraged his land-diggers and his canoe-paddlers and his canoe builders. He laughed when he stacked his roots to dry in his cook house, when he packed them into his canoe, and when he counted the fine things that came back to him from Tahu Ata. He spread out open hands and laughed when he counted out the gifts asked by Tohi-kai. He hid nothing in his clothes, he tied nothing to his rafters, he covered over nothing in his food bowl. But after the fall of the sun, when his workers had gone to their houses, he sat on his terrace looking up at the back wall of his valley. His sharp eyes pierced the gloom to a hole far above. There were things hidden there even from the grandfathers of Tohi-kai. He laughed very, very softly.

Following Tohi-kai's messenger who had come to summon him to the taboo house of the Chief, Pakoko thought, 'Now he will ask me to bring my woman.' He laughed. When he had carried a digging stick to new clearings in his valley, climbing higher and higher on the slopes, he had not always been planting roots. Going up to his treasure cave through a rocky chute down which water fell drop by drop, he had been digging an opening from its roof onto the backbone of the land. With wedges and stone tools he had cut a way out to the high level. He was free to run away, unseen and unfollowed, by this secret path. Where? He had been pondering the branching paths open to a man of riches. He would choose the best.

In Chief Tohi-kai's taboo house, a man was sitting, a visitor, a fellow with a black circle on his face, a Teii! Pakoko's eyes clung to him. Could it be his younger Aunt's son, Mauhau? He was about to rub noses with him, when the man drew back. Yes, it was Mauhau, but he was staring in disgust at the three stripes crossing Pakoko's face. The Ironwood from Taiohae could not forgive this mark of the Taipi. There could be no retying of a broken rafter in this man's house. The whole thing must go into the fire. Pakoko sat down without a word. He hoped that Tohi-kai had not seen his cousin's recoil from his stripes, for Mauhau was taboo in the Taipi valley only because his own father had worn these stripes.

Plainly, Tohi-kai was not pleased at this visit. He gave no tongue to its meaning, but sat with lowered eyes waiting for Mauhau to speak.

The Teii Ironwood said, as if spitting out a bad taste, 'Chief Veo wants to see you. He has fallen from a coconut tree. He is badly crushed.'

Pakoko's breathing choked him. His father was dying! His father wanted to see him! A rain of tears on his clasped hands startled him. Was he a child again?

The Taipi Chief said, 'Chief Veo is near death. Neither the beating of drums nor the tears of a run-away son can prolong his breathing. It is useless for Pakoko to go to Taiohae.'

Pakoko ceased being a little boy crying for his father. He was a man fighting for his freedom. 'Deny my father and his angry spirit will torment you!' He threatened Tohi-kai as if he were a sorcerer promising to send an evil spirit into a victim. Seeing his friend's eyelids quiver, he leaned over and touched his knee. 'You will not be the loser,' he promised. He was thinking of a whale's tooth which he would send in exchange for his freedom.

Mauhau unexpectedly echoed, 'You will not be the loser,' but for a different cause. Chief Kiato-nui had a first-born son for whom he desired Tohi-kai's first daughter as a mate.

The two men heard this news with different ears. Pakoko was amazed that his little brother, Kiato-nui, was a father. Tohi-kai was content that he would receive a fair exchange as soon as a daughter was born to him. 'Fill Mauhau's canoe with gifts for my son-in-law,' he commanded Pakoko. 'Empty your rafters for him.'

Even as he obeyed, Pakoko laughed softly. He could throw these things away. He was a man of wealth. He was ready to exchange it for power. And his own father was opening a path for him!

6

As Pakoko entered the walls of Chief Veo's feast place at dusk, and saw the paving covered with families from all branches of Taiohae, he was struck by an old familiar fragrance. Wrapped in *tapa* to shut out the night's cold, huddled close to their little fires, the folk were eating without noise, talking now and then with soft tongues. Now one group, now another sang gently to their dying Chief. With warm *kaoha* pouring from his eyes, Pakoko stooped over a family he knew, but they trembled and drew back from him.

'Your face images,' said Mauhau with a twisted mouth.

They thought he was a Taipi! Anger stiffened him. He pushed past them and began to shout his arrival with a loud tongue. 'Oh I am Pakoko Tohi-kai Kea!' Let them hear his great names. Bye and bye they would see his wealth and feel his power.

Against the light of burning nuts inside Veo's house, a big

shadow appeared, covering the new-comer. A deep voice rolled over him like a wave. 'Come inside, Little Coconut.'

Pakoko knew that caressing tongue and his throat shrivelled at the endearment, but he stared at the unfamiliar figure with its big head, short neck, heavy body, thick arms and legs. Could these belong to little Kiato-nui? When he was pulled onto the terrace and pressed against that heaving moist breast, he felt he was suffocating. He was being drawn back into something from which he had escaped long ago. He wanted to run away from this engulfing embrace, but he was pressed forward. 'The god is about to fall,' said Kiato-nui, pushing him inside the house.

There he was noosed by a circle of eyes, wild as birds' eyes when they saw his face stripes, but quieting as they knew him. He felt them sucking him back into forgotten seas. He was their little fellow who had been lost in the mountains and found again. Forgotten was the work of summoning the god to fall, forgotten the ebbing of the old Chief's breath. His relatives poured their tears and their tremulos over the wanderer. They were making a child of him. He stood up as tall as he could and backed against the front pickets of the house. He breathed more easily when Chief Kiato-nui stamped the torches into sputtering grease and commanded the old woman with hanging skin to go back to making the god speak.

Was that a cold wind blowing through the house opening? Was it rain that tripped lightly over the thatch? *Tu!* Something fell onto the *tapa* spread on the stones. *'Ve! Ve! Ve!'* The god was whistling. The old woman began to plead with him. 'Let your friend go free!' But the shrill tongue answered, 'We shall go together. He will die.'

A sudden storm of wailing gushed through the house, swept outside and whirled across the paving.

> Oh Chief! E-e-e-e!
> Our cries are for you! Do not die! I-i-i-i!
> Let the Chief live! O-o-o-o!
> Oh Chief! E-e-e-e!

When the tempest had blown itself out in a long-drawn sigh, Kiato-nui relighted the nuts, the women began to laugh and talk, the children woke and cried for food, the men gathered around a bowl of breadfruit paste.

As Pakoko reached for his share, he saw the eyes turn to the woven band on his wrist. He laughed noisily. 'I am taboo among the man-eaters,' he boasted, but he cut the knot of the band and burned the fibres over a torch. The thing was cutting into his flesh, he explained.

'You have not said *kaoha* to your new Chief,' said Kiato-nui, laying his son in Pakoko's arms.

Was the older brother hearing again an old command, 'Here is your child, here is your work for the gods?' The thought was a weight in his stomach. He returned the little fellow to his father and got up to open the bundles of gifts sent him from Taipivai. 'Tohi-kai is pleased at the joining of these two valleys,' he said.

Kiato-nui did not touch the fine things. Indeed, he scarcely looked at them. His eyes were clinging to Pakoko's face. 'Yes,' he answered. 'I knew I must exchange a big thing for you.'

Pakoko felt the force and the heat drain out of him. Had he walked into a trap?

'Pakoko, bring me a shell of water.' Chief Veo's feeble voice put an end to this talk. His eyes were open now and they were pulling his eldest son towards him.

The son had kept his eyes turned away from the still, broken body lying in the far corner of the sleeping space. He had not dared go near, lest he lose all his strength and go and come only as he was bidden. Now he could not help sliding himself across to his father's side. But there was no shock of meeting, no grasping for old ties. The eyes had closed, the light had drained out of the face, though breathing continued. Pakoko looked down upon a face he did not know, that of an aged man with drawn skin and hollow cheeks. Was this his father?

When the red skies of morning cast a glow over the face of Chief Veo and recognition was again in his eyes, Pakoko felt no longer strange. This was indeed his father who held him by his side or sent him here and there to fetch and carry. There were many things for Pakoko to see. The canoe made to carry Veo to the skies must be lowered from the rafters for him to admire. Kiato-nui had carved the beak himself. The pattern chosen for the lashings that would bind the old Chief's bones was called

'Lightning.' Kiato-nui would make the design on his hands. He would chant its song:

> Lightning of many colors
> Overturning breadfruit leaves.

The carved level for sunning Veo's body must be completed. Kiato-nui would scratch his father's length on a breadfruit plank, but Pakoko must bring his hollowing and lining adzes. And Pakoko must listen with his father to the even strokes of stone on wood as Kiato-nui's skilful hands smoothed this last resting place.

When Chief Veo's eyes began to turn from side to side in search of this relative or that, Kiato-nui sent messengers to all the branching valleys. Without hurry but without delay, he seemed to flow among the workers he summoned to build guest houses and to dig feast ovens. Pakoko was both smoothed and rubbed raw by the drowsy heaviness of all this work. His roots were beginning to cling again to this land and he kept pulling himself loose. He was hot and cold in turn as he greeted his relatives. His sister, fat and sad-eyed, was just as she had been, so that he could not believe that the tall boy with her was her son by Priest Kohu. This frail lad, called Taa, would not let him touch him. Once, after Kohu had gone to live altogether at the sacred place, the boy had heard his mother weeping because her brother, Pakoko, had not sent for his nephew to house and feed him. From that time, Taa had cherished his anger against his uncle as if it were fire covered in a coconut sheath. Pakoko was ashamed. For a long time he had been an uncle without knowing it. Certainly, he had heard that a child had been born to his sister and Kohu, but he had forgotten it immediately. What had filled his thoughts in Taipivai? Ah! Whales' teeth! Now he thought again of the cave above that valley and of his hidden treasures inside it. Again he forgot his nephew and turned away abruptly to go outside and consider how he could use his riches to best advantage. He walked back and forth on the terrace, shivering in the sky's cold breath, slapping his arms for warmth.

Seeing a woman crawl into Chief Veo's house and toss a thin, poorly made white beard plume at the sick man's feet, knowing her in spite of her coarse *tapas* and unoiled hair and skin, Pakoko followed and sat down beside her. 'Where do you come from, Sister Hina?' he asked.

'Little Coconut!' she gasped. Seeing him shrink, she hastened to add, 'You are growing a beard!' She followed his gaze to her coarse *tapa*. 'Yes,' she said, smiling, 'my half is an insignificant fisherman of Haka-Ui, but he asks nothing and there is no other woman in my house to shout at me day and night. I am content with this.' She unrolled the bundle in her arms and gave her child her breast.

'Give her to me,' Pakoko begged in sudden hot desire to bind himself to Hina.

His sister's eyes were soft but her question was pointed. 'Have you built a house for your joined woman?'

'Not yet,' he answered, 'but . . .'

'Wait, then.' Her tongue was gentle but firm.

A sudden cry from Chief Veo broke them apart. 'Pakoko, you here.' He beckoned with his eyes. 'Now, Ehua, my woman.' He gave them each a hand, one on either side of his stiffening body. He looked up at Kiato-nui. 'You will send me swiftly as a bird to the skies?' he asked.

Blinded by tears pouring over his fat cheeks, the Chief nodded and sat down in a crumpled heap at his father's feet. Chiefess Ehua half rose to give him her seat, but Veo's cold, wet fingers held her. She was thinking that Kiato-nui had carried the old man on his back while Pakoko was running wild in the mountains, but here was Pakoko called to the head and Kiato-nui sitting at the feet. Ehua could not look at her dear half. She covered her face with her hair and wept in secret.

Pakoko bent his ears to Chief Veo's lips to hear what he was trying to murmur. He was living again that far away time when Ehua's father had been driven from Haavao by Kena's father, when he had come begging Veo's father for Brave Faces to drive out the usurper. His memories oozed fitfully through his half open mouth. 'Said my father, "I will give you refuge, but not war with your Fire Keeper. I will not turn Teiis against Teiis." Then Ehua's father said, "Very well, then, I will seek new lands, but Haavao will return to my family because the skull of my grandfather lies beneath all others on the sacred place." ' Chief

Veo turned his eyes filled with *kaoha* upon Pakoko. 'The skull . . .' he breathed as the spirit went out of his mouth.

Pakoko tore his hand away and ran outside. He pushed his way between the sitters on the terrace. He wanted to be alone, where no one could see his wet face and shaken breast. He was weeping not bitter tears of loss but sweet, healing drops. He had thought his father did not care, that he was not just, but oh how truly he had cherished his first-born son!

A storm of grieving screamed and roared around him. Conch shells shrieked, drums sobbed, old men tore their hands with clapping as they chanted:

> Oh spirit, see our devotion!
> Do not walk in this valley!
> Do not harm the friendly!
> Go quickly in your canoe to Havaiki!

But Pakoko called out, as if he were walking happily beside that feared spirit, 'Kaoha, my father!' Indeed, he seemed close to Chief Veo and far away from those who threw themselves about on the paving of the feast place. Though he stared at his mother who was showing her wild grief, rushing naked before all, cutting her tender flesh with sharp stones until the blood flowed, he scarcely saw her. As a man walking in sleep, he moved aside when Kiato-nui led four male relatives past him to Veo's taboo house where they were carrying the body to wash it. Yes, the tumult of painful joy inside him blinded and deafened him to the storm outside.

Watching Pakoko and Kiato-nui, Mother Ehua's heart trembled for her adopted son. It was Pakoko who was performing the work of a son for a father, while Kiato-nui rested in his taboo house and sipped *kava*. When the sun stuck his legs over the mountains to walk down the valley, it was Pakoko who carried the sunning board onto the terrace and saw that the aunts fanned flies from the body while the old men rubbed it with oil and pressed out the juices. It was Pakoko who carried it back at the time of fires and tied it to the rafters of the sleeping house. When Chiefess Ehua began to peel the flesh and the skin from the bones, Pakoko wrapped the strips in *tapa* and buried them in taboo land. He broke the bones apart, bundled them and lashed them with the design called 'Lightning.' He fitted the image of Veo into the death canoe and made ready the high stone terrace in a secluded clearing where Chief Veo would paddle his way to the skies. And when Ehua carried the skull in her bird-bodied bowl to the sacred place of Meau, it was Pakoko alone who accompanied her.

Returning from that holy ground where she could not walk, Mother Ehua spoke to Kiato-nui with apprehension. 'Why was it Pakoko who gave your father's skull to Priest Kohu? Why has he taken over your work?'

The Chief's broad, slow smile should have smoothed her. 'Why not?' he asked gently. 'Pakoko has learned to serve a chief. I shall make him my Fire Keeper.'

Ehua sucked in her breath sharply. 'Be careful, my son,' she warned. 'Pakoko is quick, you are slow.' When Kiato-nui's assurances of the *kaoha* between him and his brother did not quiet her liver, the woman went to her brother, Fatu. 'Pakoko is unnatural,' she said to him. 'Why all this sudden *kaoha* for his father, Veo?'

Uncle Fatu drew down his mouth in distaste. He had seen little of his foster son since he returned to Taiohae. Every time he looked at the stripes on the young man's face, he was reminded that the fellow had always been too green a breadfruit to cook. The uncle had tried to teach him. 'Cling to your land, obey your chief, respect the taboos,' he had always told him. And what had come of it? Pakoko had run away from every work that was his and had taken up wth a moon-babbler in an enemy valley. *Tschae!* There was no guessing what his work was now. 'Perhaps he will begin breaking taboos now,' snorted Fatu, without trying to quiet his sister's liver.

With the skull of Chief Veo in the covered bowl, Pakoko had climbed to the highest terrace where Priest Kohu had come to hang the precious relic in a banyan tree. When this work had been accomplished, the two brothers had sat down to talk of many things. Finally, Pakoko asked, 'Your sky-piercing house is built on the sacred place in Haavao?'

'Yes,' answered Kohu. 'That was Kiato-nui's desire.'

'Whose skull lies below all others in the sacred pit?' Pakoko asked.

'Hiatai's,' the Priest answered promptly.

That name! Pakoko knew it well. He could hear again the old Name Singer chanting it. It came in a sea far below the sea of Fatu and Ehua, far below the new sea of Pakoko and Kohu. 'That name and that skull are ours,' Pakoko whispered.

The Priest laid a thin finger on his brother's knee. 'You would claim them?'

'With the help of your power,' Pakoko answered.

The force of Kohu's joy lifted them both on a high wave. 'I will make Chiefess Kena know that a priest has power!' he cried.

'Has Kena Brave Faces?'

Priest Kohu brushed the question away. 'A few half-hearted ones, but no Ironwood to lead them. Her joined mate went back to his father's valley on Ua Pou long ago.'

Pakoko said, 'I will bring warriors and I myself will lead them.'

The flood of joy ebbed. 'You will not make this a Taipi valley!' commanded the Priest.

'I have burned Tohi-kai's wrist band,' his brother assured him. 'Besides,' he added, standing up and spreading the swallows on his shoulders, 'I have riches to exchange for the Brave Faces of another Chief.'

Kohu's eyes glittered. 'The gods give to those with open hands.'

Pakoko understood. 'When I am Chief of Haavao,' he said it for the first time out loud and repeated it in amazement, 'when I am Chief of Haavao, I will make all red things taboo for you— *tapas*, feathers, fish, whatever you desire.' He went away swinging his hips to his new song, 'The Chief of Haavao, the Chief of Haavao.'

Kiato-nui and Pakoko stood together watching the burning of Chief Veo's sleeping house. 'On this terrace you will build the house for your joined woman, Metani,' the Chief said.

There it was, out in the open. Pakoko tightened his lips. 'Metani is Chiefess of Hakapaa,' he said. 'She will not be a dweller on another Chief's terrace.'

'Very well,' agreed the younger brother. 'You will build your own house here and visit her now and then. You will be my Fire Keeper. You will take your nephew, Taa, as your foster son.'

Pakoko could not strike down those soft eyes that were glowing with *kaoha*. He searched their depths and could find no barbed hook of suspicion. Did Kiato-nui know that he was receiving instruction from Chief Veo's aged Ironwood? Did he think that Pakoko might be preparing for war with someone? The older brother could not say, 'I shall be Chief of Haavao, I shall have my own Fire Keeper, I shall build a house for my Chiefess on my own terrace.' That news must be hidden for awhile.

But Chief Kiato-nui did not expect an answer. He told his House Builder to clear Veo's terrace and start building Pakoko's house.

Turning into the Path of War in Haavao valley, Pakoko was astonished to find his cousin, Mauhau, stepping beside him.

'Where are you going?' Mauhau asked.

That old question! 'Do you remember how furious it made me when you asked me that on moon nights?' Pakoko grinned at him.

The Ironwood did not laugh. 'I would not ask for myself. I would say, "Let him go back to the other striped faces." '

'For whom, then, do you ask?' Pakoko questioned sharply.

'Naturally, for our Chief, Kiato-nui.' Mauhau slowly unwound the sling from his head and shook it free for use.

Pakoko's hair crawled. Kiato-nui meant to keep him in Taio-hae! What bait could be thrown to Mauhau? Was there any whisper that would turn him to another path? No, Mauhau had ears only for his chief. A branching path made Pakoko think of Priest Kohu. He made his tongue run along easily. 'I am going to the sacred place of Haavao to see old Kohu,' he said in the secret upside down language the cousins had used when they were boys. He breathed more easily when he heard Mauhau miss a step in his following. 'The Priest needs another paddler for Chief Veo's sky-going canoe,' he went on. 'There is a certain man I know who cuts firewood on the uplands. I have offered to lead the Clubs where they can noose him.'

There was less spring in Mauhau's step but he kept within Pakoko's shadow up to the very opening of Kohu's sky-piercing house on the topmost terrace of Haavao's sacred place. He waited with him while Priest Kohu felt his way down from level to level of his tall shaft, his crooked foot swinging awkwardly as his good foot took his weight.

Before Kohu could speak, Pakoko caught his eyes and held them. 'Here is our cousin Mauhau spying on me,' he laughed.

'Do you remember how he used to ask, "Where are you going?"'
Pakoko punched Mauhau in the stomach. 'Well, here he is, at it
again. I hope I have not broken a taboo in telling him that I
am going to lead your Clubs up above to noose another paddler
for Chief Veo's canoe.' Pakoko paused and looked hard at the
Ironwood. 'Perhaps he thinks I am lying. Surely he doesn't want
to stop me and offend my father's spirit!'

Priest Kohu's eyes rolled up and showed the whites. 'Who
dares to cross my path?' he shrilled in unearthly tones. 'I have
promised Chief Veo's spirit a swift flight to the skies. I have called
Pakoko for a certain work. Let him go forward!'

'How was I to know?' Mauhau grumbled and left them alone.

When Priest Kohu's Clubs turned back at the foot of Red
Stone Mountain, Pakoko stood for a space looking down on the
magnificent valley of Haavao. The land of Hiatai was a food
bowl overflowing with the fruits of the land. There was a sea of
canoes waiting to be hollowed from its tall *temanu* trees. There
were rolls and rolls of *tapa* and piles and piles of mats to be
beaten from its plantations of mulberry and plaited from its
groves of pandanus. There were mountains of stone to be chipped
and rolled into place for pavings, walls, terraces. Work, work,
work! And his would be the conch to summon the workers! He
could scarcely tear himself away from the work that lay sleeping
to perform that which ran to meet him.

When he had visited a certain hidden cave high above the
valley of the Taipis, he was ready to present himself to Chief
Tea-roru of the Hapaas, the father of his woman, Metani.

7

WHEN Pakoko approached the terraces of the high level folk of Hakapaa, he began to drag his feet. What if Chief Tea-roru were angry because he had never claimed his woman? Perhaps Metani herself had chosen another mate. He shook himself and stamped forward. After all, he had whales' teeth to offer for Brave Faces. He could feel them, hard and heavy, inside his girdle. He wanted to run to Metani's house, but he made himself take a by-path to the men's house.

Pushing through ferns, he found himself beside a pool in the stream, looking down upon a young woman who was bathing a little boy. Pakoko stepped back, breaking the brittle fronds, causing her to turn her head swiftly and to lose her hold on the kicking child.

'Pakoko! Catch him!' she cried.

He scooped the little fellow up in one hand and patted him to stop his coughing, but he kept his eyes on Metani's face. Certainly it was Metani. He knew her voice. He knew her face. He knew everything about her. But how had she known him?

'Your Taipi stripes are the only ones that would dare enter this valley in the light,' she answered the question in his eyes.

Was there a hint of reproach about those stripes? He did not hear it. He sat down, at ease. 'Where did you get this?' he asked, playing with the boy.

'From you,' she answered. She laughed at his bewilderment. 'Have you forgotten the night you called me through the thatch?' she reproached him. Since he could neither move nor speak, she gave him a sharp little scratch. 'But naturally I knew you! Who else would call me Metani? That is my betrothal name. Who else would wear a woven wrist band?'

He rolled over on his back and laughed and laughed. What a woman! Suddenly he sat up and reached for the little fellow. 'He is mine!' These were not words but a sea of joy that poured out of him.

'He is Paia-roru, Chief of the Hapaas,' she said with pride.

'And Hiatai, Chief of Haavao!' he added in a sudden burst of wonder.

'The woman and the child are mine!' Pakoko pounded the small sticks of the flooring of Chief Tea-roru's taboo house.

'They have worn out their mats waiting for you,' the Hapaa said with a twisted mouth. 'The house she built for you is already an old thing.'

'I shall take them to my own house.' Pakoko thrust out his jaw.

The father-in-law did the same. 'My daughter will not go to Taipivai to scrape the leavings from Tohi-kai's food bowl. Neither will she go to Taiohae to dwell on Kiato-nui's terraces.'

'Certainly not,' agreed the son-in-law. 'She is the mother of the Chief of Haavao and she will dwell in his house.' When the old man laughed at him as if he were a little boy boasting, Pakoko opened his knotted girdle and dropped a whale's tooth into his hand as if he were a common piece of mud. 'It is three fingers across,' he said.

'So it is,' said Tea-roru, turning it over and over. 'And what great thing do you ask in return? War with Chiefess Kena? But that will be a big war with all of Taiohae, perhaps even with my own brother here in Hakapaa, for his son was adopted by Kena and he will be Chief of Haavao.'

'There will be no war,' Pakoko answered. 'I ask for Brave Faces, yes, to keep Kena from kicking and scratching, but the people of Haavao will not fight taboos and names.' He made the little boy standing on his knee. 'I have given my son the name of his grandfather-far-below, the name to which the mat of Haavao belongs. He is Hiatai, Chief of Haavao.'

When Chief Tea-roru heard the story of the skull, he clapped his hollow palm against his bent elbow to make a great and joyful noise. 'It is a feast we will plan, not a war!' he cried. 'A feast to show Chief Paia-roru Hiatai to his people, the Hapaas and the Teiis!'

Three calls of Chief Tea-roru's conch shell started the uncles and aunts walking around the feast place carrying the little Chief in his long red loin cloth. For a space, Pakoko's eyes were dimmed by an old mist, as if he were looking at Kiato-nui riding above the shouting crowds, but they jumped out into bright sun when the Name Singer began to sound the names of his grandfathers. He nudged the Hapaa Chief standing next to him and moved where he could watch the face of Chiefess Kena. He could see her fan swinging this side, that side, and its sudden fall when the chanting began to climb Mother Ehua's line from old Hiatai. The tying of the new child to that old name was a spear piercing her vitals, for the power of that ancient Hiatai was still sung by his unforgetting people of Haavao. The agitated beat of her fan showed that the point had struck.

When the procession began walking seaward, the child in the center on his uncle's head, his long red girdle resting on his aunt's head behind him, Kena pushed her way to the edge of the terrace. Why was Pakoko going ahead with Hapaa Brave Faces in full war dress? What was Chief Tea-roru doing behind with another band of fighters? Kena was a fish left on the land by a going sea, flinging itself about, slapping the stones, head and tail. She fell up against her foster son. 'Where are they going?' she demanded, but she waited for no answer, knowing that 'The Whale' was too heavy and full to get up to see. She threw her fan at Kiato-nui who was watching placidly. 'Where are they going?' she repeated.

He beamed at her. 'It is the custom to show the child to the mountains and the sea.' He was very well pleased with his brother, Pakoko, who had tied a new and powerful chief to him.

'Why is the child given a name from the line of an overthrown people?' she demanded.

Mother Ehua and Uncle Fatu were groping about in a fog because of Pakoko's choice of the name, but they held up their heads at this and Fatu said, 'Hiatai was never overthrown.'

Everyone was following the procession down to the sea. Kiato-nui went slowly, heavily as a turtle. He kept a strong hand on Chiefess Kena's arm and held her close beside him. 'They are in the canoes! They are turning west!' a man in a coconut tree called down to them.

'I knew it!' Chiefess Kena cried. 'He goes to seize my land!'

Chief Kiato-nui shook all over with laughter. 'Don't you know that I have built him a house on my father's terrace? Naturally he is going there.'

'You are stupid!' Her words foamed out of her mouth. She jerked herself free from his heavy hand and ran to a knot of her Brave Faces who were whispering together. 'Unbind your slings!' she screamed at them.

Chief Kiato-nui held up his hand. 'There can be no war. Priest Kohu has made this a taboo moon.'

'Priest Kohu will blow away this cloud of taboo!' Chiefess Kena had little breath left but she managed to press out these words before she lifted her *tapas* and ran towards the western ridge of the valley.

Ironwood Mauhau said for Kiato-nui's ear alone, 'We do not know Pakoko. Is he a Taipi? Is he a Hapaa? Or is he a Teii?'

The Teii Chief answered stubbornly, 'Pakoko is my brother and my Fire Keeper.'

Uncle Fatu stood firmly beside Kiato-nui. 'Pakoko has never broken a taboo,' he asserted.

Mother Ehua said nothing but she slipped her hand into her son's fat hand and pressed it gently.

The men got into Kiato-nui's canoe. They might as well see what Pakoko was up to. He was always different. This was the thought of the feasters who went by land also. They flowed over the hills on the west and down into Taiohae, laughing at this new thing. What was it? Certainly not war with slings and spears. Perhaps a war with words! Good!

Chiefess Kena ran with her mouth open and her black hair flying, for her tortoise-shell headband had been raked off by a branch. Tramping down tough ferns, pulling herself over sharp rocks, crawling through thickets of thorny vines, she had left the path for a short way to her own terraces. When she arrived, her *tapas* were hanging in strips, her ornaments lost, her skin scratched. Pakoko would mock a naked woman covered with mud. She was Chiefess Kena of Haavao. She would show him. Quick! Her bundles! Her headwreath of red and yellow feathers! Her earrings! Her finest white *tapa!* With shaking hands she chose her precious things. Trembling and stamping she turned round and round inside a long strip of *tapa* until she was a great, fluffy ball. She grabbed her tall, hair-tufted chief's staff, kicked a litter of treasure out of her way, and stumbled onto her terrace as her Brave Faces poured onto her paving, like ants stirred up by an unknown danger. 'Bring my sky-canoe and four bearers!' she commanded. 'Bring stones and spears! Follow me to the sacred place!'

Now her people could breathe. They could form a line and run. They could pick up things and hold them.

But the common folk of Haavao, whose ancestors had belonged to this valley, kept their eyes covered until the Chiefess and her small band had gone. They had heard from their grandfathers of Hiatai, the magnificent, the well-beloved. Now here was a new Hiatai, his own shoot. Had the god sent him to this land? Chiefess Kena was no shoot of Hiatai. Her father was an outsider, Kena was a beggar, and her foster son was a thief. What one did not ask the other stole from the rafters and ovens of their dwellers. Were the folk of Haavao about to stand up whole again? They wanted to run to the sacred place, but they made themselves go slowly, mingling with those who had come by canoe, talking of ordinary things.

Being a woman, Chiefess Kena could not walk on the sacred terraces, but she sat in front of them on her sky-canoe held up on the shoulders of her bearers, and called up to Priest Kohu, who had come onto the top terrace like a great bird about to spread his wings. He made no answer and she rocked her raft in her impatience as the ceremonial procession from Hakapaa came into the clearing to the beat of high name-calling. Chiefess Kena could not forbid entrance to those names and she waited for the Diviner with wildly turning eyes.

Priest Kohu held up his bundle of god sticks, but not to stop that bold, sly shark, Pakoko, but rather to make a silence for his words, which Chiefess Kena knew before they came out of his mouth.

'This sacred place is the mat of my grandfathers-far-below,' Pakoko announced as solemnly as a Master Chanter. 'It belongs to his namesake, Hiatai.' He took his son from his uncle and placed him on the sacred stones.

Now the skies fell and thunder split the air! Kena's Braves yelled for Pakoko's death. Mauhau slapped Kiato-nui to make him wake up and ask for war. Chiefess Kena shrieked at Priest Kohu, 'Seize Pakoko and feed him to the gods!'

Priest Kohu trembled before the woman's angry eyes and crooked claws, but, seeing the red feathers in her headband, he was thrown into a frenzy of arrogance. 'Take off that red!' he cried. 'Red is taboo to me. I am the god! I want no fish. I am full of food.'

Now at last Chief Kiato-nui was driven to fury. He might have known that Kohu and Pakoko were working together. Hadn't the Priest helped his brother to run away to the valley of the Hapaas? He grew so swollen and red and breathless that he could scarcely pull himself up onto the lower terrace. 'This is cause for war,' he gasped and lifted his conch shell to his lips.

The god's whistle stopped the sounding of the shell, stopped even the breathing of the people. 'Let the slings and spears sleep!' he trilled. 'This is a taboo moon and war is forbidden.'

Chief Kiato-nui was caught in a net. He could only turn aimlessly from side to side. But Chiefess Kena saw a way out. 'Very well, we obey the taboos,' she answered the Priest. 'This land is taboo to my father's head which is buried in it.'

'Yes, Pakoko, you will not break that taboo,' Kiato-nui pleaded with his brother, turning upon him his great soft eyes that were brimming with tears.

'No,' answered Pakoko. 'We will follow that taboo to its source. The land belongs to the head which lies below all others.'

He turned to Kohu. 'Priest, dig up the stones of the skull pit. Name the heads as you come to them.'

Kena's eyes fell back into hot bowls. Had her tongue been too quick? She bit it to keep it inside her mouth while the Priest's Clubs were digging. When Kohu stooped and lifted a skull, naming it the head of her father, she let her tongue fly again. 'There it is! The land belongs to me!'

The old people nodded their heads sadly. Many had seen that skull being carried to the sacred place. But Pakoko was not beaten. He was commanding the Priest to dig deeper.

Kohu stooped and lifted out another skull, an old yellow bone. 'This is the head of Hiatai!' the voice of the god shrilled.

'Hiatai! Hiatai!' The people of Haavao saluted their grandfather. They wept for joy. Certainly the land was taboo to Hiatai.

Chiefess Kena rocked her sky-canoe and broke her staff upon its sideboards. 'That old taboo died when my father covered it with his.'

Pakoko began to sound old words: 'One day Ono came to the island of Mohotani.' The people roared with laughter. All knew the story of that god. Hadn't he claimed the land of Mohotani because the skull of his grandfather-far-below lay buried beneath all others? It was true taboo! Pakoko was a man with bowels full of light. He had won his land. His folk of Haavao began to chant that good old story of the god, Ono, their roaring voices drowning Kena's cracked shrieks and the murmuring of her few relatives.

Yes, Chiefess Kena was ended. She was driven without a war, but not without the noise of battle. All the way down to the place of refuge offered by Chief Kiato-nui, she threatened the overthrow of her enemy with the ending of the taboo moon. Her hoarse voice ran on like a stream after rain until the Chief sent his Ironwood to stop her because he was drinking *kava* and wanted to sleep.

In Kena's men's house, the new Chief Hiatai and his father and grandfather were sitting, hearing the sweet songs brought them by the valley folk who sang the night of joy away. In the cook house, busying himself with a sheath of embers, was Uncle Fatu who had obeyed Hiatai's taboo and remained to serve his offshoot as Fire Keeper. In the sleeping house, Metani and Mother Ehua were spreading fresh ferns. Ehua had started back to Meau with her dear son, Kiato-nui, but somehow she could not make her legs carry her away from the beloved land of Haavao.

In the early light of the next sun, Pakoko called to him a man from Taipivai who dwelt in Haavao with his woman. Untying a heavy knot in the tail of his loin cloth, he unwrapped a whale's tooth. 'This will balance things with Chief Tohi-kai,' he said. 'Carry it to him with my *kaoha*.'

Chief Tea-roru of the Hapaas nodded and smiled at his clever son-in-law. 'Now that is ended,' he said with satisfaction.

'No,' answered Pakoko. 'At the next harvest, I shall invite Chief Tohi-kai to my tattooing festival. I promised to show him a new thing.' He ran his hand over his face. He was tired of these stripes. He would be the only man on Nuku Hiva with a face altogether black.

IV THE CHIEF'S STAFF

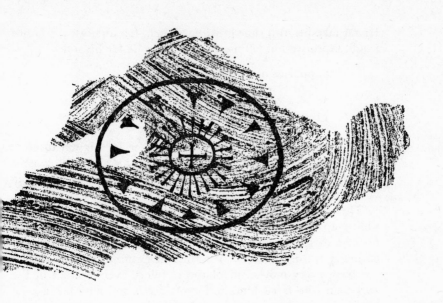

1

FROM the black shade of hibiscus trees, the eyes of the people of Taiohae gleamed, wide and fixed, as they clung to an enormous canoe which covered their sky and their sea. The thing was like a mountain with man-eating precipices, with great forests on the uplands. 'It is the wonder canoe of the old-time people,' whispered Chief Hiatai, looking up at his father who stood shading his eyes with his fan. 'The grandfathers-far-below have sent it to me,' he said.

'Perhaps,' murmured Pakoko doubtfully. Then, seeing his son's swelling lips, he consoled him. 'We will ask for it. Come.'

Hiatai drew back, pressing against his mother. 'I will wait for you here.'

Now it was the father's turn to clasp his hands in disappointment, until his woman, Metani, caught his clouded eyes and made them shine again. She was always saying to Pakoko, 'Let

Hiatai take his own time growing.' Often, for comfort, the father
would repeat to himself a song he had made for his son:

> Supporter of the skies,
> Hiatai is a chief's slender staff—
> Hair-crowned, invincible,
> Lizard-girdled, fearful.

Pakoko thought he had waited a long time for his son to grow
tall enough to hold up the skies. It was hard for him to be content
with the songs the young people made for Hiatai, calling him 'the
beautiful, fragrant wreath of Nuku Hiva'.

The Chief of Haavao forgot his son when a small canoe came
sliding down the cliffs of the father ship. All his force went into
his eyes as the clumsy craft walked backwards towards him on
curiously rolling paddles. Absorbed in examining every line of
the boat, every movement of the paddlers, every feature of the
only man who faced him, he forgot speech and movement, even
breath. He was like a tree, rooted in the land, one of hundreds of
trees that stood rigidly all along the crescent of Taiohae's sands.
They had all heard of people from the clouds who had visited the
other islands, but words had not made known to them their
splendor or their strangeness.

As five men drew near in the boat and all turned their faces
towards the land, their difference was shocking. These were not
natural men, with their skins white as coconut flesh and their
sky-clear eyes. Were they the dead returning from the skies? Even
their shouts were empty as the cries of birds. A pity that Priest
Kohu had not come down from his sky-piercing house, for he
understood the talk of birds. The Teiis struck the points of their
eyes deep into the pale ones that stared at them, hoping to find
something to catch and tie to. Not until those faded eyes wavered
and those bleached heads turned away could the landsmen discover anything familiar. Then they saw that those fellows were
ashamed and angry as they jerked their boat about. The watchers
could move now, enough to sit down, enough to whisper back
and forth.

When Pakoko's curiosity could be smothered no longer, he
stamped across the sands, splashed through breaking waves and
swam out to see the work of those outsiders who went from place

146

to place, dropping a fishing line but drawing it up without waiting for a nibble. He was the first of innumerable swimmers whose black heads bobbed up around the boat like net floaters. Pakoko thought that the sky-people were sending down a weight to find out the depth of the sea, but he went close to see whether they had drawn up anything on a hook. Others followed, and their hands grasping the sideboards tipped the boat to one side, making the occupants sit down hard. Seeing them tremble, the landsmen began to rock their boat back and forth violently, until all the swimmers were beating the sea to foam as they pressed close to join the play.

The people from the clouds were frightened all right, for their chief lifted a stick, but Pakoko pulled his arm down and held his weapon. What was this hard black stick like a bamboo with a central hole? He squinted and blew into it, smelled and licked it. He tried to pull it away, but the outsider jerked it free and, pointing it at the sky, made it flash lightning and call out, 'Puhi!' 'Beautiful! Beautiful!' cried all the swimmers, echoing its thunder by slapping the sea with their palms. But when the leader pointed it at a flock of sea birds and made it thunder, they were silent, because one of the birds fell down, gushing blood. Pakoko held the limp feathers in his hand. 'The stick has blown fire clear through the bird!' he said in awe.

While the landsmen were examining the dead bird, the small boat walked quickly to the big ship and returned with big gourds floating behind. The pale Chief pointed to the casks, cupped his hands, dipped, poured into his mouth, and swallowed. He wanted drink! When he pointed to a gourd and held up a small black stick, so hard that its point would pierce the wood of the boat, they understood that one point was offered in exchange for one gourd of water. They nodded and laughed at the cleverness of this dumb man who could talk with his hands. Clasping hands, they made themselves into long ropes and pulled the heavy, rolling boat to shore.

As they reached the shore, a commotion on the path from Meau made them all stare. There came two men with ribboned staves, clearing a way through the crowds for their chief. It was Kiato-nui, riding on a raft borne by four men-at-the-side. He sat placidly fanning himself, enjoying the sight of men and women fleeing from his path lest his sacred shadow fall upon them and destroy them, looking down with welcoming *kaoha* on the outsiders. Pakoko had often laughed at his brother's growing sacredness and whispered to Metani, 'As Kiato-nui's power shrinks, he covers his nakedness with clouds of taboo.' But now, seeing that outsiders were impressed by this display and were offering him gifts as if he were a great chief, the Chief of Haavao felt that a playful breeze was changing to a chilling wind. He began to give orders with a loud tongue to those who were floating the gourds in from the ship, bidding them take them to his own stream for water. Sliding his eyes to the corners to cover his brother, he grinned as he saw him try to stab him with petulant glances, and he drew down his mouth as he watched him fingering his strange gifts. He was as easily hurt, as easily pleased, as a child. But Pakoko was stirred to action when he saw Kiato-nui drop a hard point into Hiatai's hand. Now he would ask for the wonder canoe of the sky for his son. But Pakoko drew back in dismay when he watched Kiato-nui strip himself of his feather headdress, his whale's tooth necklace and his fan with carved handle, as the outsiders pointed to the things they wanted. Those different people from the clouds were greedy and made no true exchange. The Chief of Haavao would not repeat his brother's mistake. He was content to stand beside his workers in his running water and collect a hard point for every gourd filled, as agreed.

Meanwhile, some of Pakoko's men had discovered the wonderful hook with points that was holding the small boat firmly fastened to the sand. Scarcely able to hush their laughter, they had cut its rope and dragged the anchor away with them under water. When they had hidden it in a fisherman's house, they came back to boast of their clever thieving. The outsider who was managing the filling of the casks turned aside to see why all the landsmen were laughing. When he turned back, his buckets had disappeared. Now he knew they were laughing at him. Just then, one of his men who was being picked to pieces by curious women began to weep because they were pulling his hair. Ashamed of the sailor, the leader turned and spoke angrily to him. At that moment, Pakoko lifted his brows in a sign to Uncle Fatu, the old man whirled the confused and angry man around, Pakoko snatched his thunder and lightning blower from behind and passed it deftly to Hiatai, who vanished in the crowd. By this time the Teiis were rolling on the beach, holding their aching stomachs, gasping with laughter. Alas, this was the end of that good play, for the outsiders blew fire stones over the heads of the people on the shore and then ran away to their big ship.

Next morning, Chief Pakoko went boldly to visit the Chief of the people from the clouds. The night before he had sent a swimmer to throw a *temanu* branch tied with white *tapa* onto the high level of the wonder canoe to show that peace was desired. Today, he carried many knots of breadfruit and coconuts, baskets of taro and a few sucking pigs as a *kaoha* for the gifts seized yesterday. He laughed, as he looked across the bay at the floating island standing up red in the morning light, for the women of Taiohae were ahead of him. The sea was hidden by swimmers who held their *tapas* up on sticks to keep them dry. The ropes hanging from the ship were covered with lines of women streaming up the cliffs. Even the trunks and branches of the trees on its crests were swarming with girls who crawled about helping the men to roll and tie their sails and to smear their lashings with black gum. From the hidden level inside the hull came the laughter and cries of those who played down there. The Chief of Haavao swung his hips as if he were going to a feast, when he entered his gift-laden canoe. Seeing his paddlers lean on their blades, fearing that the mountainous ship would fall over on them because it had no outrigger to keep it upright, he laughed and waved them forward until he could grasp the dangling rope.

Pakoko was throwing a leg over the railing of the ship before he looked at the rows of dead-faced men leaning towards him. He would have fallen back into the sea if their pale hands had not pulled him up. He was sickened by their odor, confused by their rasping talk. When their Chief came, sun shining on bright disks on his breast and fringes on his shoulders, the landsman was dazzled but he began to stand up whole again. He had studied that face the day before and he knew that the man was slow and stupid. Pakoko grinned at him. After all, they had played together.

The outsider was not smiling. His light eyes were hard as skies in time of drought. He demanded the things that had been stolen, actually asked for them in the open! Not even a fisherman would be so crude. Was the fellow afraid to steal back his things or did he know he was too clumsy to succeed? On land, Pakoko would have pulled his eye lid down in derision and walked away, but here, on this high level, alone, he knew he was caught. He called down to his paddlers to bring back what had been seized.

When Uncle Fatu came with the buckets and the anchor, but without the blower which Hiatai had refused to give up, Pakoko found that he could not call out farewells and depart. Until the blower was returned, he would be held, he would even be carried off on the ship and would never again see his dear land!

Again the Chief of Haavao waited while Fatu appealed to Hiatai. The flapping sails were being drawn up, the rattling anchor chain was being coiled. Pakoko covered his uneasiness by stamping about on heavy feet, talking with a loud tongue to the wooden ears behind him, pointing to things without names. All the shining things must have come from the sun. His fingers itched to pluck them. His hands were quick, the eyes of the outsiders were slow. He would teach these rough fellows a lesson. Yes, it was easy. He ought to have laughed because he was so clever, carrying off something under his cape, but, seeing Uncle Fatu appear with the blower, he began to weep. Indeed, he clung to the old man as if he had been away from his beloved land for a long time. Still, while they mingled their tears, he did not forget to give the old man his cape wrapped around the box. He knew that Fatu would jump overboard with it while he drew the outsiders around him in farewell.

True, enough. When Pakoko slid down the rope and took his seat in his canoe, there was the box in the hull. The men peering over the railing spied it also. Did they laugh and praise him for his skill as any decent man would have done? No, they blew fire-stones across the canoe until Pakoko threw the box into the sea in disgust and made his paddlers run to shore. Then, unashamed, they sent a swimmer down to pick up the floating thing.

The women of Taiohae were calling their *kaohas*. 'Come again, come again!' They were telling one another that the ardent but clumsy outsiders were like unwashed, unoiled pigs, but that their gifts were marvels from the sky, gourds clear as air, neck wreaths of sky stuff, *tapas* that did not melt in water. 'Come again, come again!' they begged.

Watching that wonder canoe vanish in the clouds, Pakoko was pricked by a thorn of shame. He had been caught stealing. It was no good to say that his skill had been admirable, that the outsiders had unfairly recovered property that was already his. He could not forget that they had emptied his hands publicly. It was not until the Master Bone Carver declared that the clever things of the different people were taboo that he began to feel comfortable again.

The masters of Haavao were gathered in the men's house trying out their new hard points when the Master Bone Carver threw down his new tool in dismay. 'This is not the way of the gods!' he cried. 'Work is long and difficult. Even the god had to noose the sun to finish his work before dark.' He picked up his rat's tooth point and felt it resting in his hand like an old friend. Its slow accomplishment had always given him a lingering pleasure. 'Yes,' he said, 'our own tools are good, those of the outsiders are bad.'

The other masters, who had been slicing and gouging and punching into wood, shell and bone as if they were cutting ripe breadfruit, mocked him. But Pakoko cried eagerly, 'You are right!' Then he wondered why he had said such a thing. He had been working on an ironwood stilt rest for Hiatai. He saw the *tiki* taking form under his hard point as easily as he could see a man stepping out of a fog. He felt the point now and it seemed dull. 'Their things are no good,' he agreed with the carver. Having said it, he felt lighter than he had since the outsiders had taken advantage of him.

The Master Chanter, who had been looking off into the sky beyond the posts, began to sing old words softly:

Atea, the dark-haired, comes forth before,
Tane, the light-haired, comes forth behind.

All the workers turned startled eyes upon the old bard. 'Tane, the light-haired.' Of course. 'The people from the clouds are the children of the god, Tane!' Pakoko exclaimed.

'You remember,' the Master Bone Carver reminded his friends, 'Level Above said to those two sons, Atea and Tane, "Close your eyes. You must not watch my taboo work." '

Yes, yes! Everyone knew that Atea had obeyed his father, but that Tane had peeped through his fingers. Now the sun shone for Pakoko. 'Tane was a taboo breaker!' he cried.

Uncle Fatu shrank back from his hard point. 'These things will bring death to the children of Atea!' he gasped. 'They were stolen from Level Above! They are taboo!'

The workers laid down their points, some as if they were hot embers, some as if they were desirable women. They made a little heap of them for the Fire Keeper to take away and bury in the sacred place.

Though Pakoko was no longer troubled by a pecking at his liver whenever he thought of his play with the outsiders, he was worried. Hiatai had let Uncle Fatu tear the stolen blower out of his arms without an outcry, but, ever since, he had kept his eyes covered from his father. Then when he had wakened one morning to find that the hard point given him by Kiato-nui had been taken from the knot in his girdle, he had choked on his rage and refused to agree that it was dangerous to touch things forbidden by the gods. After that he had settled into a melancholy so black that his household felt that a cloud had blown across the sun whenever he approached. Less and less he came near them. Day after day he went alone to the beach. On the hard sand licked smooth by the sea, he drew again and again the image of the enormous canoe from the sky. It was a true image with all its masts, branches, sails and ropes. In the light, he drew the image. In the dark, the sea wiped it away.

Pakoko did not know whether to laugh or to weep at his son's strange ways. It was not for lack of ability that the youth was wasting his time. Neglecting nothing, the father had made a god of Hiatai. He had given innumerable pigs to priests and gods to make him grow straight and strong. Indeed, he was as beautiful as a perfectly carved spear. Pakoko had fed, clothed, housed and presented gifts to all the masters of Haavao to fashion the sacred possessions of his first-born. Hiatai's ironwood club, his *temanu* canoe, his banyan *tapa* loin cloth, his black stone adze, his feather headband, his anklets and wristlets of curled hair, all were without flaw. Yet the youth took no pride in them but kept them tied to his rafters in an unopened bundle.

Never before had a young chief of Nuku Hiva been raised to such a high level. His Hapaa grandfather had tied all the small branching valleys of Hakapaa together under him. Pakoko had knotted every chief in Taiohae to him, joining Hiatai himself to one as a son-in-law, giving the boy's brothers and sisters to others, taking the sons and daughters of high level folk of other valleys as his own foster children. There lay the valleys of the Hapaas and the Teiis side by side, like a great double canoe, waiting for their Chief Hiatai to stand up on the platform between them and command their going. But Hiatai sat on the sands, staring at the sky's foundation, drawing lines without meaning, while the grandfather and the father held the steering paddles of those two great canoes, waiting.

NOTE

Although the island of Nuku Hiva had been sighted previously from a distance, it was first visited by the *Daedalus*, a supply ship in command of Lieutenant Hergest, which was carrying stores from the Falkland Islands to Monterey, and which put in to Taiohae Bay late in March, 1792.

2

ON the front stones of Pakoko's sleeping house, his woman and his mother by birth were sitting together, their hands busy, Metani's with mat making, Ehua's with flower garlands. Mother Ehua had been a rippling stream of laughter ever since she had returned to her father's valley of Haavao when her son had seized it from Kena. She had been growing young. She looked like a girl with skin fresh as a shrimp's just out of its shell. She had not turned away from her adopted son, Kiato-nui, but, as a flicker is lost in a flame, her warm *kaoha* for him was swallowed up in her burning desire for her ancestral land. Besides, Chief Kiato-nui was seldom seen by his women folk. Many suns he slept away in his taboo house. It was said he drank three men's *kava* before he began to dream. When he was awake, he did not visit his relatives or go about looking at his trees and storage holes, but sat in his men's house carving images for the grandfathers-far-below. He did not come often to Haavao to see his mother. 'Pakoko tries to make me a nobody,' he complained.

Metani knew that this was the only shadow on Ehua's path. 'You are anxious without cause,' she told her. 'Pakoko will never forget that he carried his younger brother on his hip.' That was the way of Metani, always smoothing things out. There she was, still giving breast water to her youngest, a big fellow able to run about, big enough to be sent over the mountains to Chief Tohi-kai of Taipivai, to whom he was promised. Could she put away a clinging hand or a begging eye? No, she had enough of everything for anybody who asked, a song for Hiatai, fine white *tapas* for her foster daughters. For her own little girls, she could always find joints of dried octopus to chew or packages of bread-fruit to slip into their baskets when they went down to the rocks by the sea for tiny fish left in shallow pools. For Pakoko himself, her hands were always open, always being emptied. Because it was his hot desire to possess whales' teeth and ever more whales' teeth, she had just last moon sent all her ornaments by Uncle Fatu to Chief Hono on Tahu Ata for exchange, for news had come that a dead whale had been cast upon the shore there. 'I need no ornaments,' she had said.

No, a sea shell needs no ornament. Lying on his mat at one end of the house, enjoying his family through nostrils and eyes, Pakoko was murmuring, 'A sea shell with the light shining through, that is my woman Metani.' That was his thought which was broken by the tumult of an arrival on his terrace.

It was Uncle Fatu returning from Tahu Ata, not with laughter but with wailing. All Pakoko's dwellers ran out of their houses to meet the old man but he waved them back as he plodded across the feast place. Shaking and breathing in gulps after his hurried climb from the beach, he could not speak, or he would not, because he must first tell Chief Pakoko his terrible news. Seeing his nephew jumping down from his terrace and running towards him, he raised his trembling voice in such a clamor that children began to cry with him. Still he made no words that could be understood, even when Pakoko asked, 'Where are my whale's teeth?' He simply held up empty hands and wailed the louder, for he could see that the folk of Haavao were running from above and below and from either side of the valley to hear his word.

It seemed as if the old man who had sat behind others for so long, humble and unheard, must now stretch out his frenzy of grief until all were there to listen to him.

At last he proclaimed again and again, 'Chief Hono is dead! Chief Hono is dead!' Through a new freshet of tears, he could see that Pakoko was shocked and silent, but that was only a beginning. Now he went on to rouse him to anger. 'Chief Hono died at the hands of the people from the clouds!' he cried.

Fatu had raised a storm, all right, and, in order to quiet it so that his story could be heard, his nephew led him to his own speaking stone and helped him to climb up and look down upon all the landsmen who sat down humbly to hear him. When the old man could see everyone, his voice rang out. 'The outsiders quarrelled with Chief Hono,' he said, 'because he moved all his women to another bay.' He threw a glance at Pakoko as if to remind him that that was Hono's way. 'And why not?' he demanded. 'A chief need not offer what is not there.' But that was not all.

Hono had given trees and woodstrikers to the strangers who wanted to build a ship like their own. For three moons, four tens of these outsiders had slept in Chief Hono's houses, picked his fruits and dipped their hands into his food bowls, yet when they had finished their ship, they had refused to let him use it for war against his enemies on Hiva Oa. At the Chief's command, his Brave Faces had made ropes and tried to tie the ship to the rocks, but the outsiders had turned their big blowers upon Hono's canoe and split it from beak to tail, sending their fire stones through the chief and his paddlers. Then they had run away, taking the new ship with them.

Hearing how the people from the clouds had refused to make a return for Chief Hono's *kaohas,* Pakoko grew red and swollen with anger. Were the outsiders wild pigs, that they would carry off work they had been fed to make? While the people wailed for the dead chief and passed from hand to hand a sheath of embers, fanning it into flames in token of their promise of revenge, Chief Pakoko ground his teeth over the uncouth ways of the visitors.

That was why, when the watchers in coconut trees called down that the outsiders had come again, the Brave Faces of Haavao had their slings tied around their wrists and their stones piled in their canoes. That was why Chief Pakoko blew his conch till its wild voice lifted his men on end and its moans made their tears flow for Chief Hono who had been struck down by the tricky people from the clouds. That was why he sent Uncle Fatu to ask the Chief of Pakiu to demand war on the visitors.

The old man found the young Chief of Pakiu on the sands with those who were filling gourds from the ship with drinking water. Fatu watched him with his mouth tied up in a disapproving knot, as he bargained for a shining axe. 'Yes,' the young man was saying, 'I will give two pigs for one axe.' Fatu interrupted with a harsh call.

As he was about to send for his pigs, the Chief heard that he must ask for war. He burst into tears. 'But Kiato-nui's people will get all the precious things! This is my axe!' he cried. He could not refuse Pakoko's request, for his own daughter was betrothed to Chief Hiatai, but he must finish this work first. He would secure the axe and then ask war.

When his men-at-the-side returned with two fat pigs, he had held his place in the crowd fighting to throw their pigs into the outsiders' canoe. His went in, shoulder pole and all, before the others. Grinning, he held out his hand for the axe. Two small hard points were dropped into it. 'No!' he yelled. 'The axe!' The man shook his head and turned to others. Hot anger rushed through the Chief of Pakiu. 'Liar!' he cried, striking that unjust man in the face.

A blower thundered. The Chief looked down at his breast, amazed. Blood was spurting from it, a hot flood running down over his stomach! A red sea slapped him in the face as he fell under the feet of landsmen and outsiders who were running away from one another.

When Chief Pakoko heard that his friend had been killed before he had even asked for war, he made his conch scream his fury and led his Braves down into the waters of the bay. Swimming and paddling, they chased the visitors to their big ship, raining stones on the water and against the high side boards. Making horrible faces at the pale eyes staring down at them, they caught hold of the ship's dangling ropes and tried to pull the mountain to shore, but they were tossed aside as the mat sails ran screaming up the masts and drank the wind with noisy gulps.

Sitting on a bunch of coconuts high above the sand, Hiatai had watched this war. 'Stones do not kill,' he whispered to himself. 'Only blowers with fire stones kill.' As he climbed slowly down the trunk, he was thinking, 'If my father refuses, my grandfather will get one for me.'

NOTE

In February, 1793, the *Daedalus* returned to Taiohae under the command of Lieutenant Hanson, stopping on its way from the North West Coast of America to New South Wales.

Meanwhile, an American fur trading ship under Captain Josiah Roberts of Boston had spent several months at Tahu Ata building a small vessel. During a contest between the crew and the natives, Chief Hono was killed.

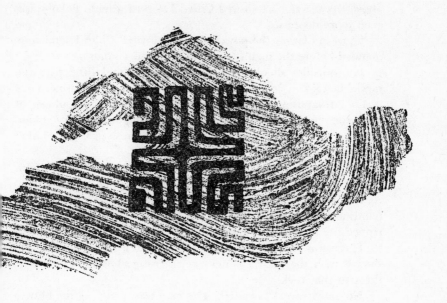

3

WHEN Pakoko's son, Hiatai, next watched the tail of a disappearing ship returning to distant seas, he capered along the shore for he saw that his grandfather, Tea-roru, was bringing with him in his canoe a man with skin white as coconut.

'Who is that in the Hapaa canoe?' his father demanded, breathless from running down from the mountains where he had been setting traps for wild boars.

Hiatai's loud answer startled him. 'That is my Ironwood!'

Pakoko was amazed at his son's shining eyes and easy-running tongue. Where was the boy ashamed, who hung his head and spoke with a hesitating tongue? Seeing this young man of spirit, the father was lifted on a flowering wave of joy until he thought of what the youth had said. An outsider to lead his warriors! Incredible! Seeing then the blower which the fellow held high above the sea as he followed Chief Tea-roru ashore, Pakoko was even more depressed.

'Show my father the power of your blower!' Chief Hiatai commanded before the man's feet were on the dry sands.

The outsider shook his head. 'It is just for killing pigs and birds,' he said, 'a *kaoha* from the Captain of the ship to me.'

Eo! All landsmen were astonished that the stranger had caught their tongue. They laughed at his lame tongue but they understood him. 'He has been a dweller in the house of Chief Hono's son,' the Hapaa grandfather explained.

'You are my Ironwood!' Hiatai shouted. 'Hear my word! Point your blower at that banyan tree and make a hole through it.'

The fellow was sweating and his blower wavered in shaking hands as he pointed it, but when it bellowed, *'Puhi!'* its lightning ripped the bark from the tree.

There was deep silence for a space, then a storm of yells and shouts, with the Hapaa Chief's voice rising above. 'Blow a hole through that rock!'

'No, no. Its work is ended.' The man was wrapping the blower and two small bags in his coat. 'The power of this thing is nothing. I have come to tell you of the power of my God.'

Pakoko taunted him. 'True, your blower is good for one time only.'

'Lies!' Hiatai's tongue struck at his father. 'Your slings are not good at all!'

Red anger burned the father's eyes. Hiatai was crazy, praising the things of others, making little of his own. 'I say the blower will not work again,' he repeated through closed teeth.

'Blow a hole in that stone!' the youth commanded.

The outsider obeyed as one moving in uneasy sleep. He put a pinch of white earth from his sack into the hollow of his blower, dropped a ball and pounded leaves on top, then pointed the stick. Thunder and lightning! The rock broke into small pieces!

Pakoko had watched every move. Before the man lowered his smoking blower, he snatched his small sack of powder and threw it into the sea. 'Now show your god's power!' he commanded.

Did this wonderful Ironwood of Hiatai destroy his enemy? He called on his god, turning his face to the sky and moving his lips, but he did not point his blower again. The landsmen began to laugh at him. Not Hiatai. He was furious. He snatched the blower, pointed it at Pakoko and pulled the knob. Its voice sounded, '*Ta*,' as gently as a falling leaf. No thunder, no lightning, no fire-stones, just, '*Ta*.'

The father stared at his son. The boy who always sat quietly, who came when called, who never stepped in front, had attacked him! Now he was shaking the stranger until his teeth knocked together. He was commanding him to obey. Pakoko was proud of his spirited son.

The man looked at Hiatai with soft eyes. 'Friend,' he said, 'you ask for a worthless thing, but I have a great new thing to tell you.'

'Make that blower work again!' The Teiis shrank back from their Chief's heat as if they had stepped unexpectedly on a hot oven stone, but the outsider came nearer. 'The blower will not work without powder,' he said steadily.

All breathing stopped as Hiatai raised his arm. Would he strike the man or his father? Neither. With crooked fingers he seized the blower and with his nails tried to tear it to pieces. Failing, he smashed it against a rock and threw the pieces into the sea. His breath rasping through his spread nostrils, he turned away from the beach and disappeared in the dark shade.

Pakoko was tortured by the hook in his intestines. He had made the blower worthless, but had he destroyed his son? Hiatai's play had been harmless. But no! He had said, 'Your slings are no good at all.' Had the outsider sent a god inside the boy to turn him against the good things of this land? Following his son, hearing his dragging footsteps, seeing his clouded eyes and stiff face, the father could not endure his pain. 'When another ship comes, I will give pigs for a good blower for you,' he called after him. 'I will ask for many sacks of powder and tie them to the rafters where they cannot be wet or stolen.' The young man did not quicken his slow feet nor raise his hanging head. The older man called back his words as soon as he heard them come out of his mouth. 'By my head!' he cried, 'our slings are good!'

Day after day Hiatai lay on his mats, flat and still as a calm sea. Without chewing, he swallowed the food brought to him. Without unrolling his yellow *tapa*, he heard his friends calling his name on their flutes on moon nights. When Pakoko made a festival of netting smelts, Hiatai held the sugar cane torch in a limp hand but let it fall into the water when the fish began to follow the light. When his father taught him to spear the ray, he dived with his spear when told but cared not at all whether he caught or lost the fish. Not even the building of a house for his joined woman and the taking over of her valley of Pakiu because of the death of her father stirred the young Chief's interest. He neither laughed nor wept. He was like a dead man.

In despair, Pakoko sent to the Hapaa chief for the outsider. Perhaps he could be taught the work of Fire Keeper for the youth. Alas, the man had run away. Some said he had gone to Tahu Ata. Some said his god had come for him, walking on the water.

Finally Hiatai's mother said to his father, her liver weary with anxiety but her lips bravely smiling, 'Let us take our son to my valley for a visit. Perhaps another place will wake him out of sleep.'

The thought that Hiatai was not being nourished by Haavao had been peck-pecking at Pakoko also. 'You two will go,' he agreed, 'but I cannot leave my land, for I fear she is sick.'

NOTE

In May, 1798, Captain Edmund Fanning of the brig, *Betsy*, from New England, brought to Taiohae William Pascoe Crooke, former tinsmith, whom he had rescued from Tahu Ata, where the London Missionary ship, *Duff*, had left him the year before. He had been forced to flee from that island in spite of the friendship of a chief, and likewise stayed only a short time on Nuku Hiva.

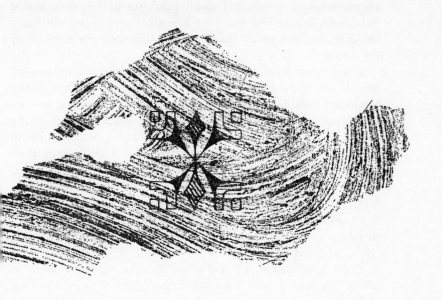

4

Pakoko did not know why he had said that his land was sick. Perhaps he wanted to hover over Haavao and draw his new lands of Pakiu under his wings. But he kept spreading his nostrils as if he smelled something bad. It would be a good thing to set aside all breadfruits for the storage holes. His ears were full of wax when the people grumbled at hanging up their picking nets. Let them eat sour old paste. They could sweeten it with yams and coconut oil and dull its sharp bite with dried rays and sharks. He had no eyes for what they did. He was watching Father Clear Space and Mother Red Soil. The skies were lazy, turning now and then, opening a little. The land drank quickly and was not satisfied. Big Breadfruit harvest yielded small children; Breadfruit Following Quickly, very small ones. The Master Planter nodded his head. Pakoko had seen truly. 'The trees just want to sit quietly for a space,' he said. The folk of the valley began to follow their Chief about from tree to tree, hoping that Breadfruit Drawn Out and Last Breadfruit would put out something better than cores. 'Soon we will be eating the wind,' they muttered.

Pakoko wondered what Priest Kohu was doing while the land was drying up. Couldn't he hear the voices of his birds? If the grandfathers-far-below were angry because Chief Hiatai desired the things of the peeping god, Tane, then it was the work of the Priest to make things right again. The father stamped up to Kohu's sky-piercing house to question him. 'Come down from your perch!' he shouted to the dim shape far above and mimicked the creaking of the bamboo uprights as its dweller descended. He snorted at his brother's tangled hair and cracked skin and torn *tapas* soiled with body juices, but when he met the Priest's piercing eyes, ah, that was different. He said then in a small voice, 'Well, where is the rain?'

Kohu stopped looking at the airs and saw the land. The red soil of his hillside was like sand. Long yellow tongues stood up stiffly in his sugar cane patch. His pandanus whirls rattled in the hot dry air. 'I did not know,' he answered feebly.

'Don't you know your work?' Pakoko was bold. 'Do the gods want a fish?'

Priest Kohu drew back into clear space, looking through his brother as if he had been a breath body. 'One, two, three moons I have been lying on the sea, listening for a new voice,' he whispered. 'Thunder in the mountains is good, but thunder from the sea is different.'

Ah. That was it. Pakoko began to tell how Hiatai had wanted to make the thunder of the Different People. Now, indeed, Kohu's eyes forgot the sky and clung to his brother's face. Blowers making thunder and lightning? Different People? Ships? He knew none of these things. Living with the gods, he had missed these works. He had heard thunder coming from the sea, that was all. As Pakoko walked back and forth, stretching his arms to show the bigness of the canoes from the moon, bellowing to imitate the voices of the blowers, Kohu followed him, drinking his words as a thirsty man sucks pulp from passion fruits. Ships that reached from headland to headland and covered the whole bay with their shadow! Sticks that blew fire-stones from great distances through birds, men, trees and stones!

Suddenly the Priest cut him short as if he had all that he could hold. He went back to his tower, flinging his weak foot in front, and drew himself up above as quickly as a rat climbs. From the tree tops the god's voice quavered, 'Bring me two fat pigs for the work of making the breadfruit grow!'

Seeing a swallow whirling in the wind around the Priest's ridge pole, hearing talk he could not understand on Kohu's trilling tongue, Pakoko tip-toed away. Now there would be rain.

Thinking he heard torrents of rain pounding the land, the Chief of Haavao came sliding down the pole from his food house. But no, the land was beaten by hundreds of feet racing towards him. Above the shouting and wailing of those who ran, Uncle Fatu was trying to make his voice heard. 'Priest Kohu is hung up on a sky ship! His breath is running out of him!'

'Pigs! More pigs! The outsiders want pigs!' One of the Priest's Clubs panted.

A word here, a word there, Pakoko caught. Kohu had taken the two fat pigs given him to make the breadfruit grow and had offered them to the outsiders for a blower! But they wanted two twenties of pigs. When the Priest refused, saying they were breeders, taboo, they had seized him and tied him by the wrists to the upright of the ship. Uncle Fatu put his shaking lips to Pakoko's ear. 'The Captain says, "Bring me two twenties of pigs or this man will hang here till he dies."'

Pakoko's teeth were pressed together. 'The pigs are taboo. They cannot be given.' He braced himself against the winds blowing against him from all sides, the old father's sobs, the shrill cries of fear. 'Will you let them eat our Priest? . . . Throw away Priest Kohu and our land will surely die! . . . What are a few pigs against a diviner? . . . Send the pigs! Send the pigs!' The Chief jumped onto his speaking stone and made his shell scream his anger. 'What do you want?' he shouted. 'The breaking of a Chief's taboo? The loss of our breeding pigs when our food bowls are empty? I say this is cause for war! Will you hear the Moon Chief's commands or mine?' When the Brave Faces gave consent to war with a mighty roar, he drew Uncle Fatu close to him. 'I will bring Kohu back myself,' he promised.

The tide of warriors, swollen by slingsmen and spearsmen who flowed from every house along the down-going path, poured onto the beach, lifted canoes from their supports, slapped them down on the water, thrust out the canoe legs to run towards the distant enemy. Alas, they had not left the land, when thunder from the ship made air, water and land tremble. The Braves were knocked flat. Sand and water gushed into their eyes and mouths. Branches of trees broke over their heads. Burrowing through sand, crashing through splintered wood, slapping away leaves, they fought their way up the slope, crawling, stumbling, running into the sheltering undergrowth.

As Pakoko stood up through a fallen tree, trying to blow his broken conch shell, a swimmer rose in shallow water and splashed towards him. 'Priest Kohu says . . . !' The Club had little breath. He began again, 'The god says, "Send pigs quickly!" ' Moaning softly, the Chief dragged his heavy feet up the path to his enclosure for pigs. Bitter as *kava* were his thoughts as he watched two twenties of breeders being tied to shoulder poles and carried away. Kohu with his double intestines, asking pigs for the gods, giving them for a blower, let him die! But he could not let his Diviner die and leave the Teiis without eyes or ears to know the desires of the gods. Kohu had woven a net from which he could not escape.

When racing feet came from the sea, the brother was all *kaoha,* arms open to receive the hurt Kohu, but only empty hands were held up to him. 'Another twenty pigs because we attacked!' Wails from innumerable throats made Pakoko shudder. Even as he bellowed, 'No! Not another pig!' he was chasing his remaining breeders, helping his men-at-the-side to tie their sharp hoofs together. When they were gone, he threw himself down in the empty enclosure and covered his ears to shut out their strangled screams as they swung upside down from the poles of their bearers. Alas, alas! No litters of new pigs, no breadfruits swelling on the trees, the people of Haavao would have to eat sand!

Pakoko bent over Kohu's limp form lying on a litter. 'You deceived me! You wanted the blower for yourself!' he whispered fiercely. But when the Priest's white lips fluttered and no word came out, he was afraid his spirit had fled. He knelt beside his brother, as if he were a little fellow again, looking at the leg that turned backwards. 'Kohu! Kohu!' he wailed. 'Do not leave me! Come back!'

Kohu's lips moved against Pakoko's ear. 'The blower was for the god—to catch his fish.'

The Chief turned this over and over, while he was covering the Priest's torn wrists with healing juices, while he was fanning away the flies, while he was feeding the sick man. When Kohu could go back to the sacred place, he questioned him. 'How about it, then? Is the god of the outsiders more powerful than ours?'

Kohu's eyes burned. 'Undoubtedly, those thieves will be punished for eating our taboo pigs. They will die of leprosy.'

Both men knew that Kohu had not answered Pakoko's question. They sat side by side on the edge of the terrace, listening to the deep silence of the valley as if trying to hear the answer of Father Clear Space and Mother Red Soil. Finally, the Priest said, 'One thing is certain. Level Above said to his two sons, Atea and Tane, "You shall not see my work." '

'Yes!' Pakoko cried, as if he were a drowning man lifted up by a strong swimmer. 'That is my thought. We will not touch the stolen works of the children of Tane.' Then, as Kohu started up valley, he called after him, 'See that you hear that word yourself. Anger sufficient has burned this land.'

The Priest nodded. 'I have been taught,' he said, looking at his scarred wrists.

5

THE sky turned to wood, the land to sand. Another Great Breadfruit harvest was tramped into the storage holes, but only half the picking nets had been filled. When the next moon of swelling came, even a child could see that there would develop only yellow and shrivelled buds. As for the litters of breeding pigs sent over the mountains from Pakoko's friend, the Taipi Chief, they were skin and bones because the people had held back their peelings and cores from them. The Chief could not blame them.

Even Master Sea was stingy. Here was a moon when winds and seas should bring fish from distant seas, but no birds were calling their arrival. Perhaps Master Sea was angry because taboo pigs had been carried over him. Certainly, the moon following the visit of the priest-hanging ship, a strange sea had sucked dry the bay of Taiohae and then vomited such a flood onto the land that houses were swept from their terraces.

Chief Pakoko called his relatives to the taboo terrace of the Master Fisherman to let the god know their need. Bringing tiny images, hooks, spears and nets, they bound them with *tapa* and made a tiny fishing just like a big one, with all packed into little canoes ready to go. Priest Kohu brought the skull of the ancient Hiatai and laid it where that grandfather could see the empty nets and the canoes waiting for good fishing. They thought of the hungry net, satisfied with a god-sent heaviness, while they sang and clapped of a work perfectly done.

The Chief held back nothing. He gave a beautiful tortoise shell headband to the mother of the Master Fisherman. He promised the women cord-makers the first net-full of fish. He warned all the women of his valley to keep their tongues, hands and stomachs asleep during the fishing. Everything had been perfectly prepared when Pakoko joined the Master and twenty chosen men as they crossed the pale sands so silently that they could hear the day's first murmur and the water's gentle licking of their canoes as they slid them out. Over the bending backs of paddlers, he could see the Master standing on the beak of the leading canoe, black against the sea's soft shining. Across the dead sea's quiet, he was suddenly stirred by the fisherman's chant of the god, Tanaoa, and mingled his own voice with the responses of the paddlers as the words were tossed from beak to tail and back again.

> I shall make myself a canoe!
>> He slapped together some beach sand.
> What kind of canoe is this which melts?
>> He slapped together some sea foam.
> Here is another which falls apart.
>> He broke off a coconut.
> Now I shall catch you in my good canoe,
>> My elder brothers, Fish-landed-in-front, Fish-landed-in-back.

When the canoes were in deep water, beyond the sister rocks, the Master gave the sign to the two big ones to unroll the net between them, while the little ones darted to either side to tie stones to its corners. Sliding then into the luminous water, he encircled it, straightening it here, untangling it there, until every eye was open, watching. He dove deep to loosen the central trap and when he rose like a bubble into the air, his face was lit by a ray that splintered the dark summit of the land. He climbed onto the beak of his canoe, shook the drops from his long black hair, unbound for work, tied a clean *tapa* between his legs and about his waist, and stood up against the clotted red sky, peering into the water for streaks of light entering the hungry net.

Three days, three nights, the canoes breathed with Master Sea, but no fish tails flowered the sea inside the net. 'No sleeping!' Pakoko warned the men who stretched themselves out in the shadow of a mat when the sun stood still above. 'No babbling!' he growled when they lay on their backs staring at the glittering moon. Drop by drop he gave them coconut water, finger by finger breadfruit paste. When not a swallow was left, he knotted his tired eyes to the Master Fisherman's and nodded his head. The Master raised his hand for the canoes to gather in their catch of soaked fibres. There was nothing else. Like ghosts, his men paddled back to the land, lifted their canoes over the lazy surf, and walked past the feasters who waited on the sands for their shares of the catch. The welcome of clapping, singing, beating of drums trailed into silence.

Chief Pakoko stared dully at the dry earth that blew up under his feet. He heard dimly the rattle of yellow leaves tossed about in a wind of scarcity. What was the desire of the angry gods? Looking across the running water that divided his land from Kiato-nui's, he saw an outsider digging into the soil with an outlandish tool. He had heard that Chiefess Kena had brought a man left by a ship to her son, a sour fellow who had gone from island to island, living with this chief and that. 'Kena wants to make an Ironwood out of this piece of driftwood,' the Brave Faces had told Pakoko and they had all laughed at the insect who could not and would not learn to jump from cliff to cliff nor even to lie in waiting without movement. People called him 'Hard To Cook' because he was stubborn and would not follow any man's path but his own. They taunted him because he was too clumsy to steal without being caught and had to plant roots for food. But no one had told Pakoko that the man was gouging Mother Red Soil with an outlandish digger. Naturally, Father Clear Space was furious. Here was just cause for the sickness of land and sea!

Wild force rushed through Pakoko's limbs. He slid down the bank, jumped the shallow pools rotting among naked rocks and climbed onto Kiato-nui's land. He yelled at the outsider, 'You are making the land sick with your foul digger! Go back to the clouds!'

The man straightened up and leaned on his stick while he regarded the Chief steadily. 'What does he want?' he asked slowly, throwing the words to those who lay in the shade nearby.

Those two knew well enough. Chiefess Kena's adopted son got up with a grunt and rolled away on his fat legs, puffing noisily through his spread nostrils. Chief Kiato-nui's first-born, hugging more tightly the thing in his arms, sprang up beside Hard To Cook.

For a space Pakoko could not tear his eyes from the garlanded thing which began to shout at him in a rough voice. It was not a pig and not a rat. The boy called it '*Peto*'. But when the Chief felt the outsider's intention to reach for his blower which leaned against a tree, he forgot the creature and sprang ahead of the slow fellow, sending the stick into the air with a vicious kick. '*Puhi!*' The blower spat thunder and lightning and hurled a fire-stone through the *peto's* leg! Then the skies fell, the outsider turning a twisted face upon the landsman as he rushed at him with upraised arms, the landsman catching him easily and holding him as if he were a child.

But the Chief of Haavao had raised a wind that sucked the High Level of Meau into its whirling heart. Above the screaming of the *peto* and the sobbing of Kiato-nui's son and the angry sputtering of the outsider rose the sounds of approaching storm. Beak leading, Chiefess Kena dove from leafy shade into the sunny clearing. Ironwood Mauhau pulled her back to let his Chief pass. Kiato-nui's bearers, crashing through the bush, carried the heavy Chief of Meau forward until he could look down on them all. The sky rider's calm vanished when he saw that his brother had picked up his precious Ironwood. 'That man is mine! You shall not steal him!' His voice broke and squeaked like a rat's.

'I don't want the fly!' Pakoko pitched the fellow onto his hands and knees. What a sight! That was the thing Kiato-nui held up, as if he were a precious whale's tooth that made him the most powerful chief on Nuku Hiva!

When Hard To Cook picked himself up, seized his blower, and stood beside the litter, slapping the dust from his clothes, Kiato-nui moaned over him as if he were sick. Then he said to Pakoko as if he were a little fellow down there running about, 'No more pecking at my Ironwood! He is taboo. Surely you will not touch what I have made sacred?'

Catching the wavering of Kiato-nui's tongue over that question, Pakoko sighed. He must still hover over this little one. 'You have been sleeping with your bowls of *kava*. You have not seen what this outsider with his outlandish tool has done to your land. Your breadfruit trees are withering, your taro roots are drying up, your fishing nets are folded. Surely you do not make sacred one who has angered the gods? Surely you will throw him away.'

Chiefess Kena darted between them. 'You will not drive this Ironwood away!' she cried.

Her son wished that he had not drunk *kava* so early in the morning. His eyes were swimming, his ears aching. 'You are crazy,' he said to Pakoko, picking at his sky canoe with long nails. 'His digger is quick. If breadfruit and taro dry up, he will give me potatoes to eat. I have given him this land to plant.'

Given him this land! How could land be given to an outsider who had no names stemming from true roots? 'The land belongs to the gods and to the father-chiefs!' Pakoko answered in alarm.

'I have given him a true name,' Chief Kiato-nui replied, making an end of pushing back and forth. He held out his hand to his shadowing Fire Keeper and, receiving his fan, began to swing it in long lazy curves.

Now Kiato-nui's son held up his *peto*, showing its bleeding leg. 'Pakoko has destroyed my namesake!' he wailed.

The father's eyelids fluttered. He called reluctantly to his outsider, 'Will the *peto* die?' When the man shook his head, Kiato-nui sighed with relief and began to fan again. 'It is nothing,' he told his son.

But Hard To Cook had another thought. His dog had been hurt and he would not let it pass. 'This cruel man must be made to pay,' he said sternly.

Well, that was just. 'What do you want?' asked the Chief.

'A father and a mother pig,' answered the outsider.

Chief Kiato-nui pushed his fan towards his Fire Keeper and

wiped the sweat from his face. He knew without looking that Pakoko was swelling with red anger.

Breeding pigs when famine was clinging to the door screens! 'I will give you pig's dung!' yelled Pakoko.

The man's eyes turned hard and sharp as he sought to gouge into the Chief of Haavao. 'You will give me these two pigs or I will send my bad spirit into you.'

The breath ran out of everyone there. Even Pakoko felt a fine quiver run through him. He felt also that he was no longer alone. All the landsmen were with him, drowning in a sea of fear. Ironwood Mauhua came close and whispered, 'He says he can bring ships from the clouds to punish us.'

Kiato-nui moved his round face from side to side on his thick neck as if he were trying to squeeze out words. 'Give—him—the pigs,' he begged.

When Pakoko had given two thin pigs and had spent a night of twisting and turning on his mat, he woke up a messenger before it was light enough to see the man's face and summoned a council of masters. He was healed of the sickness that had eaten him. He knew now that it was not Hiatai who had angered the gods. It was Hard To Cook, with his foul spells and contrary ways. He would lay the matter before Priest Kohu and the elders. He would ask for war with Kiato-nui. Ah. How hot were his intestines with the desire to seize the steering paddle of all Taiohae, to make it impossible for his easy-going brother to open Meau to the coming-and-going people from the clouds! Yes, there was a hole in the canoe of the land which must be caulked before an alien sea rushed in and swamped it. Who but Pakoko could do this work?

After the going of his messenger to talk of war, Pakoko was like a net floater bobbing up all over the valley. He visited his men's house to set his Brave Faces to mending slings and polishing spears, called on his woodstrikers to make new the strong place on the heights, commanded his fishermen to begin to dry shark's flesh for storage in the fort, talked even to the children about gathering firewood for ovens for the warriors. Before fires were lighted on his terrace, he had given all his people a moon's work. 'I will feed you after the war,' he promised, 'for this war will end the land dryness.'

Next morning he climbed the path towards the sacred place to hear whether the god had entered Priest Kohu to call for sacrifices before battle, for his messenger had not yet returned from Meau. Birds were singing without ceasing, '*Titokiri, titokiri, titokiri.*' Pakoko joined their song. He wished he could fly. 'Oh swallow up above!' he poured an old song through his open throat.

But it was not a bird which answered. '*Pupuhi!*' The voice of a blower struck the birds dumb and the song of a fire-stone close to his ear startled Pakoko. He was lying on the ground before he could think, hearing running feet pounding on the path. A shower of little stones struck him in the face as a woman slid down the slope.

'It is war!' she gasped. 'The outsider with his blower is running from tree to tree. Kiato-nui's Brave Faces are chasing our wood-strikers from the strong place!'

War! It could not be war. The gods had not given consent to war. The Priests had not offered fish nor chanted spells. The warriors had not been covered with taboo nor filled with blessed food. Warnings and challenges had not been exchanged upon the heights. This could not be war! Pakoko must make this clear. He stood up to climb to the narrow cut where the path broke through the cliffs to the high level of the land. He must quiet his wood-strikers who were screaming now. As he pushed the woman out of his way, the blower shouted at him again. The woman fell, blood gushing from her back. Pakoko leapt over her and ran up the path. He would break the neck of that coward with his bare hands!

A flood of woodstrikers came streaming down upon their Chief. Many swept past him, tossed about as if bad spirits were inside them. One stumbled against him, clung to him, coughing and spitting blood. 'We are overthrown!' he gasped.

'Stand up! Fight!' was Pakoko's answer, but even as he gave the command he was lifted up and borne seaward on the racing tide of frenzied workers. *Pupuhi!* Again the horrid sound pierced the clouds of terror breathed out by fleeing men. A Master House Builder, wedged against Pakoko's breast, went down and the sea poured over him. Bodies, living and dead, were piling up, choking the path. Those fleeing from the sling stones of Kiato-nui's men began jumping to one side into the deep ravine of the dry water course or plunging headlong into thorny thickets on the other side. Men and women rushed from their houses, dragging their household belongings, fighting for a place in the agitated current swirling past. Again and again the Chief tried to plant his feet against the raging torrent. He shouted until his voice was gone, but even its echoes were lost in the tempest of screams and wails blown seaward by the triumphant yells of the enemy.

Pakoko thought that with the help of the sea he could stop this crazy flight on the sands, but he was knee-deep in water before he could turn about. Then someone pulled him onto the tail of a canoe just as the blower hurled a last fire-stone at him and he was jerked swiftly ahead of the tide of men swimming to safety.

The Master Fisherman thrust a paddle into his Chief's hand and shouted to those who were beating the water to foam, 'To the valley of the Hapaas!'

The fisherman was right. With Hiatai's Hapaa Brave Faces, they could return to Haavao by the mountain route. Pakoko was about to dig his paddle into the sea, when a black head rose beside the canoe and a strong hand grasped the descending blade. 'Give me your name, Pakoko!' The face in the water cried.

It was Cousin Mauhau, Kiato-nui's Ironwood, Mauhau! His head lay under the sharp-edged paddle. Pakoko jerked it free, lifted it for a vicious swing. But what had the twitching mouth said? 'Give me your name, Pakoko!' He let his weapon fall gently onto the side boards and searched those ash-dry eyes.

Holding his chin above the racing waters as the canoe sped towards open sea, Mauhau panted, 'Kiato-nui has chosen an Ironwood who makes war like a wild pig. I am ended in Meau!'

Mauhau was faithful to the true ways of the grandfathers! Pakoko slid his hands down the strong arms of this brave man and pulled him up beside him and pressed him against his breast.

NOTE

In 1800, an English sailor named Robarts, who had been put ashore on Tahu Ata, possibly from the ship, *Butterworth,* came by canoe to Nuku Hiva and attached himself to Chief Kiato-nui, becoming the leader of his warriors and marrying his sister.

6

I n the high valley of Hakapaa, the Chiefess Metani made a feast
to welcome her half and his followers as if they had come in a
garlanded canoe at her invitation. Trying to make them forget
they were a miserable, uprooted people, she commanded her Fire
Keeper to spread their leaves and serve the best she had. It was
not a feast to make a song about, sour old breadfruit paste and
dried octopus, but it was fermented and made their stomachs
feel tight and full. She made Pakoko laugh by sending him a
piece of sugar cane. She brought out sheer *tapas* and polished
ornaments for all and told her drummers to stir up laughter. She
stood up very straight when she saw their eyes brighten and their
lips fall apart. When she saw her son, Hiatai, come from his
taboo house after the meal and sit beside his woman, holding her
hand in his, she was content and went with her serving women to
clean up the houses for her guests.

Pakoko's cousin, Oehitu, had brought Hiatai's little Chiefess from Pakiu by the upland path. When Kiato-nui's people had begun to plunder the houses of Haavao and Chiefess Kena had gone flying up the path to her old terraces, this younger brother of Ironwood Mauhau had also turned away from the Teiis who had joined an outsider against their own relatives. He had lowered many bundles from Pakoko's rafters and carried them to his cousin's place of refuge. He had found the small, timid Chiefess of Pakiu wandering and had taken her by the hand. He had pulled and pushed Pakoko's Mother Ehua and Uncle Fatu up the steep path to the backbone of the land, through the tall grass of the Valley of Tears, and down the rocky path into young Hiatai's high inland valley.

Pakoko had no intention of becoming driftwood cast up to rot in the mountains back of the valley of the Hapaas, nor would he allow his relatives to sleep away their exile. Day by day he had to encourage the two old ones. His mother would sit beside her brother, unmindful of the sun on her unshaded face, gazing into empty air, all her eye water dried up because of this second separation from her beloved Haavao. The aged Fatu, turning his back on the woman, would spend his suns rubbing a spear now and then with a bit of coral which was always falling from his loose old hands, always rolling where his dim eyes could not follow it. Once these had been father and mother nourishing Pakoko. Now they were lying on their backs, like children, waiting for him to turn them over. 'Crawl into the shade of the thatch,' he would call to Ehua and wait for her to turn her burned out eyes towards him in consent. 'Yes, we are going back to Haavao, perhaps tomorrow or the next day,' he would answer Uncle Fatu's daily question. But it was harder still to nourish his cousin Mauhau with hope. The Ironwood had lost his chief and his work, and alas his pride. He was like a tree uprooted whose roots were withering in dry air. 'We will soon lead Brave Faces against the usurpers of Haavao and Pakiu,' Pakoko would assure the restless Mauhau.

The driven Chief himself was rubbed raw with the waiting for Oehitu, whom he had sent as his messenger to Priest Kohu for a sign that he could strike back and regain Haavao. When he could wait no longer, he persuaded his son to call a meeting of the chiefs and masters of the Hapaas to talk of war against the usurpers of Haavao. Seating himself inside the men's house, Pakoko turned up the petalled flowers on his knees and spread the swallow wings tattooed on his shoulders with the air of a host at a great feast. He was not a lizard-eater begging from a chief's full bowl. He had whales' teeth to offer for Brave Faces. He and his cousin Mauhau were both Ironwoods, capable of leading them. But when he looked about that circle of eyes, he felt a cold sea rising about him. To encourage himself, he put his lips to the ear of the old Chief Tea-roru. 'You said to me, when I was a child, "You will be my Ironwood." Do you remember?' When the deaf old man nodded, he went on, 'Well, here I am. Give me Braves to lead.'

The eyes of his father-in-law were suddenly splashed with light, as if he were seeing how they two had driven Kena out of Haavao. Certainly, the white-head was for Pakoko's desire—while his eyes were open. But he was a very old man nearly ended, coming and going between waking and sleeping. Before he could answer, his eyes closed, his chin fell onto his breast and his breath came noisily through his mouth.

Pakoko sought his son's eyes for consent, but they were wandering in distant seas where a master could make a weapon so potent that a single one would drive an entire valley of men, its owner sitting unseen in some safe place. 'You cannot kill without a blower,' Hiatai said, stubbornly.

The father was disgusted. 'How did Ironwood Mauhau get the skull that hangs at his girdle?' he asked. Did this blind boy think that Ironwoods with thrusters and clubs or Braves with slings and spears could have been driven from Haavao by a single blower? 'The blower did not kill me!' Pakoko boasted. 'Women and woodstrikers with stone adzes, they alone were struck.' He turned to the others. 'Chiefs and Masters,' he cried, 'this is not a question just of clubs or blowers. Here is war between the orderly ways of the grandfathers and the wild ways of the outsiders. If we do not stand up and fight for our own, our own will desert us. We will wither on a dry land. Join with me! Give me Brave Faces to lead against the rat that is gnawing our roots!'

The old Chief woke with a roar. 'Give Pakoko his desire!' He

179

pounded the mat with every word. 'Give him Brave Faces—one two-hundred, two two-hundreds, three two-hundreds . . .' His tongue slept, his head fell forward, his breath wheezed through his open mouth.

'Good!' cried his son-in-law. 'I want five two-hundreds.'

A deep silence swallowed the echo of his words as the men facing the open front of the long house lifted their eyes to the new-comer who stood there. It was the Hapaa Diviner, Priest Tini. As the son and grandson of Chief Tea-roru's brother made a place for their relative between them, Pakoko knew that the three would be a great stone blocking his path. The two older men were brothers of the big-eater nicknamed Whale, whom Chiefess Kena had adopted. The younger was the promised mate of Kiato-nui's daughter. Naturally they were against this war, but only the Priest could stop it.

But Priest Tini's easy-running tongue spoke not of his own desires, nor of the desires of his gods. He said, 'Pakoko's messenger, Oehitu, is on the path.'

Pakoko knew before Oehitu opened his mouth that his tongue was mouldy with bad news. Was it because he began to babble like running water dashing aimlessly against stones? 'Kiato-nui has given his youngest sister to Hard To Cook . . . That filthy taboo-breaker gives her pig to eat and dips his hand into the same bowl with her . . . Kiato-nui's nephew is nothing but a man-at-the-side to the outsider, carrying his blower for him in the day, sleeping beside it in the night . . . Whale has made all the folk of Haavao angry because he has given the storage holes his name and he alone has paste to eat in this time of land-dryness.' Would this stream of talk never dry up? Pakoko dammed it with a loud question, 'When do we go over the mountains to attack?'

The messenger whispered his reply with a dry tongue. 'Chiefess Kena has given a name to the path over the mountains. It is called, "Kena's vulva".'

The breath was knocked out of every man there except the Priest. Tini said firmly, 'Then the talk of war is ended.'

Pakoko's pulse was pounding, his head tight. Was it at this Priest's suggestion that Kena had polluted the path and closed it to the feet of men tabooed for war? Pakoko searched for a way to go around this stone. He found it and cried out, 'The way by sea is not forbidden! We will attack by canoes!' Slyly he pinched Chief Tea-roru as he spoke.

'Yes, attack by sea!' echoed the old man, jerking upright, awake for a space. 'You will burn down three tens of *temanu* trees and summon two hundred woodstrikers to make war canoes.'

'It is for Chief Hiatai to say,' insisted the son of the old Chief's brother, watching Tea-roru fall asleep again.

' Hiatai!' Pakoko commanded with a loud tongue.

'Whatever you desire,' answered the young Chief wearily.

Now Pakoko was like a young man full of sap as he hovered over the building of his war canoes. He watched the sky-piercing *temanu* tree bend her lofty head when the master had asked the god's permission to make her fall. He dug his adze deep into the prostrate trunk. Strike! Strike down the outsider whose roots were in distant lands!

This was a slow-going work in drought. Pakoko kept the Brave Faces running about through the upper valley to find food for the woodstrikers, some with digging sticks scratching for wild yams and other roots, some with axes to cut trunks of tree ferns, some with baskets for new leaves and curled fern shoots, some with sharp bamboos to cut sugar cane and sprouts of convolvulus vines. He turned Ironwood Mauhau's restless wandering towards a search for the droppings of birds and made him lie in wait with his sling for their return to their perch. He sent the Master Fisherman to stretch heavy, red nets to catch sharks by their fins if they swam past the headland in the night. The determined Chief himself stood with upraised club to beat off thieves while the scant handfuls of poor food were being wrapped like precious things in packages for the workers. When he set up Chief Hiatai's taboo signs over the big breadfruit storage holes, keeping only one open for use, naming only one man to gouge out the hard, soil-reddened paste, he heard the Hapaas who were not at work for him growling.

One day Pakoko woke to silence instead of the rhythmic beating of stone on wood and heard the Master Canoe Builder's fearful complaint. 'The other masters are angry. They say that you seize their food to pay for your war canoes. They say that they may have to eat those who are swollen with their food.'

Pakoko was a shark's skin, springing back and sounding loudly when beaten. The Hapaas were stupid. It was for them, too, this going of his war canoes against Taiohae, this destroying of the outsider. For them also would come the opening of the skies, the drinking of the land and the fruiting of the trees. But since they could not see beyond their flat stomachs, very well, he would puff them up. To the masters of every kind of work he sent an invitation to dwell in Chief Hiatai's men's house, saying, 'All who work for the Chief will be fed.' Then to all folk in the valley, he sent this word, 'Everyone who asks may have the work of a master free.'

Thus the Teii caught every Hapaa on his glittering hook. Those who had feathers, bones, shells, fibres, brought them to the men's house and waited contentedly while their beautiful ornaments grew under skilled hands. The yellow robed youngsters ran about like ants, scraping the rocks by the sea, stripping bushes of leaves, digging up roots to feed the masters and themselves while they took turns having images struck on their skins. Every day there was an image showing festival; every night, dancing, drumming, sweet name-calling on flutes. The valley was given over to feasting without food, well, very little food. Pakoko was watching the slow ebbing of the breadfruit paste in the storage holes, pushing ahead the work of his war canoes in a race with the falling tide; but when Tea-roru's brother's son complained, 'You are crazy to empty the paste holes with all this feasting,' he answered with a laugh, 'Seeing men with white hands, the gods will open their own.'

When the shell of the first canoe was hollowed and smoothed, Pakoko thought no more of stomachs, flat or heavy. At the fall of that sun, he climbed inside his precious hull and lay all through the white-starred black night pouring his strength and virility into his swift bird of prey. Hearing the murmur of first light, he stood up, empty, and warmed his back in the spreading radiance. Listening to Master Sea's whispering, 'Go! Go! Go!' he woke his workers with his laughter. While a procession of carvers brought their parts, beak, tail, side-boards, out-rigger, seats, bailers, paddles, each with its potent name, and the master's helpers fitted and lashed them into place, Pakoko made a song and a dance of the going of his war canoe.

> My canoe, my canoe is coming to land,
> Borne on the racing sea.
> Its beak pierces Taiohae,
> Its tail brushes the opening skies.

Even while his song of work accomplished rose into serene space, Hiatai's conch began to wail far up valley. Now here, now there, tremulos of weeping gushed up. A freshet of sorrow was spreading, running down over the land towards the sea, smothering the joy on the sand, drowning one sea in another. 'Dead! Dead! Chief Tea-roru is dead!' This was the song of death that flowed over the song of war and covered it altogether.

While the woodstrikers went about cutting apart the pieces of the war canoe to hang up in the owners' houses during the taboo moons of death feasts, they marveled at the strong *kaoha* of this Teii for his father-in-law. Seeing Pakoko clinging to his canoe, beating his head against its edges until it bled, hearing his cries of anguish, 'Oh Chief, powerful and good, go quickly in your canoe to Havaiki!' they whispered to one another, 'Chief Pakoko is not even stingy with his grief.'

Go quickly? Pakoko could not hasten the orderly coming and going of stars and moons and their appropriate feast of 'broken breathing,' of 'bathing the body,' of 'tears,' of 'spirit standing up,' of 'going far without stopping,' of 'diving to the land below,' of 'wrapping the bones in the mat,' of 'dancing with uplifted hands.' Go quickly? Pakoko could not throw a branch in Metani's path when she told him she had seen her father's retching spirit holding out bony hands for food, when she commanded all storage holes to be emptied and all remaining pigs killed for feasts and more feasts. He could not refuse to swing his fan with the drums that beat like rain nor to pour his sap into innumerable mothers while the old men chanted, 'Tea-roru, watch our play! Send breadfruit buds and little fish!' He could not even protest the tying of the knot with Chief Kiato-nui when Tea-roru's brother's son sent for the daughter betrothed to his son, so that the dead Chief might know that all loose ends had been fastened. Go quickly? Where could Pakoko go but through the accustomed work and then creep down to the sand and crawl into the hollow back of his waiting canoe for open-eyed sleep? Go quickly? Who? Where? Was it Tea-roru going to join his grandfathers, satisfied with the sweet *kaohas* of his grieving relatives, eager to send in exchange new life to the dead soil of Hakapaa? Or was it Pakoko going with a sea of consecrated canoes to Taiohae to cleanse the land so that it might sprout again? Who was going quickly? Who knew in this thick fog?

It was while the driven Chief of Haavao sat one day in his canoe shell, staring out to sea where he distinctly saw his dear lost land, that a canoe came around the headland and stepped quickly over the water of the bay on its many legs. Pakoko leapt up, wakened from his dream. What bad thing was this? A woman sat in that canoe, sat upon the sea path from Taiohae! Before he could see her face, he knew that it was Chief Kiato-nui's daughter coming to join her betrothed. He screamed at her, 'The Chiefess Kena sent you by sea!'

The young woman trembled, seeing this man with flaming eyes, who stamped about making the water splash over her fine *tapas*, but she stuck out her chin and questioned impudently, 'Why not? The outsiders say that women can ride in canoes.'

The outsiders were without knowledge, but Chiefess Kena knew well enough that this woman had defiled the water path for those tabooed for war. She knew she had made driftwood of Pakoko's war canoes for as long as Kiato-nui's daughter lived in Hakapaa. Again that woman had overturned Pakoko! But again he rebounded like a pounded shark's skin. 'No taboos on land or sea can hold me back from driving the outsiders from Taiohae!' he cried. What though he could not see another path? He would make one!

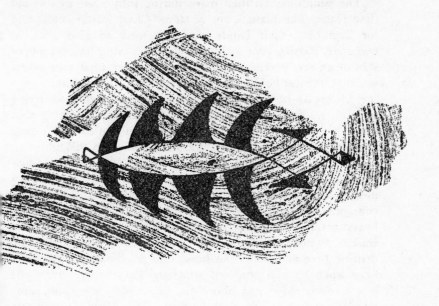

7

RED Soil herself was dragging the landsmen down to one death with her, making of Pakoko's boast aimless prattle. Again and again and again the sun stood up, splashed the land with a burning flood and fell into the sea. The moon climbed the sky and slid into the black. Only the stars were different. Thus a man watching could say, 'Ten and three moons have been drowned', because the stars marching with them had come and gone. Cross, Little Eyes, Banyan Bird, Sparkling, Pig, Big Litter, Hook, Tail, Three Together, Two Males, Four Little Fish, these stars appeared and vanished. How many times? Those who tied a knot in a string for every moon wearied of it. Some said three, some said four, some said six thirteens of moons crossed the dry skies. No one could say truly, for no breadfruit pickings marked any of them. The juices of the land dried up, the juices of men the same.

The people lay on their mats, staring with white eyes at old time feasts. The masters ate whatever Chief Hiatai could find for them, but their hands were too weak to give work in exchange. Pakoko kept to his taboo house, lying like the empty skin of an eel. Waking, he tried to remember what reproach it was that he must hold until the morrow, but he could not. Sleeping, his breath body wandered among mountains of food, trying to recall words of power that would fill his empty picking nets, but in vain. Whenever he slid down the pole to the hot stones, he found his woman, Metani, waiting for him, to shake him, to make him hear her words, 'Your desire is to drive the outsider from the land.' That put force into him and he stumbled to his men's house, calling hoarsely to his Brave Faces, 'Forward, courage!' But their answers were many and true. 'My spear is heavy, my arm weak . . . Only full stomachs can fight . . . Sleepwalkers do not know the path . . .' Alas, even Ironwood Mauhau, drifting here and there like wood dragged by water, shook his head when Pakoko proposed attacking Taiohae by way of the low western ridge just above the sea cliffs. 'We could only trickle over one by one, drop by drop, while Hard To Cook sat on Kiato-nui's terrace and blew stones through us.' It always ended by Pakoko's sitting down to talk this over, then just sitting to watch the patterns on the house posts flashing in the sun until they turned to shining fish jumping from a sparkling sea into a new net.

One day the hungry Chief found himself chewing and sucking warm, juicy flesh. Mauhau was feeding him from a covered bowl. The sight woke him. This was the kind of bowl in which one kept the flesh of a man killed in revenge! He lifted the cover and could not tear his eyes away.

'Well, why not?' his cousin demanded. 'Kena's spies have no right to wander in this valley.'

Pakoko drew down his brows and started to push the bowl away, when he saw the red eyes of his Brave Faces staring at it. He said to Mauhau, 'Spread leaves for them.' Before they dipped their hands into the bowl, he chanted solemnly, 'This is to give you strength to go against Chiefess Kena.' Then he slapped the cover onto the empty bowl and said, 'Not another!'

But the men began to whisper together and to bring out coils of coconut fibre cord. The Chief saw that they were cutting off lengths, making slip knots. In dread he demanded, 'For what fish do you make those nooses?'

Not looking at him, Mauhau answered, 'Old women are ended anyway.'

'Who is old, who is young?' Pakoko asked. 'Some might say that we are old. No, make an end of this bad beginning.' He was ashamed that he had slept when he should have been hovering over the land, coaxing the trees for true food. He asked his woman for her father's staff and fan, and with these sacred signs of power he went through the valley shouting orders. 'Follow the stars! They still stand up and lie down. They still point out true work. Men working truly, the gods will also.' Because Sparkling and Pig were in the sky and he knew without doubt that this was breadfruit growing moon, he covered land and sea with taboo. People laughed at him but he was firm. When the constellation Banyan Bird came over the sky's foundation, he asked them, 'Isn't this the harvest moon? Why aren't you shouldering your picking nets?' When they called him crazy, he drove them with his staff to get their nets.

Now the gods made a strange answer. Chief Tohi-kai came from Taipivai in a canoe filled with breadfruit paste. 'It is from the big hole you dug for me,' he said, after he had rubbed noses with his old friend and namesake.

Just to see this bleary old man made Pakoko feel young and active. And when Tohi-kai settled down in his friend's house to enjoy a feast of the breadfruit he had brought, he felt the sting of an old disappointment and had to look down at his wrist to make sure that he wore no fibre band that bound him to an improvident chief in an enemy valley. He was free, he laughed, he held nothing back from his friend.

Perhaps the gods were pleased at Pakoko's open hands, for they also made a feast for the Taipi Chief and for all the people of Hakapaa, such a feast of fish as men would sing of from father to son.

Watchers, whom the Chief had placed on rocky headlands to look for sea birds following fish, ran all out of breath, gasping, 'Porpoises!' Every man who could pull himself into a canoe and lift a paddle strained and puffed to head off the big fish that were jumping across the entrance to the bay and turn them into their family waters. The exhausted Hapaas leaned over the side boards, clapping stones, pursuing the porpoises with a shocking clamor, driving them towards the shore. The bay was asprout with black fins and tails as the frenzied creatures climbed one another in haste to beat their noses to bloody pulp upon the sharp rocks or to fling their heavy bodies upon the bright dry sands.

The crescent of the land swarmed with valley folk waiting with sharp bamboos to cut those fat juicy fish into pieces and pile them mountain high all along the curve from headland to headland. No shares were called. There was enough for all, again and again. Pakoko built a house of coconut leaves down by the beach, so that he and his family and his friend could sleep there and eat with their desire. When the hot sun had rotted the torn and trampled flesh, they washed off the maggots in clean sea water and went on eating, eating.

The Taipi Chief, Tohi-kai, could not eat enough. He could not make his stomach feel heavy nor fill his hanging skin. He waded farther and farther out, looking for fat fish. Far out, on a point of rocks, the coming and going sea was rolling a big unbroken fish in, out, in, out. That was his fish, for him alone, yes. He crawled over the rocks. He was a frigate bird, eating a little here, vomiting, going to another place, eating, vomiting. He flew alone, this bird. He was laughing to himself. A vomit bird, that's what he was! He reached the sharp rocks where the big fish was licked by the coming and going sea. He fell into the hole in the rocks that held him fast. He tore at the hard skin of the porpoise but his hands were feeble. He was like a little fish picking at a shark. He threw his arms about the black body to drag it out of the pool, but he slipped and slid under the heavy thing. He tried to pull himself up by the slippery skin. He tried to call, but the sea rushed into his mouth, filling him at last until he was tight and heavy. He lay in the hole, arms about the dead fish, rolling forward, rolling back.

Alas, when Pakoko carried his friends's body to Taipivai, he found that Tohi-kai had emptied every storage hole in his valley. There was nothing for a feast for the dead chief's spirit, but Pakoko wept for his friend and tied a handsome whale's tooth about the image in his death canoe.

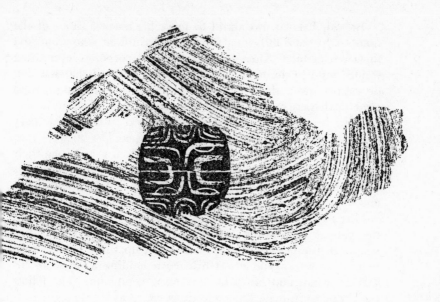

8

PAKOKO made his cousin, Oehitu, his messenger, because he could go freely back and forth between Hakapaa and his woman's house in Taiohae. One day he called his runner to his taboo house and gave him instructions. 'Here are image striking tools,' he indicated a small bundle. 'You will follow the outsider, Hard To Cook, wherever he goes. Tell him you will strike images into his skin. Make him tremble at your shadow. Make him run away on a ship.' The Chief had determined upon this work when Oehitu told him that the outsider was dying of hunger but would not eat in Kiato-nui's house because all those inside were being tattooed. Perhaps such a trembling liver could be driven away with the bone teeth of these strikers. Pakoko knew that Oehitu's work might be long, for Hard To Cook was stubborn. Still, the Chief dared not leave his own terraces to finish the outsider with one swift blow of his club. He sent his cousin away with little hope.

Indeed, Pakoko was afraid to leave his houses, afraid of the nooses that were following women and children who wandered in search of food. After the great feast of porpoises, everything seemed sand in the mouth. Many pushed away all that was dug or scraped from the soil. Some could not chew roots because their teeth were falling out. Others, sickened by their own bad-smelling breath, thought that everything was rotten. Big hungry eyes followed everything that moved, old people who went into the bush and squatted for a long time, children who missed their paths as their thin legs carried them aside to rest, with big heads fallen on their pointed breasts. Pakoko walked back and forth and kept the count of his family.

One night he was wakened by the sound of breaking thatch, the pat-pat of running feet, and the whimpering of the old people in the next house. His hair stood up when he slid open their door screen and saw Uncle Fatu holding a noose in his shaking hands and heard his quavering complaint, 'The fellow was trying to strangle Ehua and carry her away.'

After that, Mother Ehua was always trembling, always looking behind to see if a shadow were moving, always thinking of her own food-filled valley of Haavao where no one wanted to seize her to eat. She kept spreading her nostrils to smell its fragrant air. She was drawn towards that place of refuge, foot after foot, a little nearer, a little nearer. One day, when she had escaped Pakoko's watchful eyes, she felt a hand pinching her. In terror, she began to run, stirring up the red dust as she climbed to the high level, swishing through the dry grass of the Valley of Tears, making the little stones roll down into her own valley of Haavao. Yes, here it was, her good land! Now she was safe. She trailed her little feet through the murmuring leaves. She sang with the small black birds, '*Tito-kiri! Tito-kiri! Tito-kiri!*' Singing and dancing, she did not hear the whirr of a flung noose.

Suffocating, tearing at the band tightening about her neck, she was about to faint when the shrill whistle of a god woke her to new terror. 'This fish is for the gods!' she heard before she went into the black.

But Ehua had not been seized for a feast in the skies. When the cord about her neck was loosened and her eyes groped through a lifting fog, she saw the face of her nephew, Priest

Kohu, and heard the *kaoha* in his voice. 'I have driven the fellow away,' he said gently.

'Will the gods eat me?' she asked, still dry-tongued.

'They will keep you safe on the sacred place,' he promised her, lifting her as if she were a child.

Priest Kohu had no sooner hidden his aunt in his own sleeping house and climbed to his high perch to tell the gods why the woman was there, than he heard a *kaako* bird calling her name. Shivering, he slid quickly down an upright and ran to her mat. Yes, the bird had spoken truly. The spirit had gone out of her mouth as gently as a butterfly leaves its sack.

Pakoko was content when he knew that his mother's bones were safe on the sacred place of her beloved land, but Uncle Fatu was uneasy because no feasts were being given for his sister's spirit. He stole the Master Fisherman's spear and went on trembling legs to look for an offering in the sea. Day after day he groped about in shallow water. At least something moved. He struck. Yes, his spear was quivering. He raised the points cautiously. Was he seeing a true thing, a red fish? Saliva began to drip from his hanging lips. His eyes darted from side to side. No one was near. He stooped until the water wet his chin. Then, covering his face with his bent arm, he pretended to look deep into the sea, but he was eating that sacred red fish, taboo to priests and chiefs, eating quickly, swallowing without chewing, sucking in sea water with the juicy flesh.

As Fatu returned to the land, his eyes were whirling. What was that flashing across the water? A god? With a tail of fire! He fell on his hand and knees and crawled over the beach boulders. His teeth knocked together. His breathing came in windy gusts. Thinking he saw Priest Tini walking towards him, he lay still and buried his face in the sand. Could those piercing eyes see the red fish in his stomach? When the god had passed, the guilty man tried to run away, but his shaking bones would not stand up. He crawled into the bush, tearing the dry skin of palms and knees on thorns. Did his breath smell of fish? Indeed, his whole body was smeared with fish. Anyone could smell him! He tore off his *tapas* and rolled in the dust but he could not rub out that smell. Was the Priest sniffing the fish-polluted air, pressing close upon him? Where was that Chief who would tell the

Priest that Fatu was not a taboo breaker? What was his name? Fatu tried to call his foster son, but he could not remember his name. He could only say through white foam that dripped from his open mouth, '*Vovovovovovovo.*' Where was his house? He could not find the path. He stumbled from place to place, hiding under leaves when he heard a step, rolling, rolling in the dirt to rub away the smell of fish. He did not know burning light from cold dark. He was always shivering, always hungry, yet always eating. Many fish he ate, one caught in a breadfruit grove, another digging roots on the high level of the land, another asleep on a deserted terrace. None of them were red. He left the red fish for the Priest.

People said that a wild woman was running about in the valley, devouring all who strayed from the paths. Pakoko and his cousin Mauhau, knowing that Uncle Fatu had vanished, feared that he had been seized. They went looking for him and found him in a cave, dead, yes, but not eaten. It was he who had been feasting! Quickly, the two cousins dug a deep hole and laid the old man and the remains of his victim inside it.

When Chief Pakoko received another visit from his cousin, Oehitu, he scarcely listened to his news from Taiohae. He was moving his household down from Metani's terraces to dwell in their son's sleeping house. All the high level folk were swarming onto Chief Hiatai's stones, gathering like sweet-water flies on a hollow tree. They had planted taboo sticks at the corners of his walls to remind common water not to set foot on land sacred to the Chief. The Brave Faces were taking turns sitting in front of the houses through the dark, keeping torches burning, listening for feet walking softly or hands picking at thatch. Pakoko nodded as Oehitu talked to him, walking beside him on the path to Hiatai's house, but his ears were filled with wax.

Metani touched him. 'A new ship came to Taiohae,' she said, 'but Hard To Cook would not go away.' Pakoko's eyes came slowly back from painful dreams and questioned her. 'The outsider,' she answered.

'You have driven the outsider away?' Pakoko asked sharply, seeing Oehitu clearly now.

'He would not leave his woman and his new child.' Oehitu

could only add another bad thing. 'When his food was ended, he dragged himself into Kiato-nui's men's house and gave consent to the tattooing—but only one design on his breast. He is still naked and indecent.'

'Yes,' the weary Chief said, as if he had breath for no more.

The Chiefess said, 'Pakoko cannot lead Brave Faces against him just now. Chief Hiatai's woman has her first child in her stomach. When the little one has come out and been nourished, then he will talk of war.'

'Yes,' sighed Pakoko, pushing his heavy feet through the hot dust.

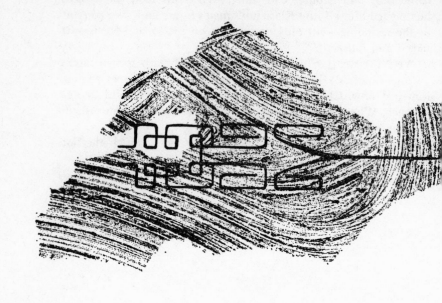

9

PAKOKO was not given the work of nourishing his pregnant daughter-in-law and his unborn grandchild. It was to Hiatai that the little Chiefess turned, tearful and trembling whenever she saw babies with bloated stomachs or heard their thin cries. As she drooped, Hiatai stood up, his hands quick to fetch her desires, his tongue loud to give her orders. When he had built the birth house for her, he would not let his father sit before it in the night. He himself walked back and forth. When his woman's pains started, he would not let his mother enter the taboo house. 'I know the way of helping my woman,' he said. Indeed, things were upside down, with Pakoko lying on his mat and Hiatai working for the gods.

When the grandfather was told to blow his shell and let the valley folk know that his grandchild was a boy, Pakoko forgot all his weariness and feeling of uselessness. He went from house to house, begging food to strengthen the child. But Chief Hiatai made little of his father's work. He had brought no hot ripe breadfruit to the new mother. How then could her breast water come? He had offered no mashed shrimps to the little Chief. Naturally, the child's juices did not flow. Pakoko was a feeble old man, good for nothing. Chief Hiatai must turn to another. Priest Tini was a man of power. He could call for a fish for the gods. He could put a stop to the trembling of the little fellow and the shrinking of his hot dry skin.

Yes, true. But after Priest Tini had promised the gods a feast, his Clubs could find no fish for them. Not even in bright sun or moon would people leave their houses in those hungry days. They clung to their own terraces in clusters, like shell fish to rocks, and could not be pried loose. Watching, Pakoko knew that Priest Tini had no power, but that he himself could bring the gods the only flesh that would persuade them to keep breath in the sickly child. Not even to Metani did he speak of his intention. While she slept he slipped his hand through the loop of his club handle and started through the morning's shades to bring the outsider, Hard To Cook, back for the gods.

It was blinding white day when he crawled onto the western ridge and crept among the hot rocks from shade to shade, hiding from the sun above and spying eyes below. When he was on the down going path, he lay flat for a space, watering with his tears the uncovered bones of his dear land of Taiohae. Stumbling then from trunk to trunk of dry-leaved breadfruit trees, he wept over their barrenness. Horrified at his grandson's pitiful weakness, he had started to Taiohae as a Priest's Club seeking an offering, forgetting anger over the death of the land. Now he was an Ironwood with contorted face, seeking revenge. He stood up boldly and shouted with all his breath, 'Blood! Blood!' He stamped down the path, looking for no cover, and followed the open shore as it curved from Hakapehi to Meau. He felt the eyes of fishermen following him, but no tongue was raised against him, no feet ran after him.

When he climbed onto Chief Kiato-nui's terrace and stood with his back to the sun, looking into the shade of the men's house, he saw all the eyes stretched wide, all the hands standing still between food bowls and open mouths. Was his anger terrifying? He did not know that his face was like a dried skull with glittering shell eyes. Anger still burned him but his anger turned against his own knees because they began to tremble, against his own tongue because it cried out, 'Little Brother, make a place for me at your feast!' He could not wait for Kiato-nui's short fat finger to point to the mat beside him but sank down, weakened by the smell of food. Laying his club across his knees, he turned to the Chief beside him and lost his breath suddenly. There was the upturned moon face, the eyes gushing *kaoha*.

'Your bones are sharp,' moaned Kiato-nui.

'Your skin is dry,' Pakoko grieved, clinging to that face ravaged with *kava*-drinking and hunger.

The two brothers nosed one another, sucking in the good smell. All the relatives crowded around them, touching the visitor, crying over him, until Chief Kiato-nui waved them away. 'Let him eat,' he said, 'he is sick with sand.'

Pakoko reached with the others towards a canoe of dark rancid breadfruit paste. He had known, without looking, that the pale eyes and fair skin of the outsider glimmered in the gloom of the thatch, and now he saw a white hand reaching towards the food. He had almost forgotten why he had come here. Now he was full of light! He knew his path. He moved his own hand towards the canoe, dipped it into the paste as the white hand dipped, raised the food to his mouth as the white hand was raised. When the food was in their mouths, Pakoko began to strangle. He rushed to the house from and spat out his mouthful beyond the stones. 'Fifth!' he sputtered. 'We have been defiled. A naked hand has dipped into a food bowl with hands that are covered with images!'

Every man there, save Chief Kiato-nui and the stranger, jumped to his feet, but not one raised an arm against Pakoko when he hung over the outsider with his club. Indeed, they bared their teeth at the fellow who sat with unchewed paste dripping from his white lips.

Kiato-nui said through his mouthful of paste, 'The taboo is not for outsiders.'

'Why not?' demanded Pakoko. 'Landsmen must obey the taboos or die. It is my right to kill this man to protect myself.' Having said this with a loud tongue, he gripped his club and waited as a wood striker waits for the tree to fall when he has struck the last blow.

Yes, the tree was coming down with a tremendous noise of cracking and splintering. Pakoko could feel the consent of masters and relatives. They were not listening to Kiato-nui's words beaten out. 'He is my man! He is taboo!' They were tired of this man's being inside and outside the taboos all at the same time. They were tired of his eating their food and making no return. Kiato-nui's nephew, who had made himself a man-at-the-side to Hard To Cook, wondered why he had bowed down to a nobody. 'Without powder and fire-stones for your blower, you are a trembling coward!' he taunted him. The Master Image Striker brushed his fingers contemptuously across the single pattern on the fellow's breast. 'You are nothing but a naked fisherman begging food from a chief's scraps,' he scoffed. The hungry men began to call for flesh. 'Rats are good to eat. Let us eat the rat that eats our food!' The Fire Keeper began to name their shares. 'The thigh is for Ironwood Motu. One shoulder is for Ironwood Muina. The heart and the palms are for the Master Chanter.'

The outsider's begging eyes clung to Kiato-nui's face. The Chief put his arms around his friend and wept. Pakoko raised his club.

Suddenly a shrill, trembling cry came from the roof of the house. The voice of a god wailed, 'This flesh is for me!'

Pakoko could not strike with that chilling sound in his ears, but he looked about for a trickster. Ah. It was through the quivering throat of his nephew, Taa, that the cry had come. Taa had always looked at his uncle with bad eyes. He had always blamed him for not taking him into his household. Did the jealous youth think he could come between his uncle and his just vengeance? Pakoko swung towards him to accuse him, but the Master Chanter caught his arm.

'Taa is now Priest of Meau,' he warned him. 'When old Hoho died, the god chose this son of Priest Kohu.'

Pakoko leaned on his fallen club, as his force drained out of him. He could scarcely lift his hand to wipe away the sweat that poured into his eyes. Or was it a fog that made it impossible for him to see where he was going? He knew that Taa was leading the outsider away and that Kiato-nui was following, weeping stormily, but he saw and heard everything as if it were a dream. He wanted to run away from the praises of all these men who thought that the god would feast now and be satisfied and send a return gift of fruits to men. The thought pecking at Pakoko's liver was a different one. Taa would never hang this man up on the god's hook. He would merely give him a place of refuge. The offering that had been within Pakoko's grasp had been snatched from him. Twice-defeated, he must return to Hakapaa, not running to get away from the shame quickly, but dragging his feet in exhaustion, tormented every step of the way by fear that the outsiders had caught the spirit of this dear land in an unbreakable net.

When he reached Hiatai's terrace and saw the small body of his grandson lying stiff and cold on a sunning board, he nodded his head, as if he had seen this bad thing also in his dream.

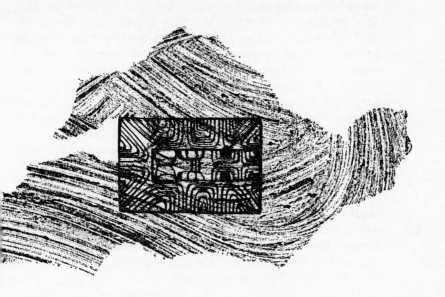

10

CHIEFESS Metani would not let Pakoko sit on his heels looking with white eyes at processions of outsiders. She pulled him along with her to hunt for food. One day they would go down by the sea, the woman holding a gourd of sea water, the man swimming for seaweed to drop into it or diving for shell fish that clung to drowned rocks or luring an octopus from its hole. Another day they would walk the dry rocks of watercourses, looking for eels asleep in stagnant pools, for over-hanging leaves to soak and braise. Another day they would go to the high level to dig roots or climb for *ihi* nuts. They were always together, without speaking, without touching, just breathing together. They were like the lashes of a closed eye.

They were going about without force or feeling, from root to root, from leaf to leaf, when runners came from several paths looking for Pakoko. They were all men from Taiohae who were taboo in the valley of the Hapaas. They were breathless but they were laughing. They were all calling out the same word, but, like little winds coming from all sides at once, they made no headway. Metani caught a word here, Pakoko a word there, and when they could put them together, they also began to laugh. They laughed and laughed. They could not stop laughing. The sea of joy picked them up and carried them down to Hiatai's terraces. Weak with laughing, they repeated the new word to all the Hapaas gathered there. 'The outsider has gone away on a ship! He has taken his woman and two children with him!'

Had the dwellers in these houses forgotten how to laugh? Chief Hiatai turned his eyes towards his mother and father, but they were empty as sleeping water staring at cloudless sky. His small woman, a drooping leaf swaying sadly, saw nothing but her empty arms. His serving people merely held out their hands for Metani's basket of roots. Pakoko threw the basket away in contempt. 'That is nothing but pig's food now!' he cried. 'Now we shall have rain! Now we shall feast!'

As Metani went about picking up the scattered roots, Pakoko ran to the cook house to talk to the Fire Keeper about digging ovens for feasts to come. Half-way across the stones he met his cousin, Oehitu. Good. Here was the messenger with the whole story. He searched the man's white, twitching face and felt claws grab his intestines. The new word was not good, but very, very bad.

Oehitu could scarcely speak. 'The Chiefess Kena.' he gasped. 'She is angry. She says, "Pakoko had driven Kiato-nui's outsider away." ' Seeing the Chief grin, he lifted a heavy hand. 'No, no! You will not laugh. Kena says her father's spirit has come back and is clinging to her like a lover, begging for food, promising to work for her.' The messenger struggled for breath and covered his eyes as Pakoko's sharpened. 'Kena has commanded her bad spirit to go . . . to go inside . . .'

'Yes?' demanded the Chief, pinching his arm as if to squeeze out the dreaded sounds.

'Inside the Chiefess Metani!' Oehitu sobbed.

Metani! Pakoko rushed to his woman, lifted her up, scattering once again the roots in her basket, and carried her inside the sleeping house. He made her drop her *tapas* and stand before him while he examined her flesh, bit by bit. What was that red spot behind her ear? Had the bad spirit bitten her and entered there? He ran his hands over her stomach. Was it swelling? Was the spirit inside, pretending to be a growing child? While he handled her, he wailed, 'Metani! Metani! My pearl shell!'

Wide-eyed, open-mouthed, Metani quivered under her half's trembling fingers. When he commanded it, she tried to drink a potion he mixed for her but she could scarcely swallow with her stiffening throat. Her limbs would no longer hold her up and she slid through his hands and lay like seaweed at his feet.

The women of Metani's household ran away to hide, lest that bad spirit leave the Chiefess for another. Chief Hiatai built a hasty coconut leaf shelter and moved his own woman inside it. Only Pakoko and his cousins, Mauhau and Oehitu, remained in the big sleeping house where the tortured woman stared into the air. Together they fought the dead man's spirit sent by Chiefess Kena and tended the stricken woman. When Pakoko was sure that Metani's stomach was swelling, he sent Mauhau for a Master of Healing to give her a bitter drink of pounded barks and to beat her head with *noni* leaves. 'Out! Out, evil spirit!' the Master commanded, and when bad tastes and smells were of no avail, he stuffed Metani's ears and nose with chewed leaves to stifle the wicked intruder. 'Who are you?' he demanded again and again.

Finally, a thin cry whistled through Metani's drawn lips. 'I am the father of Kena. I am sent by Kena.'

There it was! It was true! Pakoko selected a perfect whale's tooth from his covered box and gave it to Oehitu for Chiefess Kena. 'Ask her to call the spirit back!' he commanded. Returning with nothing but Kena's senseless question, 'What spirit?' Pakoko's messenger was given two whale's teeth to tempt the hostile Chiefess. But again the offer was refused. 'Only fishermen wear whales' teeth now,' said Kena contemptuously. Pakoko looked at his box of precious treasures. Had the outsiders made pig's dung of these also, giving them everywhere for sandal wood? He must give land then. 'Tell her that Chief Hiatai will give her land if she will recall her father's spirit.' But Oehitu brought nothing back but the memory of Kena's wild laughing and her saying, 'I cannot make my father hear. He was always deaf.'

The Master of Healing said, 'Kena has lost control of her spirit. If he asks more than she can give, he will turn against her.'

Pakoko would not bow down to any evil spirit. He commanded the Master of Healing to proceed with a more powerful rite. Walking back and forth to calm his agitated liver, Pakoko watched the master dig a ditch beside the terrace and fill it with firewood and healing leaves. When the flames had grown and branched, he carried his precious woman outside and seated her on sticks crossed over the ditch. He groaned and covered his eyes when the skin began to blister. Weeping, he knelt beside her, begging her to endure until the blood began to flow. But when the red drops splashed and sputtered on the fire and Metani still lay as one dead, he snatched her from the cruel heat, knowing that the spirit had refused to toss her about, seeking escape.

There was no hope now and Pakoko obeyed Metani's begging eyes without comment. Because it would please her to hear the adzes striking wood to make her a fine sky-going canoe, Pakoko sent for a master to do that work but they both knew that she could not ride in it to the land of abundance. Her body must be hidden quickly in the earth where it would not be used to harm other women. She tapped her fingers on the mat with the *ta, ta, ta* of the adzes, and smiled at him and he smiled at her. He sat as near as possible without being contaminated by the blood which flowed without ceasing. Day and night he fanned her, while her breath body sometimes left her as one dead, sometimes opened her eyes to him.

One night he was reaching for a new midrib of nuts before the old light died in sputtering grease, but she held him back, whispering, 'I know you in the dark, Pakoko.'

He knew she was thinking of that sweet night of play when he had climbed the man-eating precipice from Taipivai to see her and had withheld his name. He leaned over her to hear more and felt the breath come out of her mouth, flutter against his lips and fly away.

Pakoko drew back, shivering violently, but he could not get up until Mauhau helped him. 'Quick!' he heard his cousin's command. 'Into the hole!' He obeyed without thought, holding out his arms for the weight put into them. Ah, she was heavy, even with Mauhau to help. Heavy. She did not want to go into that dark hole. Alas! Her cold flesh was clinging to Pakoko's flesh, her soft hair was caressing his breast, as he followed Mauhau through the black night, the heavy weight tying them together. Was it to the sky they were carrying Chiefess Metani? Alas! The stars held them back, hard and sharp as spear points. Only Mother Red Soil opened her arms. Feeling his woman sliding down into the black, Pakoko would have followed her into the hole that Oehitu had dug, but Mauhau jerked him back. He fell in the dry grass and lay as still as the body which the two cousins were covering, as dry as the stones they were heaping upon it.

11

THE death of Chiefess Metani turned everything upside down in Hakapaa. What had been covered over was on top for all to see. Priest Tini went walking about, saying to this house-holder and that, 'It is because of Pakoko, the Teii, that our Chiefess is dead. It was to punish him that Chiefess Kena sent the bad spirit into Metani.' Chief Tea-roru's brother's son talked to the elders. 'By what right does this Teii carry the staff and fan and blow the conch of a Hapaa chief? I am the one who should stand firm behind Chief Paia-roru Hiatai.' And his son, visiting the Brave Faces in the men's house, said, 'Pakoko has always tried to stir up war between me and my father-in-law, Kiato-nui. We must let this death of Metani pass.'

Pakoko was beyond hearing the noise of the wind that was rising against him. But for Mauhau and Oehitu, he would have lain day and night beside the stones that were crushing the flesh and bones of his woman. Again and again, Mauhau led him back to his taboo house. Again and again, Oehitu tried to open his ears to the storm whirling about him. 'The Hapaas say that we are outsiders in their valley, rats stealing their food. Priest Tini says he has seen a land of abundance in distant seas. He says we must go land-seeking.'

A flicker of anger burned in Pakoko's ash-dull eyes. 'Pull up my roots? Wither in a strange place? No!' He turned back to his grief, forgetting anger.

One day Pakoko was roused by a wild, trilling voice outside his house and the murmur of many feet in dry leaves. He peeped through his bamboos and saw the Diviner rushing from side to side, eyes wide and white, mouth filled with foam, arms whirling his powerful ironwood stick. His low-bowing men and his burden-bearers were dancing before and behind him. Hiatai's dwellers, caught in surprise, were cowering with covered eyes. The sight tore away the clouds of confusion from Pakoko's empty eyes. Once again he was a shark's skin stretched over a drum, sounding powerfully when struck. With young, springy muscles he let himself down through the hole in the floor and crossed the stones to the edge of his terrace.

The Priest raised quivering hands and pointed to the tall gaunt man. 'This is the man! I have seen him in my *kava* bowl paddling away to a land of abundance in distant seas.'

The god's cry was a drum that stopped all breathing, but Pakoko's voice was a drum that quickened breath as he began to stir up those who listened. 'Who is this priest who says he has seen abundance in a distant land?' he questioned. 'Priest Tini cannot see abundance in his own valley of Hakapaa. How can he see abundance far away? Priest Tini promises me abundance, but I am a Teii. What does he promise his own Hapaas? Harvests of sand? That is what he has given you. Perhaps Priest Tini has lost his power. Ask him why he cannot bring rain to this thirsty valley.'

'Yes, Priest Tini, answer that!' A voice from behind a wall shouted boldly, giving courage to tongues that had slept a long time. 'Why haven't you cracked open the hard sky? . . . Why haven't you given drink to the land? . . . Why have you let our trees drop their leaves? . . . Why have you let the juices of landsmen dry up?'

Pakoko raised his voice above the tumult and quickened its beat. 'It is the custom to test the power of a priest who fails. It is a good custom.'

'Yes, it is good!' A storm of approval swept the people from the walls and terraces onto the paving where Priest Tini and his men-at-the-side were rushing about, leaping, screaming, wailing, refusing to hear.

'Who will throw a spear at the birds on this priest's sky-piercing house? Who will knock down the signs of a power that is gone?' Pakoko pounded the questions into the bowels of every man there.

'I am your man! . . . My spear is true! . . . I will pierce his empty shells!' Ten, twenty, forty Brave Faces climbed up beside Pakoko, shouting their consent.

Priest Tini uttered a scream that made even Pakoko's drumming die. 'Before this moon goes into the black, I will bring rain!' Like a flock of birds, he and his helpers darted across the paving and flew from level to level of the sacred place beyond.

How quietly, how slowly the pregnant moon swelled! Without going about, almost without breathing, the Hapaas waited for the Priest to show his power. As the fifteenth night was fleeing, the drums began to beat on the sacred place to let people know that a fish had been caught for the gods. Householders went from fire to fire, destroying even the embers, then crept into dark houses and covered their heads. Pakoko put on his long-tailed girdle, took his fan, and joined the procession of chanters walking to the sacred place. While the Diviner's helpers were crossing the terrace, carrying coconut leaf baskets on their shoulders, while they were climbing to the backbone of the land, he sat in the circle singing with the fathers,

> Give us rain!
> Give us breadfruit!

Drums, fans, tongues were pulsing together as Priest Tini's burden-bearers, black against the blood-stained sky of morning, walked along the crests, holding up their empty baskets to be filled.

> Give us rain!
> Here is your man!
> Here is your peace gift!
> Give us breadfruit!

Now the Priest's Clubs carried the offering to the pile of fire wood that blossomed red in the center of that circle of chanted power. As they tied the arms and legs of the victim to four posts, his head fell back. The face was empty-eyed, open mouthed, but Pakoko knew it! It was Priest Kohu of Haavao!

Pakoko's flesh crawled and his hair stood up. Rage against the Hapaa Priest choked him. Lamentation for his brother rose like vomit in his throat, but he could not let it gush out. He could not falter nor drop a word of the spell being sounded for the ears of the gods. Back and forth, back and forth, he made his fan swing. Out, out, out, he forced the words, 'Give us rain! Give us breadfruit!' In his vitals he felt the twisting fibres of pain. It was to punish him that Priest Tini had seized the Teii priest. 'Oh Kohu, I have always brought you harm!' This was his thought while his tongue sang smoothly, 'Here is your man! Here is your peace gift!'

The god's answer came confidently from Priest Tini's mouth. 'I am content. The land-dryness is ended. Rain will moisten the land, fruits will bend the branches, excrement will flow from the people.'

When three suns had stuck their legs through the wooden sky, Mauhau began to polish his spear. Caressing the point, he whispered, 'You will strike the red bird from Priest Tini's house.'

Pakoko shook his head. 'Put away your spear, friend,' he said. 'Priest Tini will not fail. Kohu is such a feast as the gods have never before eaten. They will send rain.'

True. On the twentieth night of the moon, the Hapaas were wakened by a good smell in their nostrils. They ran out onto their terraces, laughing and crying, and held up their faces to the healing rain.

NOTE

In May, 1804, Robarts refused to go away on the *Nadesha* with the Russian navigator, A. J. von Krusenstern, because of the birth of an infant to his wife. It was not until 1806 that he left on the ship, *Lucy*, taking his woman and two children to Tahiti.

V BROKEN CLUBS

1

For thirteen moons the Hapaas were lovers playing with Red Soil, sucking her sweetness, bathing in her moisture, delighting in her fruits. Men stirred up the mud of taro terraces with their digging sticks, letting their children splash without hindrance in the good black slime. Others collected new sprouts and joints of breadfruit, bamboo, hibiscus, mulberry, sugar cane, and planted them in leaf-filled holes, caressing the tender growth with soft fingers. Masters loosened coconut fibres in running water, seasoned blocks of green wood in black mud. Women dragged out their *tapa* logs and beaters, tested old oven stones, replaced their cracked food bowls with new ones. Oh, the good work of men and land, together after long separation!

Naturally, the Hapaas forgot about the long war with drought and famine and the unnatural death of their Chiefess Metani and the seizure of their Chief's lands of Haavao and Pakiu. Even

Chief Hiatai, who had shaved his head save for a single long lock in token of his desire to avenge his mother's death, was beginning to let his hair grow again. He was content with his new child, a little girl who grew fat with good food brought her from every house in the valley. As Pakoko began to look at the sun without fear, perhaps he, too, might have forgotten the evil dream had not his cousin, Oehitu, brought him news from Taiohae that opened old wounds and kindled old embers.

Chiefess Kena was dead! The spirit she had turned against others had turned against her because she had refused to feed him longer. Hearing this, Pakoko's knees felt weak, as if a support had been withdrawn. How long she had kept his fire burning brightly against the things that were wrong in Taiohae! He knew that his son would say, 'Now my mother's death has been balanced by Kena's death and we may forget revenge.' But the father would not let himself sit down and drown in a shallow sea of forgetting. Things were still wrong in Taiohae. Kiato-nui had welcomed new outsiders, given them houses and lands, allowed them to go about the valley encouraging the landsmen to drop their own good works and cut sandal wood for their ships. In Haavao, Kena's adopted son, Whale, had been stoned from the Chief's house because he had stolen fish from children, and Priest Taa was guiding the canoe of that valley from his sky-piercing house. 'The folk of Haavao are afraid to leave their houses,' Oehitu said.

Sitting in his taboo house with Oehitu and Mauhau, Pakoko covered his eyes even from these relatives who breathed with him. He knew they were thinking, 'If Hiatai had the thing that makes a chief, he would seize his valley of Haavao.' He said with too loud a tongue, 'I will not bother my son about this thing. He and his Hapaa relatives have their hands full, making the little new Chiefess strong to take her grandmother's place. There is another way. The Hapaa Brave Faces are beginning to quarrel over women, they are weary of sitting on their heels and filling their stomachs. They are ready for a great new work. But the conch which calls for war must be blown in Taiohae.'

Oehitu shook his head sadly. 'Chief Kiato-nui is content with things as they are.'

'He will not be!' cried Pakoko, bursting suddenly into light and heat. 'He will call for war when you take him this message. Tell him I have said, "The bones of Chiefess Kena are a woman's filthy mat!"' Into this curse, the embittered man breathed the vile odors that had sickened him ever since, as a child, he had felt Kena's evil power. Having said this horrible thing, he knew that Kena had not escaped him by dying, that he could still raise his arm against her. Having said it, he knew that his breath had been cleansed and sweetened, so that he might whisper into his woman's flower-like ear, 'Metani, I have not forgotten!'

Mauhau thought, 'Pakoko saw things to come as truly as a Diviner.' He was going from house to house where the Brave Faces of Hakapaa were gathered, grinding fine the edges of their paddle-headed slicers, sharpening the points of their thorn-edged spears. He was carrying Pakoko's call for the fighters to assemble for the ceremonies before battle. He was counting the men summoned by the chiefs who had given consent to Chief Kiato-nui's demand for war. Eight two-hundreds with slings, six two-hundreds with spears, two two-hundreds with clubs, all were burning to revenge the death of their Chiefess Metani and to seize again their Chief's lands. They were singing while they fashioned their weapons.

> Stand up, fight!
> Fight with the sacred sling!
> Fight with Huuti's burning points!
> Fight with the ironwood head of Tu!
> Stand up in fury, fight!

At the great fall of the sun, when Pakoko welcomed these thousands down on the flushed sands beside the blood-red sea, he was like a sleeper who wakes and finds his dream true. He knew every step before he took it: the plunge with these consecrated men into the cleansing salt water; the solemn march up to the sacred place where every man thrust his new peeled hibiscus stick into Priest Tini's thatch and received his assurance of victory over the Teiis, who had stoned a Hapaa Chief from his valley and demanded war from peace-loving Chief Paia-roru Hiatai; the breathless climb in the dusk to the Hapaa strong-place beside the Valley of Tears; the feast before battle when strong men consumed the flesh and bones of pigs and left not one bite upon their leaves to betray them.

When they had eaten half the night away, Pakoko stood up, his eyes flashing such lightning that those desiring sleep sat up to hear. His piercing tongue jabbed them to fury, until the very air trembled and groaned and wailed over the wounds of old wrongs. He made them see again the seizure of Chief Hiatai's valleys of Haavao and Pakiu by Hard To Cook and Kiato-nui's treacherous Braves. He led their agony of grief over Chiefess Metani's death into screams for revenge.

'Our anger must be satisfied!' roared the Braves in unison.

'There is more!' Their leader made them hear his words that dropped as slowly as blood from a reopened wound. 'Chief Kiato-nui has given lands and names to the children of Tane, taboo-breakers from the beginning. He has thrown away the true work of the old-time masters and asked for the worthless rubbish of liars and cheats. He has given his daughters to outsiders and looked away from the empty houses of landsmen. Are we insects, that we let this one Chief betray our land and our people?'

A sudden scream brought the men to their feet. 'Blood!' Mauhau yelled. 'Give us blood!'

'Evil for evil! That is just!' answered those who were pushing their way to the opening in the walls of the fort. They could not wait for the dawn to dim the fires inside. They stamped on the hard ground, eager for their Ironwood's command to cross the high plateau to the edge of Taiohae valley and call down their challenge to the rotten rats below.

Pakoko was the flower of a wave pushed forward by a flooding sea of hundreds of warriors who raced down the western ridge, roaring the battle song of Tu. He was twirling his short pointed ironwood. Not for him a club. His arm was strong, his legs swift. He was going into battle with a thruster so short that he must smell his enemy's breath before he struck. Now and then he thought he saw his woman, Metani, running ahead, her *tapas* gleaming in the light, disappearing in the shade, her little feet stirring up whirls of dust. Intent on following that dear breath body, he suddenly felt himself alone in a silence unbroken by stamping feet and taunting yells. Had the tumultuous sea of warriors halted on the edge of the bowl of enemy land? The Ironwood faltered in his whirring flight and looked back.

What were his Braves staring at? He followed their gaze. On the family waters of Taiohae floated an enormous ship. Pakoko thought his head would burst. 'Have you never seen driftwood before?' he yelled. 'Forward!' He might have been calling, '*Ka, ka, ka.*' Through a mist of grief and anger, he watched his birds of prey perch like pigeons on the upland rocks to see the dance of the Different People along the sands of Taiohae from headland to headland. Strong foot, weak foot, strong foot, weak foot, they stepped together, while their outlandish drums rattled and their great blowers belched fire and thunder from their ship.

All eyes turned towards a man who was climbing the path towards the ridge, a landsman with a branch tied with white. Pakoko hung his head in shame, seeing his face, for it was his own son-in-law.

The man himself was ashamed and tangled his words so that the Hapaas, crowding close to hear, had to pick them apart and straighten them out. This was a Menike ship. The Chief of the outsiders was called Pota. Pota had sent this message, 'If the Hapaas enter Taiohae for war, I will punish them.' Interrupted by mocking laughter, the Teii messenger raised his voice in vain. 'Pota says he is strong. He says he can drive you off the island.' Unable to make himself heard, he caught his relative's hand. 'Hear Pota,' he begged. 'He says, "Those who bring me pigs and fruits are friends. Those who come with slings and spears are enemies." '

The taunts of the Hapaas, who were screaming insults and shaking their behinds at the insects down on the sands, ceased suddenly as five big ships like the one floating below came around the Sister and stopped with a great flapping of sails and clanging of chains and anchors. Again they squatted to watch the small boats springing away from the big ones, emptying themselves upon the land.

Standing like a mountain wreathed in dark clouds, Pakoko looked down on his son-in-law, accusingly. 'Kiato-nui has given them land. They are bringing their bundles,' he said.

The Teii murmured, as if not wanting to hear his own voice, 'The Chief has given Pota his name, his daughter, Pae-tini, his hill, Tu Hiva. He has promised him houses.' Then the man burst into anger himself and struck at Pakoko. 'What else could Kiato-nui do? Tell me that!'

'I will show you,' answered Pakoko, through shut teeth. He turned to his men with a wild cry, *'Peo! Peo!'* which lifted them to their feet. *'Peo! Peo!'* They mingled their cries with his and followed him over the rim of Taiohae and down the slopes calling out as if they were chasing wild pigs, *'Peo! Peo!'* They cut the skins of breadfruit trees as they ran through the groves. They tramped down grasses and broke branches as they raced to the hill, Tu Hiva. *'Peo! Peo!'* They mocked the voices of the big blowers which began to hurl fire-stones at them. They sneered at the stones and spears flung hastily by Teiis who scrambled to find weapons laid aside. *'Peo! Peo!'* They were weak with laughter when they climbed back to their ridge.

Flushed and breathless, Pakoko could scarcely give his son-in-law a message for Pota. 'Ask that stuffed skin why he didn't punish us. Tell him that next time we will carry off his bundles and burn his ships.' The Ironwood caught his breath and said sternly, 'Say to him, "When you have overthrown the Hapaas, we will talk about pigs and fruits. Not before." '

Joy flowered in dance and song when an answer from Taiohae was brought to the Hapaa Braves in their strong place. 'Tomorrow,' said Chief Kiato-nui, 'Pota will punish you and wipe out the insult to my mother's bones.'

When the morning's sun splintered the crests, Pakoko's look-outs saw the outsiders crawling up the slopes as if they had no muscles to stand up. They hadn't the strength to carry their blowers but had loaded them on Teii men-at-the-side. Kiato-nui's Ironwood was carrying the Menike's flag as if it were an iron-wood thruster. Insects, all of them! The Hapaas danced back and forth, pointing to their strong place beside the Valley of Tears, beckoning Pota's slow lungs to follow them up the ridge. They stuck out their tongues and made ugly faces at the fire-stones blown at them. 'Come on!' they dared them. 'There are pigs and fruits in our strong place. Come, take them!' they ran behind their logs and climbed onto their levels. 'Here we are!' they screamed at those who paused at the edge of the tall grass. 'Raindrops!' they jeered, when fire-stones were blown against their logs. 'Why do you stand still?' they taunted the leader who waded into the running tide of grass, the Ironwood and the flag beside him.

Pota's Head Man had not long to wait for the man who was eager to make war with him. Pakoko raised his feathers above the waves of grass, lifted his needle-pointed ironwood thruster high, and walked towards his enemy. Quivering, hair pricking his skin, as he felt the force of hundreds of eyes upon him, eyes of friends behind, of foes ahead, he walked without faltering. How loud the rattle of his own head feathers! How sharp the sting of his hair skirt against his legs! His hair cape was heavy, hot. He sharpened his eyes to ferocious points. He knew they were gleaming from his dark tattooing. He was frightful! His distorted face was striking terror into that trembling liver who stood like a tree with branch-like blower pointing at him. Wild joy tore through the Ironwood's throat, the cry of a bird about to dive on a fish. He quickened his feet, flying forward with ironwood beak outstretched to rip open his prey. He heard Priest Tini's encouragement trilling in his ears, 'The enemy is overthrown! Pakoko pierces his intestines!'

But Pakoko did not get near enough to his enemy to smell his breath, and the slings, spears and clubs who ran in their accustomed ranks following his footprints could not loose their weapons. The Ironwood's leap forward stirred up a storm of thunder and lightning which roared and blazed through the small Valley of Tears. Wave after wave of fire-stones pounded the advancing Hapaas, beating them to bloody pulp, making firewood of their cherished weapons. Pakoko tried to grip his thruster for the kill, but his arm hung limply and his stick swung aimlessly on his wrist-loop. Blood flowed over his shoulder and oozed between his toes. He was dizzy. As he fell, he saw Kiato-nui's Ironwood throw down the flag of the outsiders, seize a club from a fallen Hapaa, and spring towards him. Far away in the sky, he heard the shrill cry of the Teii god pulsing through the lips of his nephew, Taa. 'The Hapaas are driven. Pakoko's brains are scattered!' Yes, the grinning club was hovering over him and he could not move.

But he was moving, sliding on his back! Hands gripping his ankles were pulling him from the tangle of arms and legs and broken spears. He saw Mauhau's face floating near. He slept.

When Pakoko opened his eyes again, he was looking up at the red and black lashing called 'kava bowl,' and he knew that he was lying in his own house. 'Was I struck?' he asked.

'The fire-stones went through your shoulder,' answered Mauhau.

'Those blowers cannot kill,' the wounded man snorted.

Mauhau's reply was bitter as kava. 'There are five Hapaas lying dead on the sacred place of Taiohae and many more carried to their houses here.'

'Lies!' gasped Pakoko. 'We were eight two-hundreds against perhaps two twenties. It is impossible!'

Mauhau answered as if he were driven crazy by an evil spirit inside him. 'We cannot fight with rubbish!' He snatched his club and broke it across a rock.

Pakoko sat up and struck his cousin across the mouth. Then he fell back, fainting, as the hot blood spurted over his breast.

When Pakoko knew the 'kava bowl' again, he heard the wailing of his son. 'The blowers have killed my father.'

'They have not!' the father snapped.

'Certainly not,' a familiar voice agreed.

Pakoko saw the Teii Master of Healing bending over a coconut shell of mashed sea and land fruits that were steaming on charcoal embers. 'How are you here—in this valley of enemies?' he asked feebly.

'There are no enemies!' muttered the Master as if he smelled something bad. 'Pota has knotted together ironwood and firewood as if they were equal, chiefs and fishermen, relatives and enemies, landsmen and outsiders. We are as tangled as a bird's nest. There is only one High Chief. That is Pota, the Menike. Even gods bow down to him and beg him to seize their pigs and fruits.' Seeing Pakoko turn questioning eyes on Chief Hiatai, the Master hastily lifted his patient so that the rising steam could enter the wound. This was no time for the sick man to throw himself about because his son had been the first to send a peace branch and offerings to the outsider. The Master went on muttering. 'If I were a Master House Builder, I would refuse to make dwellings for Pota and his men. I would say, "I do not know how."'

Chief Hiatai, who had been picking at the matting with trembling fingers, raised red eyes and glared at the Master. 'That is no answer!' he cried. 'Blowers are the only answer. Without blowers we are insects. We must come when called, we must empty our food bowls for these beggars, we must send our rafters and posts to house uninvited guests.' Swollen and sodden, Hiatai's handsome face was awash with tears. His tongue ran wild. He turned against his father. 'You refused pigs, but what did you give? You gave five Hapaa Brave Faces to the hook of the Teii gods!' Breath failing him, he beat the mat with his palms. 'Is that—your—answer?' he gasped.

Pakoko covered his face with his hands and wept. He knew no answer.

NOTE

In October, 1813, Captain David Porter, U.S.N., who had carried the war between Americans and the English into South Pacific waters in an attempt to destroy the enemy's whaling industry, entered Taiohae bay to refit the prizes he had captured. In order to keep peace during his stay, he espoused the cause of Chief Kiato-nui against the Hapaas, defeated them, brought the resisting Taipis also into submission, and made all tribes of Nuku Hiva tributary to Taiohae. He built a fort on the hill Tu Hiva, mounted cannon, and took possession of the island in the name of the United States. The declaration of possession follows:

'It is hereby made known to the world, that I, David Porter, a captain in the navy of the United States of America, and now in command of the United States' frigate the Essex, have on the part of the said United States, taken possession of the island called by the natives Nooaheevah, generally known by the name of Sir Henry Martin's island, but now called Madison's Island. That by the request and assistance of the friendly tribes residing in the valley of Tieuhoy, as well as of the tribes residing on the mountains, whom we have conquered and rendered tributary to our flag, I have caused the village of Madison to be built, consisting of six convenient houses, a rope walk, bakery and other appurtenances, and for the protection of the same, as well as for that of the friendly natives, I have constructed a fort, calculated for mounting sixteen guns, whereon I have mounted four, and called the same Fort Madison.

Our rights to this island being founded on priority of discovery, conquest, and possession, cannot be disputed. But the natives, to secure to themselves that friendly protection which their defenceless situation so much required, have requested to be admitted into the great American family, whose pure republican policy approaches so near our own. And in order to encourage these views to their own interest and happiness, as well as to render secure our claim to an island valuable, on many considerations, I have taken on myself to promise them they shall be so adopted; that our chief shall be their chief; and they have given assurances that such of their brethren as may hereafter visit them from the United States, shall enjoy a welcome and hospitable reception among them, and be furnished with whatever refreshments and supplies the island may afford; that they will protect them against all their enemies, and, as far as lies in their power, prevent the subjects of Great Britain (knowing them to be such) from coming among them until peace shall take place between the two nations.

Presents, consisting of the produce of the island to a great amount, have been brought in by every tribe in the island, not excepting the most remote, and have been enumerated as follows:'

After giving the inaccurately spelled names of all the tribes of Nuku Hiva, the declaration continues:

'Most of the above have requested to be taken under the protection of our flag, and all have been willing to purchase, on any terms, a friendship, which promises them so many advantages.

Influenced by considerations of humanity, which promise speedy civilization to a race of men who enjoy every mental and bodily endowment which nature can bestow, and which requires only art to perfect, as well as by views of policy, which secure to my country a fruitful and populous island, possessing every advantage of security and supplies for vessels, and which, of all others, is the most happily situated, as respects climate and local position, I do declare that I have, in the most solemn manner, under the American flag display in Fort Madison, and in the presence of numerous witnesses, taken possession of the said island, called Madison's Island, for the use of the United States, whereof I am a citizen; and that the act of taking possession was announced by a salute of seventeen guns from the artillery of Fort Madison, and returned by the shipping of the harbour, which is hereafter to be called Massachusetts Bay. And that our claim to this island may not be hereafter disputed, I have buried in a bottle, at the foot of the flagstaff in Fort Madison, a copy of this instrument, together with several pieces of money, the coin of the United States.'

Signatures include: David Porter, John Downes, James P. Wilmer, S. D. McKnight, John G. Cowel, David P. Adams, John M. Gamble, Richard K. Hoffman, John M. Maury, M. W. Bostwick, William Smith, William H. Odenheimer, Wilson P. Hunt, P. de Mester and Benjamin Clapp.

2

STRETCHED at ease on his stone seat in front of his house, carving a new club, just to shame Mauhau, Pakoko welcomed his cousin, Oehitu, with a twisted smile. He had no desire to hear talk of Taiohae, that valley of the Different People, guarded by four enormous blowers planted on the hill, Tu Hiva. He wanted to go on thinking of his son, Hiatai, when he was a little fellow who heard his father's words and watched for his nod.

But Oehitu waited for no invitation to talk. He had run all the way from Haavao to tell Pakoko that the Taipis had repulsed Pota and his allies when they tried to enter their valley. The defeated Ironwood knew that the sons of his old friend, Chief Tohi-kai, had refused to send pigs to the arrogant outsiders, but he had not been told that Chief Hiatai had joined with Chief Kiato-nui and Pota to punish the stubborn Taipis.

'Each Chief gave ten war canoes with thirty Brave Faces in each and Pota sent a ship,' Oehitu cried.

'They attacked by sea!' Pakoko slapped his thigh and laughed. 'Naturally, they could not climb the sea wall.'

It was true, they had been turned back by those stones. Now Pakoko was a great man because he had built that wall. The Hapaas forgot that he had led them to defeat and begged him to teach the Master Stone Builder how to protect the valley of Hakapaa. The Taipi Diviner came asking, 'Is it true that blowers cannot work if their powder is wet?' and returned to his sky-piercing tower to pray for rain. Pota could not make the Taipis afraid of a land attack, not with their man-eating precipice and rain to protect them.

Pakoko woke from deep sleep, hearing water rushing over the land. 'The Taipi Priest will drown us,' he thought, and, smiling, fell asleep again. Waking when the light was shining on the drip from soaking thatch, he went out onto his terrace to see what birds were making a noise on the ridge above. *Tuh!* Innumerable outsiders were running about up there! They were hopping around fires to dry themselves. Certainly, their powder had been ruined by the night's rain. What a laugh! The Hapaas began to come out of their houses to look up, laughing, at the fools who thought they could climb down into Taipivai without being stoned to death. They began to mount the slopes themselves to see this great game, every man with his sling bound around his forehead, ready to join the strong side.

Mauhau overtook Pakoko, going slowly because of his weakness, but pushing himself, ashamed that a fire-stone had made an old man of him. 'Why do you go up above to see your friends in Taipivai destroyed?' Mauhau asked, ashamed also that blowers had made his ironwood club ridiculous, and lashing at his cousin with a stinging tongue.

Pakoko struck back. 'If you were a man with hair on your legs you would fight with Taipis against these outsiders.'

Mauhau's eyes reddened. 'I have never had three stripes tattooed on my face,' he said.

'The Taipis are not our enemies! They are landsmen, too!' Pakoko exclaimed. Having said this, he was amazed at himself.

How often he had called for the death of other tribesmen and now he was thinking that all landsmen were the same!

Their little quarrel was pinched off in the bud as the murmur of people clinging to the rim of the valley of the Taipis swelled to a tumult. 'The Menikes are climbing down the cliffs!' they screamed. Teiis and Hapaas who had refused to go with Pota's Menikes began to pat the earth with eager feet and to yell insults down upon their unseen Taipi enemies. The Teii Priest, Taa, began to trill from a tree, 'Death to the Taipis!'

Leaning and supporting, Pakoko and Mauhau pushed their way through the crowds. Mauhau muttered, 'Why do we look at the work of the blowers?' And Pakoko snapped back, 'They will not work. Their powder is wet.'

Instantly, Pakoko's boast was answered by the thunder of blowers echoing among the rocks. He felt sick and weak, but when Priest Taa clamored his joy that rain had no power against Pota's blowers and shouted, 'Blow, fire-stones, blow through the rotten Taipi rats!' he gathered his breath against his spell. 'Blow into the air, fire-stones, blow into the air!' Pakoko cried.

The Teii Priest slid down from his tree and ran back and forth, his quivering hands held high, his tongue trilling. 'Pota overthrows Kiato-nui's enemies!' The Hapaa Priest, seeing that the outsiders were at the bottom of the precipice, enlaced his voice with the Teii's. 'The fire-stones of the Menikes are piercing the Taipis!' They two roused the people to a frenzy of desire to see their old-time enemies overthrown. 'Blow the Taipi rats to bits! Scatter the pieces!' they yelled.

Pakoko's voice was a small stone dropped into a seething whirlpool. Even his own ears refused to listen. He could see that the Taipis were flinging stones and spears from behind a wall, but that the outsiders were advancing without stopping in a spreading fire-flowered wave that leapt the wall and broke over the ambushed landsmen in a spray of deadly stones. He could see the Taipis snatching the fallen, running with them to other walls. He could see flames sprouting, branching, on this terrace, on that, houses smoking, leaping skyward in red agony, falling into dead ash. He covered his eyes and moaned.

Mauhau threw himself down and beat his palms sore. 'We are untaught children!' he groaned.

Both Priests were yelling now, 'The Taipis are driven! The Taipis are driven!' They turned to the leaping landsmen. 'The valley is open to all!'

Their words lifted the Teiis and the Hapaas over the edge of the precipice, sent them flowing down its face like water. They followed the flaming path of the outsiders, stripping bark from breadfruit trees, overthrowing the big images on the sacred places, flinging burning sticks into the thatch of taboo sheds sheltering dead chiefs in their sky-canoes. They cut bundles of *tapa* sticks, gathered knots of coconuts and breadfruit, stripped treasure poles and rafters, carried off drums, carved bowls, canoe paddles. Never before had they entered this great valley save by invitation. Now they stripped it clean, one wave after another flowing down the cliffs and fighting its way back through following seas, hampered by bundles and insane haste.

Pakoko could not keep his eyes closed. The fires below drew him as a moth is drawn, and ate him, leaving his active eyes dull stones in blackened bowls, turning his lithe body to a heavy stump as useless as the charred post that stood up where Tohi-kai's house had been. He might have stood there until burned to a dead cinder, had not the two Priests mingled their voices in a chant of triumph. Their words fanned up his fires of life again. He rushed upon them, accusing them. 'It is you two who have overthrown our relatives and friends! It is you two who gave power to the outsider, Pota! Shame! Shame!' Somehow they had put power into him. He was an angry man, determined to find a priest who would support the landsmen, who would not confuse the gods with false cries for help.

3

THREE men were whispering in Pakoko's long-legged taboo house. Below on the terrace, the evening fires had fallen low. Late comers had stumbled through the dusk and slid the wood across their house openings to shut out the prying eyes of ghostly wild women, beginning to wink in the dark-roofed night. Pakoko and his two cousins lit no nut tapers, made no movement that might not have been that of a sleeper turning now and then, breathed no sound louder than the snoring of an old man.

Pakoko was saying, 'Then we are agreed. Kiato-nui must be put down, not by war—but by another way.'

The three men felt the cold fingers of the night reaching for them through the cracks between the floor logs. They shivered and drew closer together. Yes, they gave consent. The same thought had been fermenting in the stomachs of Mauhau and

Oehitu. The Ironwood saw one death for all landsmen in the unequal struggle into which Kiato-nui had plunged them. The messenger saw a bad end in the tangling of family lines and the removal of restrictions which Kiato-nui permitted. Tears stung Mauhau's eyes as he nodded, admitting that the friend and chief of his boyhood was such soft wood that he would give his name, his chief's staff, even his land, to any outsider who offered him gifts or fought his enemies for him. Oehitu had another thought. 'Kiato-nui is a child who has walked into a noose without seeing it and now he cannot loosen the knot.'

'We must end this confusion,' Pakoko said. 'Kiato-nui must surrender his lands to me.'

Mauhau dug his nails into his palms to keep from crying aloud. 'You are a great Ironwood, a wise Chief who listens, but you cannot drive the outsiders from Taiohae!'

'They will drive each other away,' Pakoko declared, signing to Oehitu to explain.

'Pota has gone away,' he said. 'He has left a friend with twenty-one men, three ships and four big blowers. But Red Nose says . . .'

'Who is Red Nose?' asked Mauhau.

'Oh well,' answered Oehitu, 'just another Fire Keeper Kiato-nui has picked up from a ship. He is a Peketane. He says his people are at war with the Menikes. He says the workers who built Pota's walls are Peketanes seized in battle. They are kept tied by the ankles in the dark. Red Nose says that he will untie them when the moon is in the black and the Menikes are sleeping on the land with our women. Then the Peketane prisoners will kill Pota's friend, steal his ships and sail away, and the Teiis will kill the Menikes on the land.'

Certainly this was good news, but then there would be Red Nose and the Peketanes and Kiato-nui waiting to give his loin cloth to the next outsider who came. Yes, they all knew that. They rested for a space, as swimmers cling to an overturned canoe before striking out on the long hard going to land. Pakoko had said, 'Kiato-nui must be put down, but not by war.' They all knew there was another way, but they all drew back from speaking of it.

Finally Pakoko whispered, 'There is a god who can persuade

Kiato-nui to give me his lands.' Saying it, he felt his hair stand up. He dared not breathe the name. Even to think it made him shiver and look sideways. But the others understood. He did not have to name the god, nor the ugly Sorcerer who could call him to taste a bait and eat a man's spirit. Pakoko said with sudden heat, 'Kiato-nui must be frightened until he gives, but not killed.' The others nodded.

Mauhau complained, 'Kiato-nui is very careful of his belongings.'

Oehitu added, 'His Fire Keeper picks up even his nail parings before they fall to the stones.'

Pakoko smiled. 'I will pick up the bait where the Peketane cannot follow his Chief. You have told me that Kiato-nui goes onto the Menike ship to have his hair cut. I will go to see the wonderful things on that ship.'

Pakoko joined the crowds flowing down through Taiohae to watch the work of the Different People on the shore. He wore no finery, carried no insignia, chanted no names to claim his right to enter the valley. He was just one of the nobodies who looked at things that should have been taboo to them. His face was as unfamiliar to them as theirs were to him. He ground his teeth to keep back a curse that would send them scurrying to their rat holes. Oehitu had told him that Pota had given permission to men without weapons to go where they pleased. Indeed, he himself was going because of this, but the sight of this disorderly mob disregarding property and stealing privileges angered him.

His anger filled him up so that he could not think for a space of his recent visit to the Sorcerer, a horror that was heavy in his stomach. He was not afraid to attempt the bold theft of Kiato-nui's hair with the sharp shell cutter he wore hidden in his girdle, but he trembled whenever he thought of putting his brother's spirit into the slippery hands of the net-tying priest. What he had seen in the Sorcerer's retreat had sickened him: his sagging coconut-mat shelter in the black shade of *ihi* trees, his filthy garments black with slime and smelling of dried excrement, his dead legs, which he lifted with bony hands as he dragged himself about, his boy, a gray-haired mis-shapen half-wit, who brought him food. The Priest's eyes had circled about him without aim, his whining tongue had denied any knowledge of spells even when Pakoko promised to keep his oven filled with good things to eat; but when he had been told that it was Chief Kiato-nu's hair which was to be buried in a putrid hole to rot, he had turned steady eyes on Pakoko and said with a straight tongue, 'Friend, this is good work. I had a daughter who rubbed my bad legs and kept me decent, but she has run away to live in the house of Kiato-nui's outsider. I will catch his spirit gladly.' It was this saying and the hunger in the man's cruel eyes that had frightened Pakoko. He had answered, 'Chief Kiato-nui is not to be killed. As soon as he agrees to give me all of his land, you will return his hair to him.' Before he left that evil place, he had said, 'If Kiato-nui dies, you shall die also.' But still, he had to keep pushing away his fear of this Priest. He was glad to fill himself with anger against the meanderings of prying spies from other valleys.

Pakoko found Chief Kiato-nui on one of the Menike ships, standing before a big image-making shell. He was looking at his face, now this side, now that, with cheeks puffed out, with cheeks sucked in, with eye rims pulled down, with tongue stuck out. He was twisting and untwisting his long top hair, making it stand up, making it lie down. He was spreading his beard over his chest, then plaiting it in two tight braids. Suddenly, he saw two faces in the shell, a long face with sparkling eyes and shining teeth beside his own round moon. Backing away from the sudden appearance, he bumped into the man behind him and lost his breath in a frightened groan.

Pakoko said softly, 'How handsome you are, my brother.'

Kiato-nui spun around and grinned feebly. 'Pota's hair was short,' he said in hushed embarrassment. 'The Bone Mender is going to cut mine like it.'

'You are not afraid!' the older brother cried.

The younger brother laughed as if Pakoko had been a child.

'I am Kiato-nui Pota,' he reminded him. 'Pota's man will not harm me.' He held the long lock up straight. 'He will cut that off in one stroke without pulling a single hair.'

Pakoko pulled his eye rim down to show the white. 'You fool me!'

Kiato-nui made a derisive mouth in reply. 'Wait and see, Know-nothing!'

Pakoko stuck out his tongue at the face imaged beside his own in the shining disk. Kiato-nui stuck out his tongue in reply. They both laughed. Pakoko pulled out the hair from his own twist and let it fall. Kiato-nui followed the movement. They giggled together. Pakoko rolled his eyes towards the sky; Kiato-nui, the same. Those two kept on making bad faces at one another in the mirror until the Bone Mender came to cut the Teii Chief's hair. Then Pakoko backed off, crying, 'I am afraid!' and ran away, followed by Kiato-nui's bellowing laughter.

But Kiato-nui did not laugh long. When he had spread the end of his loin cloth over his fat knee and the Bone Mender had given him the shorn lock to wrap inside it and tie firmly for safety, he stared at the white hairs. They were cut at both ends! 'The tips! Where are the tips of my hair?' he panted.

The outsider was surprised. 'That is all I cut,' he said.

Kiato-nui knew well enough what had become of the tips of his hair, but his tongue was too stiff to make the Bone Mender understand. He ran about in circles looking for the rope that hung over the side boards, and scraped the skin from his palms as he slid down into his own canoe. Now his throat was stiff and he could not make a sound. He kicked his paddlers to make them go fast. Putting his sore hands to his aching head, he shivered at the prick of the short stiff hairs on top. As he stumbled across the sands, his breath tore painfully through his aching breast. He tried to run but his weak knees would not hold him up. He sat down heavily, tears streaming over his heavy cheeks. 'My sky-canoe!' he gasped, and when he was lifted on the litter to the shoulders of his men-at-the-side, he whispered, 'To the house of the Teii Sorcerer.' Quickly, quickly, he must engage this man to work for him.

Again Pakoko spent the night with Mauhau in his food house, while Oehitu went to spy on Kiato-nui. The half-wit had brought word from the Hapaa Sorcerer that the stricken Chief had sent his Priest with an offer of the valleys of Haavao and Pakiu in return for his hair. His own dear valleys had been laid at his feet, as if they were a gift wrapped in a coconut sheath, but Pakoko had refused them. 'Wait for all of Taiohae,' had been his word. Now he was keeping his fingers active, stringing nuts on coconut midribs, lighting tapers, sticking them up on all sides. He could not get enough light to wipe out the visions of the dark, the cruel eyes of the Sorcerer glistening with joy over Kiato-nui's punishment, his bony fingers tying fibres into an unbreakable net, his lips moved by unsounded, vicious words, his strong arms dragging him round and round a putrid hole in which lay a leaf-wrapped package of white hairs. When the light of the next sun dimmed the smoky flames of the greasy nuts, he climbed down from his house to walk back and forth in bright day, waiting, waiting.

Oehitu came in the afternoon with word that Kiato-nui had asked the Menikes to attack the Hapaas and bring back his hair.

'Now we shall all be killed,' moaned Mauhau.

Pakoko was not afraid of that. He could see that Oehitu brought no request for war. He guessed that the Menikes were afraid to leave their ships, afraid of Red Nose and the Peketane captives. He was astonished when his messenger told him that there would be no war because the Menikes laughed at Kiato-nui's fears. He had not known they were such ignorant children.

'They have their own spells,' said Oehitu, 'but they have no power against ours. They pierced Kiato-nui and took a gourd full of blood from him but they could not stop the pains in his head and breast.' Seeing the horror in his cousins' eyes, the messenger added hastily, 'At least the Chief has found out that his friends will not help him.'

Kiato-nui himself was a child. Someone should be standing firm behind him. His older brother should be hovering over him. Pakoko was miserable, thinking of the blood held by the people from the clouds, of the hair hidden by the wicked Priest. He walked back and forth, waiting, hoping that his brother would not resist too long.

At the time of fires, when the weary Chief was about to drag his aching legs up the notched log again, he was drawn back to the edge of his terrace by a noise in the gloom below. There was the Sorcerer's boy, scratching about as if he had lost something. 'He is dead! He is dead!' His whimpering oozed out with his saliva.

Had the Priest killed Kiato-nui? 'Hush!' commanded Pakoko hoarsely. With a sugar cane torch dipped into fire, he ran after the half-wit, fixing his eyes on his scurrying heels as they twinkled in and out of the light along the weed-choked, leafy cavern to the Priest's house. Pakoko dared not think of anything but those foot prints and when he reached the coconut shed he had no words. His cry of terror brought no answer from the black shadows of the roof. He flung his torch against the dried leaves but no one dragged himself outside, as the roof of fire fell among the leaning posts. But the light showed a thing hanging from a tree nearby. 'Whose work is this?' Pakoko demanded, looking closely at the swinging Sorcerer.

The mis-shapen gray-head slid into the light. 'My father made me lift him into the tree. Then he fell and the noose caught him.' He wagged his head from side to side. 'Dead! Dead!' he sobbed.

Pakoko trembled but he moved slowly and stroked the arm of the fellow to quiet his grief. 'Where did your father bury the hair?' he whispered. A pointing finger guided him to the hole. It was empty! 'Someone stole the bait?' he asked.

The crazy fellow shook his head. 'My father dug it up and gave it to—to—I forget.'

'Did Kiato-nui promise to give all his land?' he demanded. Seeing that the fellow was frightened, backing away as he shook his head, Pakoko smothered his desire to crush this rotten fruit, to squeeze out the truth. 'Here is a sweet smell for you,' he said softly, tossing him a bag of fragrant herbs torn from his own neck.

The half-wit sucked the odors noisily. 'Many *kaohas* are given me,' he babbled. 'Red Nose said to me, "What *kaoha* do you want?" And I said, "Blow a fire-stone through a bird." And he did.'

'Was Red Nose here?' asked Pakoko in a whisper.

'Certainly. He was going to blow a fire-stone through my father, but my father gave him the hair and then he went away.'

Pakoko leaned against a tree because his knees were weak. Red Nose with a blower had broken the power of a sorcerer! Naturally, the Priest had hung himself. Were blowers to make an end of them all, priests, ironwoods, chiefs alike? No! They need not drown in a shallow sea. Even in a storm men could float until the current brought them to some shore. Anger against the poor thing hanging from the tree shook him. 'Why did you give him the hair?' he cried. 'Death from a fire-stone is easy! At least you could have died with the knowledge of that hole in your stomach. At least you could have saved Taiohae for landsmen!'

4

THE Hapaas were stiff from sitting on their mats, deafened by the roar of rain outside and of voices inside their houses. This was not fine taro-flowering mist of lingering caresses, nor heavy rain with quickly broken back, nor rain of the night afraid of light, but big water rushing over the land day and night, moon after moon. Waterfalls hung like vines on the cliffs, streams jumped from level to level all the way down from the backbone to the sea. Enormous stones were rolling, big trees swimming, red soil gushing. Down below, the strong sea hurled itself against the running water until the lower land was awash. While the land drank deep, men waited for her bounty, trying to drown the noise of the rain with their own noises, fretful crying, shrill laughter, harsh commands, the steady drone of chanting, the sharp flutter of hand clapping, the rhythmic scraping of stone on wood.

Pakoko and his son, Hiatai, were the only men who went far from their houses while the skies were open. They did not go together from house to house, but separately, and with different thoughts. It seemed as if the father had forgotten all about blowers and fire-stones and powder and could think of nothing but slings and spears and clubs. When he sat inside his own house, he carved clubs, clubs and more clubs. When he visited masters and braves, he told them how many clubs he had made and encouraged them to fashion piles and piles of weapons. Yes, they nodded and smiled, but they began to talk of other things. Sometimes they laughed at him, even pulled their eye lids down in derision. Children began to jump out at him, crying, *'Peo!'* as if he were a wild pig. But he did not cease making his turns about the valley.

The son followed in the older man's footprints, sitting beside the food bowls where his father had sat. People said, 'Chief Paia-roru Hiatai is the man now, Pakoko the little boy.' Indeed, while the father was playing with clubs as children play with seashells, the son was boldly planning to seize Taiohae. Ever since the Menike, Sandal Wood Man, had fled to Hakapaa for refuge, Hiatai had known his path. He was no longer just a handsome wreath displayed at feasts but a supporting staff to lean on.

Sandal Wood Man had run away from Taiohae because Red Nose had freed the Peketane captives and stirred up war against the Menikes. Every Hapaa who could walk had come to Chief Hiatai's terrace to hear Sandal Wood Man tell the story of that great battle, when the Peketane captives had seized one of Pota's ships and sailed away in it. The Hapaas had listened with half-shut eyes and silent tongues when Sandal Wood Man told how Pota's friend had been mistreated and how he had had to burn the second ship and sail away in the third, but they were all feeling suddenly free and had to hold themselves still while they heard of the Menike defeat. Sandal Wood Man was a Menike and their Chief Hiatai had just made him taboo in their valley. They dared not let him see their joy over what had happened to the Menikes who were trapped on shore. 'The Teiis were wild beasts,' he said, 'stoning them to death, trampling them into the sands, fastening them on huge hooks, jerking them in and out of water like fish!' Perhaps the man had seen the fire glinting behind the black lashes of those quiet Hapaas, for he had warned them, 'Pota will come back to punish the landsmen who killed his Menikes.'

It was then that Chief Paia-roru Hiatai had said to Sandal Wood Man, 'Give me a blower and I will punish the Teiis for him.'

'I have no blower,' the man said. 'I came away with empty hands.'

'When your ship comes, the Captain will give me many blowers for my sandal wood,' Hiatai had persisted.

'Friend,' the Menike had answered, 'He will give you many fine things for your sandal wood, but not blowers.'

'Not one stick for anything but blowers!' the Chief had said with a loud tongue. He had said it again and again to Sandal Wood Man. He kept on saying it to his relatives when he went from house to house to encourage them to cut the wood and store it before the coming of the Menike ship.

Sandal Wood Man was a quiet guest in Hiatai's men's house. Whenever the muddy skies were closed for a space and no rain fell, he climbed a peak to look across the sea to the sky's foundation, his eyes thirsting for a ship that did not come. He did not talk and he scarcely listened to the talk of the Chief's slingsmen who always followed him. They were always talking about the pigs which Pota had stolen from them and left in Kiato-nui's valley, covered with taboo. They named again and again their relatives whom Pota and his Menikes had wounded or killed. They wondered how many blowers Sandal Wood Man's Captain would give for a boatload of wood. Hearing this, the Menike always shook his head. 'None,' he said. 'War is bad.' 'The Menikes and Peketanes love war,' they always answered. 'They are worse than we are.'

When the wind turned about and drove the sparkling sea under clear skies, Chief Hiatai often walked about the valley with Sandal Wood Man. He always pointed out the piles of sandal wood waiting for the Menike ship. 'How many blowers for this pile?' he would ask. Receiving no reply, he would try another path. 'I will send to your ship fifteen men with shoulder poles bending under their bundles of wood, and you will give me a blower with powder and fire-stones in exchange.' Hiatai never tired of calculating how many blowers he would get for all the sandal wood in his valley. When a Peketane ship passed the valley of Hakapaa and turned into the family waters of Taiohae and word came that the Peketanes were on top, with Pota a captive in distant lands and his hill, Tu Hiva, seized in Kiato-nui's valley, the Hapaa Chief thought he could surely rouse Sandal Wood Man to consent. 'Give me blowers and I will drive every Peketane from Nuku Hiva!' he declared. But the Menike merely pressed his lips together and looked at the empty sea with clouded eyes.

On the day that the cry went leaping up valley from tree to tree, 'Menike ship! Menike ship!' Sandal Wood Man ran like the wind to the beach, calling out to the houses he passed, 'Bring your wood!' By the time he had brought his Captain in a small boat and they two were sitting in it two arm strokes from the sands, there was a wall of sandal wood stacked all along the crescent of the shore. The Hapaas who had brought their shares covered the slopes and dripped from the overhanging trees. Chief Paia-roru Hiatai stood in front of the wood, feet planted wide apart in the coming and going sea. 'Blowers and powder!' he kept shouting to the men in the boat.

Sandal Wood Man held up an immense whale's tooth. 'See! A three-finger beauty for just one boat full of wood!' he shouted above the roar of the surf.

The mocking laughter that gushed from the slopes drowned the noise of the sea. 'Did you carve it from an old bone?' some-one screamed, knowing these tricky outsiders. Genuine or not, no one wanted an old tooth of a dead fish.

When Sandal Wood Man split a stick with a single blow of an axe and held up the shining tool, all tongues were silent and all fingers itched for the wonder, but their Chief's chant began again and all joined in, rocking with the beat of the words. 'Blowers and powder! Blowers and powder!' Who wanted an axe to cut sandal wood for an axe to cut sandal wood? They were tired of that.

The Hapaas were pretending to go away with their wood when the Menike Captain pulled Sandal Wood Man down onto his seat and stood up himself. He knew no words, but he held up a blower and a bag of powder in one hand and his five fingers of the other hand to show how many boatfuls he wanted. In crazy joy, the landsmen jumped up and down, pushed one another over and tumbled about. Chief Paia-roru Hiatai slapped the behinds of his men to make them hurry with his share of wood, while his eyes circled about to watch for trickery. In deep silence, the lips of the onlookers moved, counting every bundle of the Chief's wood as it was carried through the rolling waves, thrown into the small boat and paddled to the ship. When they had seen the great net hauled up five times, knocking against the side-boards, spilling a few sticks, they breathed out a triumphant yell and Chief Hiatai, holding up five fingers on one hand and one on the other, plunged through the foam to meet the returning boat.

Quivering as a young girl quivers when she goes for the first time to a nest in the bush, Hiatai held out his hands for his blower and powder. No *kaoha* passed between him and Sandal Wood Man. The landsman saw nothing but the shining stick laid across his arms, felt nothing but the weight of the bag of powder dropped into his hand. The outsider looked past the Chief, past the Hapaas waiting their turn on the beach, seeing something that sickened him. 'Sandal Wood Man is afraid now,' the watchers giggled, 'because the landsmen will be able to fight the outsiders.' But Chief Hiatai was beyond thinking of war just now as he caressed his blower, lying on the sands beside it in intimate joy.

Pakoko was sitting in Hiatai's men's house with ten little boys, gathered from here and there. They were chanting and clapping the story of Hu-uti who threw his reed lance through the ear of Striped Lizard on the backbone of the land. The man encouraged the children to make a big noise so that they would not hear the sharp puffing of blowers as Chief Hiatai and his Brave Faces played at war with their new weapons. The little ones had been sent inside by their fathers, lest someone kill his own son without knowing it, and Pakoko was holding them there with stirring old words, and, those failing, with quick hands. The Ironwood himself had no desire either to hear or to see this outlandish play, until a sharp puff nearby was followed by a scream of death. Then he sprang outside, while the little boys shrank together in a dark corner.

Chief Hiatai whirled about on the terrace and faced his father. Oh what a splendid son he was! Eyes sparkling, face flushed, limbs shining in a sudden bath of sweat, he stood, breathing quickly. His tongue tripped over his great joy. 'G-g-get your b-b-bundles! We are going back to Haavao. Priest T-T-Taa is dead!'

Stunned, the father fumbled about for his thoughts. Priest Taa was gone from the prow of Haavao? His taboo was ended? 'How did he die?' he asked.

The son began to tell him in great excitement. 'See! I lay on my stomach there, inside my own sleeping house. My blower lay quietly resting on the stone slab of the entrance. I watched Priest Taa going along that path to see Priest Tini. He was always spying in this valley. I touched my blower as gently as I would touch a woman. And there he is! There he is!' He pointed to a heap of *tapas* lying on the lower terrace of the sacred place.

'He is taboo here! He is your cousin!' Pakoko said in horror.

'No matter. He is a thief. He stole my lands.' Hiatai hardened his eyes and his tongue. He ran for his conch and blew it wildly, calling his Brave Faces. Between blasts, he shouted at his father who stood staring across the feast place at the dead Priest. 'Are you a tree with roots? Plant yourself in Haavao, not here. Get the women and children. Don't be afraid. I have fourteen men with blowers. We will overthrow every chief in every branch of Taiohae before you can walk to your house in Haavao. Follow me!'

Pakoko stood, trying to untangle his thoughts. Taa had been killed by Hiatai. Not by a club, not face to face. Shame, shame! Now Haavao, land so long desired, so many times fought for, was to be retaken by unseen men pointing blowers at unwarned relatives. No! He at least was not a coward. He was not afraid to swing a club. He stamped into the men's house and selected a weapon.

Just to carry this ironwood head with the blazing eyes put spring into his legs. Bring the women and children, indeed! He walked away from them without trying. He overtook Mauhau, hurrying after the Brave Faces. 'Where is your club?' Pakoko demanded, and forced the sullen-eyed Ironwood to return for one.

He began to smell the sweet air of Haavao. 'The pandanus trees are in bloom!' he cried, quickening his feet. When he passed Red Stone Mountain and turned into the down-going Path of War, he spread out his arms as if to hold all of Taiohae in their eager clasp. As he started down into the great bowl, so long forbidden, he began to run, to jump from rock to rock. He whooped with joy, 'Who-ah-hee-hoo!' Blowers or no blowers, he could not help it. His feet were on his own land!

NOTE

The Englishman, Wilson, who caused Lieutenant Gamble so much trouble, was described by Captain Porter as 'a white man tattooed and in loin cloth, who had lived on various islands of the group for many years, spoke the language fluently,' was 'inoffensive, honest, good-hearted,' and 'had a strong attachment for rum'.

Captain Porter left Taiohae on the *Essex* on January 15, 1814. Lieutenant of Marines, John Gamble, remained with twenty-one men, his own ship, *Greenwich*, a store ship, *Sir Andrew Hammond*, and a prison ship, *Seringapatam*. Four months later, Gamble's stay came to a tragic end when thirteen mutineers and six prisoners, all English, sailed away on the *Seringapatam*, under the British flag, and Gamble had to set fire to the *Greenwich* and escape on the *Hammond* with a single seaman.

Ross, an American sent to Nuku Hiva by Mr Wilcock, consul of the United States to Canton, to facilitate the traffic in sandal wood to vessels of his country, was supposed by Lieutenant Gamble to have perished with other Americans stoned to death by the Teiis at the time of his departure, but he survived and continued his work for several years. Camille de Roquefeuil, who visited Taiohae in a merchant ship, *Bordelais*, in December, 1817, describes Ross as 'a good influence, unlike the deserters', and quotes him as saying that the character of the natives had completely changed since their contact with the whites.

In August, 1814, Captain Sir Thomas Staines, commanding

H.M. frigates, *Briton* and *Tagus,* came to Taiohae, investigated the Nuku Hivan situation to determine if the tales told by officers of the *Essex* at Valparaiso, where Porter had been taken as a prisoner, were correct. He dug up the bottle buried by Porter, found his document and coins and claimed the island for England in a parting ceremony. 'By consent of all tribes, except the Taipis who would make no concession or acknowledgement to any other power, the island was taken possession of in the name of His Britannic Majesty; a royal salute was fired from the *Tagus* and the *Briton,* and the Union displayed on a staff at the royal palace.'

VI   UNBOUND GOD STICKS

1

'No,' Pakoko had answered when Mauhau asked him to come see what Hiatai had destroyed in the seaward lands of Taiohae. 'I will never look upon the foot traces of landsmen who carry blowers. I will never step on sands that have been trampled by the hard shoes of outsiders.' Moons had turned, suns had fallen, stars had floated beyond the sky's foundation, and Pakoko had remained in his valley of Haavao. He had never seen the uprooted stones of the sacred place of Meau, nor the burned posts that had been the carved images of the grandfathers. He had lived in a valley untouched by ugly new things.

Pakoko had not seen his son's face since that day of return to Haavao, when he had come running and shouting, 'We have killed thirty Teiis and sent them over the mountains to Priest Tini!' The grandfathers must have vomited those innumerable offerings, but Hiatai had not been satisfied. He was still looking for sandal wood in the mountains, still driving his woodstrikers to cut it and pile it ready for the ships, still bargaining for more and more blowers and powder. Day after day he trained his Brave Faces to strike marks on the cliffs, which he called 'the valley of the Taipis.' Alas, alas! Was it his desire to conquer all of Nuku Hiva?

When Chief Kiato-nui came begging Pakoko to lead the chanting at a life-strengthening festival for his new great-grandson, Moana, the older brother could not refuse to descend to the old feast place. 'You are the only Teii who can put power into this insignificant child and his possessions,' whined the younger.

Pakoko was shocked to see this white-haired man who slumped in a heap on his sky-canoe, pick-picking at his skin that was scaly from *kava* drinking. He was ashamed to hear him complain that no one but outsiders considered his desires, ashamed that he spoke of the new offspring as insignificant. 'He is a shoot of four great root stocks!' Pakoko said. 'He has names to call in all the valleys of Nuku Hiva.'

Kiato-nui drew down his mouth and moaned, 'The Hapaa Chief, Piai-roru, makes him a nobody.'

Pakoko winced as his brother used Hiatai's Hapaa name, yet it was just. Hiatai was a Hapaa conqueror who cared nothing for his Teii roots. He did not dwell in the land he had seized. As long as pigs, breadfruit and ornaments were sent to him at every harvest, he did not think of Taiohae. Not even bringing his coconut sheaths to collect what he wanted, he had given this work to others: to his cousin, Haape, in Meau, where Kiato-nui was a dweller without power; to his sister, Pae-tini in the twin valleys; to another cousin in Hoata; and to Pakoko in Pakiu and Haavao.

The Chief of Haavao did not want to see the stricken lands down by the sea, but he was now the only Master Chanter in Taiohae and he must perform his work when called. In truth, his brother's request fanned ash-white embers into flickering flame. Perhaps he could nourish this little one and build him into a strong chief who could hold together the families of Taiohae. He thought, 'My life is flowing swiftly away. I must leave someone who will turn his back on the sea and hold firm.'

Aloud he said, 'Come, let us plan a great feast for the child, Moana.'

Staring at Kiato-nui's love-lighted face, as he was carried away, Pakoko was deeply moved, not by that waning moon that beamed *kaoha* so easily, but by the rush of sap in his own body. He was new again, ready to make a great chief and save the landsmen! Not since he came from the taboo house where the aged Master Chanter had taught him, had he known such lightness. He had entered that house of instruction wearied and tormented by poisonous questions. What new trickery were the outsiders preparing for the landsmen? What good spells would break their bad spells? What words of power would divert their fire-stones into the earth and into the air? What nets would entangle them in unbreakable meshes? What bait would draw out the bad spirits that made men sick and ate their flesh bit by bit? Who knew? Were the grandfathers-far-below empty of power? Were the grandchildren insignificant? Were the old taboos lies? Battered by winds coming from every side, Pakoko had cried out aloud, 'Oh Clear Space! Oh Red Soil! Hold me fast between!'

When he had taken the sustaining drink of the voyager and was embarked on the sea of ancient wisdom, he had begun to be smoothed by its calm. Sounding the words of earth-growing, he had begun to feel the regular breath of the land flowing through him, the warmth of the fiery foundation spreading through his chilled limbs. As the old man had guided him down into the depths and up into the heights, he had touched the foundation, the clinging roots, the spreading branches, the little dancing leaves of his people and the clear space of Level Above. Thereafter, he had sat quietly as a bird on a sheltered branch, unshaken by winds, hidden by clouds of taboo. When he could see common things again, when he had left the taboo house and washed away his untouchableness in the sea, he had returned to his own valley of Haavao to stand up whole, a post firmly planted and supporting the roof of his land.

On the day of the rites for little Moana, as Pakoko left his own terrace, wearing his coconut leaf cape and headband, he looked at his bundle of sticks lashed together. 'What power I hold in my hand!' he thought. He felt as if he could touch the little fellow with his gift from the three gods of the sky and make him a full grown man. He carried also the fan given him long ago by his father-in-law. He lifted it as if saluting the spirit of that great Chief. 'When I told you I would be a Master Chanter, you said, "An old man's work." Well, here I am, an old man.' He laughed, looking down proudly at his glossy white beard. Then he waved *kaoha* to his new woman and the child in her arms and walked off with the spring of a dancer.

Down below, the sight of a ship from the clouds sitting asleep on the family waters of Taiohae rudely unsealed his taboo-clouded eyes. Certainly he had heard of the constant comings and goings in the bay, but, since Hiatai gave to his cousin, Haape, the right to govern his share of sea and sand, Pakoko could only vomit such knowledge so that it would not make him sick. Now, he tore his eyes away from the clumsy, forested raft and fixed them on Two Sisters. Tomorrow those rocks would be standing firm, but the floating driftwood would have vanished. Forward, courage! He stamped solidly onto the paving laid so long ago by the Taipi Master Stone Builder and refused to see its crooked and up-ended stones and broken walls. Climbing to his place with the old men, where Moana's wreathed and ribboned shrine had been erected, the Master Chanter sat down with a sigh, determined to see only the patterns given by the gods.

But he kept thinking of the empty terrace of the high born women, which he had passed. Where were they? How many times he had stopped up his ears when Oehitu brought him news of the shore people! Now he remembered some of these sayings. His daughter, adopted by Kiato-nui, no longer attended feasts . . . She wrinkled her nose as if she smelled something bad . . . Her outsider would not let her be seen by other men. Anger that outsiders should regulate the women made Pakoko snap open his eyes to see what was going on around him.

He stared at the Chief's terrace. Was that his own brother, that black stomach bursting out of a red coat with yellow fringes on the shoulders? That white head lowering itself under an outlandish cloth stretched above on poles? Was he lame that he had his legs propped up on a high seat? 'Who is the clown?' he asked the ancient sitting next him.

The old fellow snickered. 'That is Kiato-nui Pota,' he sneered. 'That is Pota's high seat. Those are Pota's cast off things.'

Pakoko loosened the neck band of his cape and turned his eyes away from the shameful sight of a landsman imitating an outsider, and from the pale skins and weak eyes that crowded around him. But the feast place itself was like a rat's nest. An outsider with a livid skin covered all over with black hair was pointing out their seats to the landsmen. 'Blood Spitter', he was called. 'Sick,' muttered the Master to Pakoko, 'left by his ship to die.' Everything was tangled. This naked outsider wearing a loin-cloth and waving a *tapa*-tied staff of authority, did he think he was a landsman? And the Teiis, wearing hard shoes strung about their necks, tobacco pipes stuck through their ear holes, black hats on their heads, wrappings covering their brilliant tattooing, were they trying to be outsiders?

The Master Chanter closed his eyes in disgust and started singing with a loud tongue. His swinging fan set the old men rocking, this side, that side, as they mingled their red voices with his.

> Profound, the Level Above,
> Up-turned, the Level Below.
> They seize, they join,
> They cling, they sleep enlaced.
> The child-bearing depths
> Bring forth Clear Space.

Soon the grand old words had cleared Pakoko's eyes. He could see the seeds planted by Clear Space in the mothers of trees thrusting up their trunks, Ironwood offering her limbs for the young child's weapons, Banyan her skin for his loin cloth, Temanu her body for his canoe.

Opening his eyes to bless these gifts laid before the shrine for Moana, Pakoko's fan stopped in sudden horror. These things were not true! A blower! A piece of red cloth! A ship's boat! The gods had not sent these outlandish things! What strength could there be in them? The same thought was in the stomachs of all the masters who sang with the Master Chanter. This child, Moana, this sprout of four rootstocks, had been robbed of his heritage from the beginning, His birth had not been called to land and sea by a chief's conch, but by a blower which offended the gods. The old men shook their heads sadly, fearfully. Pakoko started his fan again with a weak hand. Could he blow the breath of life into a child so strangely nourished?

When earth and leaves were removed from the ovens, the Master Chanter hovered near, waiting to clear away the taboo from the food for this feast. He could see that it was not a rich man's feast with mountains of food to throw away after the guests had stuffed themselves. Looking at the few pigs that had been roasted, Pakoko began to feel sorry for his brother. Not only Hiatai, but all of the chiefs of Nuku Hiva had made a food-beggar of Kiato-nui. When fear of Pota's return had been forgotten, every tribe had sent raiding parties to bring back the pigs the Menike had seized and left wandering about Taiohae with clipped ears as a sign of his taboo. Certainly the taboo of an outsider had no power. Poor, blind, Kiato-nui!

As Pakoko stepped forward to free the food, according to the custom, he was shaken by three sharp thunder claps. *'Pupuhi! Pupuhi! Pupuhi!'* puffed the blower in Blood Spitter's hands. Everyone was thrown into a panic. The Master Chanter forgot the opening words of the rite, the old men dropped their fans, the drummers left their hands hanging in the air, the people fell on their faces. Only Kiato-nui swelled up with pleasure and broke the silence with a heavy tongue. 'The skies are clear. The food is freed!' he cried. The people did not know what to do when they heard the feet of the food-bearers trotting towards them. They dared not look at the Master Chanter whose work had been taken from him. They pressed their faces upon the stones when they heard him shout, 'This food is still taboo! It will make you sick!'

Kiato-nui laughed at him. He reached for the pig that had been laid in front of him, tore off a leg and gave it to the Captain of the visiting ship. Then he called to Pakoko, 'There is only one captain on a ship, only one who gives orders. Here I am the captain. Yes?' he turned to his friend beside him.

The outsider nodded, waved the pig's leg and began to eat. The folk on the paving reached for their shares. The outsiders were not afraid. Pakoko was old-fashioned. He had lived too long in the mountains.

Pakoko returned to his seat with the old men, a huddled group, silent and confused. This would never do! No one could take away from them the true old words. He closed his eyes and began to chant.

When fires were lighted, the noise on Kiato-nui's terrace had grown to a tempest. The people from the whaling ship were singing and shouting. Their captain was calling *kaohas* to his friend, Kiato-nui, to his friends, the Teiis. He was walking back and forth, bellowing to the crowds below, pointing at the enormous gourds of bad-smelling drink that had been brought from his ship. 'Come, come! Drink! Good!' he cried.

Fathers, mothers, little ones, crowded about the gourds, dipping out the drink into coconut shells, pouring it into their open throats. Hot! Hot! They jumped and screamed as the fire ran down inside them. They began to throw hot roasted bread-fruits at one another. They tore off their clothes and smeared themselves with the soft paste. They made frightful faces and leapt upon one another, striking and gouging with half-gnawed pig bones, tearing at one another with crooked fingers. When they saw the outsiders jumping down from the Chief's terrace to seize the little dancers, who were being unwrapped for their offering to the gods, they followed them into the bush, fighting with them for possession of the delicate children.

Pakoko's closed eyes and muttered chants could no longer shut out the nightmare of screaming children, moaning women and raging men. He forgot that he was a Master Chanter and held his sticks as if they were an Ironwood's thruster. Picking his way among the tangled heaps of fighting and clinging men and women, avoiding the pools of vomit and excrement, he crossed the paving, climbed his brother's terraces and entered the sleeping house of the child, Moana. Carrying the little fellow pressed against his breast, he faced Chief Kiato-nui. 'I am taking this child to feed,' he said through tight lips. Allowing no time for an answer, he turned away from the red-faced clown who sat with his arms twined about the Captain and from the stinking rot that fouled his land.

2

Pakoko had not looked back as he left Meau, vowing it was for the last time, but the filth had not yet been cleared from that horrid feast when he was recalled to his brother's terraces by the wailing of conch shells and the wild cries of grief that spread like wind-driven fire throughout the whole valley of Taiohae. Chief Kiato-nui was dead! Dead from *kava* drinking, some said. Dead from the burning drink of the Menikes, others said.

The older brother found everything in confusion on the Meau stones. No one knew when the breath body had left that bloated skin. No one had honored the Chief with gifts or a feast, no one had called *kaohas* to his wandering spirit or danced naked in grief-showing. Who indeed should do these things? Kiato-nui's woman had died during the long drought. His daughters lived in other valleys. Pae-tini's outsider would not let her come near a dead body. Chief Haape had gone to tell his cousin, Chief Paia-roru Hiatai, that Pakoko had stolen young Moana. Other relatives were still sleeping heavily after the feast.

Only the outsider, Blood Spitter, was moving about as if he knew his path. He was making a hideous noise as he fashioned a big wooden box with his strange tools, stopping only to cough and labor for breath. The Master Chanter punched him with his god sticks. 'This is a taboo time,' he said. 'No work.'

The man looked up at him through tears! Had the fellow *kaoha* for Kiato-nui? Pakoko stared at him, and touched him more gently when he went back to striking the wood. 'Taboo,' he said again.

'We can't leave the body lying in the house,' the man answered, and, after a fit of coughing, pointed to the hillside. 'I have dug a hole there.'

The old man fixed his eyes on the box and the hole with horror. What was the thought of this wild pig? Did he want to show Kiato-nui's spirit that he despised him? These outsiders were children of darkness. Nothing they did could be seen clearly. He drove the fellow away with his god sticks and had the box burned for fire wood.

While the taboo moon climbed slowly into the black again, Pakoko did the work of the Master Chanter for Chief Kiato-nui's death feasts. He knew that Blood Spitter was always within reach of his eyes, but he never looked at him. Still, he knew that the fellow's eyes were blurred and his lips trembling. Many others sat about, frequently lifting their voices in bursts of song or tremulos of weeping, but Pakoko never heard a sound from the outsider, except his hollow coughing. By the time he was ready to burn the dead chief's house and belongings, he could look at the man without anger. When he was about to throw Kiato-nui's fan into the flames and heard Blood Spitter begging for it, he put aside his fear that he wanted it as bait for his brother's spirit. Naturally, he did not let him have the fan, but he gave him one of his own because of his disappointment. When he carried his brother's skull to the sacred place, he did not drive him back until they reached the lower terrace and then he stopped to hear his word, because he saw that he had begging eyes.

'My Chief is dead,' he said, 'my good Chief. Now I am alone. I am sick. I have no house.'

It was a true word. Pakoko answered, 'There is the house Kiato-nui built for Moana. It is yours. And I will send you food.'

Climbing the terraces to the sacred banyan tree on top, the Master Chanter was thinking, 'The *kaoha* of an outsider is the same as the *kaoha* of a landsman.' To his brother's wandering spirit, he said, 'This is my *kaoha* for you, Kiato-nui. I will feed your friend.'

When Pakoko came down from fastening the skull in the banyan tree, he had forgotten the sick outsider. The sight of the empty priest's house had filled him with shame and fear. In all Taiohae there was no diviner, no one to care for these sacred bones, no one to point out the men to be caught as paddlers for the dead Chief's canoe, no one to call for gifts for his entrance into the skies. 'Kiato-nui will be angry,' he thought. 'He will come back to do us harm.'

This was no new anxiety for the Chief of Haavao. Ever since his son had killed Priest Taa with a blower, the sky-piercing house in this valley had been empty. Pakoko had been waiting for a sign that the gods had chosen young Veketu, Priest Taa's son, to take his father's place. Veketu had slept on the mat of his grandfather, Priest Kohu, as soon as he was weaned. He had gathered wood for the sacred fire for his father, Priest Taa, as soon as he could pick up things when told. He had been nourished by his mother, Priestess Mata-heva, until she had been called to the sacred place of Hakaui. 'As surely as a young coconut ripens, this boy will become a diviner,' Pakoko thought, but no god had entered him yet, either to move or to speak through him. The lad himself was sick with desire to climb the sky-piercing house of his grandfather and his father. Perhaps if the gods saw him dancing before and behind a priest, they would mark him for their own. Pakoko determined to send him to serve Priest Kepua, his son whom Chief Tohi-kai of Taipivai had adopted.

'See that you make yourself known to Kohu and Taa, as well as the Taipi gods,' the old man said to Veketu on the morning that he pushed the youngster out of the nest in Haavao and started him over the mountains to the great eastern valley. 'If they make a sign that they have seen you, Priest Kepua will teach you to eat the air and sleep on the sea and know the talk of the three birds of the sky.'

'I have always known these things!' Veketu boasted.

Pakoko had to lower that bundle from too high a rafter. 'There are three skies, child,' he said gently, 'with new things in each, and a man is old before he climbs to the top.'

'I shall fly to the top!' the youth sang out. He started to run on his way, but his feet began to drag after a space and he turned his head over his shoulder. Seeing the old man standing like a tall, rooted tree, he ran back to twine his arms, vine-like, about that solid trunk.

'Go!' commanded Pakoko with a rough tongue, freeing himself. This time he turned around and went back to his house. He struck the bushes on either side with his staff, as if he were a child playing. He was thinking, 'Now there will be two to carry me on their backs, a chief and a priest.'

3

SEVEN Big Breadfruit gatherings the people of Haavao and Pakiu had eaten without asking a single food friend from another valley. Their land was altogether taboo to outsiders, guarded by men with clubs. Down by the sea, many landsmen pointed up above, saying, 'Only wild pigs live up there.' But there were others who whispered wistfully, 'The drums of the old time people are beating up above.' Still others said nothing but crept in the dark up the Path of War, carrying branches tied with white, begging to speak to Chief Pakoko. Some of these were fishermen who asked for work in Haavao's taboo waters, because all others were constantly being defiled by women who rode over them in canoes. Some were masters who could not work where people laughed at them, canoe builders who would not change to the patterns of outsiders, *tapa* beaters who despised outlandish cloth, planters who desired to enforce the old taboos. Some were men whose women had left them to live in the houses of outsiders. Some were healers whose gods knew no remedies for the strange diseases that were destroying the shoreward people. Yes, Pakoko made a nest in the uplands, in which all wanderers could rest and feel the wings of true gods hovering over them.

In this nest, the Chief nourished young Moana. He himself laid the thin, crying child in the morning dews, bathed him in a new stone-lined pool in the running water, covered him over with the vital sands of Tiki, cleansed him in the brine of the god, Tanaoa. For the boy, growing too quickly for his strength, he performed all the rites given by the gods and fed him daily with the true sayings of the ancients. While nut tapers burned in the men's house, drawing masters and warriors from dark corners into a circle of shining faces, he kept the little fellow content with old tales, of the child who flew across the sea on a palm leaf, of the uncle who sought a mate for his niece, with skin white as coconut flesh and fragrant as all the seeds of Nuku Hiva, of the woman whose spirit wandered in the depths below and brought back new songs. Yes, many were the chants which the grandfather and the grandchild and the landsmen who had shut themselves apart from lies sang together.

Haavao was the nest to which Priest Veketu would soon return. When the Taipi Priest had sent a messenger to tell Pakoko that the youth had been pointed out by the gods, the old man had given a feast for the word-bringer and loaded him with gifts. He had made him tell him again and again how the young man had caught his foot in a banyan root when dancing, how he had struck his head against a stone as he fell, how Priest Kepua and all his attendants had seen the god jerking his limbs. 'What did he say when he opened his eyes?' Pakoko had asked again and again, just to hear the good word. 'It was my father, Taa, who tripped me. He asked me why I was not sitting on the high level of his house.' Those were his words. Now at last Veketu was being taught and the Teiis would no longer hang their heads in shame and fear because they had no seer.

Leaning against his stone rest, Pakoko was watching Ironwood Mauhau teach Moana how to skip a reed lance across a mound of earth, when he became aware that a procession was entering his feast place. It was led by Chief Haape, Hiatai's cousin on his mother's side, who governed his affairs in Meau. The little man was in a hurry, making his thin lame legs outrun his breathing. He mumbled his greeting and brushed aside Pakoko's return. 'Quick!' he panted. 'Bring Moana. The Menikes will make him High Chief of all Nuku Hiva.'

Before Pakoko could understand this strange saying, Moana had thrown away his lance, rushed to Haape and leapt upon him, clinging with arms and legs. 'I am ready,' the boy cried.

But the Chief of Haavao would not move. He signalled to Mauhau to take the kicking, pouting child into the men's house and he made Haape sit down and drink a bowl of *kava* before he began to clear up this cloudy talk. Then he leaned back, closed his eyes, and heard that a Menike *manowa* had come, that the Captain was not Pota but that he had asked for Pota's friend, Chief Kiato-nui, then for the dead Chief's off-spring, that he had invited Prince Moana and all chiefs and priests of Nuku Hiva to come onto the ship.

Fire glinted between the tangled lashes of Pakoko's eyes. He remembered a ship that had hung a priest up by his wrists, another that had stolen the son of a chief as a worker. 'Will you let them steal our high level and leave us a people without guidance?' he demanded.

The little man twisted his hands together. 'The Captain says his blowers are not for war but to bring peace. Hear his very words, "We ask nothing in return for our gifts but *kaoha*. Give wood and water to Menike ships, do them no harm, and we will keep peace with you." '

The old man pulled his eye lid down in derision. 'Give the fellow a coconut leaf and a turtle. These are the signs of peace, not our chiefs and priests.'

'But the chiefs and priests are to give consent to Moana as High Chief over all. That is the way of it in the island of the Menikes—many tribes, one chief over all.'

The Chief of Haavao yawned. 'We know how to tie our own tribes together. The outsiders have nothing to do with this.'

But Chief Haape would not be sent away as if he were a food

beggar. 'The Captain says that war is bad. He says that here is a way to make Moana King of Nuku Hiva without war.'

'King!' Pakoko spat out the outlandish word with distaste. But he chewed on this thought. He also knew that war was bad. He also knew that all landsmen were one people and should be tied together. 'What will Chief Paia-roru Hiatai say?' he asked finally. 'He is always for war.'

Haape's eyelids fluttered. 'Yes,' he admitted. 'Chief Paia-roru asked the Captain for a big blower to plant on the backbone of the land. It was his desire to make all tribes submit to him, but when the Captain refused, Hiatai gave his consent to Moana.' With a quick jerk of his arm, the small man pecked Pakoko on his knee with his long finger nails. 'He is not a fool, your son. He will join to High Chief Moana the little girl he adopted from his sister, Pae-tini.'

The old man wriggled with pleasure over Hiatai's cleverness. The little girl, being the daughter of a Taipi chief and Kiato-nui's adopted child, would bring the people of Taipivai under Moana. Plainly, the great Hapaa-Teii Chief, Paia-roru Hiatai, would stand firm behind the High Chief and Chiefess of Nuku Hiva. Pakoko grinned at Haape and called Moana. 'Come,' he said, 'we will go with Chief Haape.'

Even to the great rite of the peace of the knotted loin cloth, the Chief of Haavao went looking for lies from the outsiders. He could not forget how Pota had loved war. When he had sat on this floating island of a ship as it moved majestically from bay to bay picking up chiefs and priests, he had made little of the Menike's talk of peace. Hadn't every landsman there relatives who had been killed or wounded by Pota and his Menikes? Pakoko joined the procession of chiefs and priests as they entered the Valley of Tears to tie the peace, but he could not help looking at the Taipi warriors who scowled from the ridge as if they alone, perhaps, knew truth from lies.

When the Menike Priest lifted his hand for silence and began to chant with a sweet voice, Pakoko sat down with the others to hear. There was a man who tried to make true words out of these outlandish sounds, but nothing but moon babbling came of it. Who was 'lost in a land of darkness?' Did he mean the landsmen? Couldn't the man see the sun? 'There is only one

God.' The outsiders had only one god! His name was Iehova, this Priest's grandfather, perhaps. What about giving him 'a broken heart?' Perhaps the Menike Priest ate the heart, but the priests of the landsmen ate the eyes also. Why was Iehova angry at the landsmen who had never even heard his name? If he had wanted the landsmen to hear his word, he would have sent his son to Nuku Hiva also, and the landsmen wouldn't have mistreated him and killed him. What was this thing of Iehova called 'lamb?' The man making the talk clear said it was like a dog or a goat. How could it wash away bad things? The landsmen were rolling on the ground, laughing, but Pakoko said, 'Hush. Let us hear the Priest's beautiful red voice.'

When the interpreter said, 'He asks Iehova to show you *kaoha*, to save you from fire through the death of his son, Iesu Kirito,' young Priest Veketu said, 'Now I understand. He has killed his fish, Kirito, and offered him to Iehova.'

The Menike Priest was red and dripping wet. His eyes were turning about. Was he angry or afraid? Ah, he was angry. Iehova was angry. 'He says that Iehova will throw you into fire if you kill men and eat them.'

Priest Tini of the Hapaas tried to smooth the outsider's anger. 'Tell him I will forbid this bad thing when I die.'

'Who is this Kirito?' Priest Veketu persisted. 'Is he Iehova's priest?'

Since the Menike had no breath for answering but was showing his exhaustion, like a man who has run uphill, Priest Hania of Hakaui, said politely, 'I know Iehova. He is in Tahiti. The people there have burned their images and taken Iehova for their god. He is god of thunder.' That was why it thundered before the coming of a ship of the outsiders. That was why blowers made thunder. It would be a good thing to have the god of thunder. 'Let us take Iehova for our god also. We are always getting new gods. I myself will be a god when I die.' Priest Hania smiled his *kaoha* at the Menike Priest.

But the outsider was not friendly. He said an ugly thing. He said, 'All your gods, all your chants, all your offerings are lies!' His face was white, his eyes red and his lips were pressed tightly together.

Priest Hania said, steadily smiling, 'Good. We will have Iehova for our god.' His lips and his tongue were sweet for the outsiders, but his eyes and breath stirred up flames in the landsmen.

Perhaps the Menike Priest felt the heat of the fire that licked him. He suddenly made his voice like cool water poured over the hot embers. 'Friends,' he said, 'many people in my land desire good for you. They want to leave their houses, their relatives and their possessions to come to this land to teach you, to bring you the knowledge of the true God, so that you may go to the land of spirits and live forever.' He looked from face to face with soft eyes. 'Is it your desire that these men and women of light come here?'

Now Pakoko knew that this glittering hook drawn across the waters had a sharp and dangerous barb. 'No!' he shouted, but his voice was drowned in a wind of cries. 'Good! Good!'

'It is for King Moana to say!' Chief Haape raised a shrill voice above all others.

The boy looked up from the shining tassels he was fingering on the Captain's shoulders. 'Good!' he agreed. 'Tell the Menike fathers and mothers to come.'

Walking back over the mountains with his son, Hiatai, Pakoko kept pace with his long steps as if he also were a young man, but he knew his power was waning, even before the younger man said, 'Moana will live with Haape now, down by the sea where I can watch him.'

Well, it was natural that a new sea should cover up an old one, he thought, as he tramped the twilit way to his upland valley. It had always been so. He must remember that he was an old man who was ended.

NOTE

In July, 1829, the United States warship *Vincennes*, commanded by Captain Finch, called at Taiohae on a peaceful mission designed to assure American ships calling at Nuku Hiva of friendly hospitality. In order to keep the island itself at peace, the Captain and the Chaplain, Rev. Charles Stewart, insisted upon a federation of all tribes under 'King' Moana, the eight year old great-grandson of Kiato-nui. The Chaplain preached the doctrines of Christianity and secured an invitation for missionaries to come to Taiohae.

4

THE sky-piercing house on the sacred place of Haavao was no
longer empty. New mats of thatch covered its long roofs.
New bundles of god sticks and stuffed red birds had been
mounted on its ridge pole, as a sign to the three gods of the
sky and their bird messengers that a new seer was waiting for
their coming. Trembling with eagerness, Priest Veketu had
scarcely touched the cross pieces as he climbed the poles to the
high platform, which his grandfather, Kohu, had reached with
such slow awkwardness with his broken foot. Pakoko's eyes had
misted as he watched the soles of the young man's feet disappearing in the shaft above him. He felt as if he could sit down
and rest for a long, long time.

Now, perhaps, the boy, Moana, living down by the careless
coming-and-going sea, would be protected by the youth, Veketu,
firmly planted on the remote mountains. Alas, when Chief

Hiatai had restored the child to the terraces of Meau, he had not watched over him but had given that right to Chief Haape. Pakoko had been pushed away by the little man who hovered over Moana. Soon the boy himself had pretended that his ears were full of wax whenever the grandfather spoke.

Chief Haape was a short man, ashamed of having to look up at the faces around him. Now that disease made his legs weak, he followed Chief Kiato-nui's custom of riding on the shoulders of bearers. Whenever outsiders came asking for Pota's friend, he always sat on his litter looking down on them, while he let them know that he had taken the dead chief's place. He always pointed to the little High Chief to whom outsiders and landsmen alike had given consent, but he always boasted, 'Naturally, he is only a little fellow and I must speak for him.'

To win the *kaoha* of outsiders, Chief Haape threw them his possessions, as if he were a sea carrying sand to a new place. When at last the Menike fathers and mothers came to teach the landsmen about Iehova, he summoned workers to build houses for them and gave his own to them while they waited. To young Moana, he whispered, 'See their many boxes filled with fine things. Soon they will make a return.' He sent the young Chief and his friends from house to house to forbid work on every seventh day because there must be silence when the outsiders bowed down to their god. Seeing that the captains of visiting ships came to hear the Menike Priests tell stories of Iehova and his son, he invited them all to sit inside his men's house and nodded gladly when they praised him. Running his fingers over the fine dress of his visitors, he whined that he was ashamed of his own poor things. 'Iehova will think I do not respect him,' he said. Then he lifted the hands of the captains onto his head to thank them for the wrappings they gave him. Indeed, they were open handed. When Chief Haape had squeezed and fastened himself inside all that he could stand, he had others to give his friends, so that they also could come to see the Menikes talk to their god.

Priest Veketu stopped listening to his birds to hear the talk that trickled through the great valley of Taiohae and even into sealed Haavao. He came down to Chief Pakoko's house to complain. 'These Menikes tell the people that I am nothing but a man like themselves. They say that our images are nothing but wood and stone. They say our taboo foods are nothing but ordinary fowls and pigs that may be eaten at any time.' The young Priest interlaced his fingers and his eyes were troubled.

'Yes,' answered Pakoko. 'I heard. I was there, in the banyan tree above them.' He began to laugh. 'I called down to the fellow with the book, "Then we will eat Iehova." That tripped his tongue for a space.' But Veketu was still trembling. 'Nobody believes those lies,' the grandfather smoothed him.

'The people sit at the strange Priest's feet, Chief Haape says Iehova is good, Chief Moana sings with the mothers the sounds that call their god.' The young Priest poured out his anxiety.

'Tschae!' Pakoko made little of this devotion. 'All they want is presents and *kaoha* from the outsiders. Next time, come with me and laugh.'

The Master Chanter and the Priest of the Teiis lay on their backs and rolled from side to side with laughter. The Menike Priest was entertaining the folk of Taiohae down on the Meau feast place. He might have been the god, Tiki, playing his tricks. When he closed his eyes and chanted, someone yelled, 'Is your god blind?' When he flung out his arms, the yellow-stained young people made a dance of it. When he opened up the 'good book', an old man stopped rolling coconut fibres on his thigh to call out, 'The book is bad but powder is good,' and everybody chanted, 'The book is bad but powder is good.' Pakoko called out, 'Show us that Iehova has power. Ask him to point out the thief who stole your axe.' Everybody knew that Pakoko himself had taken that axe off the wall before the eyes of the Menikes. They all roared with laughter. A Brave Face, asleep with his mouth open and his nose sounding forth, woke with a start to hear the story of the land of spirits. 'That will be a good place for cowards afraid to fight and lazy fellows too tired to climb a coconut tree,' he bellowed. Mothers were singing to their restless children, old people were coughing and calling harsh complaints over the hardness of the stones, young people were whispering. The Teiis were tired of this play. They began to drift away from the feast place.

'You see,' said Pakoko to Priest Veketu, 'the Menike is a moon babbler. Soon he will lose his voice shouting into an empty cave.'

'Yes,' answered the young man, but he went close to the Menike Priest and said with a hard, piercing tongue, 'Perhaps your god is good for you. Keep him, then. Our own gods are good for us.'

One day, everybody stopped laughing at the entertainment Chief Haape offered every seventh day. He went too far. Perhaps the Chief thought that the outsiders made little of him, since they kept refusing to give him their child in adoption. Perhaps he wanted to show them that he was a brave man, unafraid of old taboos—'lies', the outsiders called them. Chief Haape gave a feast and ate a sacred fowl and a red pig reserved for the spirit of Priest Kohu alone. He turned away from the frightened eyes of the landsmen who saw this dreadful thing and sunned himself in the beams of the Menikes.

The word of Chief Haape's insult to the god, Kohu, leapt from house to house up valley to the slender spire where Priest Veketu stretched himself into the clear. The Master Chanter met the Diviner half way on the path. Neither one could let this bad thing pass and it was agreed that Pakoko would warn Haape of the sickness and death that must come to him.

After Pakoko's visit, Chief Haape was different. He began to look at the Menikes with hard eyes. He said he could not find workers to finish their houses. 'They expect a return,' he told them, 'red cloth, fish hooks, files, perhaps'. When he found they had none of these things, he muttered, 'They are people without things, nobodies.' What had they given the Chief himself for all his *kaoha*? Not even the child, and he had offered to make him a chief! Why had he offended his own god for such food-beggars? He shivered, thinking of Pakoko's words, 'You will surely die for breaking this taboo.' He began to beg the Menike Priests to make Iehova heal him. That would be only just. He had eaten the red food to please Iehova, but now Iehova would not heal him. The pains in his legs kept him awake in the night and weeping in the day. He began to call out loud, 'The gods of the landsmen are true. Iehova is pig's dung.' Nobody was surprised when Chief Haape died, but he called out with his last breath, 'Iehova has no power to heal me.' Perhaps that reached the ears of Priest Kohu in the sky.

Priest Veketu showed his power now. He called for three men to accompany the dead Chief's spirit to the skies and his Clubs found them fishing on the rocks below the sea wall of Taipivai. When the Taipis threatened revenge, Pakoko let the outsiders hear that the Taipis would come. 'The Taipis will destroy the Menikes!' people began to whisper. Even those strange Priests must have seen that Iehova was a nobody without power in this island. They went away on a ship with all their women and children and boxes.

NOTE

In August, 1833, an American mission, sent from Hawaii as a result of the Rev. Charles Stewart's urging and other representations of the need for Christianizing the Marquesas Islands, arrived in Taiohae and stayed until the following April, when they became convinced of their duty to abandon this field to the London Missionary Society, which was already established in areas nearby.

5

STRANGE. The talk of Iehova was not ended in Taiohae. First, there was the coming of a Menike *manowa* to punish Pakoko for killing a black man from their land. The fellow had been caught stealing potatoes reserved for the Chief. Naturally, Pakoko had killed him. Naturally, the Menikes demanded an exchange for their dead. This was just. Nobody complained. They hid their Chief in the mountains and sent pigs to the ship. The *manowa* went away satisfied. But the landsmen were not content. They whispered together in little knots. Had Iehova seen Pakoko swing his club against this thief? Had he sent his ship to seek revenge? Chief Moana boasted, 'My god, Iehova, is a jealous god. He will punish anyone who goes against him.'

Indeed, young Moana was talking a great deal about Iehova. He had learned of the Menike mothers how to look at the book called 'good' to find in it the calls to Iehova. 'A-e-i-o-u!' he chanted now in *kaoha* to Iehova. He tried to find other songs in the book given him by the Menikes. He asked help from a young Peketane, Glass Eyes, who had made the talk clear for the outsiders. These two young men began to wander about the valley, arms enlaced, whispering together about the wonderful things of the people who followed Iehova.

Pakoko was cruelly agitated. He had warned Moana's uncle that young ears are easily tickled, but he had refused to separate the friends. Everybody liked Glass Eyes. He was always polite. He made just returns for gifts. 'He keeps Moana from running wild with night moths,' the uncle said. But the Chief of Haavao thought of his brother, Kiato-nui, who gave his name to every new comer. He had seen the same radiant *kaoha* on Moana's upturned face when he had followed the Menike priests. Indeed he had been sickened the day of Moana's joining to Hiatai's adopted daughter in Hakapaa, when the young Chief had scarcely glanced at the girl but had fastened his eyes on the outsider as if he were adoring the sun. Was there some bad god who entered into landsmen to make them despise their own roots?

Priest Veketu had tried in vain to nourish this shoot of four great roots of Nuku Hiva. He had offered many victims to the gods to put force into him so that his trunk would stand up in any wind, when he cut his hair, when he bathed, when he went on a journey, but each time the youth seemed to turn further away from the good ways of his people. He laughed at the old way of planting new shoots on the fifteenth night of the moon and at the prohibition on fishing during breadfruit growing moons, because the Menikes who planted potatoes laughed at these things. During the visit of a fellow called Shoes, who wore even his hard shoes all the time, Moana refused to play in the bush on moon nights, because Shoes said it was indecent. Glass Eyes made Moana afraid of the bad spirit, Setani, who threw into his fiery oven all those who disobeyed the god, Iehova.

Pakoko thought perhaps it was this bad spirit, Setani, who was eating Moana's strength. He went to discuss this thing with Priest Veketu. 'Can't you pull this bad god out of Moana?' he asked.

The Priest answered with a strangled cry. 'Do you also question my power? Throw your spear, then, at the birds on my roof!'

The grandfather was astonished at his trembling. 'I have not accused you,' he said softly.

'Nobody throws a spear,' Veketu said bitterly, 'but everyone doubts me.' He began to beat his palms together. 'It is true. I am full of darkness. Who is this Iehova, god of thunder? Who is Setani, god of fire?'

Pakoko smoothed himself quickly. 'Naturally, you do not know them,' he said lightly. 'Those names belong to other families in distant lands.' He slapped his thigh in sudden discovery. 'Perhaps Iehova and Setani think Moana is an outsider because he is without tattooing!'

The stale breath ran out of Priest Veketu and he gulped in the sudden fresh air. He laughed as he watched Pakoko go off to make preparations for the great work of image-striking. He thought he heard the sky god calling for a Brave Face for the feast of image showing, when Chief Moana would be marked as a landsman for all to see. He climbed up above eagerly to sit in the clear, waiting for the name of the man whom he could send to the skies simply by pointing his finger at him.

There was something bad going on in the taboo house of image-striking. Loud angry voices were raised when only the murmured prayer of the Master should be heard. This was the time when the newly tattooed should be receiving the strength of an Ironwood and the grace of a dancer from the sacred flesh sent them by Priest Veketu. Yet a wild storm was tearing the silence of the rite to shreds.

As Chief Pakoko approached the taboo house, Moana and the Master burst out of it, pushing and clawing at each other. 'You will not make me eat the flesh of a man!' the young Chief was screaming. Never since the gods had taught men the work of image-striking had anything like this occurred. The Master Chanter felt like a leaf swept up by a wind, when Moana raced past him and commanded the servers to open the feast oven. 'Pig is good food!' he declared. 'I will eat pig!' Seeing the workers stooping, hands gripping the bark they had dragged from the oven, unable to move, he leaned over himself and pulled off the covering leaves. 'There, that one!' he pointed to the roasted animal.

Pakoko found his speech at last. 'Would you swallow the power of a pig or a man?' he asked.

'Those old lies are ended!' Moana shouted. 'Iehova says, "No more fish for false gods, no more eating of men!" '

Pakoko was stepping forward to put his hand over the mouth of this mad child, when a sound not of men but of gods shook the tree tops. Swelling to a roar, then pinched to a thin whistle, spirit wailing was drawing near. The free young people who had been tattooed crept inside their taboo house. The feasters on the paving closed their eyes and stopped breathing. Even Pakoko's skin crawled as the god, Veketu, descended from his perch.

Moana could scarcely find air to breathe but he spread his legs as he stood up in front of the oven and lifted his chin against the awful wind blowing down upon him. He did not shrink back. Indeed, he leaned towards Priest Veketu and shook his fist at him when he halted on the other side of the oven. 'You gave me a man to eat!' he cried. 'You wanted Iehova to punish me in his fiery oven! But I did not eat your bait. I will not be caught!'

'You will eat the flesh sent by the gods!' the Priest commanded. He stepped down into the oven, set his bare feet upon the hot stones and walked across, the fire-breath swirling about his legs, lifting his cape. He struck at the Chief with his god sticks.

But Moana gripped the sacred bundle himself and stared at Veketu without blinking. 'Priest Veketu! Priest Woodlouse!' he mocked him. 'Your gods have no power. They are nothing but sticks!' He wrenched the bound bundle from the Priest's hand and flung it down on the stones.

The people clung to the earth, pressing their faces flat. But the god, Veketu, did not destroy them in a tempest of anger. He trembled and stood staring at his unbound sticks, scattered on the paving.

Pakoko darted at the fool who had shamed the god, seized him and shook him till his teeth rattled. 'What the god asks, not even the High Chief can refuse!' he cried. 'Ask what you will,' he said to Veketu. 'Moana will wipe out this insult.'

But Priest Veketu was unable to ask anything. Not until the grandfather's blazing eyes lighted a feeble flame was he able to move. Then he whirled away in a rush of wind, his faint tremulo risng to a long-drawn wail.

Hanging limply over Pakoko's arm, Moana spoke with the hoarseness of a child who has cried a long time. 'I will go away from this black land. I will go where Iehova's people live in the light.' He freed himself from the old man's grasp and looked with contempt upon the people who lay on the paving. 'I will come back on a *manowa* with big blowers,' he shouted. 'Then I will make you take Iehova for your god, all of you!'

'Go to your houses,' Pakoko commanded his people. 'Your High Chief is sick. I will send for a Master Healer.' But there was a different thought inside him. It would be a good thing for Moana to go away to distant lands. 'He will go with his friend, Glass Eyes. They will slip away quietly in the night.'

NOTE

The date and exact circumstances of Moana's departure from Nuku Hiva are not definitely known. He was not on the island when the French sloops of war, *Astrolabe* and *Zelee*, visited Taiohae in 1838 and it was said at the time that he had departed with an English missionary to live in Rarotonga at the mission school and later in England, and that he had promised to return on a warship to enforce his new ideas. Later, Max Radiguet, secretary to the chief of staff when Admiral du Petit Thouars took possession of the island, quoted Moana as saying that he 'had seen England near and France from afar'. He also wrote that his religious tutors profited by taking Moana to England, making him assistant cook on the voyage, and exhibiting him in London for two pence. However, inquiries of the London Missionary Society have uncovered only the information that Moana was living with Rev. G. Stallworthy at Tahu Ata in 1839.

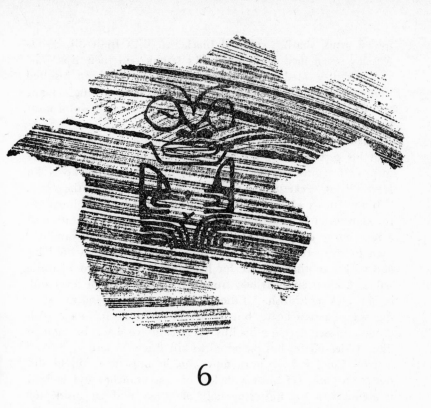

6

'Jehova is powerful? Kohu is insignificant?' These were the questions whispered in Priest Veketu's ears after the disappearance of Chief Moana and his Peketane friend. The Priest could not understand his birds because of this noise. Was this the whispering of the three birds of the sky or the whispering of his own tongue? He did not know. Sitting on his high perch, ten arm lengths above the land, he looked up at the image burned on the level above him. It was the hole in the sky through which Fai had dropped fire to men. He held up his palms, like a child asking for breadfruit paste. When no light fell, he dropped his heavy hands. The whispering! The whispering again! He reached for his *kava* bowl. He was about to kick it onto the stones below because its liquid was always dull, when he saw an image clearing in its depths. He drank in the sight thirstily. It was a carved stone, a great *tiki* with closed eyes and folded arms, sharply cut and blackened with fresh oil. At its feet lay seven men with fish hooks fastened in their lips. The god, Kohu, wanted a new image. Kohu who had been insulted wanted seven fish! The anger of the god against Chief Haape and Chief Moana must be smothered. The power of Kohu must be renewed. 'I see! I see!' cried Priest Veketu.

Pakoko shut himself inside his food house, but he could not shut his ears to the whispers of friends who climbed up there to protest against the big angry wind that was tearing up Nuku Hiva. 'Priest Veketu is a tern fishing in all waters!' they said. 'No one knows where he will dive next.' First he had blown fire through seven Hapaa Brave Faces to offer at the consecration of a new image carved for the god, Kohu. Then he had caught a man to carry the dead Priest's loin cloth, another to hold his god sticks, another to care for his ironwood staff. From hostile tribes, from friendly tribes, from low level and high level folk he was picking his fish. All the chiefs were enraged and threatening war. Pakoko heard but he sat as silent as an image with tongue pressed between his lips. At last the word was brought to him, 'Chief Hiatai has promised to kill Priest Veketu.'

Now Chief Pakoko must move, no, he must run, but he did not see a path. He built a shelter of new branches and hedged it about with the fluttering flags of taboo, and sat inside for seven days without food or sleep, waiting for the light. On the eighth day he went to the sacred place to invite Priest Veketu to come to this house for instruction. When he saw the frightful face and the foam-flecked lips of the young man, he was not agitated. He took the crooked, grasping fingers into his own hands as if they had been the soft ones of a little child. 'Come,' he said gently. 'I have been commanded to teach you.'

The Priest was swollen with power so that everything he could see lay below him. 'What have you to teach me?' he taunted him.

'I am the only Teii who knows the seas which have climbed onto this land from the beginning until this day,' Pakoko answered without anger. 'Now I am old. When I am sucked back under another sea, there will be no one to chant the names which link the landsmen with their source, no one to nourish them with the ancient wisdom. It has never been the custom to give the work of a seer and a bard to the same man, but these are troubled days when one man must do the work of two, and you are able.' All the while, the grandfather was leading the young Priest away from his high terraces down towards the small shelter he had built. When he had made Veketu wash off old juices and bad smells, he brought him into the taboo house and drew the screen across the opening.

During the moons of instruction, as Pakoko made the young man repeat again and again the calming words that had sustained the landsmen from sea to sea, he saw the blood mist clear from Veketu's maddened eyes. He watched him draw in the tern's hungry beak, tuck it under his wing, and rest on still water. Seeing him whole again, he sent him back to his high place.

The old Chief had forgotten Hiatai's threat against the Priest until Mauhau said, 'Your son came to kill Veketu. The skies fell when he saw your taboo sticks protecting him. But when the Priest's Clubs gave him their blowers, one for every Hapaa seized for the god, Chief Hiatai went away, satisfied.' Perhaps Mauhau was laughing at his old friend when he added, 'What power there is in blowers!'

7

Pakoko was very, very tired. He did not leap up to hear the murmuring of each new day but lay in his sleeping house until long after the faces of men were plainly to be seen. He lay for a very long time in his bathing pool, just floating, knowing that the sun had splintered the mountain, that he was wreathed in leaves, that he was walking in the clear. He took a very long time to sun himself, oil his skin, fasten his white beard properly, tie his clean loin cloth. He was tired because there was nothing he could do but wait.

When the old Chief of Haavao had seen the tail of his voyaging canoe swallowed by the dark as it slid away from Nuku Hiva carrying Moana and his Peketane friend to outsiders who lived on Tahu Ata, he had not waited the night out to find the High Chief's successor. It was wasted time mourning over Moana. Someone had made a song which said, 'Moana is an outsider.'

True, and now he had gone to his own. But in Hakapaa a child was coming who would take his place, and Pakoko had gone over the mountains to ask for this little one in the stomach of Hiatai's adopted daughter, who was Moana's woman. Alas, he had found a mother coughing away her life-breath mingled with blood, and a child inside her which no longer moved. There was no time for grief. Cloudy fears whipped the old man to haste. He went immediately to the far western valley of Hakaui, taking with him the consent of all chiefs that Pae-tini's second daughter, Vae-kehu, should take her dying sister's place as High Chiefess of all Nuku Hiva.

This anxiety cleared away, the pecking at Pakoko's liver had continued. He had trembled at the dark clouds of sickness which were hovering over the land. He had gone about his own valley with the priestesses who knew how to pull out all the bad gods known to the grandfathers, how to make a god fall where he could be questioned about healing remedies for old time sicknesses. With them he had seen the dreadful diseases sent by the gods of the outsiders. In his dreams he kept seeing them: people crawling far back into their houses to spit blood behind the head log where it would not be touched; men climbing to their taboo houses to get away from the bad smells and the holes in the flesh of their women; mothers ashamed of their children who came out like birds without feathers, without hair, without finger nails, with skin stretched tight over crooked bones; women on every terrace rubbing away the putrid flesh from the crumbling bones of relatives who had died. Through the long days while he sat on his terrace, he kept up a low murmur of old chants so that he would not hear the coughing that broke the unnatural silence of his valley.

The old Chief had encouraged the priestesses to perform their work for these poor people. 'Do not believe the loud-tongued lies of the outsiders who say these diseases cannot be healed,' he begged them. 'You be-little the power of your own gods. You make the people question your learning. They are asking, "Have our healers forgotten potent mixtures and true words?"' Pakoko had put force into many of these women, but, everytime they tried to heal, the god they had invoked would say, 'I have struck my foot against a stone,' and go away, refusing to work. Finally, he had built them a taboo house and sent them inside to fast and refresh themselves with old spells. He had composed himself to wait.

One day, forcing himself to walk slowly back and forth on his terrace, he paused before a small house he had built for his foster nephew, a son of his cousin, Oehitu. He had not seen this young man sliding in and out like a shadow for perhaps a moon. The uncle was ashamed of his neglect. He stood looking at the screen propped in front of the opening. He was thinking of the day long ago when he had brought this youth to his house. 'Feed my child,' his mother had begged. Pakoko could see her now as she squatted beside the path, clasping her son between swollen legs. She was the first one he had seen with face ravaged by the new disease. He had not known her. He had looked at the blemished child, whose arms hung down like broken branches, but he had seen only his brilliant eyes. Puku's eyes had not begged. They had commanded, and Pakoko had lifted the boy onto his hip, saying, 'Yes, I will feed him.'

The uncle smiled as he reached for the door screen. Puku had brought him joy. As the youth grew and the bad spirit inside him began to bend him over so that he could not run and play with the young people, Pakoko had taught him to chant and it seemed as if Puku had no desire for good arms and legs as long as he had a tongue that could sound old words. Looking into his bright quick eyes, the uncle had often forgotten that the young man was tortured by an evil god. As he pushed aside the screen now, he chanted playfully, 'Come, Tanaoa, stand erect on the shining sands!'

The light from the opening fell upon Puku's face and upon his eyes, dull, asleep! Had eye night come to him? Through the heavy silence, the young man's voice sounded like a shell coming across water through night. 'Gliding away, Tanaoa, from the sands,' he answered.

'No!' Pakoko cried out. 'By my head, you shall be made whole again!' Torn by grief, he could wait no longer for silent gods to speak. He called to the women inside the taboo house, 'Come out! Here is work for you!' When they came, he could see that they were ashamed. 'Is there one among you who has the courage to whip out the vile god that is eating my nephew, Puku?' he demanded.

The women were silent, hanging their heads. Then one looked up. 'It is better to die of shame than of neglect,' she said. 'I will try.'

When the sick young man heard that his women relatives were waiting on the terrace to take part in the rite of healing, hot tears ran into his raw flesh. 'No,' he begged, knowing that his manhood would be destroyed.

'Tanaoa, *aia!*' Pakoko encouraged him as he laid him gently on a mat and covered him with leaves of banana and coconut and a fresh white *tapa*.

The Priestess raised a cluster of *ti* leaves as a sign to a young woman to come forward. 'You are defiled!' she screamed at the filthy god inside Puku when the girl dropped her *tapas* and sprang onto the sick man's quivering body. 'Come out!' she commanded in a frenzy, beating with her *ti* leaves while the girl jumped upon the soft flesh in vain. When no god came out, shrieking and tossing aside the still form of Puku, his uncle commanded, 'Go on beating!'

The Priestess turned sick eyes upon the old man. 'You can beat out this god if you know his name!' she cried. 'I do not know it. The grandfathers-far-below do not know it. I know who sends the good sickness of blindness. I know that the blind are lifted to the skies by the pitying gods. But this eye-night is different. I do not know who sends this sickness that melts bones and makes skin shine yellow and red. Perhaps it is Setani. Perhaps he will throw Puku into Iehova's fiery oven. Who knows? Let the outsiders beat out their own vile spirit!'

As the poor woman threw away her stalk of *ti* leaves and rushed away sobbing, someone pushed through the crowds who watched. 'I am a Priest of Iehova. I will take your nephew,' a strange voice said, curiously mouthing the words.

'It is the Katorika Priest,' the whisper was breathed about.

Pakoko was stunned. He had never seen this fellow face to face, though he had often heard his feet on his path. He knew there were three foreign priests, just alike, entirely wrapped in black except for hands and faces. He knew that they lived in houses given them by Chiefess Pae-tini in the twin valleys and that they were called Wee-wees because they always answered, 'Oui, oui.' This one was different only because his strong foot turned with every step and grated on the land. Hearing those uneven steps, Pakoko had questioned often, 'Where is that fellow going?' It was always 'to ask Priest Veketu the names of trees and birds and pigs.' The Master Planter had told Pakoko that this Katorika Priest always left a question with Priest Veketu that made him beat his palms together and bite his nails. The Master had said, 'The outsider is trying to confuse our Priest. His lips are always fluttering over black spells as he goes about our valley. He is like a black spider spinning a web to catch all of us.' Now here was the black cloud hovering over Pakoko's dear foster child, saying, 'I will take him!' The Chief of Haavao had neither club nor sling at hand, but he struck with vile words. 'Go away, you filthy woman's mat!'

The insult did not touch the man. He stooped over the sick man and spoke with soft smooth tongue. 'Iehova will give you everlasting life.'

Was the spider with his fluttering lips entangling Puku in his spell? The sick man raised his head. 'Perhaps Iehova can make me whole,' he panted.

Pakoko was reaching for the Priest's thick neck when Veketu's piercing voice stopped him. Here was another who had been hiding in the crowd, watching. 'If the Katorika's god has power, let him show it,' he commanded.

Amazement, shame, anger tore Pakoko to pieces until he saw the cunning in Priest Veketu's eyes. He had laid an open noose at the feet of the outsider. If Iehova could not heal Puku, he and his priests would be ended in this land! 'Yes, let Iehova show his power!' the old man agreed.

'Friend, what is your thought?' That was the question rustling like an uneasy bird all through the valley. Would Iehova heal Puku? What was the Katorika doing to the sick man down below in his shut house? Masters, Brave Faces, fishermen, old people and young, all sat idly, waiting to hear.

At last Pakoko's cousin, Oehitu, came up the path, carrying Puku on his back. Everyone stood up to see. Alas, the sick man was not walking. The words of the Katorika were wind, after all.

Puku raised his head and called out to them, his face shining like water under sun. 'He has poured sacred water on my head and given me a place in the skies!' he called.

What did he mean? The folk swung from foot to foot, closer and closer to the Chief's terrace. They saw the old man receive his nephew and carry him inside his house. They saw Priest Veketu fly down from his sky and enter also. They waited, squatting silently on the paving.

Pakoko knelt beside the young man. 'You are not standing up!' His cry was split, triumph on one side, grief on the other. Priest Veketu stood apart, darkly smiling. Now he knew that Iehova's Priest had no power over this sickness.

'Hear the way of the Katorika's work!' Puku called out. 'His voice was a high sea swelling under me, lifting me up into clear space. I saw the god on his high seat in the sky. "Throw away the evil that is in you. Weep!" the Priest said to me, and I wept. "Hear Iehova only!" he said, and I opened my ears. "I give you a name," he said. "You are Piero."'

Pakoko's tongue pierced his joy. 'If you gave your name in exchange, he will take your bones and skin as well as your spirit and eat you altogether.'

Puku still floated serenely. 'No, that is not the way of it. The name is known to Iesu and to his father, Iehova. When I die, I have a name to sound that will give me entrance to their bright land above.'

'Lies!' The old man's breast was torn with anguish for his nephew, but he could not let this pass. 'Only the sick whose trouble is given by the gods can enter the skies.'

Puku raised himself on one elbow and declared solemnly, 'Hear the truth. Chiefs, priests, braves killed in battle, victims offered to the gods, those with good sicknesses, all are burning in the land of fiery bottom. Only those with names known to Iesu are called into his light. And I am the first.'

'What names are those—Iehova, Iesu, Piero?' Priest Veketu's sudden shrill question struck through the fog of Pakoko's anger and grief.

'The names of nobodies. The three gods of the sky have never heard them,' declared the old Chief, trying to blow a cold wind on Veketu's fever.

'The three gods of the sky are evil spirits leading the lands-men into black paths,' Puku spoke across his uncle and stretched out his hand to the Priest. 'Veketu, my cousin, throw out the evil gods that drive you wild.'

The Priest fell on his knees beside the sick man and covered his face with trembling hands. 'I hear many names,' he sobbed. 'Which are true?'

The Chief pulled Veketu to his feet. 'Iesu is a bad spirit. The Katorika has sent him inside my poor nephew to destroy him. Call him out! Crush him!' he commanded.

'Do not anger Iesu!' the sick man begged.

Priest Veketu freed himself and struck at Pakoko with his ironwood staff. 'Go away! My work is with the sick man alone.'

Driven by a menacing god with rolling white eyes and rasping tongue, the Chief backed out of the house and saw the screen pushed across the opening. He could only wait outside, gnawed by fears for his two young relatives.

Days and nights, Priest Veketu kept all others from that house. He sat beside Puku, questioning long, questioning short. 'What things have you seen? What sounds have you heard? What hidden things do you know?'

When the sick man tried to answer, he grew confused and groped about in circles. Many times he fainted, stifled in the hot breath of his questioner. Waking one day to find Veketu's eyes had caught him on barbed hooks, he cried out, 'Iesu! Iesu! Here am I, Piero! Carry me to the skies! Quickly!' He pulled at the Priest's *tapa*. 'Take me again to the house of the Kato-rika,' he begged.

Veketu lifted him onto his own back and ran with him all the way to that house in the twin valleys, eager to see for himself what had been hidden from him. Forced to remain outside, he made a hole in the thatch and sat close to see and to hear. The beating of the Katorika's lovely red voice came to him clearly, making his flesh crawl with its beauty, He could see white *tapa*, white hands, shining drops of oil, a bright flame of a candle, appearing and disappearing as the black robe uncovered and covered them. He could see an image, a small light thing, twisted in agony. Was this an image of Puku? Was he being made a god? When the sick man cried out, 'I see the god!' Veketu waited no longer but broke through the thatch into the house. He could see no god. There was only the Katorika Priest who knelt to close Puku's mouth, whence his spirit had fled. Veketu backed away and ran like the wind to tell Pakoko. 'The outsider has let Puku die!'

Sudden tears wet Pakoko's cheeks, but he lifted his chin and breathed deeply. At least, Priest Veketu would stand up whole now, knowing that the Katorika Priest was without power, knowing that he alone could care for the dead man's bones. He said to Oehitu, 'Go tell the Katorika that Puku's spirit has appeared to me and asked that his body be sent to Priest Veketu on the sacred place.' Then he blew his conch, announcing the death of his nephew to all the folk of Taiohae who waited to hear the answer to their questioning.

But Priest Veketu was not standing up whole, terrible in power. It was whispered about that he had not wrapped Puku's bones and hung them up, that he did not climb every day to the peak of his house but sat idly at its base. The old Chief of Haavao, worn out with the swinging to and fro of this wind-tossed reed, climbed wearily to his high terrace. It was true. The Priest was sitting with his hands on his knees, slow tears rolling from his closed lids. 'Have the gods no work for you?' he demanded.

The grandson turned his head from side to side. 'I do not know,' he said hopelessly. 'Puku knew. He saw. His new name took him in.'

Pakoko was disgusted. 'You know the true names, all of them. Can the Priest of Iehova match you? Have you heard him dig to the roots or ascend to the source?'

Priest Veketu looked at the old man as if he saw him now. 'I have not challenged him to sound the names,' he answered.

'Challenge him, then!' said the grandfather sharply. 'In all Nuku Hiva there is not a Master Chanter who can overthrow you. Show him your great knowledge. Trip him up. Shame him.'

The young man stood up. His eyes began to sparkle. He dressed himself in ceremonial *tapas*, in cape and cap of coconut leaves. 'You will go with me, grandfather?' he asked.

Pakoko laughed. 'I want to see that boaster die of shame,' he said, following the Priest on the downward path.

The Katorika was a man like any other. He called out to his visitors, 'Come in! Come in!' and ran about spreading mats for them. He made them look at his beautiful things. There was a tiny image on the wall, a woman with a child in her arms. The landsmen could not take their eyes from her white skin and bright *tapas*. 'That is the Mother of God,' said the Katorika.

'What god?' Pakoko demanded.

'Iesu is her son,' the outsider answered.

'No name at all,' snapped the old man. 'Your god has no name to sound for entrance in our land.'

'Your names are called to enter a valley of Nuku Hiva,' came the quick reply, 'but Iesu's name must be sounded to enter the path to the skies.'

'Nonsense!' the Chief snorted. 'Priest Veketu knows depths and heights where you cannot follow.' He waved his hand at his young relative. 'Begin with me and go to the source of all,' he commanded.

Priest Veketu closed his eyes and raised his voice, stepping down name by name. Pakoko lay on his back, watching the outsider sliding his fingers along the balls on his string. Veketu needed no knotted cords to remember. His stomach was full of names. No one could cross him or trip him or turn him aside. This puffed up outsider would be lost. He would die of shame, surely. Pakoko smiled. But, as the throbbing tones of the landsman's voice caught him in their majestic rhythm, he forgot the Katorika and went with Priest Veketu from men to heroes, to gods, to sands, rocks and waters, to levels and roots, to light and dark, and into the clear void where breathing stopped.

The rapt serenity of the landsmen was suddenly shattered by a pulsing flow of tone from the Katorika's throat, as he named his beads from Iesu to Adam to Iehova. Clearly, the fellow was not ashamed. He followed his own path with confidence. But Priest Veketu began to tremble. He had emptied his stomach. He had no name to throw across this unknown path. He was lost. He could no longer endure the unending stream of mighty names flung at him by the outsider. He could no longer sit there, powerless to stop it, unable to understand it. He must run away to hide his shame. He fled from that house.

Chief Pakoko stopped the chanting of that moon-babbler of

bird talk with an angry roar. 'Swallow your lies and die of them!' he shouted and stamped out of the house.

Pakoko's anger at Priest Veketu's trembling before a flood of outlandish sounds turned to anxiety when Mauhau told him that Veketu had gone to the sacred place at the time of fires, walking like an old man without muscles. The grandfather could not sleep. He twisted about on his mat and groaned. Finally, he wrapped himself in *tapas* and went out into the cold, spirit-filled night. Perhaps the lad was sick. It was a good thing to go see him. He quickened his feet. He was showing his breathing when he reached the top terrace of the sacred place but he ran towards the sleeping house. The last nut of a taper was burning feebly inside. In its flickering light, Pakoko saw Veketu sitting against an end post, his head thrown back, his open eyes catching the winking flame.

'Veketu, my grandson!' the old man called softly. He crawled towards him. When he did not move, he touched his knee. It was cold! Veketu was dead! Pakoko did not cry out either in grief or in rage. 'Yes,' he said, as if he had known, 'Priest Veketu is dead.' Looking at the flame eating the last nut of the taper, seeing it vanish in the dark, he muttered, 'My work also is ended.'

NOTE

In February, 1839, three Catholic priests of the Congregation des Sacrés-Coeurs de Picpus came to Taiohae. Their first convert was baptised the following May and died a month later.

VII   THE DEATH CANOE

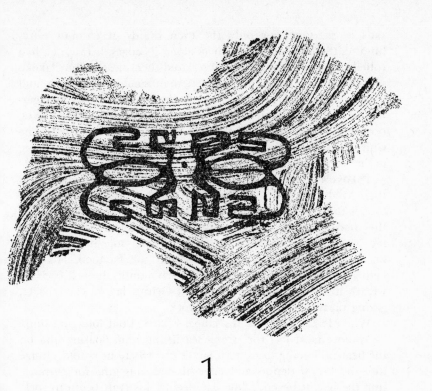

1

'BRING my wave-jumping canoe!' Pakoko shouted to his cousins, Mauhau and Oehitu, before he had crossed the paving upon his return from the last rites for Priest Veketu. He had not had time to enjoy this beautiful work before. Naturally, he had long ago realized that he was the last of his sea to linger on the land, that he must be ready to float on his retreating waters as they were sucked back into the deeps, and he had asked for a swift-winged sea bird to be made for that last voyage. While he still had work, he had scarcely thought of it, but now he cried eagerly, 'Let me have a look at my sky-going canoe.'

When the two old men had brought the carved and polished hull for the third old man, they three sat looking at it. One saw only the adzed grooves that rippled its surface in the quiet sun-light, because he had rubbed those fine patterns with his own rat's tooth. One saw only the even braids of coconut fibres binding the tropic bird's feathers along its edges, because he had rolled them on his thigh and interlaced them neatly. But Pakoko saw a land in distant seas where handsome young men and sweet-scented young women, wrapped in yellow *tapas* and garlanded with pandanus fruits, were dancing and eating. Yes, certainly, it was an island of play! Was it play he wanted? The Chief quivered with silent laughter over an old memory. 'Bring me my nose flute,' he said.

Pakoko's daughters popped out of their sleeping house when their aged father, sitting contentedly in his death canoe, began to call their names on his flute. They stood staring at him as if they had never seen him before. His adopted son ran from the men's house and squatted in front of him, solemnly watching his fingers fluttering over the holes in the bamboo. His hot-bellied woman, laughing with wide open mouth, threw a fragrant wreath into the canoe. Mauhau and Oehitu lay on their backs, gazing rapturously at their handiwork.

When Pakoko slept in his canoe, stretched out long and limp, he could almost feel the strong sea lifting him, floating him on the beautiful going to western land's end where he would plunge into the lowest depths and offer his precious gifts for entrance into the height beyond. One day, feeling his craft begin to rock, he thought, 'Now my canoe that jumps the waves is breasting the western sea at last.' But no. Oehitu's face was peering at him over the edge. Pakoko pushed him away and turned his back. 'I am tired of hearing that another ship has come.' They were always coming, but they were always going. He could not be bothered.

'Moana has come back,' his cousin made him hear.

The old Chief gripped the sideboards and pulled himself up. 'With a *manowa?*' he asked at last. Many times the folk of Taiohae had hidden themselves in trees and caves, fearing that Moana had returned with a warship and big blowers.

'No. With a Peketane Priest,' Oehitu answered.

The old man sighed as he got up. 'Tie my canoe to the rafters,' he said wearily.

Descending seaward, Pakoko drew the folk of his valley after him as smelts are drawn by a flaming torch. They ran alongside, telling him what they had seen. 'As soon as Moana jumped onto the land, he threw down his bundles and called out to the sailors in the boat, "Now you will carry, for here I am Chief." . . . Standing in front of his house, Moana said, "I will burn this rubbish and you will build me a proper house of stone." . . . We thought he was an outsider until he bellowed for his Fire Keeper to heat the oven stones . . . He said to the Peketane Priest, "In your land you eat when you have money, here we eat when we are hungry." '

A master pulled at the Chief's arm. 'Will he make us burn our gods?'

'Not while there is breath in me,' the old man answered.

The Chief of Haavao sat apart on the terrace where the welcoming feast was spread. He had not spoken a word, but he was there, in the corners of all eyes. He had never taken his own eyes off the wanderer who had returned. He was digging into him, down to his very roots. He found it impossible to catch Moana's eyes that were running from side to side. What was the fellow afraid of? He sent men-at-the-side running needlessly. He spoke with too loud a tongue, naming himself too often as High Chief of Nuku Hiva, turning too often towards the red-haired outsider to be sure he was heard. Had the outsiders shamed him, made him feel small in their land? Certainly Moana was not like Kiato-nui who had dripped *kaoha* over his outsiders and nodded whenever they spoke. It seemed as if there were a struggle between these two, both wanting to go first.

When Pakoko turned his eyes upon the Peketane Priest, the man was quick to feel their piercing points. He made a sharp return, but, finding his clear hard eyes caught and held, he wrenched them free and spoke to the old man. 'High Chief Moana has come back to bring good to his people,' he said, making true landsmen's words carefully. Pakoko made no sign that he had heard, but turned to the food on his leaves. He had seen many things: the Peketane's intestines were not double, he did not speak to deceive, but his arm would be upraised against everything the landsmen called good, against Moana himself when he crossed him. Good. Moana himself would drive the man away.

As if to answer Pakoko's unspoken thought, Chief Moana called across to him, 'My friend has left his beautiful land to come to this ugly place of rocks, to help me make everything new.' No one flinched under these wounding words, but the young man bounded up and opened his arms to his seated relatives, as if he knew he must heal them quickly. Tall and thin, swaying from foot to foot, his queer yellow skin flushed, he told them what lay in distant seas. His roving eyes were fixed on air, as he began to make everyone see the islands of the Peketanes, their enormous stone houses, their clean, hard paths, their rolling carts and man-mounted pigs called horses. He praised his outlandish clothing, taking it off piece by piece, naming it, pulling it to show its strength. He was making a song and a dance of it and he set his listeners to rocking with his repeated words, 'Beautiful, beautiful, strong, strong.'

'Strong is his desire for these things in distant lands. Why didn't he stay there?' thought Pakoko. 'He is an outsider, but he doesn't know it.'

The young Chief, at ease now, floating on a friendly tide, began to ridicule the things of the landsmen. He picked at the finery of his uncle, Niehitu, who sat next him, brushing a careless hand through the white beard plume on his head. 'Look at this worn-out hair, thrown away by some old man before you were born!' He ran his fingers across his band of porpoise teeth. 'Rotten old points from a dead fish!' He dipped the tail of his loin cloth into water and tore it to shreds. 'Rags!' He jerked up his uncle's arm and pointed a shaking finger at the images tattooed there. 'In London,' he rasped, 'the people pay two pence to look at these vile marks of a savage!'

'Ah, they have made him ashamed,' thought Pakoko.

Moana brushed away angry tears and snatched a bottle tucked into his uncle's girdle. He emptied the hot drink into his mouth before his red-haired friend could seize the bottle. He avoided Red Hair's begging eyes and shouted flaming words across his head. 'You will burn all these mouldy things and your flimsy houses. I will make everything new, beautiful and strong. Red Hair will show me how and Iehova will bless me.' As a low growl of complaint from his seated relatives swelled to an angry howling, his voice broke into shrill splinters that pierced only his own ears.

The outsider tried to calm the tempest. 'Your High Chief desires only good for you,' he cried. 'He is upset to see his relatives wandering in paths of darkness.'

Moana struck again, like lightning. 'I know the ways of light. I know what is good. You will hear my commands and I will make you a great people. All tribes, all islands will follow me and no other.' He threw this directly at Pakoko.

'No!' Long drawn, like the sounding of a conch, the word was blown upon him from the high-born on the terrace and from the common water on the paving below.

Moana felt the sand sliding from beneath his feet but he dug in his toes. 'I was chosen by the grandfathers as High Chief of all Nuku Hiva!' he shouted.

'You were chosen by the outsiders.' Pakoko had spoken at last.

All faces turned towards the calm old man, who had spoken with force but without anger. Ah, here was a chief indeed, a father chief, with quiet eyes and a white beard spread over his breast, rising and falling gently with his unhurried breathing. 'Hear Pakoko!' someone cried. 'Pakoko! Let us follow Pakoko! Let us sit in the shadow of this wise man! Yes, Pakoko is our High Chief!' The cries made a ball that rolled through the crowd.

The old Chief rose with dignity. 'Yes, my children,' he answered them, 'I am High Chief for those who follow the ways of the grandfathers.'

When Moana saw the people rising to follow Pakoko away from his stones, he danced his anger. 'This is cause for war!' he screamed.

'Old paths are worth fighting for,' was the old man's last word as he left that place, leading his children.

The Peketane tried to stop them. 'Moana is confused. Iehova does not bring war, but peace.'

Moana turned his anger upon his friend. 'In your land, you gave the orders,' he shouted. 'Here, it is I! I say, War!'

NOTE

M. L'Abbé Mathias Gracia, who was a member of the Catholic Mission to Nuku Hiva from 1839 to 1842, writes that Moana returned on December 3, 1839, with an English Protestant missionary, R. Thompson, who expected to convert the islands because of his friendship with the High Chief.

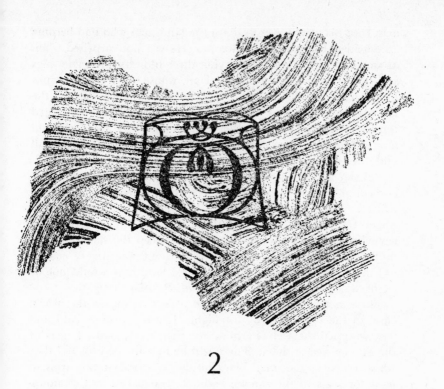

2

THE chiefs of Nuku Hiva laughed at Moana's call for war. Who would fight for him? Nobody but food-beggars, lizard-eaters, dwellers on his lands who were afraid to run away, old people who had been tied to his family, namesakes who could not refuse him, lichen who had escaped from other chiefs, all driftwood. Not even the outsiders dwelling on his lands would stand with the Peketane Priest. 'Priests and their taboos are not wanted here,' they said. Not even the Katorika Priests would tie themselves to the red-haired Protetane. It was said they belonged to tribes that were at war with one another. 'Moana will go away again with his outsider,' the chiefs said.

But Pakoko feared a different thing. He knew the strength of Moana's pride and jealousy. He also knew the strength of the hot drink offered him every night by his uncle, Niehitu. Like a sharp-beaked heron waiting motionless beside a stream, the old man kept his bright eyes fixed on the landsman who had become an outsider. He was waiting for war. He was not surprised when Moana took a whale boat, carrying three blowers and many pigs and turtles to the valley of Hoo Umi, whose chief was Pae-tini's joined half, and tied afresh the old knot of alliance between the far eastern valley and Kiato-nui's offspring. Pakoko welcomed the messengers from the other chiefs, who had heard the old man's warning at last. 'Moana will stir up a big wind,' he had said. 'Let us make fast our houses to stand firm.'

Pakoko asked his son, Hiatai, for men with blowers. What else could he do? They had not been taught to swing a club or whirr a spear, alas, but they could kill. They were ready to enter upper Haavao with their deadly fire-stones. The Taipis would come in a sea of consecrated canoes to sweep the shore clear of *mihis*. 'They cannot live among us without wanting to change us,' the hard-shelled Taipis complained, and they would not be changed. Ironwood could not be bent, Pakoko thought.

For a moon, Moana's people had been sleeping on the beach, close to the canoes, ready for flight. The old people, cold and wet, wrapped themselves around the little ones, as the fingers of the rain clawed at them. 'There will be but one end for us,' they whispered over the small black heads. 'We are without arms to fight for seats in the canoes, without legs to run to the mountains to hide. We will be eaten.' They mingled their groans with the whimpering of the children. 'We will have to tear up our roots and wither in distant lands,' the old men grumbled, as they squatted under flimsy shelters and ate their fish raw before it could be snatched by the hungry. Only the young women lay without anxiety, pillowed on bundles of finery, waiting for new houses to beckon them, waiting for outsiders with their rich gifts and soft ways with women, waiting to eat what they pleased and go where they wished.

None of the priests was helping Moana. The spells of the black-robed Katorikas were not for fighting, but for passing the time as they waited in their leaf shelters on the beach, where they had gone when Moana took their house for storing his blowers and powder. The Protetane red-head followed his Chief, protesting, when he went from house to house demanding blowers, begging him to throw them into the sea and carry a peace branch instead. When Moana finally lit the war by destroying a house full of Pakoko's relatives asleep in the night, and brought the avenging flood of Brave Faces howling down from Haavao, Red Hair could only crawl after his Chief. 'Moana! An evil spirit is inside you!' he cried. 'Setani is roaring in this valley. Stop this war!'

Chief Moana paused in his long-legged running about to taunt him. 'You say the god, Iehova, binds the power of Setani. Why isn't he doing his work?' Oh but the young man was angry at this powerless priest, and when the man fainted at the sight of a Brave Face smashing the head of a man and drinking his spurting blood, the Chief shook him awake, crying, 'If a Peketane *manowa* had come to fight for us, we wouldn't have to do these bad things.' Indeed, Moana cared not at all when he heard that the trembling red-head had crept over the mountains to another valley and given all his clothes to a fisherman to paddle him to Tahu Ata. The fellow was soft wood. Iehova was a spear without a point.

The storm that Moana had stirred up had to blow itself out. It went raging over the mountains to Hakaui, when the young Chief, throwing away his blower and running naked, fled there for refuge with relatives. Pakoko watched his son, Hiatai, leading his victorious Hapaas up the Path of War in pursuit. The father was proud of his straight-backed, sure-footed son. He was turning to Mauhau to voice his admiration, when Hiatai, in passing, lifted his blower in greeting. The gesture, the glance, were a flash of light to those keen old eyes. Hiatai worshipped the blower! It was his god! Had Iehova, god of thunder, god of blowers and *menowa,* entered into Hiatai to make him work for him? Pakoko hid his eyes from Mauhau and went silently to his food house.

When Pakoko saw his son again, he was battered by winds blowing from so many directions, that he did not at first see him clearly. The aged Chief had been summoned to the family waters of Taiohae to meet with all the chiefs of Nuku Hiva on a Ferane ship. He could not believe this message of Oehitu. He had been confident that Moana was a captive in Hakaui. He had watched a ship carry the Katorika Priests away from Taiohae. Now here it was, back again, having scooped up in its net from Hakaui pursued and pursuers alike. Here was that Ferane warship commanding Teiis and Taipis to join the Hapaas and Taioas on board in making peace with King Moana! Pakoko was too angry to speak until he saw his son coming up the path. Then he cried joyfully, 'At least there are two of us who will not obey the outsiders! Come, son, we will stand together!'

Chief Hiatai's heavy feet did not pause or turn aside from their slow climbing. Naturally he was disappointed, having been robbed of his victory. The father went to him quickly, calling over his shoulder to Mauhau, 'Bring us a bowl of *kava*.' He began to step along with Hiatai. 'We are not overthrown, my son,' he said. 'No knot the chiefs tie without us will hold beyond the sailing of that Ferane ship.' Pakoko could not stop that steady pounding up the path. He caught the younger man's hand and was chilled by its cold dampness. When he managed to look into Hiatai's empty eyes, he felt as if he had turned to stone.

Hiatai jerked his hand away. 'The outsiders are men, we are rats and mice,' he muttered between stiff lips. 'Rats and mice!' With a high, sharp cry, he began to run.

The father let his son go away without stretching out a hand or lifting his voice. Perhaps he had held him so long in so fierce a grip that when he let go his muscles were numb. Did a woman feel so when she had carried a child inside her for many moons, only to find it dead when it came out? She would not touch it, even with her eyes. So Pakoko stared at the flickering of light and dark on the path, seeing nothing more. As he turned back to his terrace, he heard again that despairing wail, 'Rats and mice!' His sudden anger was like a drink of fermented breadfruit, putting bubbling force into him. He stamped his feet on the stones. 'We are men!' he shouted to his astonished cousins. 'No *kava*!' He waved away the bowl Mauhau was bringing. 'I must keep awake!'

Without a twitch of skin, Pakoko heard the story of the meeting on the Ferane ship, when the chiefs came to tell their father chief how they had nodded and smiled at everything in order to make the warship go away quickly. They thought they were clever, the outsiders stupid, and that now they would go their own way, until the old man asked them, 'Have you gotten rid of the Katorika Priests?' That had not gone so well. Moana had been forced to return to them their house and all the things he and his people had taken out of it. 'Never mind,' said Pakoko, 'I will take care of the priests.'

The Chief of Haavao was lavish in his attentions to the Katorikas. He watched them carefully as if they were pigs fattening for a feast, but instead of feeding them what they desired he fed them what they detested. He tricked them into long journeys to houses which had not sent for them but drove them away with insults when they arrived. He sent his cleverest thieves to make their food and clothing, even their books and knotted strings, vanish under their very eyes. He built a large open bower nearby and kept it full of chanters and dancers who kept a steady wind of old words blowing through the priests' house, who threw off their *tapas* and showed their beautiful tattooing whenever they came out-of-doors. He sent young women to spy upon them when they bathed, to beg for entrance into their house when they ate, to burrow through thatch and slide onto their mats when they slept. Pakoko did his best to entertain these outsiders, and when they had had enough they paddled away to another island in a canoe which he had kept waiting on the sands. All Nuku Hiva rejoiced.

NOTE

In May, 1840, the French warship, *Pylade,* under Captain Bernard, came to Nuku Hiva during the course of a ferocious war provoked by Moana. The English missionary, Thompson, had fled to Tahu Ata to be with Mr Stallworthy, and the Catholic priests had been driven from their house and were living on the beach, ready to flee. The Commandant forced restitution of the goods stolen from the missionaries and cemented a general peace among all tribes. Pakoko, Chief of Haavao, remained hostile to this peace and to the missionaries who had tried to win him. About the end of 1841, the three missionaries of Taiohae had to go to Uapou.

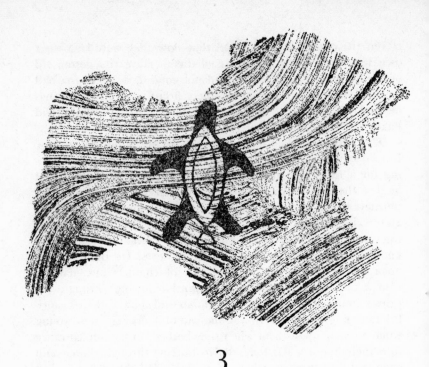

3

MOANA could think of only one thing at a time. His desire to raise Iehova to a high place had grown cold as his desire to raise himself grew hot. He had always been one to grumble about getting his share and he could no longer endure seeing Pakoko receiving everything he wanted. The outsiders had brought him nothing. Now he would seize his own, according to an old custom of the landsmen. His woman had died while he was away, but she had a sister to whom he was entitled for the asking. Vae-kehu was the daughter of a Teii Chiefess and a Chief of Hoo Umi. She was the foster daughter of the Chief of Hakaui. With her in his house, Moana would not be snubbed by the high level of Nuku Hiva. He saw her beside him on his terrace, dressed in the beautiful red cloth he would give her, receiving gifts from all families of this island, yes, and of other islands. She was his by ancient right and he would have her, by theft, if necessary.

Was Pakoko sleeping in his death canoe when Moana stole the High Chiefess of Nuku Hiva from her foster parents? No one knew the thoughts of that solid old man who looked with still eyes on all comings and goings alike. Vae-kehu was his granddaughter. Naturally, he carried welcoming gifts to her when she appeared in Moana's house in Taiohae, a tiny green dove with a red cap that would nestle against her neck, an exquisitely chased tortoise-shell crown that had belonged to his own woman, Metani. There were tears in his eyes as she turned her lovely head this side and that to be admired. 'Just like Metani,' he breathed.

The grandfather often stopped in his walks about the valley to sit on Vae-kehu's terrace while she threaded flowers and songs on filaments of laughter. He always wore a crisp white *tapa,* a glossy leaf bound around his head, and carried his elegant fan with which he could speak in long slow cadences or in breathtaking swirls. His red voice led the young woman into valleys of laughter and onto summits of grandeur. When Moana was there, the old man seemed to grow smoother, softer, gentler, as he sat in easy dignity on the stones, his clean white beard covering his breast, his oiled skin shining, and looked up at the rough-haired young man who sat on a chair, dressed in this and that given him by comers-and-goers, a Captain on a *manowa,* a worker on a whaler, a run-away sailor. Pakoko asked Moana a great many questions which he could not answer, but he always listened respectfully to his sharp, insulting replies. His glances towards Vae-kehu begged her to excuse this wanderer who had not been taught. He was not disturbed by Moana's jerks and twists and sudden moves. He seemed to grow calm as the young man became agitated. Sometimes, the old Chief brought with him a visitor who had wept when his Chiefess was seized by Moana, a grave young man who had played with Vae-kehu when they two were youngsters in Hakaui. Then Pakoko sat silent, while those two talked of their beloved valley until Moana flung himself off the terrace, unnoticed.

The grandfather knew when Moana was drinking with his uncle, Nie-hitu. He was afraid that he would frighten the young girl when he came to the sleeping house, red eyed and violent, or carelessly vomiting. On such nights, Pakoko often took her away with him to a house he had built for her on his own terrace, where his daughters served her and entertained her with women's talk. Vae-kehu was so young and tender a shoot. Naturally she was confused by a man who was neither outsider nor landsman. Before he sent her back to Moana's house, the old man would look into her eyes to be sure the anxiety had left them.

Pakoko was not surprised when Vae-kehu came one day at the time of fires, begging him to send her back to her foster parents in Hakaui. Her eyes were bright, her cheeks red, her chin held high. When he questioned her gently, at first she merely shook her head, but when he asked, 'Did Moana shame you?' she shivered with distaste.

'He shamed himself!' she burst out. 'He put my soiled mat on top of his head!'

Pakoko had been angered many times when Moana had broken taboos to show the landsmen that no harm would come of it, but he trembled with fear now. He forced Moana to submit to a purifying rite in the stream with Vae-kehu, holding the furious Chief in his place until the danger of leprosy and death had been removed. When the fellow had run away, calling out threats, the grandfather had said to the young Chiefess, 'Now I will take you over the mountains to Hakaui and you will never come back to Moana's vile house.'

'Will he light a war against my people there?' she asked, hesitating.

He thrust his eyes deep into hers. Was she more than a little girl who laughed and sang and wore garlands? There was a new look about her. Why, yes, it was the look that came over Metani the day of their joining feast when she had thought of her people imperilled by raids of the Taipis and had become a great chiefess before his eyes. He answered Vae-kehu as if she were an Ironwood or a Master. 'He cannot count a second time on a warship to turn us upside down.' Her doubt made him falter, 'If they do come, they will go away again, but we will still be here.' Still her eyes did not let go their fear. 'At least you will be here,' he smiled, 'you and your son, the High Chief of Nuku Hiva.' When she burst into tears and covered her face with her hands, moaning softly, 'No, no!' he repeated, 'Yes, truly.'

He took her hand and led her into the house he had built for her. Inside, was a new child nestling in the arms of a serving woman. 'This is your adopted son, Moana-tini,' he said. 'He is the son of Moana's sister. I have sent her a canoe load of treasures for him.' He had gone around Moana to bind that family to her! Pakoko knew he was clever, but he was as pleased as a child at Vae-kehu's amazement and drank her *kaoha* thirstily. Indeed, he thought she turned away a little too quickly when she reached for the little one.

'He may as well get used to me,' she said, burying her face in baby's soft flesh.

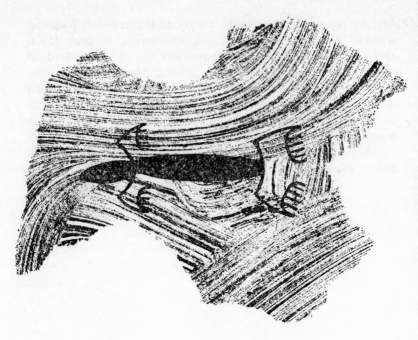

4

Pakoko had said to Vae-kehu, 'If the outsiders come again, they will go away again.' It gave him comfort to repeat this to himself when the Feranes came again, this time like a swarm of bees that covered the bay with enormous ships and the land with innumerable sailors, soldiers and priests. He kept repeating it when he sat on the high level of the Komana's ship with other chiefs, nodding and chanting 'Wee wee, wee wee' to every demand. 'Do you want to place your land under the King of the Feranes? Wee wee, wee wee. Will you give land and houses to the Katorikas? Wee, wee, wee wee. Will you give consent to Moana as King of all your islands? Wee wee, wee wee. Have you stolen Moana's woman and held her in Hakaui? Wee, wee, wee wee.' It was an ugly song, but sung smoothly and quickly, so that the outsiders would be satisfied and go away.

'They are always coming but they are always going,' Pakoko

repeated as he sat on the hill, Tu Hiva, watching the brilliant play of the soldiers and the priests. He had seen Pota raise the Menike flag on this hill. He had watched a Peketane Captain dig up Pota's paper and plant his own flag on the same spot. 'Others have vanished in the salt spray,' he muttered. 'It will be the same with the Feranes.' He made little of the sun-lighted clothing and weapons, of the thundering blowers that echoed among the rocks and the rattling drums that pattered like rain on leaves, of the conches that shouted proudly as the Ferane flag rose into the sky. But when Pakoko saw that Moana was given a flag to fasten above his own roof, he pushed through the crowds to face the Komana. 'Give me my flag,' he demanded.

'He wants a flag,' a Priest of Iehova made clear to the Komana.

'He has no right to a flag!' shouted Moana. 'I am High Chief.'

The Wee Wee brushed aside the petulant young man. Here was an old man of power with hot desire for a flag. Good. He gave it and watched, smiling and content, as Pakoko examined it to see that it was exactly like Moana's.

Pakoko wrapped the flag around him and walked with dignity to his canoe. Standing on the prow, he called back to Moana, 'Under this taboo stick of the Wee Wees, Chiefess Vae-kehu and High Chief Moana-tini are untouchable.' Then he signalled to his paddlers to go quickly to Hakaui, taking the short route between the shore and the western Sister. He meant to arrive at the house of the young woman before the Ferane long boat, which had been sent to bring her back to Taiohae.

When the long boat returned from Hakaui with gifts but no Chiefess, Moana began to pursue Captain Kole, who commanded the Feranes on the land. Every new sun he said to him, 'You must seize Vae-kehu. You are Moana. I have given you my name. It is an affront to you that your woman is held in that valley.'

'Wee wee, wee wee.' That was always Kole's answer, but he did nothing about it, for he was a man with many works, scarcely knowing which to pick up first. He was tearing down good wooden houses and building others of baked mud, digging up good plants and putting outlandish ones in the holes.

Brushed aside like a stinging fly, Moana filled his time with excitements. Every morning he mounted the horse given to him by the Komana, and, clinging to his belly with his bony knees and to his outstretched neck with his thin arms, he raced from headland to headland along the sands, feeling a rush of power make him giddy as folk ran to admire their brave Chief. 'Out of my way! Out of my way!' he shouted as he thundered past, his coat, given him by Kole, making a streak of red across their amazed eyes. These people didn't think him insignificant, not they! Every night, while the Feranes played with the women, calling them with the thunder of a big blower to come to the ship or to the mud houses to eat and drink strange things and see fire-flowers scattered among the stars, Moana retired to his taboo house to drink away his fears that the Feranes would leave before they brought the High Chiefess of Nuku Hiva back to his house.

Up above in Haavao, the aged Chief waited for the wood-gnawers who burrowed in the land to tire of it and fly away. One, two, three moons he waited, while the outsiders settled themselves more and more firmly. Pakoko began to fear that Kole's work would end and he would hear Moana's demand that he send for his woman. At last he heard that a small boat had gone to Hakaui, carrying the Komana, a Katorika Priest and Moana and he lost no time in sending his messenger over the mountains to stand firm behind Vae-kehu until he himself could arrive by sea.

Chiefess Vae-kehu received the Feranes on the terrace outside her house. She sat very straight, with eyes fixed on her tightly clasped hands. She had never been close enough to outsiders to smell them and she didn't know whether she liked their strange odor or not. Her ears were tickled by their outlandish 'kaohas', she wanted to laugh but was afraid to. She was dazzled by the sparkling headband presented to her, but she merely inclined her head without raising her eyes. Only when she heard the Komana's tongue calling to her, smooth and sweet as honey, did she steal a glance at him through her interlaced lashes. He was handsome! He admired her! Because of her confusion and surprise, she could scarcely listen to his words, made clear by the Katorika Priest. He had hoped to be welcomed by the Queen of Nuku Hiva in Taiohae. He was desolate, hurt to tears, to find her gone. He had come all the way to Hakaui to kiss her hand. She thought this was pretty talk but she lowered her face to hide the fine trembling that excited her as his eyes slid gently over her. How strong was his desire! She caught at a formal greeting for support, saying on a fluttering breath, 'This is my house, it is yours.'

'Wee,' answered the Komana, and again 'Wee', in such a tone that her eyes flew open and met his, boldly searching. He was just a man like any other, with quicker, hotter desires, perhaps. She laughed. They laughed together.

The Katorika was saying, 'The Komana has come to speak for King Moana. The King asks you to return to your place beside him.'

With a quick, bird-like turn of her small head, she looked at Moana, sitting below the terrace, cutting the heads from weeds with a switch. 'My place is here,' she said softly but firmly. She raised a delicate hand to stop the Katorika's protest. 'I was not stolen, as he says. I ran away and I will stay away.' It was a long speech and she was breathless.

The Katorika was also soft but firm. 'My child,' he said, 'it is Iehova's desire that a woman leave all others and cling only to her mate.'

'To one man only!' she exclaimed in surprise. 'But there is work for many. Who would dig the ovens and prepare the food? Who would . . .'

The Priest cut across this talk, sternly. 'The anger of Iehova is terrible against those who will not hear.'

'I know about his pit of fire,' she answered with spirit, 'but it is not for landsmen. That I know, for I have seen many who have died and they are not burning.'

The Komana frowned at the Priest. 'This is no time for— for talk,' he said. He picked up the headband he had brought as if to place it on Vae-kehu's head with an admiring gesture.

She drew back from his touch in quick fear, but took the glittering thing and placed it on her head herself. When he had unwrapped a mirror and held it before her, she cried out in delight, 'I am beautiful!'

'Beautiful!' he breathed, and made her see herself in   his

eyes. 'Let me build you a house in Taiohae,' he whispered. When she drew back, he caught her slender hand and began to admire the intricate tracery of tattooing.

Vae-kehu turned shining eyes to her serving women, who squatted behind her. 'He thinks they are beautiful, my images!' She thrust out one foot, then the other, under his lingering gaze. She rolled her *tapa* to the knees, naming her patterns one by one. He was lost in admiration! But these were nothing. She looked again at her relatives. Their eyes were shining, too. They nodded. One said, stridently, 'Her girdle is very beautiful;' another, 'There is not another like it.' Certainly, the Ferane's desire was strong! The young Chiefess sprang up and began to whirl out of her *tapa* while a woman held the end she had untied. Only the Katorika, turning his back and staring at a little book, thought her ugly. Well, who cared?

The Chiefess was displaying the delicate images encircling her back, when Pakoko's messenger, her beloved playmate from childhood, jumped onto the terrace and touched her on the arm. She felt all the warmth drain out of her. Where was she? What was she doing? Why was she entertaining outsiders and that lizard, Moana? She said politely to her visitors, 'You go. I remain here.' Tossing her unwound *tapa* to her women, she went with dignity into her house.

When the outsiders had gone away, spitting out sharp little sounds, her young friend went to meet Pakoko as he stepped from his canoe, to assure him of Vae-kehu's firmness. 'She has the thing that makes a chiefess,' the young man said.

'Why are the Feranes still here?' Pakoko asked, eyeing their boat.

'They have gone up above to see a sick chief, to get his mark on their paper.'

The old Chief was still uneasy. 'I will sit with Vae-kehu until they have gone,' he said. When he reached her terrace and found no one about but a man in the cook house who said the Chiefess had followed the Feranes to give them a sucking pig, he tapped the stones with his staff in anger. 'Go, hover over her,' he commanded the young man. 'I will wait here.' His legs were aching and stiff. He sat down, stretched them in the sun and fell asleep quickly.

The beating of feet on the path woke him. The Komana, wearing armour from the sun, was flashing past. The Katorika, like a black cloud swollen with wind, was floating behind him. Moana, swinging the sucking pig, upside down, paused to pull his lower eye-lid down in a derisive gesture meant for Pakoko. Where was the Chiefess? Forgetting his stiff legs, the grandfather sprang up in fear, and saw what was happening on the terrace. Her friend sat beside Vae-kehu's house opening, head bowed, hands hanging loosely over his knees, dejected in spirit. The serving women were standing about, weeping, holding bundles tightly pressed against their breasts. There came Vae-kehu from her house, a sun-shade bound about her forehead, a rolled mat under her arm.

The Chiefess crossed the paving to where Pakoko stood, cold and still with fear and answered his red-eyed question with a child's tremulous excuse. 'The Komana's desire is strong, grandfather. A chiefess cannot be stingy.'

'She is only a wind-tossed flower,' the old man thought bitterly, but even as he bit his lips to keep back an insult, she seemed to grow tall, to command his respect.

'These Feranes have a saying,' she told him. ' " From the high-born, more is asked than from the low-born." Is that true?'

Did she think this a wise saying, Pakoko wondered savagely. Any fool knew that the high-born had plenty, the low-born nothing to give.

'I am the Queen of Nuku Hiva,' she said. 'The Feranes have made Moana the King. With the King and the Queen divided, there will always be war, always war.' She shuddered. 'With the King and the Queen joined, there will be peace. You know this is true.' When he could not deny it, she went on, 'I am the highest, I must give most.' Her tongue tripped over the next words and she looked about her through tears. 'I must leave behind me my valley, my friend, my little son.' She saw the old man's sudden gratitude. 'Yes, Moana-tini will be safe here, with my foster parents.'

Pakoko had no answer. Perhaps it was with relief that he

watched her take the down-going path to the boat waiting on the sands. She had taken away his work. Now he could rest.

NOTE

Louis Philippe of France, having decided to establish a port of call for ships doubling the Horn, and having determined upon Taiohae, as a result of a report of Dumont d'Urville, sent Contre-Amiral Abel du Petit-Thouars on this confidential mission to take over the islands. The Admiral arrived on the *Reine Blanche* with eight accompanying vessels and four revictualling commercial ships picked up at Valparaiso, with 200 cannons and 3,000 men, entering Taiohae bay the last day of May, 1842, after having subdued Tahu Ata and Ua Pou. On June 2, the Admiral with his retinue climbed the hill, Tu Hiva, and took possession of the islands for France.

The declaration, which was signed by the chiefs, May 31 follows:

Nous demandons a prendre le pavillon Francais et a ce que Nukuhiva, declarons a tous present et a venir, que nous reconnaissons la Souveraineté de S. M. Louis-Philippe, roi des Francais; nous lui promettons fidelité et amitié.

Nous demandons a prendre le pavillon Francais et a ce que le roi veuille bien nous accorder une garnison pour la protection de notre pavillon commun et de notre ile.

Fait à la baie de Taiohae, le 31 mai 1842, en presence de M. le Contre-Amiral Abel Dupetit-Thouars, Commandeur de la Légion d'Honneur, commandant en chef de la station de l'Ocean Pacifique; de M. Nicolas-Aime Alix, Capitaine de vaisseau, chevalier de la Légion d'Honneur, commandant la fregate la Reine-Blanche; de M. Jean Benoit-Amedée Collet, capitaine de corvette, chevalier de la Légion d'Honneur, commandant superior du groupe du nord-ouest des Marquises; et de M. Laurent-Joseph Bourla, commissaire de la division navale de l'Ocean Pacifique, qui, avec nous, ont signe la reconnaissance de la souveraineté pleine et entière que de notre libre arbitre nous faisons en ce moment.'

The Admiral brought with him François de Paule Baudison, head of the Catholic mission established on Tahu Ata.

The Admiral laid out a fort at the foot of Tu Hiva and named it 'Collet' in honor of the father of Captain Collet, who had been a contre-amiral. Moana ceded the French Tu Hiva and Hakapehi and sold Hikoei to them for 1,800 francs. The Commandant Collet remained in command when the Admiral Dupetit-Thouars left for Tahiti in August.

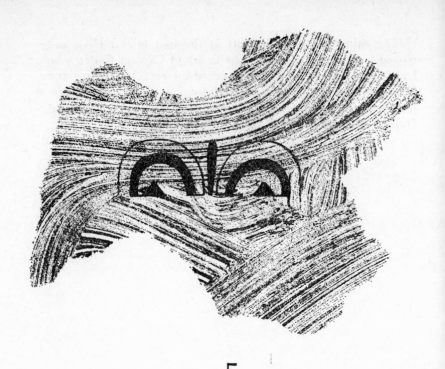

5

THE folk of Haavao did not want to disturb their old Chief
who dozed and rocked in his beautiful death canoe, but a
taboo was a taboo and who else could uphold it? His fishermen had found Moana's fishermen scooping smelts from rocks
in waters taboo to Haavao. 'They say that all waters belong now
to King Moana,' Pakoko's Master Fisherman complained to him.

Pakoko did not trail his anger through the valley to stir up
war, though this was cause for war, but he went calmly down to
talk with Queen Vae-kehu. She had said she did not want war.
The Feranes had said the same. He would see whether they were
lying or true. He was glad to find Captain Kole on the terrace
with the young woman. Now he would catch the two of them
in one hand.

When the Ferane saw that there was great anger in the fishermen who followed the aged Chief, and when he heard the tremor

in the old man's voice as he spoke with Vae-kehu, he called to his man who made words clear. 'Ask him why he is angry,' he commanded.

'For a just cause!' Pakoko asserted. 'From the night when the god Tiki raised Nuku Hiva from the sea, the fishing waters of Haavao have been set apart, taboo, for the dwellers in the valley of Haavao.'

King Moana burst out of his house where he had been listening. 'Neither the valley of Haavao nor the fishing waters of Haavao are yours,' he cried. 'You stole this land from my family.'

Kole turned to the fishermen of Haavao. 'Is this true?'

For a space, the fishermen were hung up, afraid to answer. Then, seeing that the outsider's eyes were not red, one called out, 'No, it is not true.' When the skies did not fall on them, their words began to pour out, like big water running over the land after rain. 'Haavao is the land of Hiatai, the grandfather, and of Hiatai, the grandson, and Pakoko is the father standing between. He seized his own.'

Kole's eyes sought the Queen's, and when she inclined her head, he said, 'This is a good taboo. It shall not be broken again.'

Oh, but those two had drawn the lightning of Moana's fury.

'You call me King but you treat me as lichen!' he shouted at the Ferane. 'And you,' he turned upon his woman, 'your lips smile, but they do not hide the sharp teeth underneath.' The young man's neck was throbbing and his voice broken when he accused Pakoko. 'You made a nobody of my grandfather, Kiato-nui, and you are trying to shame me before fishermen!'

'Hush!' Kole's tongue was a sharp as a puff from a blower. 'Your fishermen have broken a taboo. They must make it right.' He turned to Pakoko. 'What will be just?'

The old Chief was too astonished to answer. He thought that the word-clearer had gotten the Ferane's words wrong, until he saw that Kole's eyes were not closed to him. He sat down to talk this over, as if with a friend. 'If Moana's fishermen had eaten taboo fish, they would be very sick,' he told the Ferane, 'but since the fish are still in leaves on the sands, they may be justly shared among the folk of Haavao, according to the custom.'

'Let it be done,' said Kole, shutting Moana's mouth with a gesture.

Pakoko could not loosen his eyes. He had thought all outsiders were as like as fish eggs, but here was a face he would
know again. *'Kaoha,'* he said softly.

Kole could not loosen his eyes. Here was a landsman who
knew his path. 'Bad customs must be thrown away,' he said,
'good ones must be obeyed.'

'You do not know the customs,' said Pakoko bluntly.

Kole nodded. 'Perhaps I will make mistakes.'

'Yes,' sighed the old Chief, 'a fishing line without a weight is
tangled needlessly.'

Kole laughed. 'Very well, I need a weight. Will you be
generous?'

'Why not?' Pakoko asked. 'I know everything. You know
nothing. I will hold your line steady.' Here they were talking
like two friends! Kakata-kakata! What a thing for laughing!

Pakoko had forgotten his death canoe entirely, for his hands
were full of good work. Kole had sent a message to all valleys,
offering to settle all quarrels without war, promising protection
to all who came to his house of justice. Many came with
every sun, people who had broken apart because of lands or
names, those who had stolen and those who had lost, those who
had broken taboos and those who had buried hair for revenge.
When the Captain Kole questioned, 'What is the custom of the
grandfathers?' it was Pakoko who answered, because the outsider
had sent for him to sit inside his door and tell him the true
path of the landsmen. Crowding outside, pushing to see through
the openings, innumerable old people who had walked from
distant valleys came to hear the true talk in this house of balancing. Sometimes they whispered fiercely among themselves when
Kole said an old way was bad, but they were always smoothed in
the end by his just balancing which put a cover on war.

'Kole is a man, just like us,' the old people whispered.

'Yes,' Pakoko agreed, 'but he is a child with nothing in his
stomach. Without me, he would not know his path.'

Moana cherished his anger against Kole as if it were an ember
wrapped carefully in a coconut sheath and kept glowing. Kole
pretended that Moana was King, yet he raised Pakoko above
all others in Nuku Hiva.

314

One night, Pakoko was awakened from deep sleep by some-one stamping a sugar cane torch to blackness on his terrace. He slid open his door and stuck his head out. 'The Ferane ship has gone away,' a muffled voice spoke into his ear. Another form came swiftly and silently as the shadow of a bird flying across the moon. 'Our women say that their outsiders have gone to Tahu Ata.' From all sides, from many valleys, men with their heads covered were creeping onto the terrace, each one bringing a new word. 'Tonight we can seize Tu Hiva . . . There are only four watchers with blowers.'

Pakoko sat in the house opening, half in, half out. 'Tahu Ata is not very far away,' he said. 'Tomorrow they will return.'

'No!' Moana came stumbling and panting. 'Come! Quickly! The landsmen of Tahu Ata have driven the Feranes!'

'How do you know?' the old Chief demanded, scarcely able to make words with his swelling breath.

'I hear things that are hidden from you,' the young man answered arrogantly. 'The Feranes on Tahu Ata sent a small boat begging help. That is why the big ship went away.'

Pakoko was on his feet now, unable to hold back. The lands-men had driven the Feranes! Natural men were standing up whole again, following their own paths, sleeping with their own mates, eating their own food, building their own houses, making their own canoes! The old Chief took his club down from the wall.

'What is it?' asked deaf old Mauhau, waking suddenly and holding out his ear to catch the answer.

'Bring a sheath of fire!' someone shouted at him. 'We are going to burn the houses of the Wee Wees.'

Moana grabbed a ball of coconut fibre and began measuring off lengths for nooses. 'While you are strangling the four guards,' he said, tossing pieces to four companions, 'I will lay the torch to the house where Kole sleeps.'

'The house where Kole sleeps!' Pakoko's hands, holding out the tails of his loin cloth to jerk the knot tight, could not go on with their work. Was he going to scrape an oven for his friend, Captain Kole? The force ran out of his legs and he sat down.

'Come quickly, before the light is bright.'

Had Pakoko gone to sleep? He sat staring at air. With Kole gone, who would make a balancing between those who quarrelled? With Kole gone, who would keep Moana from stirring up winds in all directions? With Kole gone . . . 'No! Not good, this destroying of Kole!' Against his desire, the cry leapt out of him.

The men laughed at him. 'Kole has made soft wood of you.'

'Kole upholds the old taboos!' the Chief of Haavao cried.

'Kole cares nothing for our ways. All he wants is to keep men quiet while he seizes our lands and our women.' Even Mauhau crossed Pakoko's word.

Moana took command. 'Follow me,' he demanded, 'I am the King.'

Pakoko knew that he must stand firm behind the outsider, though it sickened him. He must stop this foolish attack. 'Kole is Pakoko!' he said with a strangled cry. 'I give him my name.' He stood in front of the house opening with his club, so that none might pass.

The Chief of Haavao knew that many bad eyes followed him as he went down the hill in the early morning to the house of justice where Kole sat waiting for those to come with complaints. No matter. He did not sit down just inside the door as usual, but went close to his friend. He lifted the Ferane's hands onto his own breast and said, 'You are Pakoko. You are taboo wherever my name is known. When I am gone, you will lead my people.'

A shade fell across the outsider's eyes and his tongue was gummed for a space. 'I will stay until my Chief sends for me,' he said finally.

Pakoko turned cold. 'When?' he asked with dry tongue.

'In six moons, perhaps. But another will come,' he added hastily.

Another! There was not another like Kole! The old man stumbled from the room. Had he mistaken his path?

At the door Moana passed him, glaring at him angrily because he had tied himself more closely to Kole, determined not to be outdone. He would show the Ferane that his hands also were open. 'I will give you two hundred warriors to overthrow your enemies on Tahu Ata!' he shouted.

Once Pakoko would have laughed at such a trick to hide true desires, but now he flared up, red and hot with shame for his kinsman.

'*Kaoha*,' the Ferane said, 'but no, the affair will be quickly ended. Besides, I would not ask landsmen to fight against their relatives.'

Outside the old man grinned. Kole was not deceived.

NOTE

Captain Collet left Nuku Hiva in April, 1843. He was succeeded by Captain Bruat, who arrived on the *Uranie* the following September. In July, 1844, it was necessary for Bruat to 'chastise the Hapaas'.

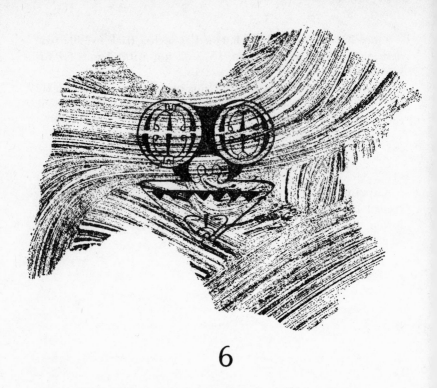

6

THE Ferane who came after Captain Kole went away did
not call Pakoko to advise him in the house of justice, but
one day the old man went just the same to explain the
custom to the new Komana. He stood outside the house opening.
The Feranes, eating inside, paid no attention to him. He sat
down to wait. He sat thinking of his son, Hiatai. When he was
alive, the father had lost his son. Now that he was dead, he had
found him. Pakoko could see him plainly, over there, just on the
edge of the clearing, waiting for him with begging eyes.

When word had come to him that the crazed Hapaa Chief
had ended his frothy babblings by leaping from the man-eating
precipice down into the valley of the Taipis, he had listened
as if someone said, 'A withered tree has fallen.' But when the
Hapaa Priestess had told him that Moana had advised the new
Komana to forbid any killing for this dead chief, he had known
that his work for his son was not ended. He must explain to the

Ferane the custom of sending men-at-the-side to the skies with their chief. After that Hiatai's breath body had come to Pakoko's terrace, begging. Yes, Hiatai was like a new child waiting for his father to raise him high. Pakoko would not fail him.

The hard tongue of the new Komana was like a hand jerking the old Chief to his feet. His man-who-made-talk-clear was saying, 'No beggars allowed on these stones.' Pakoko was puzzled and looked around for Hiatai, perhaps. He followed the Ferane to his door, trying to catch his eyes, but the man went inside, calling over his shoulder, 'What does he want?'

'Tell him I am Pakoko, Chief of Haavao,' the old man said.

The interpreter, a man called Stingy, knew Pakoko well enough, but he said, 'Moana is the only name known to this Ferane.' The fellow licked the words as if they were sweet.

Pakoko pushed him aside and called in to the Komana. 'It is about the paddlers for the canoe of the dead Hapaa Chief.'

'What about paddlers?' The Ferane, sitting at the table, was turning over the pieces of paper.

'It is the custom of the landsmen,' the old man began, speaking slowly and very loud, trying to make the outsider hear.

Stingy broke in between with a stream of outlandish talk. The Komana's face grew red and swollen and he spat out many hard sharp sounds which Stingy picked up and gathered together for Pakoko. 'He says it is the command of the Feranes—no killing for a dead chief. He says his work here is to make men out of savages. He says King Moana has the same thought.' The little-eyed speaker struck at Pakoko with the handle of his blower and added a word of his own. 'Get out, old Man-eater. You are ended here.'

The force of a young man drove Pakoko up to the high valley of the Hapaas and when he saw the Hapaa Clubs waiting on the sacred place with nooses and shoulder poles, he cried out, 'Forward, courage!'

'The Komana had given his consent?' the Priestess asked.

'He has said, "No killing," but he is an ignorant man who refuses instruction. He does not know that a man is happy to be chosen to enter the skies with a chief.'

'We cannot go against the Feranes,' declared Hiatai's cousin, the only chief left in that valley.

'You cannot insult your dead chief!' cried Pakoko. 'Do you want Hiatai's angry spirit to return to this valley to destroy you?'

The little anger of these two men was nothing, the anger of the god was a tempest of wind and lightning. 'I have asked for seven men to paddle Chief Hiatai's canoe! I will not be crossed!' The unearthly scream was blown through the trees, the sacred fire on the upper terrace leapt up, the Priestess, like a flame herself, was whirled about by the god, her red *tapas* and long black hair trailing behind her. 'Go! Go!' she commanded the Clubs, driving them to their work with her bound sticks.

When the drums announced the capture of the first young man who would go with Chief Hiatai to the skies, Pakoko joined the elders in the chanting on the sacred place. With fan and tongue he winged words of power for a swift ascent to the gods, while the Priestess fastened the great hook in the victim's mouth and raised him into the smoke-laden banyan tree. Suddenly the bonds of sound tying men to gods were ripped apart by peals of thunder, flashes of lightning and a rain of fire stones. Every tree vomited Feranes, blowers in hand. They came hurtling forward like spears flung by an unseen hand.

Pakoko had no muscles to stand up. He saw the open hole beneath the hanging paddler and rolled across the paving and dropped into it. He burrowed under old bones and lay still in the midst of a raging battle. He felt the dead victim's weight fall upon him, was pressed deeper as stones, torn from the paving, were heaped upon the stiffening body. Stifling in putrid smells, of earth, old rottenness, dead flesh and burning wood, he tried in vain to push off the heaviness that was crushing him. Flames were reaching for him when Hiatai began to call him, 'Father, come! Here I am.' Pakoko reached for his son's hand and pulled himself slowly out of the hole.

Sitting on the edge, he stared at the banyan root he was grasping, and at the piles of blackened stones and smoking posts around him. Where was Hiatai? Where were the images of the gods? Where was the sky-piercing house of the Priestess? Rubbing his smarting eyes, he peered through the fog of fire breath at the desolate hillside. Nothing stood up.

There was Hiatai beckoning! 'I come,' the old man muttered,

stumbling to his feet and dragging them upward over the tumbled waste. Where was he going? He found himself in the Valley of Tears, scarcely able to push through the tough stems of the tall grass. He was at the foot of Red Stone Mountain, in full sun, staring down at his naked body. How had he lost his *tapas?* As he picked leaves and girdled himself, he tried to remember. Ah. The first paddler caught for Hiatai's canoe had had but three fingers on his right hand. The Priestess had called for seven paddlers. Yes, six more were needed. 'I will not fail you, my son,' the father whispered, as he turned into the path of Haavao.

7

PAKOKO had not laid aside this work for his son, as he sat, day after day, leaning against his stone rest in the sun. He was waiting for a sign from Hiatai. Often the old man could see that wandering breath body hovering near. He could smell his sweetness before his shadow fell across the stones. '*Kaoha* to the High Chief!' he often called and pointed to the seat beside him.

Ironwoods, Brave Faces, Masters, who slept in Pakoko's men's house watched him out of the corners of their eyes. Seeing him beckon, they would murmur, 'Hiatai has come.' One day, because they were all whispering together in great agitation, they did not see him go to the edge of the terrace and call out, 'Go then to western land's end and wait for the six paddlers I will send you.' They were startled when the old Chief came striding into the men's house and lifted his club down from the wall. In amazement they heard him say, 'I go now to crack open those six heads.' They had thought he was walking sky paths with his son's spirit, but he had been listening to their talk!

Mauhau crawled to him and clasped him about the knees. 'No, no!' he begged, 'Let it pass.'

Oehitu came to him also. 'When the Feranes forbid, nod. When they cover your sands with taboo, smile. When they pollute your waters, laugh. It is the only way.'

Pakoko clawed at their faces with sharp eyes. What had they been hiding from him? 'Tell me all,' he commanded Oehitu.

'Well, when the Komana and Moana covered the sands and waters of Taiohae bay with taboo . . .'

'They covered my sands and waters with taboo?' the old man broke in angrily.

'You knew!' exclaimed Oehitu. 'You told your daughters that this taboo to keep women from going to the ships at night was nothing but a lie. You told them to go if they pleased!'

Pakoko was ashamed that he had forgotten. He remembered now that he had snapped his fingers at Moana's taboo on Haavao property. Hadn't Kole established this right? Ah, but Kole was gone! 'Then what?' he demanded.

'The Feranes seized our women when they went down there.' Pakoko made no move, so his cousin continued. 'They tied them in their prison in the dark for two days.' Oehitu was afraid of being struck by the club in the Chief's hand. He moved out of reach, but the old man was still as an image. 'That is why your daughters have not been rubbing your sore legs.'

Pakoko could only turn his head from side to side as if to free it from a noose that was tightening about his neck. His son's rights denied, then his daughters'!

'Now they are going too far!' Mauhau cried harshly.

More? Pakoko was too sick to be angry. He put out a shaking hand and steadied himself against a house post, while he untangled the snarl of angry words that followed Mauhau's outburst. What he heard made him an Ironwood once more, hard and pointed. The Feranes were washing their dirty clothes in his taboo bathing pool. Now! While they talked! 'How many Feranes?' he asked as he began to lift clubs down from the wall. When he heard that there were six, he smiled with satisfaction.

Hiatai would be paddled to the skies by six outsiders! How just! 'I want five men to go with me,' he said, and grunted with satisfaction when Mauhau and Oehitu were the first to hold out their hands for clubs.

Behind bushes overhanging Pakoko's stone-lined pool, the six landsmen watched the Feranes who washed their clothes in this quiet place. The outsiders were like free young people, laughing and singing as they beat their wrappings on the red edging. *Ta! Ta! Ta!* Their sticks pounded out white foam that floated towards the sea far below. They had no ears for snapped twigs nor rustling leaves, no eyes for shadows falling over them. When six heavy blows had silenced the pounding of sticks on the rocks and the laughing of young men, the landsmen stood without moving, listening to the laughing of water playing with pebbles, watching red foam floating down towards the sea. Pakoko saw Hiatai's canoe jumping over the western waves, six men-at-the-side with skins white as coconut flesh dipping their paddles, his whale's tooth son standing firmly on the prow. He heard him say, '*Kaoha*, my father.'

'The land has drunk Ferane blood!' old Mauhau muttered, unable to believe it.

Oehitu lifted his clean black club from the running water. 'When that blood reaches the sea,' he declared, 'the land will vomit all Feranes and the sea will swallow their bones.'

'True,' said Pakoko. 'We have only begun.'

When the six had wrapped the Feranes in leaves and cut shoulder poles, they themselves carried them to the sacred place and laid them at the feet of the images of the grandfathers.

The great Ironwood of Nuku Hiva was firmly planted on the backbone of the land and a strong place of stones and heavy logs was being built around him. On the day of revenge, Pakoko had said to his five companions, 'There is no safety for us in Haavao. We will build a strong place in the mountains and draw all true landsmen to us.' Even as they had climbed the Path of War, they had been joined by Brave Faces, who snatched their weapons and ran beside them, praising them for breaking the heads of their enemies and cutting the lashings from their ankles. They had made a litter and carried Pakoko on their shoulders. 'All the warriors on Nuku Hiva are yours!' they had called up to him. Before the fall of that red sun, many stone builders and wood strikers had found that band of defiant men on the heights and chosen the place for defense. Young men had followed after, raiding the valleys for food and supplies as they ran through them. On the second day came women and children fleeing from the anger of the Feranes who had found their dead on the paving of the sacred place, still tied to the shoulder poles. They could not talk of the horror behind them and Pakoko could not question. He had smelled the smoke billowing up from below and heard the sharp screams and the low rumble of confusion spreading through his beloved valley. He had waited in vain for Mauhau to come carrying the death canoe he had returned for, he had looked for his woman and daughters among those who had escaped. He had crushed his grief and fears as a priestess crushed a bad spirit enticed from the body of a sick man. He thought only of the building of his strong place and the training of his Brave Faces.

When the first moon had sunk into the deeps, Pakoko began to feel another hook tearing him cruelly. He had asked the Hapaa and Taipi chiefs for warriors, but they had sent him only food gifts and no other sign of their ties with the High Chief Pakoko. Now that the massive fort was standing up strong and hopeful, he decided to go himself with the five who had helped him strike the first blow against the Feranes. He would make a tour of the island, gathering together a mighty force.

Praise songs rolled to meet the six as they approached the terraces of the Chief of Hakapaa. The people ran beside them, laughing and pointing to the landsmen who had shaken the Ferane tree to its roots. The Chief welcomed them as relatives, but when Pakoko said, 'I cannot finish this work without your Brave Faces to help me,' he put the old man off. 'Tomorrow we will talk of that,' he said. 'You are very tired now.'

Yes, Pakoko was tired. The pains in his stiff knees were driving him hard. If he had his death canoe, he could sleep well inside it. Mauhau knew his desire. Why was he so long in bringing it? He forced himself to lie quietly in the Hapaa Chief's sleeping house, waiting for the dawn.

In the men's house, the Hapaa masters and warriors heard their Chief's question, 'Friends, can this old man-eater overthrow the Feranes?'

One answered, 'Already six are dead.' But another said, 'And an entire valley has been destroyed to balance the six.' The grandson of Chiefess Kena, who had escaped from Taiohae, said angrily, 'This Pakoko is a nobody. He stole my grandmother's valley and now he is trying to steal King Moana's high seat. He is not our High Chief.' A Brave Face contended, 'He is a great Ironwood.' But another denied it. 'Not as great as the Ferane Komana.'

The Hapaa Chief stopped combing his beard. Not as great as the Ferane Komana, that was it, the Komana with his stone-hurling blowers on Tu Hiva, with his warship in the bay, with his innumerable warriors who could fight at great distances. What was Pakoko in comparison? Nothing. The Chief beckoned to four warriors. 'Wake Pakoko's friends,' he commanded. 'Take them to the Komana and say to him, "Here are four of the killers, sent to you by your friends, the Hapaas." ' But his tongue stuck when he tried to name the father of his dead Chief, Hiatai. 'That is all,' he said.

Pacing the stones of his terrace, waiting for the sun to splinter the peaks, the Hapaa Chief received another visitor. The Priestess, who had escaped death when Chief Hiatai's sacred place was destroyed, was carried on a litter because of her broken legs. Her face was drawn with pain and fear when she leaned over to whisper to the Chief, 'If Pakoko does not seek refuge elsewhere, the gods will send a drought to destroy this valley.' When she had gone, he went on walking the stones, twisting words this way and that, trying to make a hard thing sound soft.

When Pakoko came stamping and blowing into the bright air, clamoring for the Hapaa braves to accompany him to the heights, the Hapaa laid a hand on his arm and drew him into step beside him. 'The relatives of your namesake, Tohi-kai, are eager for your visit to their valley,' he said. 'My men-at-the-side are ready to carry you safely down the precipice.'

The old man was slow in answering, not because he did not hear, but because he tried to swallow the bitter drink without vomiting. Without asking it, he had been made High Chief of all Nuku Hiva and yet he was not welcome in his own son's valley. Breathing hard, he asked, 'You will not support my taboos?'

'Your taboos cannot be supported,' the Hapaa answered, 'because the Feranes have a more powerful Ironwood than you.'

'At least we can die for . . .' he began, but was cut off by the Chief who signalled for bearers to carry Pakoko to the valley of the Taipis. 'Where are my friends?' the old man demanded.

'They have given themselves up to the Feranes,' the Chief of the Hapaas answered and waved to his men to lift Pakoko on the litter.

As Pakoko walked the familiar path to Chief Tohi-kai's old terraces, he was greeted from every house as the great Ironwood who had struck down the Feranes. It put new force into him, made him forget for a space the deep wound inflicted by the Hapaa Chief. That was Metani's valley. He had been taboo there, safe and respected, since he was a lad. Now his taboo was ended. He was alone, unprotected. When the Hapaa bearers had set him down at the foot of the precipice, he had felt just as he did when he had run away from Taiohae to seek power in the valley of the Taipis by exchanging names with Chief Tohi-kai. But here were the folk of this once-hostile valley calling *kaohas* to him, pressing gifts upon him, as he passed their houses. He knew that he would not find Tohi-kai waiting for him on his terrace. But the dead Chief's people were calling him Tohi-kai Pakoko and some even remembered that he had been given the name of Kea, the Hard Shell. Here at least his taboo was still good.

Nearing the house of Tohi-kai's grandson, the Teii Ironwood began to chant:

> The joining is broken,
> The joining with the Feranes is broken!
> Six Ferane fish have been seized!
> The fire is spreading,
> Thousands are climbing the paths,
> Thousands with angry red eyes,
> Invincible thousands with hair on their legs.

The young Taipi Chief pulled the old man onto his stones with hands as gentle as a woman's. 'You have overthrown the Feranes!' he cried.

'Yes,' Pakoko boasted. 'With one blow I knocked out the brains of six Wee Wees.'

The young man asked, 'Are they following you with their fire-stones!'

Pakoko, looking deep into those friendly eyes, answered stoutly, 'Yes. If I sit in your canoe, I may sink it.'

The Taipi did not turn his eyes away. 'You are taboo here.' He spoke with so loud a tongue that the old Chief looked at him sharply, but then he wiped a heavy hand across his eyes as if to cleanse them of a painful memory.

The next sun came over the mountains, not with the murmur of innumerable insects and birds, but with the cracking and spitting of blowers. The Taipis looked up at the crests, thinking they saw again in a dream Pota and his Menikes about to rain fire down upon them. But no, this was not a dream. The Feranes were there, determined to seize Pakoko. In a panic, the people fled from their houses to the eastern ridge. The Brave Faces did not follow them, but they went on dragging feet to the feast place of their Chief and waited with covered eyes for his command.

Inside the men's house, the elders sat with the Chief hearing the messenger of the Feranes, the Masters clasping and unclasping their hands, the Chief lifting his chin high and hiding his eyes behind his lashes. Pakoko's eyes swept that circle of friends, rested keenly for a space on each man there.

'The Feranes have no desire for war with the Taipis,' the outsider, Stingy, was saying, 'but they say they will destroy any valley that gives Pakoko refuge.'

'One death for all of us, then,' answered the Taipi Chief.

Pakoko bent his ear. Was the Taipi's voice too high, too thin? Were the Masters clearing their throats with distaste? Were the Braves outside the open-fronted hall grumbling? How easily this aged man knew the desires of the young! Lest they see the pain in his eyes, he fixed them on their great valley that sloped away from this high place down to the sea. But it was not a valley of sunlit silences and the secret swelling of fruits and the peaceful rest of dwellers under shade that he saw. He could not forget this valley on fire, with Pota and his Menikes pouring over its back wall, rolling waves of flame ahead of them, leaving blackened posts and scorched plantations and mangled bodies behind them.

'No,' the old Ironwood said, pressing out the word with laboring breath. 'One death only.' Did he hear a long-drawn sigh of relief? It gave him courage to go on. 'I am the elder here. I am above you all. I have what they want. I will give it.'

Every man was weeping, but not one said, 'No.'

'Come, then,' said the outsider roughly to Pakoko.

'Not with you!' said the Taipi Chief, wholly certain now.

Stingy was hung up, fearing some trick. 'Has he a relative here who will go with me as hostage?'

As Priest Kepua stepped forward, Pakoko's eyes lit with fear, sought his son's face, but, meeting a calm return, he said, 'kaoha. I will come tomorrow.'

'I myself will bring him in my canoe!' cried the Taipi Chief.

Priest Kepua drew Stingy aside. 'Will he be eaten?' he asked.

Stingy sneered, 'Only a filthy landsman would eat a man.'

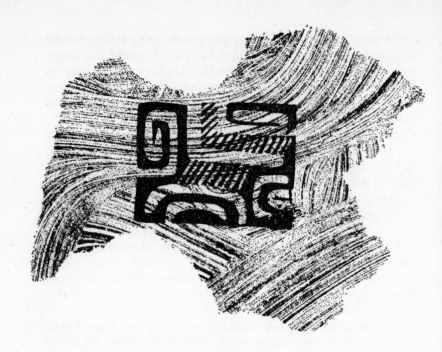

8

'**T**UTI-TUTI-TUTI!' The little drum was tapping an invitation to Pakoko's last feast. He was leaning against the stone seat of the Taipi Chief, waving his fan at the young men who were piling fire wood and big stones in the ovens, nodding to the young women who were braiding coconut leaflets around the posts of the food shed, stripping red and yellow *ti* leaves into ribbons to string under the rafters. In the coconut grove, men were slitting the throats of pigs. Down below, the fishermen were straining the sea with big nets. In the uplands, workers were digging sour paste from the big storage hole made long ago by Pakoko Tohi-kai. The Fire Keeper was touching his sheath of embers to innumerable small fires below on the paving, for the roasting of fresh sweet breadfruit. In the center of the feast place, young men and women were treading the earth, swinging from side to side, whirling and dipping with the tap-tapping of the little drum. The Song Maker sat on the edge of the terrace, making sweet words for Pakoko's ears.

> Breadfruit swelling,
> White juice dripping,
> Tree nets bursting.
> Pakoko is very ripe.
> Ta! goes his stem.
> Pakoko is the sweet breadfruit in the net.

After his going-away feast, Pakoko did not sleep. He lay quietly thinking. Yes, everything here was in perfect balance. He had given what he had and the Taipi Chief had given him a beautiful feast of *kaoha*. As soon as he could see the path, he would be on his way. He would not let his host stain himself with the fault of handing a relative over to Ferane killers. Besides, he must see his own dear land of Haavao before going to his death. He left the house of the sleeping Taipis before the mists turned red and took the upland path.

When he saw the back wall of the valley standing up in front of him, he muttered on waning breath, 'Courage, forward!' One foot, then another, that would do it! He would lie down on the near ledge and again on the far ledge. He would sleep for a space in a nest of ferns he knew. Before the sun was high he would look through the grass on the summit and pull himself up on that high level. He put his foot into the first hole, but drew back trembling. A noose was dangling on the face of the cliff. He was not a fish to be strangled and eaten by gods!

'Sit inside the loop!' a voice called faintly from far above.

He looked up until his neck ached. Were there faces in the mists? He could see nothing, but he heard a woman's high voice echoing among the rocks, chanting his genealogy. It was his own sister. Without hesitation he stepped into the noose.

Tapa-wrapped images, white shades in the shining breath of the sky, pulled him over the edge onto the backbone of the land. There was his fat old sister holding out a staff and a fan to him. There was his sister, Hina, bringing him fresh *tapas* and a shell of sweet oil. There were his Masters and Brave Faces crowding about him, crying joyously, 'We knew this would be your path.' Young women garlanded him with strings of mountain flowers.

331

Children ran back and forth, bringing him seeds and stones picked up from the path.

When they reached the foot of Red Stone Mountain and the entrance to the down-going Path of War, Pakoko felt his friendly sea retreating, as if afraid to enter their own valley of Haavao. 'You go, we remain,' someone said in a voice without an echo. 'We live up here now, in caves,' said another. The old man's answer came on a gust of anger. 'You will no longer be a floating people wandering in the mountains when I have gone to the skies. I will lead you back to Haavao.'

The Master Planter shook his head doubtfully. 'The Feranes have seized your valleys. It is said they will plant outlandish seeds.'

'I have seen the coming and going of seven outsiders on Moana's lands,' an old man said, 'and not one could make his different plants fruit.'

Pakoko laughed softly. 'Red Soil will vomit all but her true children.'

His sister began to chant the ascent of the good trees of the land. Without fear they all began to walk to the beat of those grand names of Clear Space, the father, and the many mothers of trees, Coconut, Breadfruit, Hibiscus, Bamboo, Candlenut, Pandanus, Banyan, Ironwood, Temanu.

A young woman with a child curled on her breast, touched Pakoko's arm. 'This is my thought,' she said, and everyone listened because she had slept for many moons inside the house of a Ferane, 'soon the outsiders will go away. "Wild land, wild people, ugly!" they say.'

'Yes,' agreed another, 'They say this land is the enemy of outsiders.'

'This land is the enemy of outsiders!' They all shouted this good word. Pakoko tried to repeat this hope with them, for they were coming now to the land tortured by the outsiders. He had need of clear eyes. He carried his head in the sky, seeing in the slope covered with broken branches and withered leaves land cleared for new plantations. 'Here you will plant ten forties of new breadfruit shoots,' he commanded his Master Planter. He beckoned to a wood striker. 'Pile up this wood to heat oven stones for my feast of tears.' He gathered his Brave Faces around him. 'Do not sleep your force away,' he warned. 'Build new terraces of these scattered stones, build walls around your pigs. Nine feasts of remembrance I ask, and mountains of food each time.'

Trembling cries gushed up, 'Oh Chief, do not die! Do not leave us!'

Seeing them shaken, clinging to one another, hiding their wet faces, Pakoko tried to find a strengthening word for them, but, feeling breadfruit paste oozing between his toes, he looked down and could not speak.

'Yes,' muttered the Master Planter, 'all the storage holes have been emptied.'

The Ironwood did not break. 'Feed my spirit,' he commanded, 'and I will send you breadfruit to fill every hole.' He held out his hands for his belongings. 'I will go now to my bathing pool,' he said.

His friends slid down onto the land and rolled back and forth with the pain of breaking apart. His sisters clung to his knees and wet his feet with their tears.

'*Kaoha* to all!' He went away hastily, stamping hard to drown their cries that trailed after him.

'*Kaoha nui! kaoha nui!*' Their great love found his ears, giving him fresh strength.

When he had mingled his tears with his running water and his breath with the sweetness of wild ginger overhanging it, when he had oiled himself and coiled his hair and braided his beard, he tied his handsome *tapa* about him and stepped onto the path leading to the sacred place. He wanted to thrust his staff into the thatch of the sky-piercing house and ask strength for the encounter with his enemies. There were no neatly edged smooth pavings of mounting terraces. He had to pick his way up a rough hill of broken stones to the banyan on top. He laid his hand on the skin of that great tree. 'I knew you would be here,' he whispered.

No priest lived here now but a man stumbled from the ruins, hands outstretched, feet groping, a blackened sightless face lifted to the sun. 'Is it Pakoko?' The drawn lips scarcely moved and a cupped hand went to the battered ear. It was Mauhau! Mauhau was pointing to Pakoko's death canoe, making him lie in it to be sure the fire had not warped it. Mauhau was saying, 'I will go with you as steersman.'

When Pakoko could speak above the roaring of his sea of joy, he said firmly, 'No killing of paddlers for me.' He had been thinking of this for a long time. There was a good old custom of offering sea turtles to a dead chief. He would like to have his beautiful turtles with him.

But Mauhau insisted. 'You will see. I will be with you.'

Pakoko laughed and punched him in the stomach. 'Well, we ought to be able to paddle a little canoe between us,' he said. 'But no killing of men. Tell the Priest of the Taipis.'

The Chief of Haavao went on soft, quick feet down through his valley. It seemed as if he had no weight at all. When he saw his tumbled terraces and burned houses, he murmured, 'Good.' All the things he had touched had been destroyed. He was leaving no bait to catch his spirit. He felt the wings of his canoe under him. He was going to the beautiful land of the gods!

A young woman was walking beside him. It was Vae-kehu, High Chiefess of Nuku Hiva. His eyes searched her face. 'Yes,' he said, 'your way is hard, mine is easy.'

She pressed his hand in gratitude. She had tried to turn the Komana's anger away from the aged Chief, she had tried to soften Moana's crazy jealousy. Now she found she had been caring without cause! Of course the grandfather wanted to go to the skies! But she could not let him go without telling him the thing she had done. She did not want him to come back to punish her. 'I have brought my foster son, Moana-tini, to Taio-hae,' she said. When his feet lost a beat on the path, she said in quick defense, 'I am his mother. I must hover over him as the Mother of God hovers over Iesu.' Her feet grew heavy in his silence. 'I have put him in a place of safety, in the house of the Katorikas.'

'Perhaps it is the only way,' he said at last. 'Now he will be altogether an outsider.' At the branching of the paths, one turning to Meau, the other to Tu Hiva, he stopped and drew a line across the upgoing Path of War. 'Never let him go above this mark,' he said, 'If you do not want him to return to me and my ways.' He left her, lost in a fog of confusion and a mist of grief, unable to see her path.

When Pakoko reached the terrace on top of the hill, Tu Hiva, he found Moana beating on the closed door of the house of justice. 'Open,' he cried. 'It is the King. I have come to sit with the Council of War.'

The soldier who walked back and forth with the blower on his shoulder said, 'No one enters today but the man-eater.'

Pakoko spoke over Moana's head, 'Tell the Komana that Pakoko has come.'

The Ferane backed away trembling. Moana spun about as if to dodge a blow. The one slid through the half-opened door, the other hurried to the edge of the terrace.

'What do you want from the Komana?' the grandfather called after Moana.

'Nothing!' snapped the young Chief, without looking back.

'Yes,' answered Pakoko. 'That is what you will get.'

Moana turned to shout an angry reply, but he could not lift his eyes to that venerable face nor make his tongue strike him. He ran away with long, jerky strides.

Inside the room where he had helped Kole settle quarrels, Pakoko searched the face of the new Komana. It was as quiet and blank as the face of a stone image. The eyes were never lifted to his but remained fixed on a paper on the table.

With a thick short hand, the Ferane signed to the interpreter, Stingy, to speak for him. 'Your friends, Oehitu and the others . . .'

'Where are they?' Pakoko broke in quickly.

'On the island of Ei Ao,' Stingy told him.

For the first time a shudder ran through the aged Chief. Was he also to be uprooted, torn from his island, left to wither in a strange land? He murmured a prayer to his gods, 'Let me die standing up, rooted in the land!'

Stingy continued, 'Your friends have said that six Feranes were killed by your command. Was it your word that caused these deaths?'

'Naturally,' Pakoko answered. 'I am their Chief.'

The Komana trembled with anger and raised his pale cold eyes. 'Have you no shame?'

Shame for what? 'The blow was just, Ferane!' the Chief said. 'It has always been the custom for a Chief to uphold his taboos.'

The Komana tapped the table with his fingers. 'In the name of the King of the Feranes, I must punish you for this dreadful work.'

'That is just,' the old man agreed. 'It was necessary for me to cleanse my land and my relatives with the blood of your men. Now it is necessary for you to demand a balancing. I am ready.'

The Ferane covered his eyes with his hand and sat quietly for a space. 'Go, then,' he said finally.

Go where? To a distant land, to wither? Pakoko could not bear to hear that word even on his own tongue. He asked instead, 'Do I go to my death?'

The Komana nodded, gathered up his papers and went to the window. Ten soldiers stepped forward, each with a blower.

Pakoko smiled at them. They were going to blow fire-stones through him. Good! But when a man came to tie his hands together he protested. 'How, then, could I carry my staff and my fan?'

'Free his hands,' said the Komana without turning around.

'*Kaoha*,' the old Chief called out politely as he left the house.

Pakoko could see over the heads of the soldiers as he faced them on the terrace. He could see his trees walking up the slopes of Haavao. He could see Red Stone Mountain above them, piercing the sky. With the back of his hand, he pushed away the cloth brought to cover his eyes. 'Not good, Ferane,' he begged. He turned his eyes upon the waters, the sands and the rocks of his dear land. When he had called to them in parting, '*Kaoha!*' and again, '*Kaoha nui!*' he lifted his fan, commanding the blowers of the soldiers to salute him.

NOTE

About the end of 1845, Pakoko was condemned to be shot, having been judged guilty by the council of French chiefs headed by M. Almaric, Chief of battalion of artillery. His valleys of Haavao and Pakiu were confiscated.

336

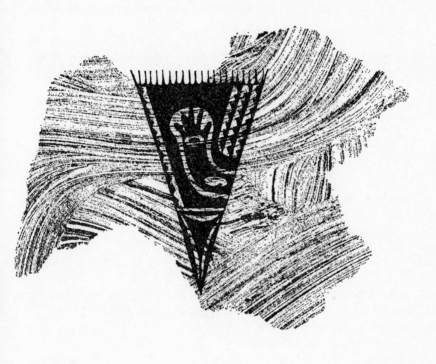

Designed by Philippa Walker, AIDIA
Text set in 10 pt lino Baskerville, two points leaded
and printed on 89 gsm Old Vale Antique paper
at The Griffin Press, Adelaide, South Australia

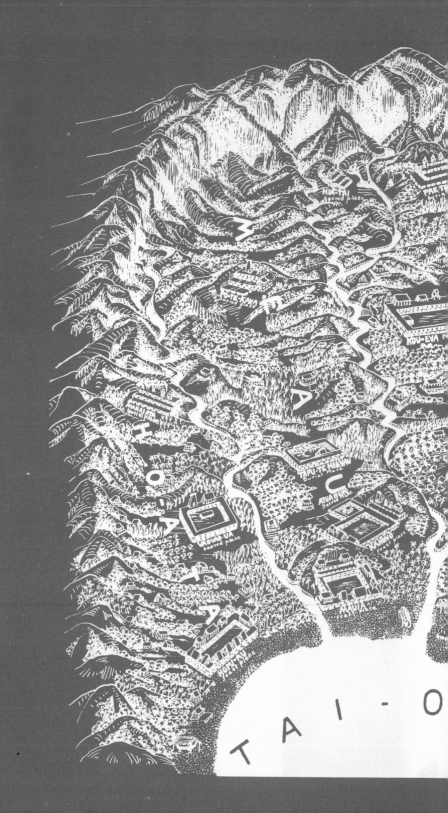